MADE

A Sempre Novel

xoxo

J.M. Darhower

JM Da

2-7

This book is a work of fiction. Any references to historical events, real people, or real places are used fictitiously. Other names, characters, places, and events are products of the author's imagination, and any resemblance to actual events or places or persons, living or dead, is entirely coincidental.

ISBN-10: 1942206070
ISBN-13: 978-1-942206-07-1

To everyone out there who read Sempre and wanted to know more about a certain mysterious hitman.

This is for you.

PROLOGUE

A drizzle fell from the overcast sky, the asphalt glistening from the spiteful evening rain. Barricades were set up around the Dirksen Federal Building in Chicago, leading from the front entrance, down the sidewalk and to the curb, a pseudo-red carpet of drab concrete. Hoards of people pressed against the flimsy metal railings, waiting with bated breath, as more gathered across the street. The overflow surrounded the 53-foot tall sculpture on the plaza, the blood red structure jutting into the gunmetal gray air.

Some of the onlookers carried notebooks, others with their finger on the button of old tape recorders, while black cameras hovered above the crowd. They all watched, and waited, and watched, and waited, for the man of the hour to show his face. Optimism shined from their vigilant eyes, but they'd be disappointed.

He'd give them nothing.

He saw them before they saw him. He'd expected the media to be circling like vultures, ready to pick him apart like dying prey, but the protestors and so-called *'fans'* puzzled him. It seemed society suffered from a case of amnesia, desensitized to men like him. Even the high brought on from a 'not guilty' verdict in such a high-profile RICO case wasn't enough to ease his tension when he saw how many had gathered for a glimpse of him.

Inhaling deeply to steel himself, Corrado Moretti opened the door and stepped out into the dreary evening to face their judgment.

Flashes of bright light blinded him as cameras went off in rapid succession. Bitter bystanders threw out insults while relentless reporters shouted questions… the same vexing questions asked every other time he found himself here.

"How do you feel?"

"Did you do it?"

"Are you innocent?"

"Can you tell me what *really* happened?"

Ignoring them as usual, Corrado kept his expression blank and head down. Flanked by armed security, his lawyer by his side, he led his wife, Celia, to a black Chevy Suburban idling along the curb. The trek took only a few seconds time, but an eternity dragged by with him stuck in the spotlight.

Corrado ushered Celia into the back of the awaiting vehicle when a female voice called out from the crowd. It was quiet, not as pushy as the others, but the words she spoke made him pause.

"What made you this way?"

He blinked away the light rain as it hit his long lashes, and after decades of no comment, he finally… *finally*… broke his silence.

"Sweetheart, I wouldn't even know where to begin."

PART I

Lonely Town

1

Soft cries filled the dim kitchen, a light above the stove illuminating the woman's gray-streaked hair and tear stained cheeks. It was early morning hours—three, maybe four. A turkey already cooked in the oven, while can goods and half-made pies covered the vast counter space, the food temporarily forgotten as the woman sat at the bar, sobbing.

It was Christmas, and seven-year-old Corrado Moretti couldn't sleep. Not because he was anxious for presents or because he wanted to catch Santa in the act. Those things might've kept other kids awake, but they meant nothing to him. Christmas to the Morettis meant a long church service and an even longer family dinner, two things Corrado hated more than anything.

No, he couldn't sleep because his parents had been fighting all night, screaming down the hallway from his bedroom. He hadn't even known his father had come home until he heard the unmistakable sound of his mother hurling things, shattering glass all over their room as she berated him for whatever he'd done while away.

Corrado stood in the kitchen doorway, staring at the troubled woman. Had she heard the fighting, too? "Why are you crying, *Zia*?"

She startled, wiping her tears as she jumped to her feet. "I didn't hear you."

"Did you get hurt?" he asked. "People cry when they're hurt."

"No." She hesitated. "Well, yes. You could say I'm hurting."

"Do you need a Band-Aid?"

The sadness remained in her eyes, but her dimpled cheeks flickered with amusement. "A bandage won't help. I'm hurt on the inside."

"Why?"

"I miss my family."

"You should go see them."

"It's not that easy."

Seemed easy to him. "If you don't want to be here, go."

"But leave you?"

Corrado shrugged. He didn't want to be there either. "I'll be okay."

Zia offered him a small smile, a hint of brightness in the dark room. Wordlessly, she filled a small cup with tap water and handed it to Corrado before leading him upstairs, the two of them tiptoeing down the hallway. Whimpers filtered out from the crack under his parents' door, soft cries and whispered words. Zia covered Corrado's ears as they passed, taking him straight to his back bedroom.

"They were fighting," Corrado said. "It was really bad."

"I know," she said. "I hoped you and your sister would sleep through it."

"I think she did." Corrado climbed into his bed. A small lamp lit up the space around him, illuminating a poster of the Chicago White Sox behind his head. "Katrina sleeps through *everything*."

"Yeah, she usually does." Zia pulled the blankets around him to tuck him in. "You two may be twins, but you're nothing alike."

"Mom says she's the good one. She likes her more than me."

"That's because Miss Erika's an idiot."

Corrado's eyes widened, an abrupt laugh bursting from him. He covered his mouth to muffle the sound, not wanting his parents to hear.

"I shouldn't have said that," Zia said, shamefaced, "but you're a good kid. You have a heart of gold, Corrado."

"If that were true, my mom would love me… or *somebody* would." Corrado frowned, too upset to go to sleep. "Will you tell me a story? Please?"

Zia hesitated before sitting down on the corner of the bed beside him. "Hmm, have you heard *The Steadfast Tin Soldier*?"

Corrado shook his head.

"Well, let's see… a little boy, around your age, got a set of toy tin soldiers for his birthday," she started. "One of the soldiers was different from all the others—he only had one leg. That flawed soldier noticed a pretty, paper ballerina. She stood on a single leg too, and the soldier instantly fell for her. He thought she must be like him and could understand his struggle. It was love at first sight."

Corrado grimaced. Zia chuckled at his childish reaction, pressing her pointer finger against his scrunched up nose as she continued.

"Although he loved her from the first time he saw her, he said nothing. He couldn't. It wasn't in his nature, you see. He's a soldier, and soldiers don't show their feelings. So he chose to watch her from afar. That first night, a goblin warned the soldier to keep his eyes off the ballerina, but the soldier ignored. Can you blame him? He was smitten! The next day, a gust of strong wind sent the soldier falling from a window and into the street below. Two little boys found the soldier, stuck him in a paper boat, and sailed him straight into the gutter."

"Why?"

Zia shrugged. "Why do you boys do anything you do? The boat washed right into a storm drain, where a filthy rat demanded the soldier pay a toll. The soldier ignored him."

"His nature again?"

"Of course," she said. "He was worn and tired by then, but he kept on going. He never gave up. The boat washed into a canal, where the tin soldier was swallowed by a fish."

"What kind of fish?"

"A big one? I don't know. All I know is that fish was eventually caught and cut open, and the tin soldier found himself once again standing on the table near that paper ballerina."

Corrado's expression lit up. "He made it back home!"

"Yes, but..." Zia eyed him peculiarly, as if contemplating whether or not to go on. "...the little boy threw the tin soldier straight into the stove."

Gasping, Corrado's eyes widened. "What?"

"The soldier thought he had lost the ballerina forever, but a gust of wind blew her into the fire with him... maybe the same wind that blew him over the ledge to begin with. She was consumed at once, burning to ash right beside him, as the tin soldier melted into the shape of a heart."

Corrado gaped at the woman as she finished the story, horrified at the ending. "They *died*? That makes no sense!"

"Oh, it makes plenty of sense," Zia said. "Maybe someday you'll understand it."

She softly kissed his forehead, ruffling his untidy dark curls, before heading for the door. She glanced back at him as he snuggled with his gray Batman comforter. "Get some sleep, okay? No more getting up."

"Yes, ma'am."

"And Corrado? I can't speak for your mother, but I can say for sure that someone does love you."

"Who?"

"Me, little man. *I* love you."

She walked out, shutting the door behind her. Within a matter of minutes, the silence swept Corrado away. He slept hard, dreamlessly, but was startled awake hours later by an eruption of noise. Curses echoed through the house, footsteps running the hallways and all around downstairs. Corrado rubbed his tired eyes as his bedroom door flew open and slammed into the wall.

Erika Moretti appeared, eyes wild, breathing shallow. "Is she in here?"

"Kat?" Corrado guessed.

"No, not Katrina. That bitch of a slave!"

Corrado blinked rapidly. *Zia*?

Erika groaned at his prolonged silence and stormed away without demanding a response. Alarmed, Corrado climbed out of bed and made his way downstairs. His father, Vito, stood at the bottom of the stairs, leaning against the banister as he puffed on a thick cigar, his favorite gray fedora slightly cockeyed on his head. Corrado paused beside him, eyeing the man warily. There were claw marks on his cheek.

"Hey, kid." Vito's voice was steady, as cool as could be. "How long has it been? Two weeks? A month?"

"Since Thanksgiving."

"That's what I thought," Vito said. "You look like you've grown a foot since then. You keep it up, you'll be taller than me."

Corrado stared at him, unsure of what to say. Wrinkles marked the man's weary face, more than Corrado remembered there being. Maybe they both changed some while he was away.

His mother burst in the front door from outside then, her bare feet dirty, her eyes even wilder than before. "She's gone! There's no sign of her anywhere!"

"*Zia*?" Corrado asked.

The lone word set Erika off. She snatched Corrado's arm and violently yanked him toward her, shaking him. "*Zia*? Aunt? That woman isn't your goddamn family, boy. She's nothing, you hear me? Nothing!"

Tears prickled his eyes. "Yes."

"Calm down, Erika," Vito said. "Leave him alone."

"Calm down?" Letting go of Corrado, she turned her rage on her husband. She punched him in the chest, knocking him roughly back against the winding banister. "Are you deaf? The bitch is gone!"

Vito continued to puff on his cigar, his face a mask of indifference. "She won't get very far."

Erika stalked upstairs, her feet like steel against the wooden floor. Once she was gone, Vito pushed away from the stairs. "Merry Christmas, kid."

"Merry Christmas, Dad."

"Maybe after this clears up, we'll play a little ball later," Vito said. "How about that? Just you and me."

They didn't go to church that day. Corrado stayed in his room, clad in his worn Batman pajamas all morning and afternoon, reading books and playing with his toys.

Best Christmas ever.

Around nightfall, another commotion rocked the house. Corrado made his way downstairs again, finding the front door wide open. Curiously, he crept onto the porch, his bare feet abruptly stopping at what was happening.

Zia crouched in the yard, filthy and bloody, struggling against a thick chain wrapped around her neck. Erika held the end of it, jerking her like a dog on a leash, before wrapping it around the porch railing, tethering her there. Without hesitation, Erika grabbed a baseball bat from the yard and wailed on the woman, viciously assaulting her. Screams shattered the night air, coupled with the sickening crunch of bones as blood splattered.

Corrado could only stare, his feet cemented to the porch in horror. *Zia*, he chanted in his head, unable to get his voice to work. *Not Zia. Please don't hurt Zia anymore.*

Hearing the noises, Katrina stepped out on the porch, pausing beside her brother as she fiddled the ends of her long black hair. Her eyes widened as she watched, her lips twisting with a single breathy word: "Wow."

Erika didn't stop until the shrieking silenced, until the woman no longer fought back, her limp body a heap beside the porch. The bat was cracked down the middle, nearly split in two. Erika threw it in the grass, bypassing the kids without speaking as she stormed inside.

Vito approached from out in the yard, surveying the carnage before heading after his wife. His hand clamped down on Corrado's shoulder as he passed. "Guess we'll need to get you a new bat before we can play ball now, huh?"

Katrina and Corrado stood in silence, staring down at the motionless woman.

"Is she, uh…?" Katrina looked to Corrado with wide-eyes. "Is she alive?"

"I don't know," he said. "I don't think so."

A riveted smile jerked the corner of her lips. "Wow."

Katrina skipped inside while Corrado stepped off the porch, approaching Zia. He knelt down and reached for her, hesitating, his hand hovering mid-air, before pushing her matted hair out of the way. Her eyes were closed, her face relaxed. No grimace, no scowl, no tears. Except for the blood, she appeared fast asleep.

"Zia?" he whispered. "Are you dead now?"

Zia didn't move. She didn't speak. She didn't even breathe. She remained still and mute as Corrado tried to shake the woman awake.

Traumatized, Corrado headed inside the house when she wouldn't budge. The kitchen was hazy, the smoke detector blaring from the ceiling. Vito pulled the overcooked turkey from the oven, cursing as it burned his hand. He threw it on the counter, fanning the thick smoke.

"Guess we won't be having dinner tonight," he muttered to himself, startling when he spotted his son standing there, stoic, silent. Vito's eyes scanned him, his gaze settling on Corrado's balled-up fists. "You got blood on your hands."

Vito pulled him over to the sink, using soap and water to scrub Corrado's hands. Corrado fought back tears as he watched the red circle the drain. "Zia needs a Band-Aid."

"A bandage ain't gonna help her, kid."

"But she's hurt on the outside now."

"Look, it's best you don't get attached," Vito said. "You don't go crying that this turkey died, do you? No, you eat it… Well, not *this* one, but you know what I'm saying. The circle of life, it's cruel, but it's unavoidable. If the shark didn't eat the man, the man would eat the shark. That's just how it goes."

The next evening, the family gathered together in the dining room for dinner at precisely eight o'clock. Erika took her usual seat at the head of the table, a chair nobody else ever occupied, while Vito chose to sit as far away from her as possible, on the opposite end. Corrado and Katrina sat across from each other somewhere in the middle, a few empty seats between them and both parents.

Corrado stared down at his food, eyeing the burnt grilled cheese and thick tomato soup with disgust. Katrina scraped the black from her sandwich, creating a mess of tiny charred breadcrumbs, the grating sound echoing through the otherwise stone silent room.

Hunger pangs pinched Corrado's sides as he watched his sister nibble a bit, salvaging the meal. They hadn't eaten at all the day before, but as starving as he was, he couldn't force himself to eat any of it. His father wasn't eating, either, instead swirling his spoon around in his tomato soup, pulling up a spoonful and tipping it over, watching as it poured back into his bowl. The soup splashed out, small splatters of red staining the white tablecloth.

Seeing it made Corrado's stomach hurt worse.

"This soup is cold, Erika," Vito said. "What did you do, pour it straight from a can into the bowl?"

"Oh, quit complaining," she said dismissively, clutching a glass filled to the brim with red wine. She sipped it, completely ignoring the food on her plate. "Eat it or don't. I don't care."

"Of course you don't care." Vito threw his spoon down. "If you did, you'd put more effort into taking care of your kids."

Erika scoffed. "You want to criticize my parenting, Vito? I didn't see you in that fucking kitchen trying to make them dinner."

"Had I known how incompetent you were? I would've." Vito leaned back in his chair, his gaze shifting from his food to his wife. "I guess I forgot, unless it comes in a bottle with a vintage label, it means nothing to you."

"Fuck you," Erika spat. "You have no right to talk that way when you're never even here! You worry about your kids so much, then why don't you take the little fuckers with you? Huh? Why don't you take them to Chicago? Why leave them with me if I'm so goddamn incompetent?"

"Maybe I will," Vito said. "God knows, they'd be better off."

Erika jumped up, shoving her chair back. "You… you…"

"Me, what?" Vito challenged, cocking an eyebrow at her. "Spit it out, or are you too drunk to think of the words? What's that, a bottle and a half already today?"

Enraged, Erika snatched a hold of the tablecloth and yanked on it. All four plates skidded her way as Vito's glass fell over, the water spilling all over the table and onto his lap. Cursing, he shoved his chair back and stood, brushing the ice cubes from his soaked pants. "You bitch!"

"Looks like you pissed yourself, Vito," Erika said, still holding her glass of wine, having not let go of it. "You might want to have that checked out, you little dick motherfucker."

Vito, nostrils flaring, lunged across the room, but Erika slipped away before he got to her. Corrado sat there, staring down at the table, his heart racing, as his sister sniffled, fighting the tears streaming down her flushed cheeks.

"Don't cry, sweetheart," Vito said, frustration in his voice as he ran his hands down his face. "Come on, let's go out for pizza. We can go to that place down on Fillmore, the one with the arcade. You can play some games. How's that sound?"

Neither kid answered, but they both stood obediently and headed for the downstairs closet to get their coats and put on their shoes. No shoes on in the house… it was Erika's biggest rule, one her and Vito both seemed exempt from, but the kids were made to follow it.

Vito changed clothes, pulling on a fresh pair of slacks from his always-packed suitcase. He put on his fedora and grabbed his keys.

"Is Mom coming with us?" Katrina asked, her eyes puffy.

"Not this time," Vito said.

They piled into Vito's brand new shiny black Lincoln Continental, Katrina up front with their father as Corrado climbed into the back alone. The drive to the pizzeria took about ten minutes, the place packed on a Friday night. Vito parked in the only empty spot in the lot and led the kids inside, finding a small table off to the side. Vito squeezed into the orange plastic booth and pulled out a pocket full of change, dropping it on the table. He snatched some quarters for himself before motioning toward the rest. "Have a ball."

Katrina grabbed handfuls and ran off, heading straight for the bowling game, while Corrado picked up the leftover coins and wandered around the arcade. He played a few games of pinball and tried his hand at the crane game, his eyes continually drifting between his sister and his father. Each time Vito would be sitting there, shaking his leg, not paying attention… until one time Corrado looked, and he was gone.

Panic bubbled inside of him as he stepped away from his game, seeking out his father in the crowd. Vito stood along the wall, crowding a payphone, the receiver to his ear. He paced around as far as the cord would go, his mouth frantically moving as he fed coins into it.

He stopped pacing after a few minutes, his eyes darting around. He spotted his son standing there and waved him over. "You got a quarter left? Let me hold it."

Corrado handed the coin over. Vito stuck it into the slot, shaking his head as his focus turned back to his call. "I'm still here. I'm at an arcade with my kids. Yeah, I know, I shouldn't have called… I just, I don't know what to do. They're my kids, you know? But I get it, Boss. I get what you're saying. Gotta do what we gotta do."

Corrado lingered for a moment before strolling away, wandering over to a game of Duck Hunt. He put a dime into the coin slot, having to step on a stool to reach the attached rifle. Lining it up, he waited until the birds flew by on the screen before squeezing the trigger, trying to shoot them. A few ducks fell but most breezed on past, unscathed.

"You're pretty good, kid."

Corrado jumped, nearly falling off the stool as he faced his father. Vito smirked, motioning for Corrado to get down. Vito swiped another coin from him—this time, a dime—and fed the slot. He grabbed the rifle, aiming it as the game came to life.

Pop. Pop. Pop.

Ducks fell in rapid succession. A bell went off, declaring a perfect score, and Vito laughed. "Now *that's* how it's done."

His hand clamped down on Corrado's shoulder as he led him back over to their booth. As soon as they sat down, the waitress came by with drinks and a large cheese pizza.

"Katrina!" Vito called out. "Come on, baby girl. Get some grub before I eat it all."

They ate and played more games, not leaving until the arcade closed. They drove back home, Katrina excitedly yapping the entire time, and Vito stopped Corrado on the front porch. "You alright? I don't think you've said a word all night."

Immediately, Corrado's gaze drifted past his father to the spot where Zia had died the day before. She had disappeared overnight, vanishing while Corrado slept. Tears stung his eyes as he bit his lip to keep them in… biting down so hard he broke the fragile skin. The rusty metallic taste of blood coated his tongue, and he grimaced, but didn't utter a single word.

What was he supposed to say?

"It's been a long day," Vito said. "Let's just go inside, kid."

As soon as they opened the front door, Erika's voice reached them, singsong and light-hearted, the words slurring together. "There you are! I've been worried!"

She reached for Katrina, hugging her tightly, and motioned for Corrado to join them. He remained in place, refusing to move, until his father shoved him forward. Begrudgingly, Corrado stepped toward his mother, bracing himself as she wrapped an arm around him, holding his breath to avoid smelling the alcohol he knew would reek on her breath.

After letting go of the kids, Erika turned to Vito, her eyelids heavy. "Vito."

"Erika."

She staggered forward, grabbing his shirt and pulling him toward her. "My big, strong, handsome man."

Corrado grimaced as their lips smashed together, the pair moaning and groaning as they sloppily kissed. Erika's hands laced through Vito's dark hair, knocking the hat from his head.

Corrado didn't stick around to see what would happen next. He sprinted up the stairs, going straight to his bedroom and closing the door. After putting on his pajamas, he climbed into bed, leaving the small lamp lit so not to be left in the dark.

It didn't take long before the house again erupted in chaos—

an hour, maybe two. Doors slammed and glass smashed, shrieks filling the air. He covered his ears with his pillow, trying to block out their fighting, but it was useless. It grew louder and louder each passing minute as Erika screamed at the top of her lungs, flinging every curse Corrado had ever heard at his father.

His door cracked open after a while and quietly closed again, little feet scampering across the floor before his bed shifted. He remained still as his sister climbed in beside him, yanking some of the cover onto the other side to hide beneath it.

"Corrado?" she whispered, her voice quivering. "I'm scared."

"Go to sleep, Kat," he muttered. "They'll get bored and stop soon."

A few minutes later, Katrina's deep snores filled his room, and not long after the fighting slowed to a trickle. When all became quiet, Corrado snuck downstairs, careful not to step on anything broken in his bare feet. The house had been ransacked—pictures torn from walls, vases smashed, furniture flipped over. Corrado scanned the house, through the mess noticing his father's suitcase propped against the wall in the foyer. Vito lingered in the living room. The lights were off, but the moonlight illuminated his face as he clutched a picture frame, staring at a photo of the four of them.

Vito set it down, jumping when he noticed Corrado lurking in his path. He clutched his chest. "How do you do that? I never hear you…"

Corrado stepped aside to let his father pass. "You're leaving?"

"Yeah, I have to get back to Chicago."

"How long will you be gone? When will you be back?"

"I don't know."

"Can I go with you?"

"Not this time."

"Why?"

"You know better than to ask so many questions." Vito grabbed his hat and put it on. "Be good, kid. If you can't be good, don't get caught."

Corrado watched as his father picked up his suitcase.

"*Arrivederci*," Vito said.

"Goodbye," Corrado muttered.

His rough hand patted Corrado on the head. "Good job. Keep practicing that Italian. Never know when it might come in handy."

Vito walked out, climbing into his Lincoln and driving away, disappearing into the darkness. An ache burned Corrado's chest, an emptiness nagging at the pit of his clenched stomach.

He wouldn't see his father again for almost a year.

There were more women in Zia's wake, appearing overnight in the Moretti household to take on the burden of cooking and cleaning. Corrado never spoke to them; he never let them get too close. Sometimes they died, sometimes they disappeared, but never did they stick around long enough for him to remember their names. He pretended they didn't exist as he withdrew further into himself, accepting the painful reality that had slapped him in the face that Christmas day.

It's best you don't get attached.

His mother's harsh streak, her mental and physical abuse, grew worse as Corrado's father's absences grew longer. Things crumbled around them, often literally, the house in pieces as Erika destroyed everything in a bitter rage. She took her anger out on the kids, Corrado enduring the brunt of it to spare his sister.

He figured he was doomed, but maybe Katrina had a fighting chance.

2

Warm air filtered through the wide-open bedroom window one evening in the early spring of 1971. The temperature lingered around eighty degrees outside, even higher inside the darkened, bleak house. Nine-year-old Corrado lay tangled in his sheets, sweat soaking his half-clothed body. It was too hot to fall into a deep sleep, too suffocating to breathe, too muggy to relax. He'd tossed and turned for hours.

The dark made him restless.

The electricity was off. Despite the numerous notices that had appeared at the house, Erika acted shocked when the worker showed up that afternoon to disconnect it. She scoffed and insisted it was a mistake, belittled the man and berated him, but she didn't dare beg. Never that. She'd simply stood at the front door, watching. Once the electricity was off, she'd grabbed a bottle of wine from the kitchen and stomped off to her bedroom alone.

They hadn't heard a peep from her since.

It was eerily silent with no power in the house. Corrado was used to the subtle sounds: air blowing from vents, the hum of appliances, the static of televisions and radios. Even his bedside lamp emitted a sort of low buzz, a sound he'd never noticed until he'd tried to sleep without it.

Impossible.

He lay there with his eyes squeezed shut in an attempt to fall asleep, when a low groan rebounded through the still bedroom.

A creaking floorboard.

Corrado's eyes shot open just in time to make out the form hovering over him. His heart stalled for a beat before hammering fast and hard in his chest. He sat upright, eyes wide with alarm, and faintly made out his mother's face in the soft glow of the moonlight. She stood deathly silent, as unmoving as a marble statue, as she stared at him, clutching a white pillow with both hands.

"Mom?" His voice was a panicked croak. "What are you doing?"

Her expression, cold and detached, melted as she slowly lowered the pillow. "Just checking to see if you were still breathing."

The stench of alcohol was thick on her breath as she spoke. She made a point to fluff the pillow before setting it on the bed behind him. Grasping his shoulders, she pushed him down onto it, and grabbed his blankets. Despite the fact that it was scorching hot, she covered him up, tucking him in so tightly he could hardly move.

Erika staggered out of the room without saying another word. Corrado just lay there, staring at the doorway in the darkness.

It was the first time he'd had to consider the fact that his own mother might try to kill him someday. Had he been asleep, had he not sensed her, had that floorboard not creaked...

He shuttered to think of what she might've done.

Corrado didn't dare close his eyes again that night.

Corrado stood in front of the darkened refrigerator, grimacing at the odors spilling out of it. He grabbed the milk, gagging and coughing when he caught a whiff of the rancid spoiled scent. He set the carton beside were Katrina sat on the counter, swinging her legs, watching him.

"Anything?" she asked impatiently.

He shook his head. Nothing.

The electricity remained off with no sign their mother planned to do anything about it. The most recent woman to come stay with them had vanished days ago. Corrado wasn't sure if she'd run away, or been fired, or if she might have died, but her absence meant they had no choice but to fend for themselves. School days they'd had lunch at least, but today, Saturday, they were all on their own.

He moved on to the pantry next, but little remained in there. Picking up an old box of Cheerios, he shook it, hearing a bit of cereal left on the bottom. He tossed the box to his sister, who opened it and reached inside, grabbing a handful of the remnants. She popped some in her mouth, talking as she noisily chewed. "This is stale. Isn't there something else? Anything?"

Corrado eyed the contents: a dented can of peaches, a bag of dry beans, and some kind of processed can meat. "Not really."

Katrina groaned dramatically, throwing the box of cereal down beside her. "Ugh, I'm going to die!"

Corrado shut the pantry door. "You're not going to die."

"Yes, I am! I'm going to starve to death!"

Corrado kept his patience, sensing panic beneath the immature whining. She was scared, and rightfully so.

He went upstairs, hesitating outside of his mother's bedroom. Slowly, he raised his hand and tapped on her door, listening intently for sounds inside. There was nothing—no response, no movement—so he knocked again. When she didn't respond that time, he carefully opened the door. "Mom?"

Erika lay sprawled out face down on her bed, not moving, hardly wearing enough clothes to cover herself. The air in the room was musty and humid, the odor nearly as putrid as the refrigerator had been. A surge of panic ran through Corrado as he stared at her, wide-eyed, unable to tell if she were breathing. He walked over and grasped her arm, feeling her clammy skin. He shook her hard, feeling like he was only able to breathe when she did.

She grumbled, peeking an eye open. "What?"

"We're hungry."

"Then eat something."

"There is nothing. And the lights are still off. It's been a whole week already."

She groaned as she rolled away from him. "You brats are always complaining. I don't know what you expect from me."

I expect you to be a mom, and get out of bed, and put on some more clothes, and take a bath so you don't stink so much, and make the lights come back on, and feed us so my sister doesn't starve to death!

The thoughts angrily ran through Corrado's head, but the words didn't come from his mouth. He remained silent, unmoving, until his mother fell back into a deep sleep, lying so still it was like she wasn't breathing again.

For a moment, in his fury, he wished she wasn't.

Frustrated, Corrado's stomach growled, his gaze zeroing in on the white purse on top of the dresser. He peeked back at his mother, double-checking she wasn't awake, before tiptoeing over to it. He dug around, his heart racing when he pulled out a crumpled wad of dollar bills. He shoved them in the pocket of his dirty jeans before bolting out of the room.

Katrina still sat on the counter when he returned to the kitchen. "Mom gave me some money so we can go get something to eat."

Her eyes lit up. "Where?"

He shrugged. "The pizza place?"

It was the only restaurant they ever went to.

"How are we going to get there?"

"We can walk. It takes a couple minutes driving, so it won't take much longer walking, I think."

The two put on their shoes and Corrado grabbed his mother's house keys from the stand in the living room, in case they got locked out, and hesitated before snatching a scrap of paper from the corkboard in the hallway above the telephone. It, too, had been disconnected days before the electricity went out.

The few-minutes journey actually took them almost two hours. Their legs were tired, their bodies drenched in sweat, when they stepped foot into the busy pizzeria. Corrado dug in his pocket, laying all his money out on the front counter.

Seven dollars.

"A small cheese pizza," he said. "And two colas."

The teenage boy rang up his order. "Total's $5.40."

He pushed the cash toward him. "Can I have the rest in coins?"

"Sure."

The boy gave Corrado his receipt and a handful of change. He gave half of it to Katrina, who ran off to play games, while Corrado headed over to the payphone. He put a bunch of coins in it, not sure how much it cost, as he pulled the scrap of paper from his pocket.

Chicago, it said, written in his father's handwriting, with a phone number beneath it. He dialed, making sure he pushed the right buttons, and clutched the big receiver to his ear as it rang and rang.

"Moretti."

Vito sounded out of breath as he answered.

"Dad?"

Silence for a moment, then a woman's voice rang out in the background before Vito shushed her. "Shut up, V. It's my kid." Something rustled as he focused on the call. "Everything okay?"

"Yes, but we need some stuff to eat," Corrado said. "Things we don't have to cook on the stove, because we can't use it until they give us some lights back."

"What?"

"We need food at home," he repeated.

"Yeah, groceries, I got that part. But what do you mean about getting the lights back?"

"We don't have any," he said. "The man turned them off."

Tense silence took over before Vito spoke again, a hard edge to his voice. "You telling me you ain't got no electric?"

"Yes."

"Where's your mother? Put her on the damn phone."

"She's not here," he said. "She's at home in bed."

"In bed? Where the hell are you?"

"Walked to the pizzeria."

"By yourself?"

"No. Kat's with me, too."

Vito laughed dryly, muttering under his breath. Curses flew from his mouth, back-to-back, one after another. "That goddamn woman. I tell her to fucking call if she needs anything. Bullshit. What the hell did she do with my money? Drink it all away?"

Corrado switched the receiver to the other ear as a lady came on the line, saying he had one minute remaining. He searched his pockets for more coins, but he had none left.

"The phone lady said I have to go. Can you send some food? But not milk or anything, since we can't use the fridge."

"Don't worry about it, kid. I'll handle it."

"Thanks, Dad."

Corrado hung up, heading to an empty orange booth when their pizza was ready. Corrado took one piece, slowly picking at it, while Katrina greedily devoured the other five. He was still hungry, but he didn't take any from his sister, not wanting her to starve.

Once they were out of food and money, the two made the trek home. They walked slower this time, in no rush to get back to the stuffy house, so it approached nightfall when they finally arrived. They stepped inside the front door as Erika walked out of the kitchen, wearing her robe, carrying a sealed bottle of wine under her arm. In her hand she clutched the dented can of peaches, the top removed, a fork stuck in them. "Where have you been?"

"Outside," Corrado said before Katrina could answer. "Playing."

"Good," Erika muttered. "Fresh air's what you need. Keeps you out of my hair."

They remained silent until their mother stomped back upstairs. Katrina turned to Corrado then, raising her eyebrows. "Mom didn't give you that money, did she?"

He slowly shook his head.

"Didn't think so."

He headed up to his bedroom and took off his shirt before collapsing onto the bed, not bothering to change out of his jeans. Exhaustion dragged him into a deep sleep, but it didn't last long.

His bedroom door flew open, crashing into the wall and waking Corrado. It was dark now, the only light in the room from the open window. He sat up abruptly, eyes darting to the doorway as his mother burst in. His heart raced as he tried to make sense of things, his adrenaline pumping overtime.

Erika descended upon him, no hesitation in her footsteps, one of Vito's thick leather belts in her hand. Corrado tried to move away from her when he spotted it, but he was too late. She snatched his arm with her free hand, twisting it as she pinned him down on the bed. "You think you can lie to me and get away with it, you little shit? Huh? You think you can *steal* from me? You're just like your father!"

Before he could reply, before he could defend himself, she raised the belt, the first blow striking him in the chest. A sharp sting rippled across his skin, seeping into his muscles, seizing his lungs as he let out an agonized screech. He tried to get away from her, sliding off the side of the bed and collapsing onto the hard wooden floor, his shoulder throbbing as she twisted his arm further.

She savagely whipped him as he huddled into a ball, trying to shield himself from the beating. Strike after strike hit his back, a few even connecting with his head and face. Tears stung his eyes, involuntarily running down his flushed cheeks, as he struggled to hold in the sobs bubbling deep in his chest.

Squeezing his eyes shut, he tried to block out the sound of the cracks, the pain of ripping flesh, the flashes of memory. His mother didn't stop until her arm grew tired, the blows weaker as Corrado's body grew numb, his mind detaching. He forced himself to go somewhere else, to think of something else, to not focus on the brutal sting.

Not a word was spoken as Erika walked out, dragging the belt behind her, leaving him on the floor, his face coated with tears.

He raised his head after a bit, his eyes drawn to the doorway. Katrina stood out in the hallway, watching him, that familiar look of wonder in her eyes he'd seen before.

"You," he ground out, his voice scratchy. She'd *told.* "How could you?"

She shrugged. "The more she hates you, the more she likes me."

Corrado stayed in bed that night and most of the next afternoon, huddled under his Batman comforter, not wanting to see the sunshine, not wanting to face the day. He heard movement around the house, cheerful voices downstairs, even his sister's laughter across the hall, but no one bothered him. No one called for him. No one came to check on him at all.

Evening approached when he heard heavy footsteps down the hallway. He lay still, holding his breath as they neared his room. They stopped right outside, long, torturous seconds passing before the knob jiggled. Corrado closed his eyes, imagining his mother's anger that he blocked it with his desk.

She had caught him off guard twice. He wouldn't make the same mistake again.

Someone shoved against the door, trying to force it open, but it wouldn't budge. "You in there, kid?"

Corrado's eyes opened at the sound of his father's voice. Throwing the blankets off, he climbed out of the bed, hobbling as he made his way across the room. He shifted his desk back in place and cracked open the door, peeking his head out to meet his father's gaze.

"Hey," Vito said. "Why'd you have the door blocked? What if there's a fire? How you gonna get out if..."

Vito trailed off. His expression changed, his posture stiffening as the calmness drained from his eyes. With no warning, he slammed his hand against the partially opened door, forcing it open the rest of the way. Corrado winced as his father roughly grasped his chin. "What happened to your face?"

"What?"

"You got these red marks. You get in a fight at school?"

Corrado shook his head.

"Well?" Vito prompted. "What happened then?"

His voice was quiet as he tried to respond, stammering.

"Was it your mother?" Vito raised his eyebrows. "She beat you?"

Corrado didn't respond, but Vito knew.

Letting go, Vito studied Corrado, surveying his severely marked skin. He motioned for Corrado to spin around and let out a low whistle at the welts, the deep gashes and streaks of dried blood covering his bare back.

"Where's your mother, anyway? Her car ain't here."

Corrado shrugged. He hadn't even known she'd left.

"She didn't tell you where she was going?"

"No."

"She must've taken Kat with her," he said. "Your gym shoes were the only ones downstairs."

"Oh."

Vito stared at him, clicking his tongue. Corrado's face heated like a furnace, tears prickling his eyes from shame.

"Come on," Vito said, his voice a forced calmness that betrayed his fiery eyes. "I brought a pizza home. Let's go eat."

Corrado followed his father downstairs to the kitchen, where a large pizza box lay on the counter. The greasy scent filled the air when Vito opened it. Sausage and mushrooms—Corrado's favorite kind.

Vito grabbed a plate and handed it to him. "Dig in."

Corrado took one slice, but his father grabbed two more and slapped them on his plate. He took a seat on one of the stools at the bar, eating as Vito opened the fridge. More covered the shelves now—things to drink. Corrado's brow furrowed, confused, considering the refrigerator still wasn't working.

"Habit, you know," Vito explained as he pulled out a glass bottle of coke and popped the top off, as if he'd sensed Corrado's confusion. "Can't keep them cool, but that's where they go, so that's where they went."

He laughed, but there was no humor to it as he slid the drink to Corrado. The soda was still sort of chilled, the outside of the bottle sweating from condensation.

Vito grabbed a can of Budweiser from the fridge and opened it, taking a swig. He grimaced in disgust, shaking his head, but it didn't dissuade him from taking a second drink. He set it down then and grabbed a slice of pizza, leaning against the counter as he gnawed on it.

"The Sox look good this year," Vito said casually. "They got that Tony Muser guy now. Good move, if you ask me..."

Small talk filled the kitchen, setting Corrado at ease as his father ran down the White Sox roster, talking up the team. "They're gonna pull ahead this season. We're going to the World Series, kid. I can feel it."

Corrado smiled at that.

He finished his fifth slice of pizza when the front door opened, and Katrina ran inside. She hesitated in the foyer, dropping a shopping bag on the floor. "Daddy?"

"In here," Vito yelled from the kitchen, taking a sip from his second warm beer.

Katrina burst in, heading straight for their father, wrapping her arms around him in a tight hug.

Vito patted her back, his eyes on the doorway as Erika stepped into view. "Erika."

"Vito," she said. "What brings you home?"

"Oh, I think you know."

Erika's eyes narrowed suspiciously, darting straight to Corrado. His shoulders slumped, body trying to fold into itself as he wished he could disappear.

Vito pulled Katrina away from him, motioning toward the rest of the pizza. "Why don't you grab a slice and head on upstairs so your mother and I can talk?"

Katrina glanced at the pizza and wrinkled her nose. "I don't like sausage."

"Pick it off."

"Gross, and mushrooms!"

"Pick them off, too."

"But—"

"You heard me, Kat. You can't always have it your way."

Katrina stared at their father for a second, frowning as he cut off her whining. She grabbed a piece of pizza and stormed out, her feet stomping on the stairs. Corrado slid off of his stool, his head down as he scampered toward the doorway.

"Hey, kid."

Corrado looked at his father.

"You look like you grew another foot."

Smiling, he turned back around and slipped from the room.

He barely had enough time to make it to his bedroom before fighting ignited downstairs. It was different this time, as Vito's usual passive voice rose above the chaos, enraged and terrifying.

"You think it's okay to beat my son? You think it's okay to hit him like a man? How about I beat you that way, huh? How about I hit you like a fucking man!"

Corrado huddled under his blanket again, trying not to listen to them, but it was impossible to block out all of the shouting.

"You can't pay the bills, you can't feed my kids, but you can go shopping? You can spend my money on this bullshit—your expensive shoes, your fucking vintage wine—but you can't keep the goddamn electric going?"

Corrado's door creaked opened, the loose floorboard groaning again. He didn't look, knowing it could only be his sister. She stood there beside his bed, and Corrado sensed her gaze on where he laid, dead center of the bed, but he didn't move, didn't scoot over to give her room.

He had nothing to say to her after what she'd done to him.

Katrina went away eventually, going back to her room alone.

"I do everything for you… *everything*! You never had to work a day in your life because of me! All I ask is you keep my kids fed, and you don't even have to do that! I give you someone to do it for you! And you can't keep them around for more than a couple days without losing control!"

The fighting went on and on, non-stop for hours, increasingly incoherent as they yelled about things Corrado didn't understand. The house was pitch black when it slowed to a trickle, finally growing silent, not a peep downstairs from either parent. After awhile his bedroom door opened again, heavy footsteps treading through the room. Someone sat down on the end of the bed and snatched the comforter off Corrado's head.

"Come on, kid." Vito's voice was scratchy from the relentless shouting. "Don't do that. We Moretti men don't hide. We don't cower from anyone."

Corrado sat up carefully, eyeing his father in the darkened room. From the soft glow of the moon, he noticed scratches on Vito's skin from his mother's fingernails.

"Your mother said you stole from her, that you lied about it. That true?"

He hesitated before slowly nodding.

"I told her she ain't give you no choice," Vito continued, not surprised by his answer. He knew he had. "You throw a man into a war and he's gonna kill, you know? Gotta do what we gotta do, any means necessary to make it out alive. And besides, people should never be punished for protecting family, no matter what."

Vito ran his hands down his face before standing back up. "You can't go to school looking like that. They'll think you live in a bad home, and we can't have them thinking that. We can't have them thinking they can take you away from me. So you'll have to take a few days off, you know, until it heals up a bit. *Capice*?"

"I understand."

"Good." Vito started for the door, pausing to look back at him. "I'm proud of you, kid."

Proud?

Corrado stared at his father as he walked out. It was the first time he'd ever said that to him.

3

Early the next morning, Corrado awoke to cool air blowing in his room, rattling the metal vent. A warm glow swaddled the bed from his lamp, casting light upon his weary face.

He was so groggy it took a minute for it to click.

Electricity.

Climbing out of bed, he slowly made his way down the stairs, hearing the radio playing from the living room. Frank Sinatra. The place was in order, all signs of last night's fighting gone. The smell of breakfast wafted through the house, bacon sizzling as the toaster popped up.

Corrado stepped into the kitchen, finding his sister sitting on a stool at the bar, dressed for school with her pink bag already on her back. She sipped a glass of orange juice, the plate in front of her practically licked clean.

Erika stood in front of the stove scrambling eggs, her hair a messy bun on top of her head. She dumped some eggs onto an empty plate as her eyes caught Corrado's.

"Just in time," she said, setting the plate on the bar. "Come eat your breakfast."

He hesitated. "Me?"

"Of course," she said. "Who else?"

Corrado slid onto the empty stool, picking up a fork and stabbing at the eggs. He tentatively took a small bite. They were rubbery and bland, but he choked them down, grateful to have some at all.

The lights were back on. They had food to eat.

His father *had* handled everything.

Katrina finished her glass of juice as Vito strolled into the kitchen, dressed flawlessly in a dark suit, wearing his fedora, humming along to the tune on the radio. "Come on, sweetheart. I'll drop you off at school."

"Do I have to go?" Katrina asked.

"Yes," Erika and Vito answered at the same time.

"It's not fair!" she said. "Corrado gets to stay home!"

Vito shot her a disbelieving look. "You really wanna go there? Because I'm sure your brother would've been happy to trade places with you the other night, but you don't hear him whining about it, do you?"

"But—"

"Enough," Vito said. "Get in the car. You and I need to have a talk about ratting out people."

Sighing theatrically, Katrina jumped down from her stool and stomped out. Vito pulled out his keys and kissed his wife briefly before heading for the door.

Corrado sat still, staring down at his plate and poking at his remaining eggs as he listened to his father's Lincoln pull down the driveway. His mother stood right in front of him.

"You should go outside," she said. "It's a beautiful day."

She didn't wait for him to respond before walking out of the kitchen and heading upstairs.

Corrado took his mother's advice. He sat on the porch, still clad in his pajamas, when his sister got home later that day. The school bus dropped her off at the end of the long dirt driveway, and he watched as she made the trek toward him.

She hesitated as she reached the porch, kicking around in the dirt with her Mary Janes, before sitting down beside him. She frowned, her chin resting in the palms of her hands.

"You think he's coming back?" she asked.

Corrado stared down at the remnants of tire tracks. "Maybe."

They sat together for a while, watching, waiting, for something that didn't come. Katrina eventually gave up. "Well, I don't care if he does."

She was lying, but he didn't call her out on it.

Corrado continued to sit there by himself after she went inside, not getting up until sunset. He went inside and went right up to his room, going straight to bed.

Nobody called him down for dinner.

He's probably back in Chicago. Left without saying goodbye again.

He drifted off to sleep, waking early in the morning to a rustling in the doorway. Vito stood there, observing him.

Corrado sat up swiftly as he gaped at his father. "Dad?"

"You thought I left, did you?"

Vito's voice sounded earnest. Corrado couldn't lie. "Yes."

"I ain't going nowhere if I can help it," Vito said. "Don't worry, kid."

Could it be true? Would his father stay?

"Get up," Vito said. "You're coming with me today."

Once, the year before, Corrado's teacher at the private academy they attended asked the class a simple question:

What do your parents do for a living?

His classmate's answers were predictable—teachers, lawyers, doctors, even a few casino workers. It was close to Vegas, after all.

"My mother stays home," Corrado said when it was his turn.

"Your father?" the teacher asked. "Where does he work?"

"Chicago," he replied.

"And what does he do there?"

Corrado stared blankly at the teacher.

He had no answer for that.

When he got home from school that day, he'd asked his mother. Her amused laughter filled the house, so intense that it brought tears to her eyes. "You want to know how your father makes his money?"

"Yes."

"He does it very carefully."

"He's careful for a living," he'd later told his teacher. "That's what my mom says, anyway."

She'd looked at him with pity, like she thought he didn't understand. And he didn't. Not really.

Katrina had the same assignment. She told the teacher their father was a spy, going undercover on missions that took him away for months at a time. The lady laughed it off, but Corrado wondered if maybe Katrina actually believed it.

After all, Vito was a secretive man. He never talked business whenever the kids were around. He could've done anything, been anyone, and they'd have never known.

He could've been James Bond.

So Corrado was shocked that morning when he stepped out onto the front porch and asked his father where they were going.

"Work," Vito said.

Work.

Corrado climbed into the passenger seat of the Lincoln. His father started the car and shoved an eight-track tape into the player. Frank Sinatra's voice vibrated the speakers, loud and grainy, as Corrado rolled his window down.

Warm wind blew in Corrado's face, ruffling his dark hair as his father drove toward the highway, singing along to the music. Corrado relaxed back in his seat, a smile ghosting across his lips.

Despite living in the area his entire short life, Corrado had never been to the heart of Las Vegas before. Eyes peeled to the scenery, he watched in awe as they crept past casinos along the strip—past Sahara, Riviera, and Stardust, past Frontier, Sands, and Caesar's Palace—before stopping when they reached The Fabulous Flamingo. The lights on the tall fluorescent pink sign twinkled as Vito pulled into the parking lot, swinging to a stop right at the front door.

Vito cut the engine and climbed out of the car. Vito kept his door open, tossing the keys to a man standing along the sidewalk.

"Don't scratch the paint."

"Yes, sir."

Corrado followed his father, eyes wide with fascination as a man nodded at Vito before opening the door for him. "Mr. Moretti."

Vito said nothing as he strode inside. The man at the door eyed Corrado curiously, brow furrowing, but he uttered not a word as Corrado followed his father inside the casino.

Stepping through those doors for the first time was like entering another dimension. The world Corrado grew up in, dull and bordering on downright dreary, ceased to exist as lights and sounds flooded his senses. Vibrant tables and multi-colored slot machines filled the massive room, offset by the pale pink walls and subtle yellow lighting. The clatter of spinning roulette wheels and cranking slot machine arms mixed with the chatter of dozens of people, standing around in groups, clutching buckets of casino chips. Shuttering lights flashed as bells and whistles went off, machines spewing coins so rapidly it startled Corrado.

They headed through the chaos, straight to a large office down a hallway in the back of the casino. Vito opened the door without knocking, startling an older man sitting behind a desk.

He jumped to attention, pushing the chair back. "Mr. Moretti, I thought you'd left town."

"You thought wrong." Vito took off his hat and set it atop a coat rack beside the door. He strolled over, plopping down in the chair the man had vacated, barely giving him a chance to move out of the way. Vito motioned toward another chair off to the side. "Have a seat, kid."

Tentatively, Corrado sat on the edge of the chair, his eyes darting between his father and the other man.

"Uh, I'll give you some privacy," the man said.

"Yeah, you do that," Vito called, a dimpled smirk lighting up his face. "And bring me a drink, will you? Scotch, straight up. Top shelf. Don't bullshit me."

"Of course, sir."

"And something for my kid. A pop or whatnot." Vito's eyes

darted to Corrado. "What's your favorite?"

"Cactus Cooler."

Vito stared at him blankly for a moment before turning to the man. "You heard the kid. Cactus Cooler."

"Uh, yes, sir. Right away."

The man walked out, muttering under his breath. The sounds from the casino muffled to a droning whisper once the door latched behind him. Vito kicked his feet up on the desk as he leaned back in the chair, his hands clasped together at the back of his head. "We'll see how long it takes him to dig up one of those coolers."

"Are you his boss?" Corrado asked hesitantly.

"Depends on what you mean by that."

"Well..." What did he mean? "Do you run this place?"

"I run this *town*, kid."

"How?"

"Carefully."

Carefully.

Corrado stared at him, remembering his mother saying that word. Vito noticed his son's baffled expression and sat up, his feet again dropping back down to the floor. He leaned forward, his expression serious. "You learn about the Boston Tea Party in school yet?"

"No."

"The people didn't want their tea taxed by the British, so they dumped all the tea out in protest. Screw you and your tea, they said. The British lost control of their empire. And well, I don't plan to lose control of mine anytime soon, so I make sure I'm careful." A light laugh escaped Vito's lips as he relaxed again. "You know, when I collect my taxes."

Corrado remained confused, but he didn't ask his father anything more. Vito hated being questioned.

The man returned with their drinks—a glass of scotch and a cold can of Cactus Cooler, the price tag from a local shop still affixed to it—followed shortly thereafter with another visitor. This man, tall and lanky, wearing a casual gray suit, clutched a manila envelope. He handed it to Vito, who opened it and pulled out a thick stack of cash. Corrado stared at it, audibly gasping and choking on his drink when he noticed the amount of money in his father's hand.

Vito painstakingly counted it by hand, bill by bill, dollar by dollar, as the man stood in front of the desk. There had to be thousands of dollars. It took ten minutes of strained silence, the only noise in the room the sounds from the casino filtering around the cracks in the door, before Vito was satisfied. He returned most of the cash to the envelope, save for a few stray bills, and opened a drawer in the desk, tossing it in. He handed the leftover money back to the visitor.

Without a single word spoken, the man left.

"They say if you give a man an inch, he'll demand a foot," Vito said, "but I find if you steal a foot from a man, he's grateful to be given an inch."

Corrado still didn't understand—not really—but one thing was sure to him then. His father may not have been James Bond, but he was definitely someone special. He felt like he had witnessed Bruce Wayne put on his Batman suit for the first time.

And that left Corrado spellbound.

They spent all afternoon in the casino office, sipping drinks as a steady flow of men visited. Each brought with them stacks of money, very little spoken beyond the occasional small talk. Corrado made himself at home, scooting his chair closer to the desk... closer to his father.

He had no idea where the money had come from, or why they were giving it to Vito, but as stacks and stacks of envelopes piled up in the desk drawer, all Corrado thought about was how the electricity should never go off again.

His dad was *rich*.

"Cactus Cooler," Vito muttered, picking up the half-empty can from the corner of the desk. Corrado's third soda of the day. "Your mother would kill me if she knew I let you drink so much of this crap."

"I don't think she'd care," Corrado said.

"Oh, she would," Vito insisted. "She has issues—there's no denying that—but family means a lot to her."

Impulsively, Corrado touched his face, knowing the bruises and red marks were still visible.

"Yeah, I know," Vito said, as if he had read Corrado's mind. "She has a funny way of showing it, huh?"

Vito stood then and strolled over to the door, grabbing his hat from the coat rack. "Come on, lets get out of here. I'm starving, kid, and somewhere in this town there's a juicy steak with my name on it."

Every day that week, Corrado went to work with his father at the casino, where the two sipped on drinks and bonded. Corrado drew on scraps of paper while Vito conducted his business. *He's a casino worker, or maybe some kind of banker.* He even entertained that his father may be a politician. *Maybe he's the mayor of Las Vegas!* But nowhere in the bustle of day-to-day activity—the exchanges of cash, the silent meetings—did Corrado ever once entertain the word *Mafia.*

Everyone knew the Mafia was bad, and well, Corrado believed his father was the greatest man alive. His father splurged and took him to fancy restaurants all week long, spoiling him with junk food like never before, grinning proudly when he showed him off. His father was the most passive person he knew, especially compared to his mother.

Erika whirled wildly like a tornado, whereas Vito drifted along like a spring breeze. Never once had his father raised a hand to him, or anyone else that he'd ever seen. He'd lost his temper a few times, like when he'd gotten home and seen the aftermath of the beating, but even then, he'd restrained himself from hurting anyone.

Thoughts of that evening, his mother's assault when he'd stolen money from her, slowly faded from Corrado's mind. The bruises and welts eventually disappeared, the sting long gone. Corrado waited, and waited, for his father to leave again, for them to tell him he had to go back to school, for life to return to how it had been, but the day didn't come. Days turned into weeks, and they settled into a new routine, one where Vito became a permanent fixture.

And his constant presence pacified Erika.

Corrado couldn't remember a time when that ever happened before. His family felt like a real family, a happy family, and it was all because of his father coming home.

If Corrado hadn't idolized the man before, he did now.

4

"On tonight's show, Italian-American Civil Rights League founder Joe Colombo will be joining us to—"

"Rat!" Vito spat as he sat up, his back straight, his eyes narrowed at the television. "He's gonna start singing like a canary!"

They were all gathered around in the living room like they did every other night at that time, watching *The Dick Cavett Show.* Vito and Erika lounged on the couch while the kids lay on the floor, sharing a bowl of popcorn.

"Can you believe it?" Vito said. "The balls of this fucking guy!"

"Relax." Erika rubbed his back. "He isn't there to talk about—"

"It doesn't matter," he said. "You don't go talk on national television! You just don't! You gotta be careful! This ain't *careful*!"

Corrado stared at the screen, confused as to what upset his father. He'd never heard of any Colombo guy before and didn't know what it mattered. What was the big deal?

"Turn it off," Vito declared, his voice hard. "Right now."

"But it's Dick Cavett!" Katrina whined, staring at their father with pleading eyes.

"I don't care," Vito said. "We don't watch that man anymore."

"But—"

"You heard me, Kat!" Vito shook his finger at her, his eyes ablaze. "Never again!"

Corrado reached for the dial and changed the channel, tuning to Johnny Carson instead. Katrina huffed, snatching a handful of popcorn as she turned her attention back to the television.

No one said a word through the program, and Vito's posture remained stiff. He bounced his leg, his expression hard as he seemed to stare through the television, not truly watching it. The show wasn't even over yet when his rough voice shouted out. "Go to bed, kids."

Katrina started to argue, but Corrado grabbed her arm and shook his head, warning her not to do it. She pushed away, shooting daggers at him, as she stomped upstairs.

Corrado slowly made his way upstairs behind her and hadn't even gotten to his room when he heard his father yelling. Corrado's shoulders tensed, waiting for his mother to yell back, but his father's voice was the only one he heard. He couldn't understand what he said, Italian words flying from his lips too fast and furious for him to translate, mixing with names he'd never heard before. He stood there in the hallway, too intrigued to move, when a creak on the stairs captured his attention. Turning, he saw his mother appear on the second floor, as his father's voice grew louder downstairs.

"Did you see it? Can you believe it? What kinda cockroach goes on television like that? *Digraziato!*"

Erika raised an eyebrow at Corrado. "Didn't you hear your father? Go to bed."

"Yes, ma'am," he muttered, heading into his room before she had to say anything else to him.

There was a soft, timid knock on the casino door the next afternoon. Vito hollered for them to come in, his eyes fixed on a newspaper on the desk. He had been tense all morning, not acknowledging Corrado the whole drive into Vegas, not even offering him a drink when they arrived.

The door opened, a young guy in a gray suit stepping inside. "You wanted to see me?"

Vito cringed as the man addressed him.

"Hey, kid, do me a favor, will you?" Vito glanced across the office at Corrado, speaking to him for the first time as he ignored his visitor. Corrado was doodling on a time sheet he'd found on the desk.

Corrado looked at his father curiously. "Sure."

Vito opened the bottom drawer—the one overflowing with envelopes of cash—and pulled out a small bag. It clinked and clanked as he pushed it across the desk. "Run this over to the cashier's cage. Tell them it's from Moretti. Wait there until they give you the cash."

Corrado snatched up the bag, surprised by how heavy it was. Casino chips—white, green, and mostly red, but some black. He held it with both hands, lugging it past the visitor.

"Here you go, shorty," the guy said, holding the door open.

The casino was busy. Corrado weaved through the crowd, heading straight for the cages at the front of the building. He was the only kid in the place, since they weren't allowed on the casino floor. Gamblers towered above him as he waited in the line, having seen his father cash out chips a few times.

When his turn came, he struggled lifting the bag so the cashier could reach it. She eyed him peculiarly like she wanted to object, but the moment he said 'Moretti' her expression changed. Quickly, studiously, she counted the chips and handed him a stack of bills.

"Thank you," Corrado said, taking the money.

The cashier smiled sweetly. "You're welcome."

Corrado strolled straight back to the office and immediately opened the door. He took a step inside, freezing and dropping the cash with a gasp. Groans echoed through the space as his father pinned the man in the gray suit against the wall, a pistol shoved beneath his chin. Blood oozed from the guy's mouth, his cheek swollen from a blow to the face.

Vito didn't notice Corrado, too wrapped up in the situation. "I'll kill you right now! I swear I will!"

"I'll have it tomorrow!" the man cried. "I will!"

"You said that yesterday," Vito spat. "I should've blown your fucking head off then."

"Please," he begged. "I'll have the money. Just give me one more day! That's all I need!"

Corrado's heart raced. "Dad?"

The moment his voice sounded, Vito grew rigid. His head snapped in his direction, a fire in his eyes Corrado had never seen before. Almost as if by some instinct, Vito turned the gun on him. "Don't you know to fucking knock?"

A gun. His father had a *gun*. And it was aimed at *him*.

Panicked, Corrado bolted right back out the door, slamming it behind him. He stood in the hallway, on the verge of hyperventilating as he leaned against the wall.

He'd been wrong. Maybe his father wasn't a spring breeze. Maybe the man was actually a hurricane.

Minutes passed before two guys came running down the hall straight toward him. Corrado pressed himself tighter against the wall, trying to be invisible, not wanting to be seen. Not wanting to be in the way. The men barely noticed him as they ran into the office. Within a matter of seconds, they returned carrying the man. He was bloodied, his eyes closed and body limp. The men quickly left with him, disappearing out a back door.

Vito strutted out of the office then and lingered in the doorway, concealing the pistol in his jacket. He pressed his hand on the top of Corrado's head, ruffling his hair. "You really gotta learn to knock, kid."

Corrado swallowed thickly. "Is he, uh...?"

"Dead?" Vito asked. Corrado nodded hesitantly as Vito led him back into the office. "Nah, he's just taking a little nap."

Vito sent Corrado on numerous errands over the next few days to get him out of the office. It started small—cashing out chips, grabbing drinks, and delivering paperwork—but before long he was passing messages and covertly placing bets. More visitors came and went during that time, some on their own accord, others carried out through the back door.

Corrado didn't question it, but his curiosity grew and grew. Not a banker, not a casino worker, and definitely not a politician...

what could his father be? Vito didn't hide so much from him anymore, openly toying with his gun a mere few feet from Corrado.

Police officer? No.

Maybe he's a secret agent, after all.

One thing was for sure, though. After that first time, after what he had seen, Corrado never forgot to knock on a door again.

They were sitting in the office one afternoon when there was some commotion out in the hallway. Vito's eyes darted to the door as his hand flew into his coat, gripping his pistol. He started to react when the door shoved open, a man Corrado didn't recognize appearing.

He looked as old as Vito, with darkly tanned skin and jet-black hair slicked back on his head. He was sturdy with a mustache and wore a dark suit. Something about him drove Corrado to attention, an air of superiority surrounding the man. He held his head high, no hesitation, nothing but confidence as he stepped inside the office without awaiting an invitation.

He wasn't like the other men who visited. He showed no fear.

Corrado expected his father to get angry, seeing as how the man hadn't knocked, but Vito seemed taken aback instead. His hand released his weapon as he stood, shoving his chair back. "Mr. DeMarco, uh, sir."

Corrado blinked a few times at the uncertainty in his father's voice. He'd never heard him stammer before.

"Moretti," the man said, his voice flat, all business.

"I didn't know you were coming."

Mr. DeMarco said nothing. He stared at Vito before shifting his gaze toward Corrado, a bit of unfriendliness in his expression. "What is it, take your kid to work day? Did I miss the memo? I would've brought mine."

"No, I just figured..." Vito trailed off, switching his attention to Corrado mid-thought instead. Reaching into his pocket, he pulled out some loose change. "Take a walk, kid. Grab yourself one of the coolers. I'll come get you later."

Wordlessly, Corrado grabbed the money and headed out.

"Sorry, Boss," he heard his father say when he stepped into the hallway.

"It's fine," the man said. "He just shouldn't be here for this."

Corrado had no idea what *'this'* was and had no intention of sticking around to find out. That guy made his dad more like pesky Robin than powerful Batman. He strolled through the casino, heading toward a small restaurant in the lobby. A closed sign hung at the entrance, but a bartender lurked behind the bar.

Contemplating, Corrado slipped inside and approached the bar. The bartender glanced at him with surprise when he climbed up on a stool. "You Moretti's son?"

Corrado nodded.

"Figured," he replied. "What can I get for you?"

"Do you have Cactus Cooler?"

The man frowned. "Sure don't. I have Coke, though."

"That's okay."

Corrado spilled out his handful of change on the bar, but the bartender ignored the money, pouring a Coke. "It's on me."

Sipping his soda, Corrado glanced around the darkened place as the bartender prepared for opening. Minutes of silence passed before footsteps approached behind him. Vito's shoulders were uncharacteristically slumped as he climbed onto the stool beside him, waving for the bartender and ordering scotch.

He downed his drink in one large gulp.

"That work?" Vito asked, motioning toward a radio behind the bar. The bartender nodded, pouring Vito another drink. "Turn it on. The Sox are playing in California today."

Corrado lit up at those words. The White Sox? The bartender fiddled with the radio for a bit to get a station to come in that broadcasted the game. The reception was fuzzy, but it came in clear enough for them to listen.

They spent the afternoon with the White Sox as they demolished the Angels, beating them thirteen to nothing. Vito grew deeper into a depression the longer they sat there, despite the staggering win.

"Come on," Vito said, standing when the game came to an end. "Let's go home."

Corrado followed him, noticing Mr. DeMarco at a blackjack table in the casino with a group of men. "Who is that guy, Dad?"

Vito cast him a wary glance. "That's my boss."

"You have a boss?"

"Yeah, we all got someone we answer to."

Corrado watched Mr. DeMarco, admiring how everyone seemed to hover around him yet keep a certain distance, as if both attracted to the man and terrified of him. "Who does he answer to?"

"I don't know, kid. God, maybe?"

Corrado sat right in front of the television, a bowl of dry Fruit Loops on the floor in front of him, his eyes fixated on the grainy, flickering screen as the late night news came on.

"Alleged New York Mob Boss Joseph Colombo was shot tonight at the second annual rally of the Italian-American Civil Rights League. Witnesses say..."

"Yo, yo, yo, turn that up!" Vito shouted as he sprinted into the room, throwing himself down on the couch so roughly it shifted a few inches. He relaxed back, one arm over his wife's shoulder as his free hand brusquely waved for Corrado to obey him.

Corrado reached for the dial on the television and turned the volume up a few notches.

"...Colombo was heading to the podium to give a scheduled speech when he was shot three times. A second unidentified assailant in the crowd then shot the suspect dead before escaping."

"I'll be a son of a bitch," Vito said. "Can you believe it?"

"What, Daddy?" Katrina asked, lying on her stomach on the floor near Corrado. *Colombo.* He'd heard that name before.

"Just history in the making, baby girl," he declared. "The start of something big."

Erika groaned, not as amused by the news. "Time for bed."

They whined in harmony. Bedtime wasn't for two hours.

"Let them stay up," Vito said. "That Dick Cavett's about to come on."

"I thought you didn't like him anymore," Erika said.

"Eh, maybe he ain't so bad."

Corrado and his sister stayed up well past midnight, watching Carol Burnett on *The Dick Cavett Show.* It was the first night in a week they'd all hung together as a family, the last night Corrado remembered ever spending like that. There was no fighting, no belittling, no anger or hatred. His father seemed happy, something that hadn't happened since Mr. DeMarco arrived in Las Vegas.

The calm before a storm only Vito knew was coming.

The weekend passed uneventfully. Monday morning Corrado woke up and dressed, heading downstairs for breakfast. His mother had started cooking every morning, and although it was never very good, at least they had something to eat. That was more than he could say months ago.

He hit the foyer when his mother stepped out from the kitchen, clutching a bottle of wine. He glanced between her and it with surprise.

"Better hurry," she slurred. *Drunk.* "You're gonna miss the bus."

"What?"

"Don't *'what'* me. If you miss school, your ass is in trouble."

Corrado stared at her, wide-eyed. "But Dad—"

"What about him?"

"I want to go with him."

"Too late," Erika said. "He already left."

Corrado wanted to believe he just went to work early, that he'd headed to the casino while he was still asleep, but deep down inside he knew the truth. The stench of alcohol on his mother alone was enough to tell him what he needed to know.

Vito hadn't stayed.

5

Corrado's stomach flipped and flopped as the dingy yellow school bus churned down the road, every bump sending him an inch off the cracked brown bench. He sat in the front by himself, diagonal from the bus driver, while his sister raised ruckus in the back with her friends. Katrina's voice shrieked above all others as she hollered and laughed, the constant center of attention.

The bus slowed, the air brakes screeching as they neared their long driveway. The two-story white house could be seen on the hill, appearing minuscule at that distance. Corrado glanced out the window as the bus came to a halt, eyeing the black Lincoln parked beside the porch, gleaming under the bright afternoon sunshine.

Corrado's muscles grew taut. He hadn't seen it in ages.

"Holy shit!" Katrina yelled from the back. Corrado didn't have to look at her to know she'd seen it, too. He stood when the doors creaked open, barely making it out of the seat when his sister ran past, knocking into him.

"That's no kinda language for a young lady to use," the bus driver scolded her as she bolted for the door. Corrado followed, pausing at the edge of the driveway as the bus pulled away. Katrina ran a few feet before skidding to a stop.

"Do you see it?" she asked. "Dad's home!"

"But *why* is he home?"

She dramatically rolled her eyes. "Because it's our birthday, duh! I bet they're throwing a party for us! Eleven is a big deal, you know."

Katrina ran ahead while Corrado strolled down the driveway. As he neared the house, he heard screaming inside, the familiar tale tell signs that his mother was enraged. Corrado sat down on the porch, dropping his tattered book bag on the step beside him.

Going inside was pointless. There would be no cake, no ice cream, no balloons, no presents. There would be nothing different from any other time.

He sat there for a while before the fighting stopped. He heard his mother stomping upstairs seconds before the front door thrust open, his father stepping out.

"That goddamn woman," Vito muttered, a cigarette hanging from the corner of his mouth. Stalking forward, he sat down on the step beside Corrado, stretching his long legs out in front of him.

He pulled a silver Zippo lighter from his pocket and flipped it open, striking it about a dozen times before shakily igniting the flame. He lit his cigarette, taking a deep drag before shoving the lighter back into his pocket.

Neither spoke. Corrado had no idea what to say to the man. It had been five, maybe six months since he'd seen his face. Vito used to make it home once or twice a month, but now once or twice a year felt like a downright miracle.

"Your sister said it's your birthday." Vito flicked ashes into the yard, blowing smoke his way. "Happy birthday."

Corrado only offered a slight nod.

"Sorry I forgot," he continued. "I was, you know, tied up for a long time, and then things in Chicago got out of hand. I haven't had time to think about much of anything that doesn't have to do with work. Guess that's what happens when you choose the life. Well, hell, scratch that—the life chooses you. And I'll tell you, kid… it's got me by the balls."

The life... Corrado had no idea what that meant.

Vito smoked his cigarette, throwing it down once the flame reached the filter. He stood, tramping it out, and started toward the car. "I'll be back tomorrow. I need you to pack some bags."

Something sparked in Corrado then. Hope. "Am I going with you?"

Vito laughed wryly. "No. I'm sending you and your sister away for a bit. It's not safe right now. You know, work stuff. You'll be better off somewhere else."

"Where?"

He shrugged. "Anywhere but here."

Corrado watched his father drive away, the engine roaring as the Lincoln disappeared down the road. Afterward, Corrado headed inside, stepping over everything that had been strewn around during the fighting, and went straight up to his bedroom. He meticulously folded some clothes and layered them in his book bag, finished packing in a matter of minutes.

The next morning, the Lincoln returned, parking in the same spot as the day before. Corrado sat on the porch once again, his book bag beside him. Vito climbed out of the car and strolled toward him. "If you weren't wearing different clothes, I might wonder if you sat out here all night. Is that all you're taking? One bag?"

He nodded.

"You might be gone for a while," Vito said. "You don't wanna take anything else? Your ball and glove, maybe? You always liked baseball."

Corrado just stared at his father. He hadn't played in years, not since his mother had splintered his special edition Louisville Slugger cracking the skull of a woman he'd considered family.

Realizing he wasn't going to get a response, Vito turned his focus to the house. "Katrina! Come on, girl! It's a long drive!"

The front door opened a moment later as Erika ushered her daughter outside. They hauled half a dozen bags out onto the porch, dropping them at their feet. Katrina wrapped her arms around her mother's waist, clinging to her, but Erika didn't seem to notice. Her piercing gaze, bitter and frigid, focused squarely on Vito.

"Hell of a father you are," she barked. "You deserve a medal. What kind of man does this to his kids?"

"It's just a precaution. They'll be fine where they're going."

Erika laughed bitterly. “So I stay here and *I’m* the one in danger?”

“I asked you to go,” Vito said. “I *told* you to, but you refused.”

“You’re damn right I refused,” she spat. “I won’t be driven out of my house—my *home*—because my husband’s a spineless coward who can’t keep his family safe! You’re not a real man, Vito. You’re half of one. You’re a pest, a cockroach, and I’d like nothing more than to step on you, squish you beneath my foot, and be rid of you forever.”

“Don’t start on me, Erika,” Vito warned. “I’m not going to fight with you in front of the kids.”

“Go ahead and use them as an excuse,” Erika said. “*Jamook.*”

Vito started to bite back but restrained himself, clenching his hands into fists at his sides. He took a deep breath, closing his fiery eyes. When he reopened them, his face was a mask of calm. “Get in the car, kids.”

Corrado obliged right away, climbing into the backseat. Katrina begrudgingly did the same, squeezing in beside her brother in the back. Vito threw their bags in the trunk and asked Erika to reconsider when she turned her back to him.

Vito refused to fly.

"If I was meant to be up in the air, God would've given me wings," Vito explained when they got on the road, his hands lovingly stroking the steering wheel. "This baby gets me wherever I need to be."

It was a two-day trip from Las Vegas to the east coast, to a small, secluded town called Durante, in the foothill of the mountains in North Carolina. Darkness shrouded the car when they arrived at the old plantation home tucked deep in the woods. Corrado sleepily climbed out, grabbing his book bag from the trunk as his father juggled all of Katrina’s bags.

They headed for the house as the front door opened, a woman appearing on the large porch. She was dressed impeccably in a blue dress and a pair of heels, a string of pearls around her neck. Her dark hair was proper, pulled back and curled. She dressed like she was going to a formal event, not living in the middle of nowhere.

"Gia." Vito greeted her, kissing both of her cheeks. "I'm forever indebted to you for this."

"Nonsense, we're friends," she said. "Besides, I'm sure they'll be a pleasure to have around."

"They'll be on their best behavior. Isn't that right, kids? You'll mind Mrs. DeMarco?"

DeMarco. Corrado recognized that name.

"Yes," Katrina said promptly. "I promise."

All eyes turned to Corrado. He nodded. Of course he would.

"Well, then," Mrs. DeMarco said, her gaze lingering on him for a moment. "My kids will be happy to have someone to play with. Come on in."

They followed Mrs. DeMarco into the foyer of the house. Corrado glanced around, taking in the interior. It was clean and cozy, fully furnished and well lived-in—nothing like their home back in Nevada, full of expensive, broken shells of things.

"It's a shame about Frederica and Luigi," Vito said. "I'm still reeling from the news. As soon as they told me, I knew I couldn't delay it anymore. I needed to move them. It could've been *my* family, you know?"

"Such a pity," Mrs. DeMarco said. "Who would attack a whole family? And that baby! God willing, Antonio will find who did it and make them pay."

"I'm sure he will," Vito said. "As soon as it calms down again, I'll come back for the kids."

"Just be careful out there." Mrs. DeMarco smiled warmly at him before turning to the kids. "We have two empty rooms... one on the third floor with the children and one on the second with me. Do we need to flip a coin or can you work it out yourselves?"

"I call third floor!" Katrina said.

Mrs. DeMarco peered at Corrado, eyebrows raised. He merely shrugged. He didn't care. A bed was a bed. He was there because his father said they had to be there. It wasn't sleep-away camp. He hadn't come to make friends.

"So it's settled." She motioned toward the stairs. "The doors are open. Make yourselves at home."

"This is so stupid," Katrina complained, wading in a small creek that ran behind the house. "I wish we were at home with Mom."

Their first morning in rural North Carolina had dawned an hour earlier. Katrina snuck out the back door as the sun rose, and Corrado followed her, partially curious, the other half of him compelled to keep an eye on his sister.

The murky water came mid-calf, drenching Katrina's feet. Corrado cringed at the sopping, squishing sound it made whenever she took a step. "Your new shoes are getting wet."

She rolled her eyes. "Thanks for stating the obvious, Sherlock. And that's all you have to say? Seriously?"

"What do you want me to say?"

"I don't know. Say something… *anything*!"

"Something," he muttered. "Anything."

She shot him a foul look. "Smart ass. You aren't even sorry, are you? It's your fault we're here in the first place, you know."

"How is it my fault?" How could *he* be to blame?

"Because you suck," she said, matter-of-fact, as if that answer made even a bit of sense. "And because Mom doesn't like you."

"She doesn't like anyone."

"She likes me," Katrina said defensively.

Corrado didn't bother responding. If blaming him would make her feel even the slightest bit better, so be it. She could blame him all she wanted. He'd accept it, because that's what brothers did. But at the end of the day, it wouldn't change the truth.

They were there because no one else wanted them.

The sound of twigs snapping and leaves rustling drew Corrado's attention away from his sister. He glanced around, expecting to see squirrels run through the thick brush, but instead a girl stepped out from behind a tree. He watched her inquisitively. Katrina didn't look, either not hearing or not caring, as the girl approached.

She was about their age, her long brown hair sloppily braided down her shoulder, like she'd done it herself in the dark. Wispy pieces stuck up everywhere. She wore a pair of cut off jean shorts, an oversized Chicago Cubs shirt tucked in the front of them. She smiled as she met Corrado's eyes, revealing a set of clunky metal braces. "Hi! I'm Celia Marie."

"Celia Marie?" Katrina asked, still wading in the water. "What kind of name is that?"

Celia shrugged. "The kind my parents gave me."

"Well, it's a stupid name," Katrina said. "I'm glad my parents didn't name me that."

Celia seemed taken aback by the response, but it wasn't anything out of the ordinary. Katrina never had a nice thing to say about anything.

"Well, what's *your* name?"

"Katrina Sophia," she replied. "Just like Sophia Loren. She's the best actress ever. I was named after her."

Lies. She'd been named after their grandmother.

"I don't like her that much," Celia said, crossing her arms over her chest in defiance. "I like Faye Dunaway better."

"You would," Katrina snapped, eyes narrowing as she turned her gaze toward the girl. "Faye Dunaway's stupid and stupid people like her!"

"Takes one to know one," Celia retorted, not backing down. "Stupid."

Katrina gaped at the girl, stunned someone would talk back to her. It took everything in Corrado not to laugh at his sister's expression.

"You… you… you… I hate you!" Katrina trudged up the bank of the creek and stormed past them, heading for the house, her shoes caked with thick mud. "I hope you get eaten by monsters and die!"

"Ditto!" Celia shouted after her.

Once Katrina was gone, Celia turned to Corrado cautiously. "Is she always like that?"

He nodded.

A boy approached them then, younger, less sure about Corrado's presence as he weaved through the brush. His expression was guarded, suspicious, when he appeared from behind a tree.

"This is my little brother, Vincent," Celia said, motioning toward him.

"I'm not that little," Vincent grumbled.

"You're littler than me! You're only eight, but I'm almost eleven."

Celia grabbed a hold of a tree and pulled herself up into it. She sat on a thick branch, swinging her stick-thin legs, not a trace of polish on her dirty toes.

She was unlike any girl Corrado had ever seen before. Girls wore dresses and painted their fingernails. Girls didn't climb trees and know about baseball… even if she did like a terrible team like the Cubs.

Vincent tried to climb the tree with his sister, too short to reach the branch. Celia jumped back down to help him, and Corrado took their distraction as a chance to slip away. He headed back toward the house and found Katrina alone on the back porch.

Corrado sat down beside her.

"I don't like that girl," Katrina declared.

Corrado said nothing, but a small smile tugged at his lips. Katrina may not like her, but Corrado had to admit he kind of did.

"Do you kids want some ice cream?"

Katrina and the DeMarco kids nodded excitedly. Mrs. DeMarco laughed at their eagerness and got up from the table, disappearing into the kitchen.

Corrado continued to pick at the food on his plate. Even though he hadn't eaten since leaving Las Vegas, he couldn't force anything down. It was too foreign to him in this old house. It was strange, being with these people who weren't yelling, who didn't throw anything. It was like those television families. They even prayed before they ate.

"You're quiet."

Celia's voice dropped low as she whispered across the table. Corrado knew it was directed at him, but he didn't bother saying anything.

It wasn't as if she'd asked a question, anyway.

"He's an idiot," Katrina said. "So it's better he doesn't talk. He'll just bore you to death."

Katrina closed her eyes and threw her head back, dramatically snoring, pretending to be asleep.

"That's not nice," Celia said. "He's your brother. You shouldn't talk about him like that."

"Would you rather me talk about your brother?"

Celia tensed. "You leave my brother alone."

"Or what?"

"Or… I'll smack you silly!"

Mrs. DeMarco stepped into the room, gaping at her daughter. "Celia Marie! How dare you speak to our company that way!"

"But Mom, she—"

"No buts! It doesn't matter what she did. We don't threaten guests. No ice cream for you!"

"She started it!" Vincent blurted out in defense of his sister. "She was mean first!"

Mrs. DeMarco glared at him. "Did you not hear me, young man? I said it didn't matter! None for you, either. You kids are a serious disappointment."

Vincent gasped at his mother's words, his face contorting as he began to cry. Mrs. DeMarco ignored him and dished out some ice cream for Katrina, who smiled to herself as she devoured it.

"Corrado, would you like some?"

He shook his head as Katrina interjected. "He doesn't like ice cream or anything good, really. He won't even eat chocolate."

"Is that right?" Mrs. DeMarco glanced between them. "Why?"

Katrina laughed. "I already said why. He's an idiot."

Mrs. DeMarco looked at her with surprise when she insulted him, but shrugged, not bothering to scold Katrina. She retook her seat, the table remaining silent except for the soft cries from young Vincent. It was like she didn't care her children were upset, or that they'd been wronged.

Corrado turned back to his plate of food.

Maybe it wasn't so foreign, after all.

For days, Corrado crept around the DeMarco house, staying out of the way and keeping to himself, as his sister tailored herself to the surroundings. Katrina followed Mrs. DeMarco around all day long, constantly offering to help, hanging on to the woman's every word. Nearly everything out of Katrina's mouth was laced with politeness as she batted her eyelashes, soaking up the attention.

Corrado watched, more and more sure as time passed: Katrina was plotting something.

He didn't know her end game, what she hoped to accomplish, but he knew his sister. He had been on the receiving end of her schemes more than once, and he still bore faint scars from some of them. Whatever brewed in that head of hers would be ugly, and Corrado suspected, this time, it wasn't *him* she conspired against.

It was the girl. Celia.

The DeMarco kids spent all day outside, from sun up to sun down. The only time Corrado encountered them was at meals, and he noticed it then, the looks his sister shot across the table at Celia.

She had meant it—she didn't like her.

Corrado lingered in the doorway to the kitchen one afternoon, watching as his sister stood on a stool, helping Mrs. DeMarco put away dishes. Katrina rattled on and on as they worked, telling the woman stories of things her and their mother used to do together, talking about Erika like she was the greatest woman to exist.

"You must miss her," Mrs. DeMarco commented.

"I do," Katrina said, her voice laced with genuine sadness.

"I'm sure she misses you, too."

"Of course she does."

Again, her words were sincere. She truly believed it.

Katrina grabbed the last glass and put it away before jumping down from the stool. "You know, my mom has people to do this kind of stuff for her."

"You mean a maid?"

"No."

Mrs. DeMarco leaned against the counter and crossed her arms as she gazed at Katrina peculiarly. "Huh."

"What?"

"I didn't think your father was like that."

"Like what?"

"The kind to have those kind of people in his house."

Katrina's eyes widened with alarm. "Is that wrong?"

"Depends."

"On what?"

Mrs. DeMarco shook her head. "It's nothing for a little girl to concern herself with."

"But—"

Mrs. DeMarco smiled tersely, cutting her off. "How about we bake a cake?"

Katrina stared at her for a moment before shaking her head. "No, I think I'll go outside and play instead."

"Great."

Corrado moved out of the way as Katrina strode past, heading straight for the back door. His eyes followed her, something about the expression on her face urging him to shadow her. Quietly, he stepped out back, squinting from the sunshine as he followed his sister toward the creek. The DeMarco kids were sitting beneath some trees, forming a makeshift track for Vincent's toy cars. Corrado loitered a few feet away, leaning against a tree trunk and watching as Celia dug in the dirt with her bare hands, pulling up grass and tossing twigs aside. Smudges of dirt covered her flushed cheeks, her hair falling out of a ponytail as sweat beaded along her forehead.

Katrina walked right past them without speaking and sat down on the bank of the creek. She grabbed some rocks from around her and tossed them in the water, the plop echoing out. Celia glanced behind her, eyes narrowed suspiciously as she studied Katrina, but she shrugged off her presence.

She dug a bit more, extending the track so it weaved around a small tree in the shape of a cloud.

"There," Celia said, climbing to her feet. She brushed the loose dirt from her knees. "All done."

Excited, Vincent dumped out his bucket of cars and lined them up on the track. Celia turned then, and Corrado felt her gaze. His eyes shifted from Vincent to Celia, seeing the smile on her lips.

"Hi," she said.

Hello. The word was on the tip of his tongue when his sister shifted position in his peripheral. Before he could react, the loud whack sounded. Celia cringed, stumbling a few steps as she reached behind her to grab her back.

"Ow!" she hollered, spinning around. Corrado looked over at Katrina, seeing the rock in her hand. Without even hesitating, she launched it at the girl, smacking Celia in the chest with it. Celia cried out, hardly having time to defend herself before Katrina grabbed another.

"Hey!" Vincent shouted, jumping to his feet. "Stop that!"

Katrina glared at him defiantly as she launched a third rock at Celia. This one struck her arm as she held her hands up to block herself.

"I said stop it!" Vincent yelled.

"Make me," Katrina sneered, throwing another, hitting Celia right in the knee, the blow making her stumble.

Determination marred Vincent's young face. Growling, the boy picked up one of the rocks.

"Don't do it, Vincent!" Celia hollered, but it was too late. Vincent launched it straight at Katrina with all his might, the rock hitting her in the face.

Gasping, Katrina clutched her cheek as tears sprung to her eyes. Scampering to her feet, she let out a strangled sob. "I'm telling!"

Katrina sprinted off through the trees, back toward the house, knocking into Corrado as she ran. He let out a frustrated sigh, closing his eyes. Vito's lectures about not being a rat never seemed to sink into Katrina's head.

"You shouldn't have done that, Vincent," Celia said.

"She was hurting you!"

"I'm fine," Celia said. "You're going to get in trouble, though."

"So?" Vincent said. "I don't care. She's mean, and she shouldn't hurt you!"

Corrado opened his eyes, sparing them a glance, before following his sister to diffuse the situation. He scarcely made it out of the trees when Mrs. DeMarco's shrill voice rang out through the yard. "Vincenzo Roman!"

Corrado's footsteps slowed, coming to a halt when the woman stormed out the back door, clutching a belt. Katrina stepped out behind her, still holding her cheek.

His stomach sunk. He knew from experience what would happen next.

Vincent didn't cry. His body was rigid, his shoulders squared as he marched through the back yard to face punishment. Celia ambled behind him, a troubled look on her face. Her breath painfully caught, a tear streaming down her cheek, when Mrs. DeMarco grabbed Vincent and raised the belt to strike him.

It happened so fast, yet in utter slow motion, as Corrado opened his mouth, his commanding voice echoing through the yard. "You shouldn't hit him."

All eyes shifted directly to him. Mrs. DeMarco hesitated. "Excuse me?"

"People should never be punished for protecting family," he said, reciting words his father had once told him. "No matter what."

Mrs. DeMarco stared at him, mouth agape. An eternity of strained silence passed before slowly, carefully, the woman lowered the belt and let go of Vincent. Mrs. DeMarco stood there, still staring at Corrado for a moment, before she pulled herself together. Her eyes surveyed the kids as she cleared her throat. "You all should learn to get along."

Katrina gasped. "But—"

"You heard me," Mrs. DeMarco said, silencing her as she

headed back inside. Katrina shot Corrado a furious look before following the woman.

Stunned, Vincent plopped down in the yard, staring straight ahead, as if the last few minutes had robbed him of every last drop of energy. Corrado's gaze met a pair of watery brown eyes, regarding him curiously. Corrado couldn't quite get a read on Celia. Happy? Sad? Mad?

He smiled to ease the tension. "Hello."

Celia's eyes widened as she parted her lips, as if to respond, but all that met Corrado's ears was captivating, exhilarated laughter.

"Why don't you talk?"

Corrado stood in the shade of the tree, his hands in his pockets as he watched Vincent push his cars around the dirt track. He said nothing before his gaze shifted up to Celia. She sat on a branch in the tree above him, her feet level with his head. "I can talk."

"Well, obviously you *can*, but you don't do a lot of it."

"I don't have a lot to say."

"Your sister never shuts up."

Corrado let out a laugh at that.

Celia's expression brightened at the sound. "You laugh, too?"

"When something's funny."

"And you think your sister running her mouth is funny?"

"No, but you talking about it is."

Corrado turned his attention back to Vincent when the boy growled, making engine noises as he rammed his cars together, oblivious to anything outside of them. Strange, for someone who had nearly got beaten not long ago. He recovered quickly, trudging back out to the creek and picking up where he had left off. Celia had followed her brother, and curious, Corrado trailed right along.

"Why did you help my brother?"

The question caught Corrado off guard. "I said why."

"You said he shouldn't be punished for protecting family."

He nodded.

"Why?"

Corrado looked back at the girl. "You ask a lot of questions."

"Does that bother you?"

"Yes."

She jumped down from the tree and skidded as her foot slid on some leaves. Instinctively, Corrado grabbed her before she hit the ground, keeping her upright. She gaped at him as he clutched her arm but recovered from the shock. "Why does it bother you?"

Shrugging, he let go of her. "It just does."

"Well, I like asking questions." She took a step back from him as her hand grasped her arm where he had touched her. Had he hurt her? "How else will I know things?"

"Do you always have to know things?"

A smile lit up her face. "Was that a *question*?"

He stared at her without responding. It felt as if she had tricked him some way. *How did she do that?*

"Fine," she said, looking away from him. "Mom wouldn't listen to me if I spoke up, but she listened to you, so thank you for that."

"You should thank your brother," Corrado said when Celia plopped down on the ground and grabbed a toy car. "He's the one who protected you."

"How come we've never met before?"

Corrado glanced up from his bed to the open doorway later that evening, seeing Celia lurking in the hallway. *More questions.*

"It's just," she continued, stepping into the room uninvited. Corrado's hair bristled, and he shifted away as she casually sat down on the bed beside him. "I know your dad. I see Vito all the time in Chicago."

"He works there."

"He lives there, too."

Corrado blinked a few times. "We live in Nevada."

"So why don't you live with him?"

"I do."

Celia cocked her head to the side as she studied him. "You're kind of weird."

Was she insulting him?

Celia shifted her body, drawing her legs beneath her on the bed. "Can I ask you a question?"

"You just did."

A glint of amusement touched her eyes. "Can I ask another?"

He nodded slowly.

"Why didn't your mom come with you?"

"She said she wouldn't be run out of her house."

"Didn't your dad tell her it wasn't safe?"

"Yes."

"Isn't she scared?"

"No."

She blew out a deep breath. "Even Mom's scared, and she's not scared of anything. Daddy *made* us leave when things got bad. You know, because Sal's family died and stuff. I don't want to end up like them."

Corrado stared at her. He didn't know who Sal was, but this girl was a treasure chest of information.

"You don't have to be scared," Corrado said, sensing genuine fear in her voice. "My dad says it's safe here."

Celia relaxed. "I like you, Corrado."

Those words surprised him. "I thought I was weird."

"You are," she said. "But I still like you."

Corrado still kept an eye on his sister, shadowing her throughout the house, but he found his attention drifting more and more outside as the weeks passed.

Celia and Vincent played together every day, rarely arguing. He watched them, wondering how they managed it. Corrado hardly tolerated his own sister from a distance. Katrina continued spending all of her time with Mrs. DeMarco, her looks of hatred at the dinner table now rationed between them.

A month after arriving in North Carolina, Corrado stood at the window in the living room, staring out into the back yard, when Celia grabbed an old, worn baseball glove from an outside toy box and put it on. Vincent picked up the baseball, winding his arm dramatically, before hurling the ball at his sister. Celia ducked, the glove straight in the air, as the ball whizzed past her in the yard. Silent laughter twisted her features as sunshine poured down upon her. It was a cloudless day, mild for summer, but Celia's cheeks were flushed, her long, loose hair rustling in a breeze.

Without even realizing it, Corrado found himself smiling, unable to drag his eyes away from her. The two passed the ball back and forth, Celia tossing it to Vincent underhanded, while Vincent launched it back erratically.

"Pathetic."

The low hiss came from across the room. Corrado's eyes shifted slightly, catching sight of Katrina's reflection in the grimy window.

"You're not good enough for them," Katrina said, stepping closer. "They'd never even look at you if they weren't stuck in this place, too."

Corrado's smile melted away.

"Nobody likes you," she continued. "You're nothing to them."

Looking away from his sister, his focus shifted back to Celia as she picked up the ball. She brushed her hair over her shoulder after tossing the ball to Vincent, her eyes drifting to the window. They connected with Corrado's, and she smiled warmly, waving the glove at him. Something tightened in Corrado's chest. Distracted, Vincent abandoned the game and wandered through the yard.

Wordlessly, Corrado stepped out the back door, shutting it behind him. Celia heard the click and glanced his way as he picked up the baseball, clutching it in his hand. He gazed at the dirty ball, seeing the messy signature in blue ink. *Autographed.*

"Ernie Banks," Celia said. "Best Chicago Cub to ever play the game. That was his five hundredth home run."

"You didn't catch it."

"How do you know?"

"Because you're not very good."

Celia laughed at his bluntness. "Do you play?"

"No," he said, looking from the ball to her. "Not anymore."

"Why?"

"Doesn't matter."

Celia raised the glove. "Throw it."

He shook his head.

"Come on," she insisted, punching the glove with her free hand. "Scared of being beaten by a girl?"

"Of course not."

"Then throw it."

Corrado tossed the ball underhanded, straight to her. Celia caught it without even looking.

"That was weak," she said.

"Better than you."

Her eyes narrowed. "Get a glove and I'll prove you wrong."

"I don't need one." He'd seen her feeble throwing.

"But—"

"Just throw it back."

"Fine."

Before Corrado could even prepare, Celia hurled the ball right at him. It soared to his right, and Corrado reached out to catch it. The ball struck his hand, viciously stinging his palm as pain rippled up his arm. Hissing, he let go, shaking the pain away as the ball hit the grass with a thud.

His hand felt like it had burst into flames, his fingers stinging.

Celia threw the glove down and ran over to him, grabbing his arm. "I didn't hurt you, did I?"

"Of course not," he ground out, flexing his fingers.

She poked and prodded at his hand. "Didn't break anything, I don't think."

"It's fine." He pulled away from her. "Don't worry about it."

"I'm sorry," she said. "Really, I am."

"Don't apologize." He could only blame himself. "I didn't expect you to throw so hard."

"Why? Because I'm a girl?"

"No, because you threw terribly with Vincent."

"He's my little brother. Of course I'd take it easy on him. But you, well..."

Nothing to them. "I get it."

Reaching over, Corrado grabbed the ball from the ground and tossed it to her. She caught it in her bare hand, sighing as her fingers wrapped tightly around it. "You took it easy on me."

"Yes."

"Because I'm a girl?"

"No."

Because maybe you're not nothing to me.

Independence Day.

The clear night, warm and breezy, carried sounds through the closed windows of the DeMarco household. Mrs. DeMarco sat in a chair in the living room, having turned it to face the vast window. She gazed outside, searching for something, seeing nothing.

Nothing but blackness, as far as Corrado could tell.

The bangs and cracks in the distance were loud as fireworks went off in the town of Durante, the trees blocking their view of the vibrant colors. But each noise, no matter how expected, made Mrs. DeMarco wince.

Only a dim lamp lit up the space around her. The kids gathered in the room with nothing to do. There was no television in the house. The radio was off. It was too dark to read.

"Can I go to bed now?" Vincent whined.

"No." Mrs. DeMarco's tone was clipped. It was the fifth time Vincent had asked that question, and each time the answer remained the same. *No.*

Corrado sat quietly, mostly watching Celia, as the girl peered at her mother. Katrina slouched in a chair, kicking her legs as she peeled the nail polish from her fingernails. Vincent, exhausted, curled up on the couch, giving up, and closed his eyes.

The explosions continued to go off in the distance for another hour. By the time the noise trickled to a stop, complete silence permeating the house, Vincent was fast asleep, and Katrina had somehow slipped away. Mrs. DeMarco didn't turn away from the window, her eyes still fixed on the darkness, but she waved her hand dismissively. "Go to bed."

Celia roused her brother from his deep sleep, dragging him off the couch and setting him toward the stairs. Corrado followed, his footsteps slowing when he reached the second floor, seeing Celia lingering at the bottom of the second staircase. She turned to him. "Do you think our dads are okay?"

"Yes," he said. Why wouldn't they be?

Celia frowned. "Daddy didn't call today."

"Maybe he was busy."

"It's a holiday," she said.

"It's only the Fourth of July," Corrado said.

"It doesn't matter. He's never missed any holiday before."

Corrado couldn't imagine… Vito barely made it home for Christmas. "He probably just forgot."

She shook her head. "Daddy says DeMarcos never forget anything."

"Don't be so worried," Corrado said.

"But the Russo family—"

"I don't even know who they are."

Surprise passed across Celia's face. She seemed to be about to say something when Vincent yelled for her from the third floor. Turning, she sprinted up the stairs, leaving Corrado in the hallway alone.

He headed into his bedroom and changed into his pajamas before climbing into bed. He lay there, staring at the ceiling, unable to sleep, when he heard his knob turn and the door open. Groaning, he closed his eyes as footsteps approached his bed. Not Katrina. Not tonight.

"Are you asleep already?"

Celia's voice, startlingly close, jolted him upright. He stared at her as she stood beside his bed, clutching a big book to her chest. "Celia?"

"Duh." Without needing any encouragement, she plopped down beside him and set the book between them. "How can you not know the Russos? They're related to Sal."

He shrugged, awkwardly inching away from her. "I don't even know Sal."

Celia opened the book and shifted through it. A scrapbook, Corrado noticed, as she flipped through page after page of photos and newspaper clippings. Reaching the last filled page, less than a quarter of the way through the book, she spun it to face him.

Corrado squinted, trying to read in the darkness, as he glanced down at the newspaper article. The edges were frayed, part of the article ripped like she had torn it out in a hurry. The bold headline was vibrant enough for Corrado to make out the words:

Local Prominent Family Missing, Feared Dead

Celia clicked on a small lamp, giving him light to continue reading.

On the surface, Luigi and Francesca Russo seemed to be a picture-perfect couple—he, a wealthy businessman out of Chicago; her, a stay at home mom—but the family harbored secrets of another life that are only recently coming to light.

Authorities were called to the Russo residence early Sunday morning after a priest reported the couple didn't show up for church. When police arrived, they found the back door had been broken down, the inside rifled through. Upon entering the house, police discovered a gruesome scene: blood splattered walls and shell casings on the floor, but there was no sign of either Francesca or Luigi, or their one-year-old daughter.

Friends insist there's no reason anyone would want to harm them, but further investigation revealed long-standing ties to organized crime.

Corrado stopped reading and glanced at Celia. He had questions, ones he desperately wanted to ask, but he couldn't get the words out. He didn't need to—not really. The answers were written all over her sullen face.

Turning back to the book, Corrado flipped back through the other pages, reading the bold headlines.

Shoot-out at Infamous Crime Hangout

Seven Arrested on Racketeering Charges

Murder Plot Uncovered
String of Slayings Have Underworld on Guard
Reputed Mob Boss Arrested
Mob's Waterfront Extortion Exposed
Court Papers Detail Chicago Mob Hits

The more he saw, the more absorbed he became. The hair on the back of his neck bristled as he scanned articles, noticing familiar names—Colombo, DeMarco, Antonelli—and spotted faces of men he'd encountered in passing without even realizing it. Men from his father's casino… men who had delivered stacks of cash, men who had bought Corrado drinks and patted his head like they were friends.

And there it was, as he turned the page again, the one thing he waited for through it all. A small part of him hoped not to see it, hoped he wouldn't find anything, but there, in print, was the name.

Vito Moretti.

The photo accompanying the article had faded with time, but Corrado made out his father, his face partially concealed from the camera with the collar of his coat, his gray fedora on his head. The headline above it shone bold—**Not Guilty**—but what drew Corrado's attention was the small, italicized caption below the picture.

Alleged Mafia Capo walks free.

Mafia.

He stared at that word until a small hand grasped his.

"Do you think it's all true?" she asked.

"Maybe."

"Do you really think they're okay?"

"Yes."

Her expression softened with relief as she took the book from him, flipping the pages back to the very beginning. The first article was torn, the paper yellowing, so old the words were barely visible anymore. She held it up, showing it to Corrado as he squinted, struggling to make out what it said.

Car Bomb Kills Reputed Crime Boss

The photo was vaguely recognizable as a car, smothered in flames and smoke. Corrado couldn't read much of the article, but the name DeMarco caught his eye.

"It was my *Nonno*," Celia explained, closing the scrapbook as she set it down on the bed. Her grandfather. "The newspapers said the Irish killed him. Killed my *Nonna*, too. She was in the car with him. I just remember Daddy being upset and saying he was going to make sure the Irish paid for it. The newspapers after that said he took over *Nonno*'s job… that my dad became the boss."

"My dad calls him that," Corrado said. "Boss."

Celia nodded. "I think it's true."

"Did you ask him?"

"No."

Corrado was surprised. Celia, always full of questions, didn't ask her father something she wanted to know?

She seemed to sense his confusion as she lay across his bed sideways, bunching up the comforter to use it as a pillow. Corrado hesitated but lay down facing her, doing the same.

"He says I shouldn't be so nosy," she mumbled. "My questions bother him, too."

Corrado didn't know what to say about that. He stared at her in the dim lighting, watching as her eyelids drifted closed, her breathing steady as she drifted off to sleep. He didn't move, didn't close his eyes.

Sleep evaded him all night long.

Three days later, as they sat around the dinner table, picking at pork roast and potatoes, the shrill sound of ringing shattered the silence of the house. At once, the children tensed as Mrs. DeMarco shoved her chair back and ran for the phone. She snatched it off the wall in the hallway, just within eyeshot, and brought it to her ear. "Hello?"

Her next breath was a long exhale of relief. "Antonio. Thank God."

Celia dropped her fork and jumped up to face her mother.

"Yes, I know." A smile touched Mrs. DeMarco's lips. "I never doubted it."

She listened intently before letting out a light laugh. "Yes, she's right here. Hold on."

Mrs. DeMarco held out the phone to Celia, who sprinted over to snatch a hold of it. "Daddy?"

Celia's eyes sparkled. "Yes, of course I'm being good.... yes... I miss you, too."

Her excitement grew at something before she launched into a story. It took a few minutes for her to run out of steam, her words slowing to a trickle. "I promise. Love you, too. Bye, Daddy."

Celia held the phone out toward her brother. "Vincent?"

Slowly, he pushed his chair back and walked over to grab the phone. "Hello?"

A long, exaggerated pause of silence passed as Vincent stared at the ground.

"Uh-huh," he mumbled finally. "Yes, sir."

Vincent handed the phone back to his mother and retook his seat. Mrs. DeMarco turned the corner, out of their view, and whispered into the phone, trying to find a bit of privacy. Corrado picked at his food until Mrs. DeMarco returned, taking her seat. Her eyes scanned them before ultimately settling on Corrado. "Vito's fine," she said, glancing from him to Katrina. "Just busy with work stuff."

Work stuff.

Mafia.

A heat wave struck the mountains of North Carolina, the temperature creeping into the high nineties every afternoon, as summer droned on. The sticky, humid air coated Corrado's skin like sweat as he spent his days outside. He ran around, clad in only a pair of pants, barefoot and bare chested, sunshine blasting him as it streamed through the trees, bronzing his skin.

Celia stood in the backyard one afternoon as the first of

August dawned, wearing a ruffled red bathing suit. Vincent ran around her as she clutched a hose, trying to squirt him. Their laughter rang out, jubilant, childish, both kids soaked from head to toe as their feet sunk into the muddy earth. Corrado lurked a few feet away, his dark curls damp from the wayward spray.

Vincent shrieked, running away from his sister, heading straight for the woods. Celia sprayed him as far as the hose would go before bending it, stopping the flow of water, and swinging around to face Corrado. She pointed it at him like a gun, drops of excess water dripping into the puddle around her feet.

"Surrender," she demanded, eyes sparkling, a mischievous twist of the lips. "Or else."

He stared at her.

"Last chance," she warned him.

He still said nothing.

No more than a heartbeat passed before she loosened her grip on the hose, letting the water fly. Corrado backed up a few steps, but it wasn't enough. The spray slammed into him, soaking his chest, as icy water blasted him in the face. Laughing, he lunged at her. Panic flared in Celia's eyes as she squealed, dropping the hose and throwing up her hands defensively. "I surrender."

Corrado was undeterred. Celia backed up, yelping as she slipped in the mud, nearly falling, but she caught herself as she ran. Corrado stared at her retreating form for a fraction of a second before making the decision to go after her.

He took off into a sprint, chasing her through the yard. Celia glanced behind her, squealing as she dodged and weaved, trying to evade him. She ducked into the woods, grasping the trunk of a small tree to swing around it. Corrado jumped in front of her, stopping her, his looming figure backing her against the tree.

She panted, trying to catch her breath, still dripping water. Her flushed cheeks twitched as she fought to contain her smile. "I said I surrender!"

"I didn't ask you to."

She tried to duck around him, but he moved with her, blocking her yet again. Her eyes flared wildly, darting past him with excitement as she sought out a way to escape. Left. Right. Left. Right. Corrado anticipated her every move, keeping her pinned in place, not letting her slip past.

Until finally, once, she came right at him. She stepped forward, her head tilted as she stared him in the eyes. He looked down at her, curious, and barely had time to react before she sprung up on her tiptoes and forced her lips against his.

Every inch of Corrado, warm and sweaty, froze over like a block of ice. It was over as quickly as it started, Celia ducking past him with a giggle, running through the woods back to the house.

He watched her, wavering this time before following. He caught up to her when she reached the back door, his hand catching hers when she flung it open.

"You cheated," he said.

She cast him an amused look as she headed into the house. A response had come from her lips, but Corrado didn't hear it. All he heard, all that existed when he stepped inside, was the familiar deep voice, smooth and calm. Corrado's eyes darted around for the source, his heart racing when he spotted the man in the hallway.

His father.

Vito turned their way, trying to navigate around Katrina, who clung to his waist. He smoothed her hair lovingly as he grinned, regarding his son. "Good news. You get to go home, kid."

Good news. Contrary to those words, the smile faded from Corrado's face. Home. Las Vegas. Back to his mother. Away from the DeMarcos.

Vito's expression shifted to confusion. "Nothing to say?"

Corrado looked away. "I'll go pack."

"Yeah, you do that," Vito said, prying Katrina away from him. "You, too, sweetheart. Sooner you're packed, sooner you're out of here."

He didn't have to tell her twice. Katrina bolted upstairs, taking them two at a time. Corrado slipped past Celia and followed his sister, stopping on the second floor. He packed what little he had brought, done in less than five minutes. Sitting on the edge of the bed, he clutched his backpack between his legs and stared at the floor.

A soft knock on the door caught his attention. He glanced up as it opened, seeing Celia slip inside, her braid let loose into damp waves. She had changed her clothes, wearing shorts and that dreaded Chicago Cubs shirt—the same thing she had worn the day they arrived.

"I'll write you," she said, eyeing him earnestly. "Okay?"

He nodded.

"Come on, kids!" Vito hollered. "Make it fast, will you?"

Corrado stepped around her and walked out, tossing his bag on his shoulder as Celia walked right on his heels. His father stood at the end of the staircase, swinging his keys around his finger.

"Ah, the prettiest DeMarco to ever live," Vito said, a charming grin lighting his lips as he reached over and tugged Celia's hair.

"I heard that," Mrs. DeMarco said, stepping out from the kitchen.

"Busted." Vito glanced at the woman. "I was never very good at being discreet."

"You and Antonio both," she chided.

He let out a laugh, smiling sheepishly. "Guilty."

Mrs. DeMarco shook her head, not seeming as amused, and strode off. Vito winked at Celia, nudging her chin with his hand. "I don't know where you get it, pretty girl."

Katrina's appearance on the stairs shifted Vito's attention away. Corrado stepped down into the foyer and glanced back at Celia, his father's words running through his head. He surveyed her features, her hair, her eyes, taking in the sight of her pale lips… lips that had not long ago touched his.

Pretty.

Vito snatched up Katrina's bags and lugged them out the front door. Corrado followed him onto the porch when Celia grabbed him from behind, knocking the backpack from his shoulder, as she wrapped her arms around him in a tight hug.

"Bye, Corrado," she said. "I'll see you again someday."

His stomach sank when she let go.

"Goodbye, Celia."

6

Two months can alter life in unbelievable ways.

When they made it back home at the end of summer, vast sunshine streamed through the downstairs, casting blinding glares off the damaged frames and chipped crystal, but the house itself was spotless.

Corrado squinted, surveying the dead silent surroundings, his eyes falling on a small form in the hallway. For a brief moment, when he first caught the glimpse, he was sure she was an apparition. Her alabaster skin glowed as white as the light surrounding her, matching her snow-colored dress.

Unconsciously, Corrado took a step back.

"Why is there a girl here?" Katrina asked, dropping her bags to the floor in the foyer. "And why is she wearing my dress? Oh God, Mom replaced me! She replaced us!"

"Don't be dumb, Kat," Corrado muttered, staring at the girl. He could make out nothing but her fiery red hair and green eyes. "Mom wouldn't replace us."

"How do you know?"

He didn't know. He wouldn't put anything past his mother. "Well, she wouldn't replace us with Irish kids, anyway."

Their father stepped in the house behind them and cleared his throat. "Corrado, Katrina, this is Maura. She's your mother's new, uh, help."

The girl stepped forward at the sound of her name, out of the blinding glare and into Corrado's line of sight. She was young...

younger than him. She was just a girl, no older than Vincent.

"But why's she wearing my dress?" Katrina asked again as her voice rose. "It's mine! Not hers! *Mine*!"

Erika came down the steps then, groaning dramatically. "What's with all the yelling?"

"This girl... this slave... is wearing my dress!"

Maura flinched at the hostility, her cheeks flushing bright red as tears welled in her eyes.

"That dress hardly fits you anymore," Erika said. "Besides, she needed clothes. You didn't expect me to buy her any, did you? Not like I could afford it, though, even if I wanted to. Blame your father. If he'd make some money for once..."

"Don't start, Erika," Vito warned.

Erika waved him off as she strode right past for the kitchen. Vito stood there for a moment, looking at his watch. "I gotta get going, kids."

Corrado frowned. "Already?"

"Yeah, you know, work," Vito said. "I got some stuff to handle at the casino, but I'll be back for dinner."

At least he would come back tonight.

Vito kissed the top of Katrina's head before lingering in the doorway to the kitchen. "I'm leaving, Erika."

"Of course you are," she muttered, coming back through the foyer and heading back upstairs.

Vito shook his head and walked out of the house as Katrina threw her hands up. "Unbelievable!"

She stormed off, leaving Corrado and the strange new girl alone in the hallway. Maura regarded him cautiously, her mouth opening and closing as she considered speaking.

"Hey," she said finally, her voice feeble.

A response hung on the tip of Corrado's tongue, a simple "hello" in return, but a crash upstairs made him swallow it down.

Closing his eyes, Corrado grabbed his bag.

There was no point talking to her when she would just leave eventually.

He couldn't keep anyone.

Screaming. Screaming. Screaming.

Why did there always have to be *screaming*?

"Where's the fucking money, Vito? You promised you'd have it!"

Erika's voice was so high-pitched it surprised Corrado it didn't shatter their water glasses. He kept his gaze on his plate, tired eyes fixed on his untouched food. His appetite was long gone, disappearing when his parents started bickering.

He was almost wishing now his father hadn't come back.

"Is that all you care about? Money?" Vito remained calm. He sounded defeated. Corrado couldn't recall a time his father didn't sound that way. "Figures."

"What, you expect me to care about you? Ha! You can't even handle your responsibilities! You shove them off on me!"

Responsibilities, Corrado knew, was code for him and Katrina. He chanced a peek across the table at his sister. *Welcome home.* She had her elbow propped up in front of her, her face in the palm of her hand as she shifted the food around on her plate. To most people she would've appeared bored, disinterested, but Corrado knew better. Moments like this were the only time Katrina showed vulnerability, the only time she even seemed human to him anymore. Watching her, seeing the hurt in her eyes, he almost felt bad. She was still just a kid.

But then again, so was he, and he wouldn't let it get to him. If only the screaming would stop, though. It gave him a headache.

"I sent money last week. What did you do with it all? The kids weren't even here!"

He'd clearly asked the wrong question. Erika slammed her hands down on the table, shaking it from the force of the blow. Her wine glass toppled over, spilling the red liquid. Corrado watched as it spread across the table and ran over the side, dripping onto the floor beside him.

"Are you kidding?" Erika spat. "You send me pennies and have the nerve to ask what I did with it all?"

The wine pooled near Corrado's chair, the red seeping into the floor. Maura would have a hard time getting it up, for sure.

"Pennies? I sent you thousands!"

"Two thousand. That's it! That doesn't even cover the bills!"

"It would if you wouldn't live so extravagantly."

Again, wrong thing to say.

Erika shoved her chair back as she jumped up, launching her plate of food across the room. Katrina and Corrado both ducked out of the way, but Vito didn't even flinch. It flew right past him and smashed against the wall over his shoulder, the sauce from the lasagna leaving a smear on the white paint.

Maura would have trouble cleaning that up, too.

"You call this extravagant, you little dick piece of shit? You're pathetic! I should've never married you!"

Erika grabbed the bottle of wine before storming out of the dining room, barking orders on the way. Maura scurried into the room from the kitchen and dropped to her hands and knees, blotting the wine from the floor with a white towel. Corrado watched her, seeing the cloth staining bright red, and hoped bleach would take it out or else she'd be in even more trouble.

He considered telling her that but figured it was pointless. It was already done. She couldn't take it back.

Vito sighed, the sound exaggerated. Corrado didn't need to see his father's expression to know he'd find pity in his eyes, shame for their lives, anger at their mother. Vito would frown, his lips twisted as he gnawed on the inside of his stubbly cheek before clicking his tongue. He always did that when deep in thought.

Corrado didn't know what he had to think about. Same thing happened every time. Nothing new about it.

"I have to get out of here," Vito said, standing. He walked around the table, pausing beside Corrado's chair. "Maura, sweetheart, you'll wanna throw that towel away. Bury it deep in the trash. Don't let her see."

"Yes, sir," Maura said, her voice shaking. She seemed surprised he'd suggest something to help her, but Corrado wasn't. His father was that kind of person. Corrado liked to think he was more like Vito than his mother, but the fact that he hadn't spoken up suggested otherwise.

His father pulled out his wallet and counted out some cash, setting it down on the table beside Corrado's plate. "Hold on to this in case you need it, kid."

"Yes, sir."

He patted Corrado on the head. The gesture, intended to be warm, annoyed him, and he pulled away. He wasn't a puppy. He didn't need to be pet like one.

Vito started for the door as Corrado slipped the money in his pocket. Katrina jumped up, sprinting for their father, and wrapped her arms around his waist. His footsteps faltered yet again as he hugged her, patting her back gently.

"Don't go." Katrina's voice came out as a broken whisper, but Corrado heard her plea, disturbed she would resort to begging.

Their father wouldn't stay. Didn't she realize that yet?

He never did.

"Where are you, you little bastard?"

Erika Moretti was drunk. Again.

Corrado didn't move, sitting still at his desk in his bedroom, hoping she'd get distracted and forget about him. A book lay open in front of him, but it was impossible for him to focus on any of the words.

"Your father should've taken you with him, that pathetic son of a bitch. But no, he always leaves you behind for me to deal with." Her words slurred, a bottle and a half of wine deep now, he guessed. "He knows I don't want you, that I never did."

She let out a sharp, bitter laugh that bounced off the walls and echoed straight to him, striking him in the chest despite the armor he'd built. "Vito forced me to have you just to torture me. He loves torturing me. That's all he's good at, you know. He sure can't fuck or take care of things."

She grew deathly quiet then, but Corrado detected her footsteps down the hallway. He strained his ears listening. He couldn't let her sneak up on him. On misstep, one miscalculation, and she'd have the upper hand.

His arm hairs stood on end, his skin prickling when her footsteps drew closer, pausing right in the doorway behind him. He was defenseless besides his wit, and to hear his mother tell it, he had none of that, either.

"Are you ignoring me?" she asked. He remained quiet, figuring that would be answer enough, but she didn't accept it. "I asked you a question, Corrado Alphonse. I expect a goddamn answer."

"No, ma'am," he said.

"Liar." She strolled into his room. "Give it to me. Right now."

He looked at her as she held her hand out. "Give you what?"

"You know what." She grabbed the back of his chair and yanked it out from under the desk, snatching him to his feet. He froze as she rifled through his pockets, finding the money his father left. "You're just like him."

She shook her head as she shoved him back into his seat. She raised her hand like she was going to hit him, and he flinched, throwing his arm up protectively. He braced himself for a blow that didn't come.

"Do the world a favor, Corrado," she said. "Don't have a family. You'll only fuck them up like he did."

She started to walk away when Corrado muttered under his breath, "you fucked us up worse than him."

Feet abruptly stopped. Despite her intoxication, Erika spun around gracefully and came back toward him. "What did you say?"

Corrado hesitated. *Lie*, a voice in the back of his head screamed. *Beg.* But Corrado was too far-gone to listen to it. He was worn down, mentally exhausted, and tired of putting up with her. "I said you fucked us up worse than—"

He didn't get it all out before her fist swung, striking him across the face. For a petite woman, she had a strong right hook. Corrado hardly had time to recover, to brace himself, when she pounced, wailing on him over and over with her small fists. Strike after strike stung, her blood red painted fingernails ripping at his skin as she resorted to clawing his hands away from his face. He tried to block the blows, deflecting half of them, taking the other half in stride. He didn't throw any punches, refusing to raise his hand to his mother, no matter how furious she made him.

Erika grew tired eventually and staggered away. Corrado watched her as she spit toward him, her face contorted. "You disgust me!"

Likewise, mother.

That moment, as Erika staggered from his room, altered something inside of Corrado. He rubbed his jaw, stinging from a blow, and caught sight of his sister smirking in the hallway. He knew, from the smug look on her face, that she'd instigated it yet again. She'd told their mother he had the money.

Standing, Corrado stalked to his door, glaring at his sister. "You know what, Kat?"

"What?"

"You're on your own now."

He slammed the door in her face.

Early the next morning, while everyone else was still in bed, Corrado slipped out of the house and headed into town. The walk took him two hours, the sun just rising and the streets coming alive when he strolled along the sidewalk, his hands stuffed in his pockets. Where he was going, what he was doing, he wasn't sure. But he couldn't sit around that house; he couldn't deal with them anymore.

He visited shops and sat in a park, enjoying the sunshine, ignoring his life.

As much as he didn't want to admit it, he missed North Carolina. He missed the mountains. He missed that house.

Or maybe he just missed Celia.

It was mid-afternoon when he ran into a group of boys from school: Michael Antonelli, Shawn Smith, and Charlie Klein. The three were rolling through the park on their bikes while Corrado sat alone on a bench. Charlie skidded to a stop when he spotted him, the other two following suit. "Corrado, right?"

Corrado didn't particularly like any of the boys. After a few beats, he nodded.

"Where's your sister?" Michael asked, smiling goofily.

Corrado shrugged. "Home."

"Well, whatcha up to?" Charlie asked. "We're heading to the arcade on Fillmore, if you wanna join us."

After considering it, Corrado shook his head. He'd had enough of dealing with people to last for a while, and he just wanted to be left alone.

"Your loss," Charlie said. "You change your mind, you know where to find us. The pizza's on me."

Corrado sat there quietly when the boys rode away. After a while, his stomach growled, the mention of pizza stirring up his hunger. What could it hurt?

He debated before walking the few blocks to the arcade. The place was chaotic with summer break still in full force for another few weeks.

"Corrado! Over here!"

Charlie's voice rang through the place. Corrado spotted the boys sitting in a center booth, a large pie already on the table. He joined them, slipping in the seat beside Michael.

"Glad you changed your mind," Charlie said. "Eat up, my friend."

My friend. The words struck Corrado strangely. He didn't consider Charlie a friend at all. The boy was older by two years and had a reputation as a troublemaker.

"Where you guys been this summer?" Michael asked, gnawing on a slice of pepperoni, cheese hanging from his chin.

"Away," he said.

"Missed seeing you around."

Corrado's brow furrowed, while Shawn snickered, tossing a napkin at Michael. "You missed looking at his sister, Mikey. That's all that is."

Michael tossed the napkin right back but didn't deny it.

The boys ate and chatted. Charlie dumped out a pocket full of change—at least four dollars in silver coins. Michael and Shawn grabbed some and ran off to play games, while Corrado just sat there, curiously watching Charlie. He wasn't sure why he'd been invited, but he could spot a scheming person a mile away.

His stomach growled at the smell of greasy pizza, so he reached for a slice. He took a small bite, savoring the taste, when Charlie pulled out a stack of bills. He flipped through it, and Corrado nearly choked when he spotted almost a dozen twenties mixed in the bunch. Even his father rarely left him that much. "Where'd you get all that money?"

Charlie smirked. "Earned it."

"How?"

Charlie glanced around to make sure no one was listening as he leaned closer, whispering, "by doing favors for some guys around town."

Corrado narrowed his eyes suspiciously. "Favors?"

"Yeah, you know, delivering things, running errands, sending messages. Nothing big, yet, but soon… my day's coming soon." Charlie stared at him. "Especially if I get you on board."

"Me?" Corrado was taken aback. "Why?"

"Don't act like you don't know," he responded, slipping the money back in his pocket. "We all know who your dad is."

So that was it.

"With Vito Moretti's kid involved, we'd be unstoppable. Wouldn't nobody mess with us."

Corrado's appetite faded. He set the slice of pizza down. "I'm not interested."

"Oh, come on," Charlie said. "You can't tell me the idea of making your own money isn't tempting."

Tempting, definitely. As much as Corrado tried to deny it, that was true. Having money… his own money… and a means to survive without depending on his mother. Against his better judgment, Corrado nodded. "What do I have to do?"

Charlie's smile grew. "Stick with me, and I'll show you."

The Fillmore Crew, they called themselves. Every day for the next week Corrado slipped out of his house before dawn and made the journey to town on foot, meeting up with the three boys in the park.

It started out innocently enough. They did exactly what Charlie had said: passed notes between men, delivered packages, picked up dry-cleaning, and even ordered dinner. Corrado felt like a messenger boy as he shadowed Charlie, saying nothing, mostly watching. Some tossed Charlie as little as a few coins, while others stealthily slipped him a few dollars. It was nothing substantial—a far cry from the big bills Charlie had touted, but it was something.

And it was the easiest job in the world.

Michael and Shawn did most of the brunt work, while Charlie dealt with the people face-to-face. Corrado stayed in the shadows, nodding whenever he was introduced as Vito Moretti's kid, and collected his share before heading home.

He wasn't sure if his mother even noticed his absences, considering he always made it home before dinner.

The following Friday morning, Corrado sat on the park bench when Charlie rode up alone. Corrado eyed him curiously. "Where are the others?"

Charlie climbed off his bike and secured it to a tree. "Not coming. It's payday."

Payday? Hands in his pockets, Corrado clutched onto the handful of change and scraggly bills he'd accumulated. "Isn't that every day?"

Charlie laughed as if something he'd said were funny. "You're a trip, Moretti." He nudged Corrado's arm. "Come on, let me introduce you to the boss."

Boss?

Corrado's mind ran rampant as they walked through town, toward a middle-class neighborhood. Charlie led him to a small white house on the corner, a golden colored Cadillac in the driveway.

"Be cool, okay?" Charlie said. "Mr. Barzetti's kinda paranoid."

Corrado hung back as Charlie stepped up on the porch and knocked. Some locks jingled before the door opened, a vaguely familiar man appearing. Corrado stared at him, trying to place his face.

"Mr. Barzetti, sir," Charlie said, whipping out a Manila envelope uncannily like the ones Vito collected at the casino.

Mr. Barzetti opened the envelope and pulled out a stack of cash.

Definitely like the envelopes his father collected.

Mr. Barzetti counted it before slipping a few bills to Charlie. "Here you go, shorty."

Shorty. The moment he said it, Corrado recognized the man. He'd seen him at The Flamingo, the first one he'd witnessed carried out through the back door.

Mr. Barzetti's gaze drifted off the porch toward Corrado. He narrowed his eyes briefly.

"This is my friend," Charlie said, grinning broadly. "He's—"

"Vito's kid." Mr. Barzetti's face paled as he finished Charlie's sentence. Wordlessly, he reached into the envelope again and pulled out even more bills, this stack larger than the first. He passed them to Charlie, his eyes never leaving Corrado. "Send my regards to your father. Tell him I took care of you, okay?"

Corrado nodded.

Mr. Barzetti disappeared back inside, relocking his door. Charlie stepped off the porch, cheering as he counted the money... $200.

"Whoop!" he said, splitting it right down the middle and handing Corrado half. "This is yours."

Corrado grasped the stack of twenties in his hand. "How often do you see him?"

"Every Friday."

Four hundred dollars a month... a hell of a lot of money for a kid.

Family dinner was the last thing on Corrado's mind after that. He arrived home well after dark, well past dinnertime, on his brand new bright red Schwinn Stingray. He hopped off the bike in the front yard, leaving it there, and bounded up onto the porch. Before he even made it to the door, it swung open, his mother appearing. "Where the hell have you been?"

"With friends."

"He's lying," Katrina said, stepping around their mother and onto the porch. "He has no friends."

"I do, too!"

Katrina crossed her arms over her chest. "Name one."

"Michael Antonelli."

Instantly, Katrina paled.

"Antonelli?" Erika asked, raising her eyebrows. "You've been with Frankie's kid?"

"Yes."

"Mikey's a fool," Katrina declared. "Why would you ever hang out with him?"

"Now, now," Erika said, grasping her daughter's shoulder. "Michael comes from a good bloodline."

Katrina rolled her eyes. "I can't tell."

"Hush up, girl," Erika said. "His family's connected. You'd do well to befriend him."

Katrina cringed.

Corrado stood there, unsure of what else to say. He wanted to go inside, but he didn't dare move. His mother didn't appear angry anymore, but that could change as quickly as the flip of a light switch.

"Where'd you get that bike?" she asked.

"I stole it."

The words flowed from his lips so naturally. He hadn't intended to lie. What was the point? But it certainly sounded better than the truth.

What was the truth? He wasn't sure. He'd been paid for being a Moretti. Was that normal?

"Take it back," she said, waving her hand as she headed back inside. "Now."

"Yes, ma'am."

He had no intention of returning the bike. He had bought it, earned it fair and square, and no one would take what belonged to him.

The next few weeks found Corrado sinking deeper and deeper into a life he still knew little about. Just as Charlie had predicted, Corrado's last name alone propelled the Fillmore Crew to notorious heights in the streets. Mr. Barzetti wasn't the only one calling now… whenever anyone needed a petty job done, they went straight to them.

Michael and Shawn still did the brunt of the work for chump change while Charlie and Corrado collected the big bills. Every week the money increased, from $200 to $300, from $300 to $400.

Corrado never breathed a word of it to his father, despite their request every week to pass along their regards. How could he? He hadn't seen him. Vito hadn't been back since dropping them off.

"Here you go, boys," a young waitress said, sliding a steaming hot pizza onto the table in front of Corrado. "Enjoy."

"Thanks," Charlie said, shooting her a wink as he grabbed a slice. "What's your name, sweetheart?"

She just rolled her eyes and walked away.

"Girls love me," Charlie declared.

Corrado took a bite of his slice. Girls most certainly did not love Charlie. He was gangly, his head too big for his body, his teeth too big for his mouth. He had dirty blond hair, hazel eyes, and skin that constantly seemed to be burned.

Distracted, Charlie slipped away from the table, hauling pizza with him as he chased after the waitress. Corrado stuffed himself with half a pie before heading out through the arcade, strolling straight to the Duck Hunt game. It seemed like a lifetime ago that he'd watched his father earn a perfect score, and Corrado was determined to match it someday.

Popping a dime into the slot, Corrado grabbed the gun and aimed. He pulled the trigger as ducks flew past, hitting about half, the other half going unscathed.

When the game ended, he put in another dime.

And another.

And another.

And another.

He played over and over, until his trigger finger ached. Although he was there, present in the arcade, his mind went elsewhere. He thought about his father, his mother, his sister… his life, the abuse, the anger… Celia, North Carolina… and he thought about Zia.

Zia.

Pop. Pop. Pop.

Duck after duck fell, the game dinging again and again, as everything inside of him flowed out. Numbness coated every inch of his body, his eyes fixed forward as he went blank. He was attuned to everything—every movement, every noise—but his mind was gone.

He felt nothing.

He was in the midst of his twentieth game, down to the last few ducks and near a perfect score, when something slapped him on the back. Corrado's finger slipped, the gun shifting.

The last duck flew right on by.

And just like that, every ounce of emotion flooded his system, overwhelming his senses. Colored splotches appeared in front of his eyes, obscuring his vision.

Something inside of him snapped.

Dropping the gun, he spun around. With no hesitation, he swung, a loud crack echoing through the arcade as his fist connected with something. Pain shot up Corrado's arm as a person flew backward, dropping hard.

Dead silence overtook the arcade. Everyone stopped and stared. One, two, three seconds passed before a horrifying cry echoed nearby. The sound jolted everyone into motion. Corrado blinked a few times, his vision clearing, and saw Charlie lying on the floor. His jaw was already swelling, cocked at an unnatural angle, as blood poured from his mouth.

Corrado stared at him with a mixture of horror and fascination. He'd never hit someone before. Adrenaline pumped through his veins, making his stomach churn.

"Charlie?" he called, stepping closer. "Are you okay?"

Charlie tried to talk, but he could only let out unnatural groans. People helped him off the floor, saying he needed a doctor, as someone yelled for them to call the police.

Police. The word ran through Corrado, chilling him to the bone. It seemed to have a similar effect on Charlie because he furiously shook his head, crying out in pain from the movement.

"No," Charlie ground out. "I'm fine. It was an accident."

Charlie pushed away from the crowd and headed for the exit. Corrado followed, catching up with him as he climbed on his bike.

Before Corrado could say anything, Charlie turned to him. "I'm sorry, Moretti. Really."

"For what?"

"For whatever I did," Charlie said. "I'll make it up to you, I swear I will."

Charlie rode away, leaving Corrado standing there, baffled.

He was sorry?

Corrado rode his Schwinn home in time for dinner. As he neared the house, whipping his bike onto the long driveway, he skidded to a stop in shock. There, parked in front of the house, was his father's Lincoln.

Carefully, Corrado dropped his bike beside the porch and headed inside. Maura busied herself setting the table and avoided his gaze as he flopped down in his usual seat, not waiting to be called. He sat in silence for a few minutes, watching Maura as she worked. She had a black eye, the bruise fading to a greenish haze, and she limped, her face grimacing from the pain.

He thought about asking what happened to her, but he already knew. *Erika Moretti strikes again.*

Katrina and Erika both appeared at eight o'clock on the dot. Smiles graced their faces, fresh nail polish gleaming from their nails. Tags were still affixed to Katrina's navy blue dress, and his mother uncharacteristically wore a pair of high heels around the house.

"Well, well," Erika said, taking her seat, her eyes on Corrado.

"It's kind of you to grace us with your presence."

He'd missed more dinners than he'd shown up for that week.

Vito strolled in last, his face a typical mask of indifference. He slid into his seat and started to eat without offering a greeting. He was dressed immaculately in a black three-piece suit.

"Nothing to say, son?" his mother pressed.

Instead of speaking, Corrado reached for his fork, cringing as pain shot through his wrist. His knuckles were bruising, twice the size of normal. He tried to pull his hand back away, to hide the injury, but he wasn't fast enough.

His mother noticed.

She jumped up, moving at the speed of light. It startled Corrado, and he momentarily froze, giving her the chance to snatch a hold of him. Her hand grasped his, squeezing, her manicured nails biting into the sensitive skin.

An involuntary yelp escaped his throat.

"Hurt?" she asked mockingly.

He ground his teeth together, refusing to respond.

He wouldn't give her the satisfaction.

She squeezed harder. "What happened to your hand?"

"Nothing," he said, yanking his hand away. Crippling pain ripped up his arm as he shoved away from the table. He stormed out, his feet stomping on the stairs as he went up to his room and slammed the door.

It was only a matter of time before someone came after Corrado. He sat at his desk, rocking in his chair, his heart pounding rapidly as he stared at the door. Mere minutes passed before heavy footsteps methodically headed his direction. Vito.

He wasn't sure whether to be relieved. His mother would've flipped, and the violence he tolerated, but his father...well...

Corrado wasn't sure what his father was capable of anymore.

There was a light tap on the door.

"Come in," Corrado muttered.

Vito stepped inside and strolled over to Corrado's bed, sitting on the edge of it, facing him. Corrado purposely kept his gaze away, avoiding him.

"Look at me," Vito ordered.

Corrado turned, his eyes meeting his father's.

"I know what you've been doing."

The coldness in Vito's voice washed through him. "You do?"

"Did you really think I wouldn't know? I told you, kid—I run this town. You can't be out there running my streets without me knowing, especially using *my* name to stake your claim."

"I—"

Vito held his hand up to stop him. "Do you know who I am?"

Corrado's brow furrowed. "You're my father."

"I am, but above that... before that... I'm Vito Moretti. And when you're out there, using my name, associating yourself with me, they ain't thinking about your father. They ain't thinking about the guy who got you that Sox bat for your birthday one year. They're thinking about Vito Moretti, the man they heard stories about."

"What stories?"

Vito stared at him, as if contemplating how to answer. "You remember the movie *The Haunting* we watched? You know, the one about the mansion that drove those people crazy and killed them?"

Corrado nodded. How could he forget? It was, by far, the most intense movie he had ever seen.

Granted, he wasn't allowed to watch many…

"Let's just say those men would rather face that house than Vito Moretti. They have a better chance of surviving that way."

A chill shot down Corrado's spine at those words. He tried to keep his composure, but his alarm was obvious.

"I ain't telling you that to scare you," Vito said. "Well, yeah, I am. You ought to be scared. Because when you use my name, *that's* what you're using. And if you're using it, you gotta be prepared to back it up. And kid? You ain't prepared. I know it, and they know it. And all it takes is one guy with big enough balls to call you out on it."

"But I'm not trying to—"

"It don't matter," Vito said, cutting him off. "I got a reputation that proceeds me. And if you wanna be out there, doing what you're doing, you need to do it with your own name. You need to build your own legacy. And if you can't? Well, then you ain't got no business being out there. Understand?"

Corrado nodded slowly.

"Good," Vito said. "Now tell me what happened to your hand."

Corrado flexed his fingers and grimaced at the pain. "I punched my friend."

"Your friend?"

"Yeah, Charlie Klein."

"Ah, *that* kinda friend. Did you hurt him?"

"I think I broke his face."

Vito laughed. "Must've been one hell of a punch."

"I didn't mean it. He didn't even do anything wrong."

"Don't fret it," Vito said. "But don't do it again. Only the weak use their fists. The strong use their words."

Corrado found that weird, coming from a man he'd seen beat Mr. Barzetti unconscious.

"Just remember what I said, kid." Vito stood and reached into his suit coat, pulling out a small white envelope. "This is for you. I promised I'd get it to you next time I made it home."

Vito held it out. Carefully, Corrado took it, staring at the front of the envelope as his father left the room. It was crinkled and worn, but he faintly made out his name written in pencil on the front.

Opening it, he pulled out the single piece of paper and unfolded it. A photo tumbled out from the paper, drifting to the floor. Corrado glanced down at it, seeing Celia's smiling face.

He turned back to the letter, seeing the careful cursive, the i's all dotted with little hearts.

Even before reading it, his cheeks grew warm.

Broken in two places.

Charlie's jaw was wired shut. He rambled on and on through clenched teeth, his words jumbled. Corrado could hardly understand him. He'd stayed home for days while his father was in town, trying to be on his best behavior, and had gone to the park as soon as Vito left. Charlie had rolled up on his bike, with Michael and Shawn in tow. Neither of the other boys said anything, but they'd been filled in on what happened. Their guarded eyes told Corrado that much.

"Six weeks," Charlie said. "For the next month and a half, I'll be eating with a straw."

Corrado frowned. "I didn't mean to hit you."

"Don't worry." Charlie waved it off. "These things happen."

No, they don't, Corrado thought. Friends don't put their friends in the hospital for no reason at all.

"What about school?" Corrado asked.

Charlie blanched. "My mom says I still have to go."

Summer break ended soon. Corrado was going into the seventh grade, as were Michael and Shawn, whereas Charlie was set to start high school. It wasn't much of an adjustment for Michael and Shawn, seeing as how they lived so far out in the desert that the school provided boarding for them, but Corrado dreaded it.

"Anyway, I have to go," Charlie said. "My mom's been on my ass. I'll catch you later."

Charlie rode off. Corrado expected the others to follow, but they remained on their bikes in front of him.

"Did you really mean to hit him?" Shawn whispered.

"Yeah, and where'd you learn how to fight?" Michael asked.

"We heard he flew like ten feet in the air."

"They said his jaw was practically hanging off by the time you were done with him."

Corrado shook his head. "It was an accident."

Shawn sighed. "Well, whenever Charlie gets better and the crew gets back together, we—"

Corrado cut him off. "I'm out of the crew."

Michael's eyes widened. "What? Why?"

"We had a good run, but it's time to move on. Time to grow up."

Time to make my own name.

7

Corrado sat back in the stiff wooden chair, his feet propped up on the corner of his father's desk. An old radio off to the side blared the sounds of a Frank Sinatra song, the speakers rattling as Corrado hummed along. His chair rocked on its hind legs, his hands clasped on the back of his head, his eyes closed as the lyrics washed through him.

My kind of town, Chicago is…

The office door opened, the chaos from the casino disrupting the melody. Corrado opened his eyes as Vito turned down the radio, so soft Corrado could hardly hear it anymore. His father stalked over, shoving Corrado's feet off the desk as he moved around him. The chair almost tipped as Corrado's feet hit the floor.

On his lap, Vito dropped a bag, the weight of it making him grunt. The black leather bag, round with a metal clasp, reminded him of one doctors carried when they made house calls.

Curious, Corrado peeked inside, finding it filled to the brim with old black $100 casino chips. There had to have been hundreds of thousands of dollars worth. "Do you want me to cash these in?"

"No," Vito said. "They ain't ours."

Corrado glanced in the bag again, seeing *Sands* written on the clunky chips. Sands Hotel was just down the strip, less than half a mile from The Flamingo. "Where'd you get them?"

Vito shot him a stern look. "You know better than to ask questions. Where I got them ain't none of your business. What is your business, what I want you to do, is run them down there."

"And cash them in?"

"Cash them in?" Annoyance flared Vito's voice. "Don't you listen? I said they ain't ours."

"Okay."

"Take them down there, and tell them you need to speak to Antonelli," Vito said. "They'll show you to his office."

Corrado stood, clutching the bag under his arm like a football.

"And make it fast, will you? I told your mother we'd be home for dinner tonight."

Dinner had long since passed. The clock near the doorway read a quarter after nine at night. His mother was likely already drunk and passed out in bed. "Yes, sir."

Corrado strolled down the hallway, heading for the back exit of The Flamingo to avoid the weekend crowds. Being as it was a Saturday night, the place was packed. He passed his father's bodyguards and nodded at them, but neither paid him any mind. They were busy staring out into the casino floor.

Corrado shoved open the door and slipped out into the dark backstreet, letting the metal door slam closed behind him. He hummed, the Sinatra song still stuck in his head, as he headed for the bustling strip. The moment he moved, something in his peripheral caught his attention, a slight shifting in the pitch-black alley.

A tingle swept through him, his skin prickling as the hair on his arms stood on end. He swung around, on alert, and barely had time to react when someone ran up on him. Two guys, cloaked in black from head-to-toe, both wearing ski masks, rushed him, a gleam of a gun catching Corrado's eye in a sliver of moonlight. One grabbed him from the back, tearing him away from the door, and shoved a silver revolver against the side of his neck. The other stood feet in front of him, a black pistol pointed straight at his face. The barrel of it shook as the hand clutching it trembled.

With his free hand, the man in front of him snatched a hold of the black bag, trying to pry it from Corrado's grip. He held on to it, refusing to let go. These men might hurt him, yes, but his father would *definitely* kill him if he lost the chips.

The man viciously tugged, and Corrado gripped it tighter,

anger rushing through him. He shifted, yanking the bag back and sent both guys into a frenzy. It happened fast, split seconds passing in the blink of an eye. Corrado pushed away, fumbling and dropping the bag into the alley. Flustered, the guy aimed his revolver. Grabbing his arm, Corrado twisted it, grasping the gun, his heart racing so fast his vision blurred. He forced the gun around, deflecting, the barrel facing his attacker as they fought for control. A gunshot exploded in the alley, a bullet ripping through the side of the guy's neck when Corrado managed to squeeze the trigger. The attacker let go and dropped to the ground, horrific gurgling sounds rushing from the wound in his neck.

Somehow, Corrado kept a grip on the gun. He had no time to think, no time to second-guess. The second guy hastily grabbed the bag and ran. With no hesitation, Corrado raised the pistol and fired, again and again, bullets ripping straight through the back of the assailant. He dropped hard, the bag going down with him.

The one behind him flailed on the ground, gurgling words Corrado couldn't understand. Turning to him, Corrado knelt down and grabbed the ski mask. The moment he pulled it off, a sudden rush of wooziness ran through Corrado, nauseating him. He stared at the flushed face, hazel eyes pleading with him, the ends of his blond hair stained red.

No. Corrado shook his head. *No, no, no.*

Charlie Klein.

Corrado hadn't seen him in years, not since breaking his jaw that summer, but he would recognize that face anywhere.

His grip on the gun tightened as Charlie raised a bloody hand toward him. His own friend. His friend had tried to rob him. He'd tried to kill him. If Corrado hadn't fought back, if he hadn't deflected the shot, it would've been *him* on the ground.

Numbness followed that thought, swarming his body. Instinctively, he raised the gun, his finger back on the trigger. He aimed straight for Charlie's terrified face.

The gunshot echoed through the alley, magnified to Corrado's ringing ears. He lowered the weapon again when a subtle cry in the alley pulled his attention away. Beside the Dumpster, crouched down, partially hidden, was a third guy. Dressed all in black, his ski mask perched on top of his head, his face was only faintly visible in the darkness.

Michael Antonelli.

Corrado stared at him as the backdoor to the casino flew open, Vito's bodyguards appearing. They blanched, eyes wide as they stared at Corrado. The men seemed torn between intervening and fleeing, frozen in shock. They were knocked to the side after a second when Vito burst outside. He started to speak, his mouth wide open, but no words escaped.

He stared at his son for a moment before glancing between the two boys, dead on the ground.

"You killed them," Vito said, raising his eyebrows. "You shot them both. You fucking *killed* them."

Corrado turned away from Michael to face his father. It didn't take a genius to figure out the other boy, dead in the alley, would be Shawn. Those three were inseparable.

Opening his hand, Corrado let the gun hit the dirty asphalt. He'd killed them, the only friends he'd ever had. "They were my friends."

Vito shook his head. "They weren't the kind of friends you thought they were, kid. They were friends in the life, and well, sometimes you gotta take those friends out." Vito slapped Corrado on the back, shoving him away from Charlie. "Go on. Do what I told you to do. We'll take care of this. "

In a daze, hands shaking, Corrado walked over and snatched the black bag from the alley.

Corrado didn't tell his father. Had he pointed him out, Michael would certainly be dead. But maybe, if he kept his mouth shut, he might walk away unscathed.

Corrado didn't want his blood on his hands.

The ten-minute walk to The Sands was a blur. He stepped inside the casino, telling the first person he saw that he needed to speak with Antonelli. Anxiety swirled inside of him when he spoke the name. A lady led him to an office near the front, where a stern looking man sat in a leather chair. Frankie Antonelli. Corrado set the bag in front of him, waiting to be dismissed.

Frankie glanced inside the bag. "Hope it wasn't any trouble."

"Of course not," Corrado said, his voice barely above a whisper.

Frankie pulled out a twenty and slipped it in the chest pocket of Corrado's button down shirt. He patted it. "That's for you."

Corrado nodded and slipped out of the office, pulling the money back out. Twenty-dollars. That was what taking his friends' lives had been worth.

Passing a waitress, he shoved the crinkled bill in a glass tip jar on her tray and kept on walking.

The trip back took another ten minutes. He'd been gone less than a half-hour, yet by the time he reached The Flamingo, all signs of the struggle were gone. The alley was vacant, a subtle stench of bleach assaulting his nose when he reached the back door.

Instinctively, he glanced beside the Dumpster.

Michael, too, was gone.

He headed inside, hands shoved in his pockets, his head down. Both bodyguards were alert this time, addressing Corrado as he passed, but he didn't respond. Tapping on the office door, he turned the knob and stepped inside when his father acknowledged him.

Frank Sinatra again crooned from the old radio. Vito sat behind his desk, his feet propped up now as he moved his right foot to the beat. He seemed relaxed, almost as if the last thirty minutes hadn't happened, almost as if it were just a nightmare, but the revolver he fiddled with told a different story.

"I take it everything went smoothly."

"Yes, sir."

"Let me ask you something, kid." Vito sat forward, putting the gun down on the desk as he clasped his hands together in front of him. Corrado tensed, waiting for the anger over what he'd done, but instead a small smile quirked his father's lips. "You ever think about coming to Chicago with me?"

Corrado didn't hesitate. "Every day since I was seven years old."

PART II

The Impatient Years

8

They didn't call it the Mafia. No, the undignified term, according to Vito, tainted their image.

They called it *La Cosa Nostra* instead.

The words flow beautifully from the tongue. *This thing of ours.* It's a brilliant sentiment—belonging to something powerful. Corrado had jumped into it with preconceived notions, just like most others did. He went for the money, for the power, for the respect, and he stayed because, well… he stayed because he had to.

After they invited you in, after they embraced you, there was no walking away. It's a beautiful web of glorious silk, intricately woven together with deception, which draws you in like moths to a flame. But as soon as you're close, as soon as you approach, the web snatches a hold of you and refuses to let go.

And once you're stuck, the black widow comes and fucks you good before eating you alive.

Corrado learned that lesson quickly. Despite the allure of the words, there was nothing poetic about *La Cosa Nostra.* But there wasn't a single moment, as he settled into the life, that he regretted his decision to move. It wasn't pretty. But compared to his life back in Nevada? His life with his mother? Being in Chicago was a cakewalk.

It turned out to be monotonous at the beginning. At seventeen, a high school drop out, he was back to acting like that eleven-year-old kid, running errands and delivering packages for a few dollars here and there… money that disappeared in the blink of an eye as he regularly picked up the tab for everyone. He was a peon, a disposable messenger boy, a kid with no voice and no opinion. Corrado was the bottom rung of a ladder, one that got stepped on by those on their way to the top.

He was nothing. He was nobody to them.

But he never complained. He did what was asked of him, no matter the time of day, no matter how menial the task. If a *capo* wanted food at three in the morning, Corrado was out the door in less than five minutes, searching for a place still open at that hour. He picked up dry cleaning, filled shopping lists, and even made coffee. He did it all, because the alternative was doing nothing.

"Here, kid. Got a job for you."

The moment Corrado opened the front door of his rental house on Felton Drive, a thick manila envelope was shoved at him. He groggily stumbled a few steps as he clutched it, still half-asleep. Pitch-black night hung thickly outside, cold air prickling the bare skin of his chest. It was a cloudy, dreary night… or morning, Corrado thought, since it was well past midnight.

Had he not recognized his father's voice, he would've never known who delivered the package. Vito turned away, rushing from the porch and disappearing down the street. Corrado closed the door and strolled through the downstairs of his house, his bare feet dragging against the chilly wooden floor. Flicking on a lamp in the living room, he glanced down at the package, seeing an address scribbled on the front of it. No other instructions.

"Just great," he muttered, heading upstairs to get dressed. He threw on some black slacks and a gray button-down shirt, walking a fine line between lazy and presentable, exhausted but not knowing what situation he'd walk into it. It could be as simple as handing it through a crack in a door, or as extravagant as crashing a formal party. He had to be prepared for anything.

He just wanted to go back to bed.

Grabbing a jacket, he concealed the envelope in the large

inside pocket before picking up his gun and heading out into the night. The shiny Ruger Mark II revolver slipped nicely in the holster in his jacket, hidden but fully loaded, just in case.

Unfamiliar with the address, he pulled the crinkled Chicago map from the glove box of the car he'd bought—a beat up, old black Mercedes. He unfolded it, scanning the neighborhoods until he found Kessler Street in the south side of the city. He drove there, creeping down the street until he located the address written on the package. It turned out to be a decrepit little brick building, more of a rundown business than a house, the windows boarded up, the outside crumbling.

Corrado parked along the curb in front of it, beneath a flickering streetlight, and climbed out of the car. He glanced around, studiously checking the neighborhood for any signs of trouble, but it appeared abandoned. He scanned the building, noting the exits and entrances as he approached the door. It seemed to be made of steel, a slide slot where a window usually would be.

He hesitated, finding no doorbell or knocker, before tapping on the metal. No sound came, no response or movement. He tried the knob, curious if it was unlocked, but it didn't budge. He knocked again—two, three, four times. Was anyone even here?

He took a step back, assessing, when a stirring caught his attention. It was subtle, the rustling of grass. His defenses went up, the hair on his arms standing on end. Reaching into his coat, he grasped his gun, whipping it out as he swung around.

Corrado was fast… but not fast enough.

A hard blow to the face knocked him off balance, his surroundings a blur as he stumbled. Before he could regain his composure, another strike knocked him back against the metal door, forcing the air from his lungs as someone pinned him there, an elbow going straight to his gut. A thick hand grasped his wrist, viciously pulling it backward, and Corrado gasped as a sharp pain shot up his forearm.

The gun was ripped from his flimsy grasp within a matter of seconds, the pressure restraining him releasing once he had been disarmed.

Corrado blinked, his hazy vision coming back into focus, as his own gun pressed to his forehead. "And who might *you* be?" a deep voice asked, strikingly calm.

Struggling to catch his breath, suddenly on the defense, Corrado gaped at the man in front of him. Corrado wasn't short or scrawny, but his assailant was a beast of a man, making him feel as puny as a stuffed bear. He was shrouded in darkness, an oversize hood covering his head, concealing his face. His free hand held a white plastic bag containing Chinese food containers.

"A friend," he managed to say, his jaw throbbing as he forced out the words.

"A friend," the man echoed, "of whose?"

"Yours."

"I have no friends." His answer was immediate. "Try again."

"I have something for you," Corrado said. "A package."

"Ah." The gun withdrew from his head and slipped into the man's pocket. "Why didn't you just say so?"

The man reached past him and unlocked the door, shoving it open. Corrado tried to move out of the way, but the man grasped his arm and shoved him inside, relocking the door behind them.

Heart beating rapidly, Corrado assessed the building as the man hit a switch, only one bulb working on a hanging light. The place was in shambles, even more so than the outside. The stench of chemicals and something rotting hung in the air. Chinese containers were strewn around the floor, dozens of them from a place called Lang Miens.

One room, Corrado noted. Furniture scattered throughout the space, a grimy couch and chair in front of a small television with an antenna; an old mattress in the corner with a pillow and blankets; a small heater beside a massive black trunk. Along the back, aligning the wall, were half a dozen gallon drums, some empty and tipped over, others sealed. In the back corner set a refrigerator.

He lives in this dump?

The man strolled over to the heater and lit it before removing his hood. Corrado's blood ran cold at the sight of the familiar withering, pale face and beady blue eyes.

Luca Esponzio.

Corrado had never met him before, and hoped never to have to. He'd seen his face, though, on the front of the newspaper. Reported serial killer, suspected in over fourteen disappearances, but they never found any evidence to prosecute him. People vanished into thin air after being spotted with Luca, never to be seen again.

"You say you have something for me?" Luca asked, raising an eyebrow as he stepped toward Corrado, holding out his massive right hand. It was calloused and dirty, with a gold ring wedged on his swollen middle finger.

Reaching into his coat, Corrado pulled out the envelope and handed it over. Luca opened it right in front of him, skimming through a stack of cash before pulling out a photograph. Corrado caught a quick glimpse of it, recognizing the man in the photo as a mobster in New York: Johnny Canella.

Luca stuffed everything back into the envelope as he plopped down on the couch and tossed it beside him. He pulled out his dinner, expertly using chopsticks to eat. "You like Chinese food?"

Corrado watched him curiously. "Occasionally."

"You should give Lang Miens a try." He motioned to the container. "Best Orange Chicken in Chicago."

"I'll keep that in mind."

"You do that." Luca waved him off. "Unless you have something else for me, I recommend you leave."

Corrado turned at the dismissal, taking a few steps toward the door before hesitating. "Sir?"

"Yeah?"

"My gun."

A sinister smirk twisted Luca's lips. "*My* gun now."

Corrado's stomach twisted in knots. Vito had handed him that gun after the incident at the casino, telling him to keep it, that it was lucky. Although Corrado didn't believe in luck, the gun was special to him.

Other than the long ago fractured bat, it was the only thing he remembered Vito ever *giving* him.

He wanted to argue, to demand it back, but a voice in the back of his head told him to retreat.

Corrado slipped into his car and drove away, his hands trembling against the steering wheel. He went straight home, arriving before dawn, the sky lightening but the neighborhood still startlingly dark. On his porch sat a figure, the soft orange glow of a lit cigar illuminating his father's face.

Vito glanced up as he approached. "You make out okay?"

Corrado shrugged. "I survived."

Vito flicked ashes onto the sidewalk as Corrado sat down beside him. "Looks like you're getting a nasty bruise on your cheek. You didn't draw on him, did you?"

Corrado rubbed his jaw, wincing. "Yeah, I did."

"You can kiss that gun goodbye." Vito chuckled under his breath. "Guess you'll know better next time."

He narrowed his eyes, studying his father. *Next time*? Vito peeked at him, seeing the questions in his eyes… questions he wouldn't ask. He knew better.

"The crazy bastard's good at what he does," Vito explained. "Nobody's better. And if he ain't working for you, he's working against you. Remember that."

Vito stood, clasping his son's shoulder and laughing lightly to himself. "Better find yourself another gun somewhere, kid."

No, he wanted *his* gun. And he would get it back someday.

A few days later, Corrado watched the news when a familiar face flashed on the grainy screen. Johnny Canella, reputed mob associate, had been reported missing, vanished from his bed as he slept beside his wife.

A chill shot down Corrado's spine. Luca Esponzio struck again.

Less than two weeks later, Vito showed back up at Corrado's door in the middle of the night, again carrying a thick envelope. Corrado stared at it with disbelief before getting dressed and heading out, concealing his new dull black pistol in his coat. He'd bought it off one of the local thugs, the serial numbers scratched off, the trigger stiff and hard to squeeze. He hated the feel of it, missed the ease of his revolver, but it was the best he could do under the circumstances.

He drove across town to the address on Kessler Street, stepping onto the porch and knocking on the door. Once again he heard the subtle rustling, but this time he remained still, not reacting. His heart hammered in his chest in anticipation as shadows swept across the small porch, the man stepping behind him, towering over him.

"Back again, I see."

Corrado said nothing as Luca reached past him, unlocking the door and again violently shoving him inside. He stood there, pulling out the envelope and holding it out. Luca took it, once more skimming through the cash and glancing at the included photo before taking his spot on the couch with a container of Chinese.

He clearly had a strict schedule, one he stuck to in order to keep himself straight. Following a routine cut down on the number of mistakes you likely made, but it also painted you very predictable. A trait of a true psychopath. Methodical. Organized.

"You can go," Luca said, waving him off without Corrado ever speaking.

Every few weeks he repeated the visit, so much so that by the fifth time, Luca merely opened the door, and Corrado strolled in on his own. Luca took the envelope, settling on the couch with his dinner, hardly even sparing Corrado a glance.

"You try Lang Miens yet?" he asked, obnoxiously chewing a mouthful of orange chicken.

"No."

"You don't know what you're missing," Luca said. "I could eat it every day."

More containers had piled up over the weeks. Corrado suspected he *did* eat it every day.

"I'll try it this week," Corrado said.

Luca glanced at him, eyes narrowed as if gauging whether

Corrado were lying to him. "Get on out of here. Grab some on the way home. You won't regret it."

Corrado nodded, turning to leave, when a flash of silver caught his eye. He hesitated, watching as Luca pulled out the familiar revolver.

My gun.

The man set it beside him on the couch.

It took everything in Corrado walk out the door.

Next time, he told himself.

There would be more visits, more opportunities.

But much to Corrado's surprise, the envelopes stopped being delivered.

9

Winter had come early to Chicago. A frosty wind whipped through the neighborhood, violently shaking the tall maple trees that surrounded the brick mansion at the end of Felton Drive. Thick wet flakes fell from the sky, sporadically sticking wherever they landed, while a thin layer of ice coated everything. It glistened, like a fresh topcoat of clear paint.

Corrado stood in the middle of the slick driveway, huddling between his father and a Cadillac DeVille. The Boss's car, he knew. He'd seen it drive by a few times, seen it parked outside his father's house twice, but he'd never been so close to it before.

In fact, he rarely even got this close to the Boss.

Antonio DeMarco, the Don of the Chicago syndicate, stood on his porch, surrounded by some of the most dangerous men in the country. Salvatore Capozzi, the underboss, stood statuesque on Antonio's right. He was hefty with a high-pitched voice, like an Italian Porky Pig without the stutter. On Antonio's left was Sonny Evola, his *consigliere*. Sonny was tall, six-and-a-half feet, but walked slumped over because of scoliosis.

They were the top rungs of the ladder, the men who called the shots. Corrado had encountered Antonio once before, as a child, in his father's office at The Flamingo.

He was even more intimidating in his own territory.

All around them stood *La Cosa Nostra*'s finest, most of whom Corrado didn't know. They were the most powerful Capo's, the strongest soldiers, the ones who night-after-night terrorized

Chicago's streets. As a mere street runner, Corrado knew he didn't belong there, but he'd been with his father when Vito got the call to show up.

"What we gonna do, Boss?" a capo asked. "This is getting out of control."

"I know it is," Antonio said. "Why do you think I called you here? It needs handled. *Now.*"

"I'll do it," someone chimed in from the center of the crowd. "Whatever it is. Let me do it."

Corrado had no idea what they were discussing, the meaning of the meeting lost on him. Cold seeped through his thick wool coat, the damp air feeling like ice clinging to his skin. He tried to ignore it, keeping a straight face while they talked, but it proved difficult. He wasn't yet used to the cold weather, so every snowflake made him shiver even more.

The house he stayed in was only a few blocks down the street. He considered heading home, to get out of the cold, but walking out while the bosses were talking? That was asking for a death sentence.

The Boss surveyed the crowd, not saying much of anything. Corrado's teeth chattered while he waited, another shiver ripping down his spine as his gloved hands gripped his coat tighter around himself. He rocked on his heels, anxious for dismissal, so unfocused that he didn't notice the Boss watching him until he spoke.

"Are you cold?" Antonio asked.

Corrado glanced at him, sensing the impatience in his voice. "No, sir."

"Really?" Antonio asked, raising an eyebrow. "You shivered."

"Excitement."

"Your teeth were chattering."

"Anticipation."

The curt responses flew from his lips. Beside him, his father cursed under his breath. *Not good.*

Antonio's eyes narrowed. Corrado knew little about the Boss, only the stories he'd been told and the vague childhood memory from years ago. He knew the man lacked tolerance, though, and it wasn't easy to earn his respect.

And Corrado had a sneaking suspicion based on the man's expression that what little respect he might've earned for just being there had already withered away.

"Since you seem to be so eager, I have a job for you," Antonio said. "Do you know Luca Esponzio?"

There was a sharp intake of breath from the men. Everyone in the godforsaken city knew the name. Corrado didn't know if it were a trick question, given he'd been handling business with him, and decided to tread lightly in case it was a test.

"I've heard of him," he said. "The serial killer."

"Right." Antonio glanced around at the others again and shook his head. "You see, he's being a thorn in my side, and I need it removed right away. You get what I'm saying?"

Corrado nodded. "You want him taken care of."

"Exactly. You think you can do that for me? You think you can get rid of my little problem?"

Corrado remained stoic. "Yes, sir."

Antonio dismissed him with the wave of a hand. "Do it, then."

"How will you know I did it?"

The question came out abruptly, catching Antonio off guard. He seemed torn between answering and killing him. "He wears a ring, middle finger. It's covered in diamonds, a big L in the center of it. Bring it to me."

Corrado remembered that ring. Without another word, he disappeared into the night, feeling the Boss's eyes on him as he strolled away. He reached his father's Lincoln and slipped into the passenger seat, turning the key dangling in the ignition. The heat blared, a burning stench filling the car as he cranked it the entire way up to thaw his frozen body. *To hell with walking.*

Vito climbed in beside him and slammed his hands against the steering wheel. "Fuck!"

"What?"

"You can't take on Esponzio," Vito said, raising his voice. "No fuckin' way. He's a savage. He'll chop you up in pieces and throw you in a barrel of acid. And he'll do it without even breaking a sweat! No… *no way*. You ain't doing it."

Corrado glared at his father as they drove away from the house, tires squealing as the car skidded down the icy driveway. Vito doubted him. He underestimated him.

Corrado would show him.

"The crews will get him," Vito continued. "You just lay low until it blows over. The Boss will be pissed, yeah, but he'll get over it once Esponzio's dead. He'll forgive you. He's that kind of man."

Despair laced Vito's words as his voice dropped low. Antonio DeMarco wasn't that type of man. He couldn't be to run the business. He wouldn't *forgive*.

Vito pulled up in front of Corrado's house, the car again skidding, nearly hitting a man crossing the street. The guy yelled, slamming his hands down on the hood of the Lincoln as he berated Vito about his driving. Corrado expected his father to lash out—to shoot the guy—but he merely muttered, "Fuck off!"

Corrado climbed out and stood on the curb in the darkness, watching the taillights of the Lincoln as it sped away. As soon as it disappeared from sight, Corrado pulled out his keys and took the journey to Kessler Street.

The neighborhood was quiet, as usual, the boarded-up brick building seeming as vacant as ever. Corrado parked down the street, gripping the gun in his coat as he headed onto the small porch. He took a few deep breaths, trying to prepare himself, before tapping on the door.

He waited. And knocked. And waited. And knocked. Eventually he heard the subtle rustling, barely detectable. He remained still, watching the porch around his feet and waiting for the man's hulking shadow to fall over him. It happened finally, and Corrado clutched the gun tighter, his finger hovering on the trigger. He started to greet Luca, to shoot him, when the shadow whisked away. The sound of crackling brush met his ears, accompanied by hushed voices around the side of the house.

Corrado barely had time to look at Luca when the man pulled the revolver from his coat. Gunshots shattered the night air as he blindly fired around the side of the house at whoever approached. Mere seconds passed before screams accompanied the noise and gunfire returned.

An ambush.

Someone had beaten Corrado there.

Heart thudding in his throat, Corrado dodged off the porch. He wasn't one to retreat from a fight, but he knew better than to involve himself in someone else's battle.

Furious didn't cover his feelings as he drove home. A familiar numbness coated his body as his thoughts raced. The pure resentment brewing inside of him caused a fracture, forcing a detachment between body and mind. Underestimating him was one thing… undermining him was another.

He could've done it.

He *would've* done it.

They hadn't even given him the chance.

He'd show them.

He'd show *all* of them.

"Can I get you something?"

Corrado reluctantly pulled his gaze away from the glass door of *Dolce Vita Pizza*, glancing at the boy with a filthy red apron tied around his waist. He barely looked old enough to be off the tit, much less working there.

"Water."

Corrado turned away again, thinking the boy would take a hint, but he didn't budge.

"Nothing to eat?"

"No."

"We make a fantastic deep dish pie."

"No."

From the corner of his eye, Corrado watched the boy shrug before walking away, whistling to himself. Corrado focused his attention back through the glass door, out to the quiet neighborhood. The pizzeria would be closing soon for the night, as would the small green building across the street. *Lang Miens.* The florescent sign flickered, half-lit, the dim restaurant vacant except for the couple working. A woman at the front counter, cashing out the register, while a man occasionally popped his head out from the back.

It had been two days since the ambush… and ambush that left half a crew dead and Luca Esponzio missing. Nobody knew where he'd run off to, but he hadn't gone back to his hideout on Kessler Street. He was in the wind, they believed, but Corrado knew better.

Luca was a man of habit.

Corrado glanced at his watch. Twenty minutes until midnight.

The boy returned with the water, setting it down on the table in front of Corrado. "Here you go."

Corrado nodded his thanks. He had no intention of drinking it.

The boy lingered there as if waiting for Corrado to speak, but gave up and walked away. Corrado's focus remained outside as he counted down time in his head.

At a quarter till, the woman at the register grabbed her purse and walked out the front door… exactly like the day before.

Corrado stared at the building, watching, waiting. At ten till, a cloaked form stalked down the street, heading right for Lang Miens. Luca stealthily slipped inside the restaurant, keeping his head down. He moved like a shadow, blending into his surroundings, and disappeared into the back where the lone worker waited.

Exactly like the day before.

A moment later, Luca reappeared, carrying his dinner. Orange Chicken, Corrado knew. *Just like every other day.*

After Luca vanished around the side of the building, Corrado tore his gaze away from the door. He grabbed a few dollars from his wallet and tossed them on the table, nodding politely at the boy working before leaving to go home.

Twenty-four hours later, Corrado strolled back into the pizzeria, taking the table adjacent to the door again. Before he could do anything, the boy from yesterday approached, carrying a glass of ice water. "Water," he said, setting it down on the table in front of him.

Corrado was put off by it. "Thanks."

"You want to try that deep dish today?"

"No."

"Sure?"

"Positive."

He shrugged. "Okay, then. Let me know if you change your mind. My name's John, by the way."

Corrado spared him a glance, seeing his expectant look, as if he anticipated him actually introducing himself.

Ignoring, Corrado glanced at his watch before focusing his attention outside. He couldn't be bothered with pesky pizzeria workers today. Twenty minutes until show time.

At a quarter till, the lady working at Lang Miens packed up to leave. Corrado stood, tossing a few bucks down on the table, and headed outside. After making sure the area was clear of threats, he headed across the street as the woman left. He slipped inside, cringing as a bell on the door chimed. It startled him—he hadn't accounted for it—but he didn't have time to hesitate.

"Luca, my man," the guy hollered from the back. "Your Orange Chicken is coming right up."

As he walked, Corrado unfastened his tie, pulling it off. Gripping the ends of it with both hands, he shoved the door open to the kitchen and caught the worker off guard by jumping him from behind. Corrado wound the tie tightly around his neck, pulling it from both ends with all his strength, cutting off his flow of air. He gasped, struggling to breathe, and tried to fight off the attack, but Corrado held on. In less than a minute, his body went limp, passing out from lack of oxygen. Corrado let go, not wanting to kill the man, and he dropped to the floor. His head hit the linoleum with a sickening crack.

Corrado retrieved his tie, carefully slipping it around his neck again, before glancing at his watch. Two minutes to go.

Just like clockwork, the bell above the door chimed two minutes later. Heart hammering in his chest, Corrado reached into his coat and pulled out a gun. This was it. In thirty seconds, one of them would be dead.

The door to the kitchen opened, and Corrado didn't hesitate. The moment he caught a flash of Luca's face, he aimed and squeezed the stiff trigger. The explosive gunshot echoed through the restaurant, making Corrado's ears ring as a bullet ripped through Luca's forehead, exploding out the back of his skull. Eyes as wide as saucers, he plunged to the floor instantly.

Corrado was in a haze, his hearing fuzzy as he dropped the pistol and walked the few steps over to Luca. Gloved hands grasped Luca, and Corrado tried to pry the ring off, but it wouldn't budge past the first knuckle.

Glancing around, Corrado grabbed a butcher's knife from the counter and a rag. Without giving it a second thought—knowing he'd lose the nerve if he dwelled on it—he hacked the finger with the blade, whacking it off. He wrapped it up in the rag and slipped it into his coat before patting Luca down. Reaching into the man's pocket, he pulled out the shiny Ruger Mark II revolver.

"*My* gun," he muttered, concealing it as he bolted for the door. He slipped out of the restaurant, into the darkness, giving only a brief glance behind.

A brief glance, leading straight to a set of startled young eyes watching suspiciously from the pizzeria door.

Corrado parked in front of the mansion on Felton Drive and stepped out of his car, surveying the quiet property. Most of the house was dark at this hour, except for a bright light shining from the front room. Corrado shut his car door, a shiver running through him from the bitter cold, and wrapped his coat tightly around him. When he stepped up on the porch, the curtain ruffled, alerting him to the fact that he was being watched.

He approached the door and reached toward the doorbell, but stopped before pressing it. This late at night, it wouldn't surprise him if most of the family were already asleep. Not wanting to be rude, he instead tapped on the door.

Immediately, it opened a crack, a young boy appearing. Corrado blinked a few times, vaguely recognizing the face. "Vincenzo?"

His expression flickered to annoyance. "It's Vincent."

"Vincent," Corrado said. "Is your father home?"

Vincent narrowed his eyes, studying him, deciding whether or not to answer. He was about a foot shorter than Corrado and still had a slight baby face. Thirteen, Corrado tried to remember. Maybe fourteen. He hadn't seen him since that summer in North Carolina.

After a moment, Vincent opened the door the rest of the way and waved Corrado in. "He's in his office. It's just down the hall, last door on the right."

Corrado nodded his thanks and strolled down the hall as Vincent closed the front door again. The door to the office was cracked open, a soft glow of light spilling out onto the floor. Corrado pushed it open the rest of the way, seeing Antonio lounged in his black leather office chair. His eyes were closed, a pager lying on the desk in front of him.

Waiting for the news Corrado was about to bring.

Corrado stepped into the doorway, stealthily, but Antonio seemed to sense it. Intuitive. His eyes snapped open, his hand reaching into his desk with lightning speed and whipping out a small .22 pistol. He pointed it, no hesitation, as emotions played out in his eyes. Sheer terror turned to shock before fading to suspicion.

"How'd you get in here?" Antonio asked, the gun aimed straight at Corrado's face.

"Your son let me in," he said. "He told me where to find you."

Antonio cursed under his breath. Clearly Vincent wasn't supposed to invite people in.

"What are you doing here?" Antonio spat. "You had an order! Did you think I was fucking around?"

It took a second for those words to register with Corrado. The Boss thought he'd failed.

Corrado said nothing, the anger of being underestimated again swarming inside of him as he reached into his coat. Antonio watched apprehensively, his finger still on the trigger of his gun, appearing unnerved by his presence.

Corrado pulled the rag out of his pocket, grasping it in the palm of his hand as he took two steps forward. Antonio kept the gun trained on him as he set it on the desk before taking those same two steps back. It was calculated, careful.

He didn't want to get shot, after all.

Glancing down, Antonio balked, the gun wobbling and no longer aimed at him. Luca's middle finger lay in front of him, bloody and still fresh, a grotesque shade of purple framing the gold ring. Antonio stared at it, shell-shocked. "His fucking finger!"

He hadn't expected it to be attached still.

"How…?" Antonio looked back at him. "*You*? How the hell did you do it?"

"I watched him for two days, studied him, until I could predict his next move. Then I just stayed one step ahead of him."

Corrado turned to leave without waiting for dismissal when Antonio cleared his throat. "Hey, kid."

"Yes?"

"What's your name?"

"Corrado," he replied. "Corrado Moretti."

Recognition dawned on the man's face. Corrado saw it in his eyes, practically heard his next thought: *Vito's kid.*

"Nice job, Moretti."

Corrado shook his head. "A job is a job, sir. If you're doing it right, there's nothing *nice* about it."

10

A horn blared in front of the house, loud and incessant. Corrado walked to the window and peered through the curtain, spotting the familiar black Lincoln in the driveway.

He opened the front door, not giving his father much of a look as he tried to fix his collar. His knot was sloppy, the tie completely lopsided.

Ties came in handy—last night had proven it—but he'd never get the hang of them.

The horn stopped blowing as Vito stepped out. "Un-fuckin'-believable."

Corrado groaned. "I know. I'll never learn to tie these things."

"I ain't talking about your damn tie, kid," Vito said, his voice high-pitched. Corrado glanced at him, wondering if it were excitement or anxiety fueling his words. "I wake up to the news that Esponzio is dead. Dead! The organization is gossiping like a bunch of little girls! Everybody wants to take credit, everyone's crew trying to step up, wanting the glory, you know? But nobody really knows who did it. My crew sure didn't."

Corrado remained quiet, his eyes still on his tie, but his mind absorbed his father's every word.

"But then I'm sitting at the house, and my phone rings, and it's the Boss. The Boss! He goes, 'Vito, I need you to do something for me.' And I'm down for whatever, you know? So I tell him that, and he goes, 'I need you to bring your son to me today. I wanna meet with your kid.' So I go, 'my kid?' And you know what he says?"

"What?"

"He says, 'yeah, Corrado.'" Vito's voice leveled out as he spoke his name, a staunch seriousness seeping in. "*Corrado.* At first I'm nervous, you know, because he's calling you in, but then something hits me—he knows your name."

Corrado gave up on fixing his tie and stared at Vito. "So?"

"So Antonio DeMarco doesn't care to know names. He makes a point never to learn them. Some days I wonder if he even fucking remembers mine. So I hang up the phone, and then it hits me. I know why no one can say whose crew killed Esponzio."

"Why?"

Vito pointed at him as he stepped forward. "Because it was you."

Corrado remained silent.

"Tell me you did it," Vito said, a hard edge to his voice. "Tell me you went out and killed that bastard after I specifically told you not to try it."

Corrado nodded slowly. "I did."

Every muscle in his body grew taut at the look on his father's face. He prepared for him to lash out, to rail on him for disobeying. Vito didn't like people disregarding him. But as quickly as the rage flared in Vito's eyes, it disintegrated as genuine laughter burst from his chest. His laugh was loud and boisterous as he grabbed Corrado, pulling him into a tight hug. He smacked him on the back, happiness oozing from him as he grabbed Corrado's face between his hands. Pride shined from his glossy eyes. "I knew you had it in you, kid. That's what I was talking about, you know. I told you to make a name for yourself, and you fucking did it."

Corrado didn't disagree, but his father was wrong. Antonio DeMarco may know his name, but he'd seen it in his eyes—he was still just Vito's kid.

"Come on." Vito stepped off the porch. "Can't keep the Boss waiting."

"Now?"

"Yeah, now. We got ten minutes to get there."

Corrado shut his front door, locking up the house, before following his father. He grew tense as they drove across town, sickness brewing in the pit of Corrado's stomach as they approached the neighborhood he'd lurked in three nights in a row. They cruised down the street, past police cars with lights still flashing, as yellow caution tape surrounded Lang Miens. He hoped his father would continue on, but Vito whipped the car into the first parking spot he found.

"Here?" Corrado asked incredulously.

Vito shrugged, cutting the engine. "The Boss picks the place. We just show up."

Corrado climbed out of the car, keeping his gaze away from Lang Miens as he followed his father to Dolce Vita Pizza. They stepped inside the pizzeria, and Corrado's eyes darted around, sure everyone there would recognize him. No one seemed to, though. No one even gave him a second look.

Antonio sat in a booth in the far back, away from the door but with a window view. His eyes were peeled outside, fixated across the street. Vito and Corrado slid into the booth across from him.

"It's something, isn't it?" Antonio said, turning his gaze to Corrado when they removed the caution tape. "You must have one hell of an adrenaline rush. Being here, so close, yet nobody knowing. Nobody saw. Nobody suspects."

Nobody. Corrado nodded, yet he knew it wasn't true. The suspicious eyes of the kid named John haunted his thoughts. He may not have seen it, he may not have known, but he suspected.

Corrado looked around for the boy, not finding him anywhere. There was no adrenaline rushing through him, no excitement, and no satisfaction. He felt very little.

It seemed all like a vague dream.

"I gotta tell you—I didn't think you'd do it," Antonio continued. "I still wonder how you pulled it off, but part of me doesn't wanna know. What I do know is that you got a God-given talent, and I wanna use that. I want *you* to use that. You get what I'm saying?"

Corrado slowly shook his head. "No, sir."

Antonio leaned across the table, closer to Corrado. His eyes were full of wonder as a small smirk turned his lips. He looked like a kid who just found the best prize on the bottom of his Cracker Jack box. "I want you to work for *me*. I'm offering you a chance, a way to the top, while we have an opening. You'll still have to earn your place, you know, join your father's crew, but aside from that, I'll have some special work for you."

He didn't spell it out, but Corrado got the message. He'd killed *La Cosa Nostra*'s biggest hitman. Someone had to take his place.

"Okay."

Antonio raised an eyebrow. "Okay?"

"Okay." What else was he supposed to say? He couldn't refuse him. He hadn't been around for long, but he knew enough to know that when the Boss made an offer, it was actually a demand.

Antonio remained there, unmoving, staring at Corrado inquisitively. "How do you do that?"

"Do what?"

"Stay so detached," he asked. "I've yet to see any emotion from you. You show up, calm and collected, like we're talking about the fucking weather here."

"He's always been that way," Vito chimed in from beside him.

"I don't think I've even seen him smile," Antonio continued, shaking his head. "Hell, *can* you smile?"

"Of course I can," he replied. "There just isn't any reason to."

Antonio reached across the table and grasped Corrado's shoulder, squeezing it. "I like that about you. You don't bullshit. Most guys plaster on that fake smile, you know, always laughing like a fucking clown. You can't trust them if you can't tell when they're being genuine. But you... I can tell with you."

Corrado was unsure of what to say.

His lack of a verbal response made Antonio snicker again. Sitting back in his booth, he waved them away. "You fellas get on out of here. My family will be here soon for lunch, and well, you know..."

"I understand, sir." Corrado stood. "Have a good day."

Vito said goodbye before following Corrado. They strolled out of the restaurant as Vito pulled his car keys from his pocket and started down the block. They'd made it a few steps when a car pulled up to the curb, a door opening. The sound of laughter reached Corrado's ears, light and airy, like a soft classical melody. His footsteps faltered as he glanced toward the source.

Celia DeMarco.

Bright afternoon sunlight streamed down on her. Her white dress made her skin appear much tanner than he recalled. It was chilly out, so much so that Corrado detected a slight fog surrounding every breath, but warmth surrounded her like glowing light. Happiness radiated from her as she spun in a circle, yelling something back at whoever was in the car before heading toward the restaurant. She paused at the door, hesitating as she glanced Corrado's way.

Their eyes connected.

The woman in front of him was a far cry from the girl he'd met so long ago. Awkward knobby knees and gangly limbs had given way to a curvaceous body, her clunky braces gone, replaced with a dimpled grin, complete with perfect teeth as she smiled dazzlingly at him.

But still, her hair hung over her shoulder, sloppily braided.

Celia's free hand came up, cautiously giving him a small wave.

Corrado raised his hand, awkwardly waving back, the gesture making her laugh again… this time at him. *For* him. The stunning sound faintly reached his ears as she disappeared into the pizzeria, making every inch of his body tingle at the recognition.

Without realizing it, Corrado was smiling.

He stood there, dumbfounded, before his father grasped his arm and pulled him out of his stupor.

"Guess you found your reason to smile, huh?"

Corrado straightened his expression out. "It's just nice to see a familiar face."

"Is that all it is?"

"Of course. What else would it be?"

Vito opened his mouth to respond but shut it, instead shaking his head, thinking better of answering that. "Just be careful, kid."

"Careful," Corrado echoed. "Isn't that what I do for a living now?"

"There's a witness."

Corrado watched with surprise as he approached his house, seeing his father sitting on the front porch. It was late at night, around eleven o'clock, and Corrado was just coming in from a long first day of work. Or what Antonio DeMarco called work, anyway. It was more like twelve hours of shadowing and nursing a glass of scotch he had no desire to drink. "What?"

"One of our guys on the inside of the police department said there's a witness to the Esponzio hit," Vito said as he puffed on a cigar. "Some kid saw an Italian boy loitering in the area, described him as sorta tall, dark, curly hair, late teens, maybe early twenties. Said he was handsome."

Corrado's brow furrowed. *Handsome?*

"If I didn't know any better, I'd say they were describing you," Vito said, casting him a narrowed look. "You're handsome, I guess. Look like your father a bit, and he's a good looking bastard." Vito smirked at his own joke, but his humor faded as fast as it came on. "Can't be, though. Because you wouldn't have let anyone see you, right? Had to be some mistake."

"Had to be."

Vito flicked his ashes as he stood. "That's what I thought. Figured you'd clear it up, you know… make sure nobody could identify you."

"Absolutely."

Vito strolled away as Corrado muttered under his breath. Utterly exhausted, he wanted to go to bed, but he knew he couldn't. Not now. Not until the situation was resolved. His father hadn't said that, but he didn't have to. The implication was there.

Corrado drove straight to Dolce Vita Pizza. It was a Saturday, so the place was busy even at that hour. Corrado strolled inside, pausing right in the door to survey the crowd. It took a moment before he spotted the familiar boy off to the side, clearing off a small table.

Taking a deep breath, Corrado sauntered across the pizzeria

and slid into one of the empty chairs. John went to say something, but froze when he got a good look at him. The color drained from his face as he stood up straight.

Casually, Corrado grabbed a menu from where it stuck out behind the napkin dispenser. He opened it in front of him and glanced up. "John, right?"

John hesitated. "Yes."

"Do you have a last name, John?"

An even longer pause. "Tarullo."

"John Tarullo," Corrado said, chanting the name in his mind, reciting it to memory. "You know, I can't seem to stop thinking about the other night."

The boy stiffened. "What about it?"

Corrado remained silent, surveying the menu. Settling on something, he closed it to face John. "I think I'll take that deep dish pie now. You wouldn't wanna disappoint me, right? Wouldn't hang me out to dry?"

"Right."

"Good. Make it a small, with sausage and mushroom. Light on the sauce. You think you can get that for me? And a glass of water, of course."

"Uh, sure. Anything else?"

Corrado stared him down. "No, I don't think so. I think we're good here. Aren't we, John Tarullo?"

"Sure thing."

11

Beyond the bruises and welts, cleverly concealed by an ample flow of blood, a soul is as easily traumatized as a human body. No one sees it; No one knows. But the crack of a belt against flesh, the strike of bitter words laced with venom, ricochets and lashes away at what lies beneath. Cuts appear on the soul, strong and sturdy as the thickest tempered glass, until one day, one attack is too much for it to take.

The second the strike hits, everything shatters into a million tiny fragments. Shards poke through the skin and are plucked away, unknowingly disposed of, gone forever in the blink of an eye.

The person you were doesn't exist anymore.

And just as bruises fade, the body tries to heal the soul, rebuilding what remains like a puzzle, overlooking the pieces that were lost in the assault. Again and again it happens, more pieces missing, more gaping holes left behind. Sometimes the body compensates, trying to fill the void the best it can based on the memory of a long ago snapshot, but often it shuts down and closes off, building a wall. The strikes still come, vicious and unremitting, but they don't hurt so much.

It's not easy to hurt when you hardly feel anything anymore.

The remnants of the soul become lost, trapped behind the wall with whatever darkness had leached into the fractures. No one could touch it; No one could reach it. Not with a harsh tongue, and certainly not with a gun.

But sometimes, things find a way to slip through.

Sometimes it's a smile; sometimes it's a laugh.

Sometimes it's as simple the sound of your name.

"Corrado!"

Corrado turned toward the familiar voice—a voice he would recognize anywhere—and saw Celia approach. Just after dark on a Friday night, he stood in the downstairs hallway of the DeMarco residence. Antonio had sent him out to handle some business and asked him to stop by afterward for a talk. There were other places he would've rather been, like at home in bed, but when the Boss called you in, you had to come in.

"Miss DeMarco," he said politely, nodding in greeting. Besides a few brief glances in passing while in public, it was the first time he'd encountered her since moving to Chicago.

"Celia," she said, her voice suddenly stern.

"Excuse me?"

"My name's Celia."

Why was she introducing herself? "I know your name."

"Do you?" she asked. "Because I'm pretty sure you just called me Miss DeMarco, and that isn't it."

He smiled guiltily. "Force of habit."

"Habit or not, that's no way to greet a friend."

Friend. It was a title in the life reserved for his kind. The word seemed foreign coming from her lips. Was that what she was? His *friend?*

As he considered how real friends were supposed to greet each other, Celia rushed toward him. He held out his hand, figuring he would just shake hers to be safe, but it was then that he spotted the blood.

Blood. There was blood on his hands. He wasn't even sure where it came from. He quickly shoved his filthy hands in his pockets but she didn't seem to notice his reaction as she wrapped her arms around him in a hug.

Corrado felt her warmth through her clothes and smelled her sweet perfume, the scent making him dizzy. His heart pounded rapidly and his chest tightened. His throat felt like it was closing up. Breathing was difficult. His skin tingled. He swayed.

Was he having an allergic reaction?

She pulled away from him, smiling brightly. Her radiant expression did nothing to help his condition, his knees going weak. He wanted to tell her to call 911, but no words would come out. He was stunned. Speechless.

Stunned speechless. *What's wrong with me?*

"You look good," she said, brushing at his suit coat and straightening his blue tie. "Bigger. Firmer."

Her skin flushed as she spoke.

"You, too," he managed to say. "Good, I mean. Not bigger or firmer. Although, well, you are bigger."

It wasn't coming out right.

"In the good way." Was there a good way to tell a woman she was bigger? "You're bigger in the right places."

She stared at him with shock. Even he recognized how wrong that sounded. Instinctively, almost as if some God-given male gene triggered, his eyes darted to her chest. *Definitely bigger.*

That wasn't something friends were supposed to do.

He caught himself, but not quick enough. She caught him. "So you like my, uh, bigger places?"

"Yes." The answer, while true, sounded horrible verbalized. She was the Boss's daughter. What was he doing? "Wait, no." That wasn't good, either. "I just mean—"

She cut him off with a laugh. "You should probably stop right there. Your mouth seems determined to get you in trouble."

A lot would get him in trouble in his life, his mouth being the least of his concerns, but he nodded anyway. "You might be right."

"Of course I am," she said with a wink. "Get used to that fact."

"I'll try."

"That's all we can do," she said. "Try."

She was a far cry from her father. Antonio believed there was no trying, only doing. To survive, you had to succeed, no exceptions.

"So, what are you doing here?" she asked.

"Business. You?"

"What am I doing here?" She snorted. "I live here, Corrado."

"Oh," he said, realizing what he'd asked her. It was confusing. He was flustered, barely able to form thoughts. Everything seemed foggy.

Maybe it wasn't an allergic reaction.

Maybe he was having a stroke.

He stood there, unsure of what to say, and she laughed again.

"You're cute," she said, patting his cheek. "It's good to see you."

He'd been called a lot of things lately—cold, calculating and even crazy. But cute? That wasn't one of them. "It's good to see you, too."

Antonio appeared, his footsteps faltering at the sight of Corrado and Celia standing together. "Have you two been acquainted?"

"Of course," Celia said. "We're old friends."

"Friends? The two of you?"

"Yes. Remember North Carolina, Dad? We spent two months living together there."

"Oh, yeah. Right. I'd nearly forgotten."

Celia was still touching him and dropped her hand, taking a step to the side when Antonio gave them a pointed look. He stared Corrado down for a second, silently judging in a way Corrado tried to avoid, before turning to his daughter. "Don't you have a date tonight, honey?"

Date? The moment the word registered, Corrado eyed Celia. She looked nice in a pair of jeans and a sweater, but she wasn't dressed up. What kind of date was she going on in sneakers?

"Yes, he'll be here soon," she said. "I should go finish getting ready now."

She started out, pausing to kiss her father's cheek. After she left, Antonio led Corrado to the den. He offered Corrado a drink but he declined, not wanting to prolong the visit with socializing.

Too bad socializing was all Antonio had in mind. He chatted away, but Corrado couldn't focus. The fact that he was distracted must have been obvious because after a while Antonio cleared his throat. "Are you alright, Corrado?"

"Yes, sir," he replied. "Fine."

"Are you sure?" he asked. "You're fidgeting."

Corrado glanced down, noticing he'd been wringing his hands together. "I'm just tired, sir."

Antonio stared at him, his expression blank. Corrado wasn't sure if he believed him, but he had no other explanation. He said not a word, the sudden tense silence putting him more on edge. His gaze was intense as he studied him, scrutinizing him, sizing him up.

The sound of the doorbell echoed through the house. Corrado startled, regaining his composure quickly, but the Boss noticed. He didn't move as it rang a second time, followed by the sound of footsteps on the stairs. "You couldn't answer the door?" Celia yelled from the foyer.

Her father didn't respond, too fixated on Corrado.

The boy greeted Celia when she let him inside. His voice was smooth, almost song-like, and she giggled at the sound of it.

Corrado's hair bristled. He instantly hated him.

Celia led her date into the den. Antonio's posture relaxed as he eyed the boy. "Hello."

"This is Andrew," Celia said, motioning toward him. He was an American, with shaggy blond hair. He looked like a surfer, an absurdity to Corrado. Chicago wasn't near the ocean. "Andrew, this is my father and Corrado, a friend of the family."

There was that word again. *Friend.* Unlike the first time, it didn't settle well with him then.

"Nice to meet you guys," Andrew said as he draped his arm over Celia's shoulder. Corrado's heart pounded forcefully again, even harder than before. He was touching her.

Why was he touching her?

The intense surge of blood made his skin feel like it was crawling, sickness brewing in the pit of his stomach. His vision went red and his chest burned, a voice in the back of his head screaming.

Warning. Warning. Warning.

This boy was a threat. He needed to disappear.

Maybe he was wrong. Maybe he was having a heart attack.

"You, too," Antonio said. "You kids have a nice time."

His nonchalance stunned Corrado. Didn't he sense it, too? Didn't he feel how thick the air was? Couldn't he see the red flags?

"We will," Celia said. Her eyes lingered on Corrado, almost as if she expected him to say something, before she took Andrew's hand and they exited the room.

The boy touched her again. He needed to stop doing that.

"They met at school," Antonio explained once they were gone. "His family just moved to town."

"And you think it's safe for her to be with someone you know nothing about?"

"I wouldn't say I know nothing about him. His father's a doctor and his mother's a teacher. They're from Ohio. He has a perfect GPA, plans to go to Princeton. Never been in trouble. He's harmless."

Harmless wasn't the vibe Corrado got from him. "Are we done here, sir?"

"Yes," he replied. "Get some rest. I don't like seeing you frazzled."

Corrado headed for the front door, feeling the Boss's gaze on him as he exited. It didn't matter what he said. Something was horribly wrong with the situation. Celia shouldn't have been with that boy. Dozens of reasons why passed through his mind. He imagined her hurt, or in danger. He imagined him violating her or taking her somewhere she shouldn't be. Violence. Anger. Pain. Horror. Distress. The foreign flood of emotion was intense.

But never once, in his panic, did jealousy come to mind.

"There comes a time, thief, when the jewels cease to sparkle..."

The screen lit up with the film, the sound rumbling through the lot from speakers situated on the dozens of cars. Corrado shook his head, aggravated, and tried to ignore it. Of all the places in the world, all the things they could've done, Andrew took Celia to the drive-in to see *Conan the Barbarian.*

The boy didn't deserve her. She was better than this.

Corrado parked along the back, his car partially hidden, but close enough to watch the dingy, little gray Volkswagen Bug. The two lounged inside of it, eating popcorn as they watched the film.

He hadn't even treated her to dinner. She needed more.

Corrado checked the time. Only a few minutes past ten, but it felt like days had passed since the movie began. Didn't she have a curfew? How long would this nonsense go on?

Corrado glanced back at the car and froze, his blood running cold. Andrew had his arm over Celia's shoulder as she leaned toward him. His chest ached. He wanted to crawl out of his own skin.

And then she kissed him.

Her mouth, those lips that had spoken his name just hours before, touched the blond boy's filthy, rotten mouth. All composure slipped away, every ounce of self-control Corrado possessed gone. He flung open his door and jumped out, his hand going into his coat for his gun.

It didn't matter how many people were there or what he had to do to stop it… that boy was never going to touch her again.

Corrado took a few steps in their direction, grasping his gun when someone called his name. The sound of it stalled him. His senses cleared long enough for him to realize what he was doing. He turned toward the voice, seeing Vincent standing a few feet away. He regarded Corrado suspiciously, his gaze shifting to his hand before his eyes darted toward the car his sister sat in.

"Did my father send you?" Vincent asked, panicked. "Why are you here?"

"Shouldn't I ask you that?" Corrado asked, deflecting. "Aren't you a little young to be out at this time?"

Vincent narrowed his eyes, his cheeks flushing. "I'm not much younger than you. I'm sixteen now."

Sixteen. "Well, does your father know you're here?"

"Does he know you're here, Corrado?"

Corrado stared at him as that question sunk in. Vincent raised his eyebrows, a smirk tugging the corner of his lips. He knew he had him. He could be a cocky little punk when he wanted to be.

"Go home," Corrado said, "before I decide to tell your father."

"You, too," Vincent said, taking a few steps back. "And for the record, I don't like that boy either, but I don't think killing him is going to help. It might make her mad. If you like my sister, just ask her out. At least it would be less messy... I think, anyway."

Corrado watched as Vincent walked away before glancing back at the car. Celia had pulled away from the boy and sat straight in her seat, her attention focused on the movie. The ache in his chest lessened, a bit of relief washing through him.

Was that what he wanted? To date her?

Corrado stood along the street near the high school, leaning back against his parked car with his arms crossed over his chest. It was a warm, cloudless afternoon. He was sweating profusely from the strong sunshine.

Classes had just let out and students swarmed the streets. It was a Friday, and he could hear their excitement about the weekend. They were deep in conversation about things he knew little about, like games and parties and dates.

Dates. He suspected he started sweating more at that word.

Girls strolled by, wearing skimpy clothing. Some of the guys were already going shirtless, relishing in the sun, and there he stood, dressed as usual—plain black fitted suit, black tie, and black polished shoes. Usually he fit in with his clothes, falling into the background, but now he stuck out like a sore thumb.

At least, he was pretty sure he did, considering the looks he kept getting from the students.

Everyone blended together in a sea of people. He was reconsidering his idea when the sound of familiar laughter reached his ears. He turned in the direction it came from, stunned when he saw her. She wore a pair of extremely short shorts and a flimsy white tank top, cut short to show her navel, the material so thin her black bra shined through.

Corrado was equal parts awestruck, aroused, and downright horrified. Did her father know she went into public like *that*?

When she glanced in his direction and caught his eye, he suspected Antonio didn't. She looked ashamed. Nervous. Petrified. "Corrado? What are you doing here?"

Suddenly, he was nervous, too. "I needed to speak with you."

"Is something wrong? Did something happen? Oh God, it isn't Daddy, is it?"

He realized how his imposing presence must have seemed, like he came to deliver bad news.

This wasn't going as planned.

"Your father's fine," he said, reassuring her. "It's nothing bad."

"Oh." She relaxed, and he wondered if maybe he shouldn't have said that. What if she thought it *was* a bad thing? "So, what's up?"

"I just wondered if you'd like to do something."

Her brow furrowed. "What?"

What? He hadn't figured that out yet.

"Just something," he said, "with me."

"With you? Like what?"

"Anything. But if you would rather not, I understand. I wanted to ask you before I went to your father for his blessing. I didn't want to presume..."

"Blessing for what?" The moment she asked, her eyes widened. "You mean do something, like, *together*?"

"Yes."

"Corrado Moretti, are you asking me out on a *date*?"

The word came from her lips as a squeal. He nodded hesitantly, unsure of her reaction. Was she sweating at the word, too? "Yes, I'd like to take you on one of those."

He held his breath as he waited for her to respond. He figured she'd have to think about it. He even prepared himself for an outright denial. But what he hadn't expected was for her to laugh.

"You know it's unnecessary to ask my dad, right? I mean, it's really sweet, but I'm eighteen. I'm an adult now. We don't need his permission."

She may not have needed his permission, but Corrado did. One of the most important rules in their world—you don't mess with a made man's family, especially the Boss's.

Without his blessing, Corrado would be violating a *La Cosa Nosta* commandment, and their God wasn't very forgiving. No Hail Mary's would save him from His wrath.

"So is it a 'no'?"

"No."

"Okay," he said. "I'll let you go on your way."

He turned away, but she grabbed a hold of his arm to stop him. "I said 'no', as in it wasn't a 'no'. That means it's a 'yes'."

"Oh." He gaped at her. Yes? "Would you, uh… like a ride home?"

"Sure."

"This was nice of you," Celia said as they parked in front of her house. "Thanks."

"Thank *you*," he replied, cutting the engine of the car.

He opened his door to walk her inside, but she grabbed his arm. "Not yet."

"Something wrong?"

"No. Well, yes." She glanced down at herself and groaned. "Daddy's home. He's going to be pissed about my clothes. I'm not ready to deal with him yet."

Corrado had been right. "I thought you were an adult? You don't need his permission."

She narrowed her eyes. "You think you're funny, don't you? You know how he feels about appearances. 'No daughter of mine will look like a streetwalker'."

Corrado smiled at her feeble attempt at an impression. "How did you get out of the house this morning?"

"He was still asleep, so it wasn't hard."

"Next timc take a spare set of clothes along with you."

"Wow, you're pretty good at this being sneaky thing."

"Yeah, it sort of comes along with the job."

"Do you like it?" she asked. "Your job, I mean?"

It was the first time anyone had asked him such a thing. Did he *like* it? "I like that it keeps me busy."

She laughed. "You sound like an old man with a nine-to-five office job. You're only eighteen. Live a little. Take some risks. Break some rules."

"I take risks and break rules every day."

"You do what you're told to do, Corrado. You follow orders. I'm not taking about breaking the law; I'm talking about breaking your *own* rules. Step out of your comfort zone."

"I did." He started to get defensive. "I asked you out."

"Yeah, and it took you long enough. We've known each other for years. You're slower than a turtle. At this rate, you won't have the guts to actually follow through until I'm already married."

The mere mention of her marrying someone made his heart race again. He clenched his hands into fists. "You're wrong."

"I'm always right," she said. "I told you to get used to it."

"Yeah, well, you're wrong this time. I don't just do what people want me to do."

"Prove it to me," she said, her expression serious.

He wasn't going to back down from her. Climbing out, he walked around to her side to help her out of the car. "Come on."

"What are we doing?" she asked, panic in her voice.

"Bending rules."

He reached the front door and shoved it open. The foyer was empty, same with the hallway, but in the den, off to the side, a television played.

"Celia, is that you?" Antonio called out. Footsteps started their direction immediately, and she stiffened.

"Go change," Corrado whispered, motioning toward the stairs. She bolted up them as he went toward the den to distract her father.

It was then, as he helped her deceive his Boss in order to prove her wrong, that he realized he actually was proving her right. He did exactly what she wanted him to do. She had pulled his strings and played him like a puppet.

She was calculating. Manipulative. Cunning.

She'd managed to get one over on him.

How did she do that?

She had him wrapped around her finger and he knew it right then. He knew what the ache in his chest meant. He knew why he acted so irrational. He knew why, despite everything, he couldn't be mad.

He was falling for her. *Hard.*

Antonio faltered in the foyer when his eyes fell upon Corrado. "What are you doing here?"

"I wanted to speak with you."

"So you let yourself into my house? Uninvited?"

Corrado stared at him. "Sorry, sir. I just—"

"Of course he didn't," Celia hollered, bounding down the steps in a pair of jeans and a blue blouse. "I let him in when I got home."

Antonio narrowed his eyes as he glanced between the two of them, suspicion clear in his expression. Corrado remained still, speaking not a word, not wanting to make it any worse. Antonio knew they were up to something. You couldn't rule an organization full of liars, murderers, and thieves, and not be able to spot deception.

Celia casually kissed her father's cheek before disappearing into the den. Antonio stared at Corrado a moment longer before clearing his throat. "My office."

Corrado's stomach sunk. *No.* The office was reserved strictly for business, for when Antonio slipped into boss mode. Everything about the man changed in there, from the tone of his voice to how he addressed him. Corrado didn't exist in there. In the office, he was nothing more than the youngest Moretti. "I thought we could speak in the den."

"My office," he reiterated, heading for it.

Corrado followed hesitantly, carefully shutting the door and taking a seat across from Antonio. The Boss opened his humidor and pulled out a cigar, clipping the end of it and lighting it before addressing him. "No."

"No?"

"I know what you're going to ask, and the answer's no."

Corrado had no idea what to say.

"It's nothing personal, Moretti, but I can't give you my blessing. She's my daughter, my baby girl, I know her. And you? Well..."

Corrado closed his eyes. He was scum, a lowlife, who made a living by deceiving and destroying. *Of course* he wouldn't want a man like that dating his only daughter.

"I understand, sir," he replied, as much as it pained him to say it.

"Good," Antonio said, standing and heading for the door again. "I'm glad we're on the same page. You couldn't keep your eyes to yourself, but I have faith you at least have better control of your hands."

Wordlessly, Corrado followed him out of the office. Celia lurked in the doorway of the den, watching the two of them.

Corrado nodded politely at her as he passed. "Miss DeMarco."

Celia's expression fell. "Corrado?"

He didn't stick around or try to explain. Instead, he headed straight for the door and slipped outside into the sunshine, his earlier anxiety now nothing but regret.

Regret for not being good enough for the one thing he foolishly let himself want.

12

Creak.

The low groan on the first floor roused Corrado from sleep. His eyes snapped open, suddenly alert, as the relentless noise seemed to echo through the house. A window. He often slept with them open a crack to let the air circulate, but someone shoved one open the whole way.

His heart thumped wildly in his chest as he reached onto his bedside stand and grabbed his gun. He habitually checked it, ensuring it was still loaded, and jumped out of bed. There was no time to waste getting dressed; he crept down the hallway in his plaid boxers, his bare feet lightly touching the floor, making not a sound.

The second he made it downstairs, a breeze struck him from the living room. A few steps later he appeared in the doorway, pointing his gun at the form halfway through the window. He flipped off the safety as his finger lightly touched the trigger. Two seconds. Two seconds were all it would take to blow them away.

A pair of wide brown eyes instantly met Corrado's. "Whoa, there, big guy."

Just as fast as he'd aimed, prepared to kill whoever was breaking into his house, he lowered the gun. "Dammit, Celia!"

"Nice to see you, too." She swung both legs inside but remained perched on the windowsill. "You weren't really going to shoot me, were you?"

"Yes," he said, no hesitation. "I was."

"Well, I'm lucky you didn't."

"Lucky?" Corrado stared at her with disbelief. "I would've shot you, Celia. Two more seconds and I would've *killed* you. And then your father… your father would've killed me."

"Yeah, he probably would've."

"There's no probably about it. He would've mutilated me. You… you wouldn't have felt a thing. But me…" He shuddered just thinking about it. "What are you doing here? Are you in some kind of trouble?"

"I wanted to talk to you."

Corrado gaped at her. "You broke into my house to *talk*?"

"Well, I would've called, but I don't have your number." Celia stood and strolled around the darkened living room, glancing at his belongings. "Besides, something tells me you're not the talking-on-the-phone type."

He wasn't, but it didn't negate the fact that she'd broken into his house in the middle of the night. It was reckless. Dangerous. "It couldn't wait until tomorrow? A lady shouldn't be out alone at this hour, especially *you*. You should always have an escort after dark."

He'd been stone cold serious, but his declaration made Celia burst into laughter. "Really, Corrado? Do you hear yourself? It's 1981 now. Women don't need escorts."

"But you're not just a woman," Corrado pointed out. "You're a DeMarco, and they most certainly *do* need escorts."

"Whatever." She rolled her eyes as she picked up a book from the shelf above the fireplace. Nonchalantly, she flipped through it, likely not even able to read the cover in the dark. Corrado watched her, still glued to the spot, the gun still in his hand. A continual breeze blew in the wide-open window, sending a chill down Corrado's spine. He suddenly felt indecent wearing nothing but his boxers.

He hadn't planned on entertaining company.

Without saying another word, he slipped back upstairs and threw on the first clothes he found—a pair of black slacks and a plain white t-shirt. He hesitated before slipping the gun in his waistband and headed back downstairs. A blaring light from the kitchen alerted Corrado that Celia had switched rooms. He stumbled into the doorway, shielding his eyes as he tried to adjust to the brightness, and found her scouring through his scarce cabinets.

"Do you cook?" she asked, shifting things around.

"Not usually."

"I could cook for you," she declared, moving on to the refrigerator. It had more than the cabinet but was still quite bare. "Of course, we'd have to go shopping first, since there's nothing here to make."

"I've already eaten," Corrado said.

"I didn't mean now," she replied. "I just meant sometime."

Corrado let out a deep sigh. "I don't think that's a good idea."

"Why?"

"I don't think we should spend time together."

"Why?" she asked again.

"Your father—"

"I told you… I don't need his blessing."

"But I do," Corrado said. "And I'm not getting it."

"Why?"

There was that word again… that stupid, relentless word. Hearing it grated on his nerves. He'd been taught never to question things, so why did she find it so easy to? Why couldn't she just accept things like the rest of them did?

"You should go home." Corrado turned away without answering her question. "I'll escort you."

"No."

He ignored her, heading into the foyer. He slipped his shoes on his feet and grabbed his keys before heading back to the kitchen doorway. "Come on."

"No."

"It's late," he said. "Let's go."

"No."

Frustrated, Corrado closed his eyes and counted to ten in his head before blowing out a deep breath. When he reopened his eyes, Celia had crossed her arms over her chest defiantly.

He gave her one more chance. "It's time to leave."

"No."

Saying nothing, he stalked right toward Celia, eliciting a small retreat from her. Before she escaped him, he grabbed her. It took some effort, but he managed to pick her up and start for the door. She fought against him, yelling for him to put her down, but he ignored. He weaseled the front door open and hauled her outside, setting her back on her feet on the front step. The moment she was free she tried to dart around him, but he managed to slam the door closed behind him to block her.

Flustered, Celia blew some wayward hair from her face that had been knocked loose from her braid. "Ridiculous."

"It is ridiculous," he agreed, locking up before stepping off the porch. "Come on."

He offered Celia his arm, but she ignored it and stormed past him. "I don't get it, Corrado. A few hours ago you were all about spending more time with me, now suddenly you're blowing me off."

"Your father—"

"Oh, screw my father."

Corrado abruptly stopped talking, taken aback, a small, devoted part of him enraged by her words. How dare someone speak ill of the Boss? "You don't mean that."

"I do," she insisted. "I hate him."

"You don't."

She glared at him. "Why are you putting so much weight on what he says? Didn't you hear me earlier about bending rules? Live a little. Have some fun. Do what you want."

Tempting, for sure, but it wasn't that simple. "I can't."

"You didn't have a problem earlier."

"There's a big difference between helping you with your wardrobe and blatantly disobeying an order."

"Well, I order you to take me out on a date then," she said, stopping on the sidewalk a few houses down.

"Nice try," he replied, "but it doesn't work that way."

"Why?"

He groaned at the question. "You know why."

She seemed to, considering she rolled her eyes and walked again. "It's not fair."

Life rarely is. Especially mine.

"I thought Daddy liked you," she continued. "He never has a bad word to say, so why wouldn't he want us to date?"

It was a loaded question that Corrado didn't want to get into. "It doesn't matter."

"It does," she insisted, stopping for the second time. They'd barely made it half a block. "I like you, Corrado. I *really* like you. I've been waiting for you to notice me forever, and when you finally do, *this* happens. What gives?"

Corrado stared at her as her words ran through him, a single question popping into his mind: *Why?* Why did she like him? How could she? Whatever would she see in someone like him? He kept his mouth closed, though, refusing to verbalize it. He wouldn't start questioning things now.

Instead of offering her words, he offered his arm again. This time, she took it.

The two walked silently the remaining few blocks to the DeMarco residence. Corrado took her straight to the front door and stood there, committing to stay until she was safely inside. Celia clutched the knob but hesitated, glancing back at him. "I'm not giving up."

He wasn't surprised. If he knew anything about Celia, it was the fact that she was tenacious.

"You asked me out on a date, and you're going to take me, whether you like it or not."

Despite himself, Corrado smiled at her words. Oh, he'd like it, all right… but he knew without a doubt Antonio DeMarco wouldn't.

Bright and early the next morning, before the sun had even had a chance to take its rightful place in the sky, Corrado stepped out his front door to be greeted by a familiar pair of warm brown eyes. Celia stood by the curb, leaning against the passenger door of his car.

He stared at her. "You're not supposed to be here."

"I told you I wasn't giving up."

A lengthy pause passed before Corrado grabbed the newspaper from the porch. He beat it against his hand, contemplating, before speaking again. "Go home, Miss DeMarco."

Without awaiting her response, he slipped back inside and shut the door.

Corrado stayed diligent the next few days. Antonio didn't call him for any special work, so he busied himself with petty jobs around the city with the crew. He purposely avoided everywhere he knew Celia would be, trying to push her from his thoughts and move on from his disappointment. The sting of rejection ran deep, though… not from her, but from her father. He kept musing over her question, wallowing in the truth that no matter what he did, he'd never be good enough for her.

Maybe his mother had been right about him.

A week passed. Corrado sat in his living room, a dim lamp beside him faintly illuminating the pages of *The Count of Monte Cristo.* He neared the end of the book when the telephone on the stand beside the couch rang. He tensed, the sound running through him and striking at his insides like a claw hammer.

He set his book down on the couch and picked up the phone. "Moretti speaking."

He anticipated hearing the Boss's voice, but instead a light feminine laughter met his ears. "Always so formal."

Corrado grew even tenser. "Celia?"

"The one and only."

"I thought you didn't have my number."

"I didn't, but I picked the lock in my father's office and swiped it from his Rolodex."

"You picked the lock?"

"Yep."

"You shouldn't know how to do that."

"Why, because I'm a girl?" She scoffed. "Did you forget who my father is? Breaking and entering is in my blood."

"Don't I know it," he muttered. "Do you need something?"

"Need? Not really. Want? Absolutely."

"What do you want?"

"You." She answered with self-assurance. "And I know I can't have you, not like that... but why can't we at least still be friends?"

"I'm not friendship material," he said, "any more than I'm boyfriend material. I think your father had a valid point."

"You're just saying that because he signs your paycheck."

"He doesn't pay me because I agree with him. He pays me because I have the balls to stand up to him."

"Then stand up to him."

"I can't," he said, "not like this."

"Why?"

Why… why… why…

"You're trying to kill me, Celia." He ran his hand down his face. "Literally."

"I know how to keep a secret," she said. "That's in my blood, too. And I know without a doubt that you know how, too. He wouldn't even have to know."

"You're worth more than that," Corrado said. "You deserve to be somebody's *everything*, not somebody's secret."

"I deserve to make my own choices."

"You do," he agreed, "but I *can't*."

"You can," she argued, "and you will. Because I know you, Corrado. You opened that door, and you're going to walk through it. It's only a matter of time."

Before he could conjure up some sort of response, the line went dead. Corrado set the phone down as he shook his head. He'd certainly met his match with her.

13

Corrado slid into a seat at the small table, the legs of the chair scratching against the checkered linoleum of the pizzeria. His right hand clutched the day's newspaper. He opened it, skimming through the crinkled pages, scanning the headlines for anything worthwhile. Evening had since fallen, most of the breaking news common knowledge by now, but it was the first chance he'd gotten to unwind.

Although, *unwind* was misleading for a guy like him. He was always working, always watching, always waiting. His mind remained two steps ahead, calculating his next move. He had to.

"Can I get you something?"

John's quiet voice shook as he addressed him. Corrado peered overtop the newspaper, attempting eye contact, but John refused. His gaze remained downcast.

"Small deep dish, sausage and mushroom," he said. "Light on the sauce."

"The usual, then."

The usual. Those words unnerved Corrado. He needed to stop being so predictable and made a mental note to order something different next time. Turning back to the newspaper, he continued scanning articles, blocking out most of his surroundings. John returned with a glass of ice water, sliding it onto the table before scurrying away.

Corrado flipped the page, reaching the sports section, and stopped on an article about the White Sox. He read through it, immersing himself in the latest news about the team, when the chair across from him moved. "Hello, friend."

Corrado withdrew his gaze from the text at the interruption. He dropped the newspaper, coming face-to-face with Celia as she invited herself to sit at his table. She was dressed casually, jeans and a red cardigan, her hair pulled back.

"Miss DeMarco. Have you been following me?"

"Nope," she said, motioning toward a table across the restaurant. "I was grabbing dinner with some friends from school and saw you sitting here, so I thought I'd say hello."

He glanced in the direction she'd pointed, confirming it was a group of teenage girls. "Well, hello then."

His gaze went back to the article.

"What are you doing?"

"Reading."

"Reading what?"

"An article."

"About what?"

He sighed exasperatedly, reading the same sentence for the fourth time. "The White Sox."

"Oh!" Her voice bordered on a high-pitched squeal. "Do you think they have a chance of bouncing back this season? Because let's face it—they've been terrible."

Corrado dropped the newspaper again, his brow furrowed as he stared at her. A sparkle of excitement shined from her as she rattled on and on about recent games and trades they'd made—things even Corrado had been too busy to keep up with.

"I thought you were a Cubs fan," Corrado said.

Her eyes widened slightly in surprise. "I am."

"So how do you know about the Sox?"

She shrugged. "I like baseball."

"Then you know the Sox aren't *terrible*," he said defensively. "No worse than the Cubs."

"True," she agreed. "The Cubs suck, too."

"So why are you a fan of them?"

"The Cubs are just the better team. White Sox fans are savages."

"*I'm* a Sox fan."

She stared at him, a devious twinkle in her eyes. "I know."

John returned, sliding the pan of hot pizza on the table between them. Celia was still talking, her words stumbling when she glanced at the waiter. "Johnny!"

John's eyes darted to Corrado nervously before flicking back to her, a slight flush overcoming his cheeks. "Hey, Ceily-Bear."

"I forgot you worked here," she said, reaching out and grasping his arm. The sight of her touching him, red-painted fingernails wrapping around his scrawny bicep, made a similar color coat Corrado's vision. His own grip on the newspaper tightened as he fisted the sides of it, tearing a page. The ripping sound echoed around him, but Celia didn't notice.

John did, though. His eyes once more darted to Corrado, the sudden blush draining from his face.

"You know each other?" Corrado asked, attempting to keep his voice steady, ignoring the haze that threatened to settle over him out of rage. Rage that she was touching him. Rage that he was *liking* it.

"Yeah, from school," Celia said, still beaming. "We're friends."

"Friends." That was what she'd called him… her friend. What she wanted them to be… *friends*. "How close of friends?"

John stammered, mumbling "not *that* close," while Celia just laughed. That laughter… it wasn't the genuine laughter he'd heard before. It wasn't the laughter of his childhood, the melodic sound that warmed him from the inside out. It was a bitter laughter.

Mumbling some more, John made a speedy escape. Had he even said goodbye to Celia? Corrado wasn't sure. He wasn't sure of anything except for the look in her eyes as she leaned across the table toward him, her smile turning sinister. "Oh, we're close."

"How close?" He hardly recognized his own voice, the demanding tone as the question forced its way from his lips.

"*Very* close," she whispered seductively. "So very, very close."

His jaw clenched, his eyes narrowing as his body instinctively seemed to follow her lead, moving toward her, his voice dangerously low. "You're lying."

"Am I?"

"You are," he insisted. "Tell me you're lying. Tell me that pesky little boy hasn't gotten close to you. Tell me he hasn't… that he hasn't touched you. Tell me he hasn't—"

"What if he has?"

"I'll kill him."

"Why?"

Why. That word again. As soon as it registered with Corrado's mind, he slammed his hands down on the table, nearly knocking over his drink. People close by startled at the commotion, but Celia didn't even flinch. She stared him dead in the eyes, awaiting an answer.

Demanding an answer.

"You know why."

She nodded, her shoulders relaxing as she leaned back in the chair. Reaching up, she unbuttoned the top button of her cardigan. "You're not jealous, are you?"

"No."

"Not at all?"

She unbuttoned the second button. Corrado impulsively glanced at it, his eyes trailing down her neck, seeing the hint of flesh of her chest. He stumbled a bit on a response. "No."

"Not even the tiniest bit?"

She reached for the third button as Corrado's pulse raced. "Stop that," he ground out, reaching across the table to grasp her hands as she unfastened it. He caught a flash of her bra and blinked rapidly. Fumbling with her shirt, he struggled to button it as she laughed.

This laugh… this one was familiar.

This was genuine.

This one flustered him.

She shoved his hands away and fixed her shirt. "He's a friend, Corrado. We have Chemistry together."

Those words didn't ease Corrado's tension. "You have chemistry?"

"Yes, the class." She rolled her eyes. "Not the attraction. He's a nice boy, but…"

"But you haven't?" Corrado asked. "He hasn't…?"

"No, we haven't," she said pointedly. "Not that it matters. Where do you get off threatening to kill someone for touching me?"

"Where do you get off *letting* someone touch you?" he retorted.

She balked. "Excuse me?"

"You should respect yourself more than that. Your father would—"

She looked like she wanted to slap him. "How *dare* you. My body is my own, and who I let *touch* it is my decision. Not yours, and certainly not my father's. I'm sure it's nice, this perfect little square box you live in, but I have no desire to squeeze myself inside of it. I'm not going to conform to anyone's standards. It's take it or leave it, and you've made yourself clear that you don't plan to take it. So lets just leave it, and I'll leave you alone."

Every ounce of anger inside of Corrado evaporated at the dejected tone of her voice. "Celia, wait."

"I waited a decade," she said. "And then I waited some more. I've waited enough. It's your turn to catch up."

Besides a faded photo of a six-foot-five, buzzed head, coke-bottle glasses wearing Italian man, Corrado knew little about Marcus Bellamy. A shopkeeper. A gambler. He walked with a slight limp.

That was the extent of his knowledge, but it didn't matter. It didn't matter what kind of personality he had, what he found funny, if he had a family, what he enjoyed. It was inconsequential.

Because Marcus Bellamy had to die.

The manila envelope of cash had been delivered to his house in the middle of the night, the photograph tucked inside with the name scrawled on the back. He hadn't been hard to find—the phone book gave Corrado all he needed. He drove to the address listed in the yellow pages and waited outside in the darkness until the man from the photo appeared.

Corrado tailed him across town to a small convenience store. He debated his options before exiting his car and lurking in the small alley adjacent to the store. Minutes passed before Marcus stepped out the back door, lugging a black garbage bag. He went over to the Dumpster and shoved it inside as Corrado stepped out behind him.

The single gunshot lit up the alley before the bag of trash even hit the bottom of the Dumpster. The noise was suppressed, muffled against the back of the man's head. Marcus never knew what hit him. One second he was breathing, the next he was dead.

Corrado concealed the gun in his coat and strolled from the alley, keeping his head down.

Nobody saw. Nobody knew.

Nobody suspected.

He made sure of it this time.

Corrado's slick black shoes crunched against the loose gravel of the path leading to his father's house. The black Lincoln gleamed along the curb in the dim evening light, the paint shiny almost as if it were still brand new. His father took care of the car... *more than he took care of his own family.*

Soft light glowed from the house windows. A lamp, Corrado figured. He pressed the doorbell, hearing the faint chime inside.

Corrado wasn't entirely sure why he was there. He'd been in Chicago for months and had only ventured to his father's place a few times. Vito preferred his privacy, and Corrado was more than happy to give it to him.

But he needed someone tonight.

Corrado rang the bell again, hearing another chime, followed by a shuffling inside as his father's voice shouted, "Hold your fucking horses, I'm coming."

Footsteps approached the door, followed by the sound of laughter.

Female laughter.

Corrado's insides knotted. The door flew open, a shirtless, disheveled Vito appearing, unlit cigar hanging from the corner of his mouth and fedora cockeyed on his head. Corrado barely gave him a glance, his gaze shifting past him to a woman scampering down the hallway.

A woman who was *not* Corrado's mother.

"Hey, kid!" Vito sounded genuinely surprised. He smirked, turning around. "V! Get your ass over here, woman."

Within a matter of seconds, the woman reappeared. She wore nothing but a burgundy silk robe, her curly brunette hair haphazardly pinned up. Smeared makeup covered her face, splotches worn off to expose aging skin. Not as old as Vito, but she approached middle age.

"V, this is my kid," Vito said. "We just talked about him, remember?"

"Yeah, right!" Her eyes sparkled. "I've heard a lot about you."

Corrado wished he could say the same. He stared at them, silent, stoic, as his father wrapped an arm around her petite waist. She giggled, plucking the cigar from his mouth before kissing him, smearing what was left of her pink lipstick onto his chapped lips.

"I'll let you boys talk," she said. "Great to meet you, Vito's kid."

Corrado cringed.

Vito watched her scamper away, a dopey grin on his face, before turning back to Corrado. He slapped his son on the back, squeezing his shoulder as he stepped out on the porch. "Vivian Modella. Met her years ago when she was a student at the university. She's still a looker, alright, but man… she was something back then."

Corrado was dumbfounded. "You've been seeing that woman for years?"

Vito cast him a sideways glance at the judgment in his voice. "Don't you look at me that way. We do what we gotta do. Your mother... well, your mother's your mother. I'll always love her, I'll always support her. I take care of mine, kid. But a man has needs... needs your mother ain't taking care of."

Corrado had no idea what to say. A conflicting sense of loyalty nagged at him.

"Enough about that," Vito said. "What's going on with you?"

"I, uh..." Corrado hesitated. He'd come to talk to someone

who might understand his situation, but instead, he'd found a man whose judgment he wasn't sure he trusted anymore. Did vows mean nothing to Vito? "It's nothing."

"Nothing?"

"Yeah," he said. "Forget about it."

Corrado tried to leave when his father caught his arm. "You okay, kid?"

"Fine."

"You got a birthday coming up soon, right? We ought to do something for it. Maybe catch a Sox game. You been paying attention this season? They're doing pretty good."

They're doing terrible. Celia's words ran through his mind, but he didn't verbalize them. How could he expect his father to know that when he didn't even know his birthday was still months away? "Sounds great."

Vito squeezed his shoulder again before heading back inside.

Corrado turned his gaze to the Lincoln. The streetlight had flicked on as the sky gradually darkened, giving him a better view of the car. It was rusting, Corrado realized, around the back wheels.

Respect was a funny thing. It took a lifetime to build, a lifetime to secure, but a mere moment wiped it all away. And once gone, things looked different, the rose-colored glasses that once beautified the world now a set of grimy bifocals, tainting the view. An infallible man was no longer faultless. A flawed woman had been wronged the entire time.

Maybe the perpetrator was just as much the victim.

Maybe things weren't as clear-cut as he'd thought them to be.

14

The energetic tunes from the live band filled the busy banquet hall as a Sinatra look-a-like commanded the stage. A crowd gathered along the floor, stumbling their way through a dance. Corrado lingered in the doorway of the entrance, surveying the gathering. His black jacket felt heavy, weighed down by the thick envelope shoved inside the pocket.

Vito sauntered inside, pausing beside him. He appeared relaxed, confident, and happy to be there.

Corrado would rather have been somewhere else.

"The celebration awaits, kid," Vito said. "Eat. Drink. Find a pretty girl to take home with you tonight."

Corrado's eyes were instantly drawn to the front of the room. He excused himself, strolling to the head table as he pulled the envelope from his pocket. Antonio glanced up as he advanced, assessing him before looking back away in approval.

Nobody approached without his permission. The guys scattered along the edges, incognito in all black, made sure of that. Enforcers were the most ruthless of the bunch. They were the intimidators. The murderers.

It still hadn't sunk in that Corrado was one of them.

Taking a deep breath, Corrado approached the person on the left. Celia's attention had been on the crowd until Corrado stepped in her line of sight. Almost as if it took some painstaking effort, she forced her gaze to him. She didn't smile. She said nothing.

She looked beautiful, though. Celia DeMarco wasn't just a

pretty girl. Even with such a stern expression, even with resentful, narrowed eyes, her face had a passive calming effect on him. Her navy dress fit snug, complimenting the blue graduation cap perched on the table in front of her.

Corrado cleared his throat, holding out the envelope. "Miss DeMarco."

She still said nothing. After a moment of awkward silence, she reached out and snatched it from his hand.

"Celia Marie," her mother scolded. "That's no way to act toward a friend."

"Sorry, mother," she muttered, not sounding apologetic. "Thank you, Mr. Moretti."

He nodded, stung a little at her formal addressing of him.

"It's great to see you again, Corrado," Mrs. DeMarco said, her words more genuine than Celia's had been. "Antonio says such great things about the kind of man you've turned out to be."

The praise made Corrado uncomfortable. Thankfully, Antonio chimed in before he had to respond. "Now, now, Gia, enough of that. You give the kid a big head, and he'll be no good to me."

"Nonsense," she said. "From what I've heard, he's earned his ego. Strong, passionate, and handsome to boot? He'll make some young Italian girl very lucky someday."

Uncomfortable put it lightly. Corrado was *unnerved.*

Celia hastily shoved her chair back and stomped off, high heels clicking against the wooden floor as she went. Corrado cast her a glance and frowned when she disappeared into the crowd.

"Honestly, I don't know what's wrong with that girl." Mrs. DeMarco waved her off flippantly. "We raised her better than this."

"It's probably hormones," Antonio said, picking up his glass of wine to take a sip.

His wife huffed but didn't disagree. Corrado caught Antonio's eyes, seeing the truth, silently acknowledging the real problem.

Him.

"If you'll excuse me," Corrado said, nodding politely. There was something to be said about being the source of conflict. It was the quickest way to end up eliminated, point blank.

"Of course," Antonio said.

"Go on." Mrs. DeMarco smiled. "Enjoy yourself, since it seems like my own children can't. Ungrateful brats. I don't even know where Vincenzo went!"

Corrado slipped into the crowd, relieved once out of the Boss's line of sight. He strolled over to the bar, hesitating, before sliding onto an empty stool. He waved to the bartender, asking for a glass of water, before turning to his right.

Celia.

She fidgeted with a small glass in front of her, half-full of clear liquid. Corrado ventured to guess they hadn't ordered the same drink. His suspicion was confirmed when she took a sip and grimaced.

"And here I thought the drinking age was twenty-one."

Her body stiffened at the sound of his voice. "I can do what I want."

She sounded like an entitled princess. She was in a sense. A spoiled rotten *principessa*.

"Congratulations," he said, deciding not to point that out to her. "I'm happy for you."

"Yippee," she said sarcastically, twirling a finger in the air. "I survived high school."

"It's a big deal."

"It's a piece of paper."

"It's an accomplishment."

"Whatever." She took another sip and sputtered, shoving the glass away from her. "Did you graduate?"

"I stopped going in tenth grade. I stopped caring in fifth."

"Because it wasn't a big deal."

"No, because they couldn't teach me what I needed to know."

"And you think they taught me? Yeah, sure. They squeezed in Mafia Wife 101 between economics and calculus."

He frowned. "That's not who you are."

She'd seemed to give up on her drink, but his words made her think better of it. Grabbing the glass, she tipped it back, downing the rest of it in one large gulp. She coughed, her face turning bright red, but it didn't deter her from gasping out her next words. "What makes you think I won't be just like my mother someday?"

"Because there isn't a hateful bone in your body." He cast her a sideways glance. "You put on a good facade, Miss DeMarco, but I'm not fooled. You're bigger and brighter than this world."

"You don't get it," she said. "That's like saying the stars are too bright for the sky. Maybe they are, but it doesn't matter, because that's where stars have to be. I'm *in* this world, Corrado. I always have been. And I belong here, just as much as you do."

"You're better than it."

"Yeah, well, so are you. You can't see it, but it's true." Celia waved for the bartender and asked him for another drink—vodka, straight up. Corrado wanted to interject, to order water for her instead, but thought better of it. A tenacious woman like Celia wouldn't like to be told what to do. "It was wrong of me to snap at you. I get it—I do. I know what happens when people disobey an order, and I know being with me isn't worth dying for."

He stared at her, wishing he could find the words to tell her how wrong she was about that. It was worth dying over. He lived his life in a box—she'd been right about that. A box where he felt nothing. It was only when he stepped from that box, when he treaded lightly into her domain, that he came alive. Being with her would be worth risking it all.

Risking everything, of course, except for *her*.

He wasn't a good person. Festering poison consumed him, his heart a hideous, bottomless pit, a shell incapable of giving her what she would want. Incapable of loving her like she deserved. He'd taken lives, callously, casually, and without remorse. How could he ever be enough? His own mother hadn't found him redeeming.

He was barely worth the oxygen intake.

"I'd infect you with my darkness."

"Or maybe I'd cure you of it."

"You can't know that."

"Neither can you."

He spared her another glance. A frown tugged her lips, her eyes downcast. Pouting at her own party.

"You should be celebrating," he said. "Dancing."

"Will you dance with me?"

"Not a chance. I wasn't made for dancing."

"Then we'll just sit here," she said, shrugging, "and not dance... *together*."

He shook his head, picking up his glass and swirling the ice around in the water. He stared at it, watching the ice clink against the sides as water rushed overtop of them, swarming them briefly before they resurfaced again. The water churned, round and round, matching his insides—the scarcely confined tumultuous cyclone of his soul.

"Why?" The question he hated so much... the question he'd been taught never to ask... spilled from his lips as he stared into the glass.

"Why what?"

"You hardly know me, Celia, and what you do know about me isn't pleasant. Why would you ever torture yourself pursuing me?"

"Torture?" She laughed. "You might think you're dangerous, Corrado, but you don't scare me."

There was no *think* about it. Corrado knew what he was capable of, and dangerous put it mildly. He was a man with a gun and no regard for his own life. It was hard to see what was so special about breathing when your own mother thought smothering you with a pillow was an ideal solution.

"Besides," she continued, shrugging, "you pursued me first."

"It was a mistake."

She recoiled. "Ouch."

Setting his glass down, Corrado shifted in his stool to face her. "*You* weren't a mistake. I like you, Celia, and I have no shame about that. But it couldn't work, and the mistake was thinking it could. Maybe we exist in the same world, but we live on opposite ends."

"Then we move to the middle," she insisted. "I don't see why you can't get that."

She made it sound simple. So simple, in fact, that he didn't know what to say. He shook his head, muttering, "You're far too beautiful to be so damn wise."

Her dejected look perked up as she swung her body toward

him, knees knocking against his. His eyes were immediately drawn downward to a set of creamy, bare legs. "Beautiful, huh?"

"You know you are. That's half the problem… you use it."

"Oh, I haven't used it." Her voice dropped low as she leaned toward him, slowly crossing her legs, her dress riding further up on her thighs. "Yet."

Corrado suppressed a groan and yanked his eyes away from her bare skin just in time to see Antonio's approach. Shoulders squaring, Corrado shifted his body away from Celia as the Boss surveyed the two of them. Celia remained relaxed, boldly moving closer to him in response to his subtle retreat.

Enforcers lingered behind Antonio, keeping a few feet distance to give the Boss his illusion of privacy, but Corrado knew they were listening.

"Sir," Corrado said.

"Corrado." He turned his attention to his daughter as he stepped even closer. Corrado moved his head out of the way as the Boss reached past him, snatching the glass off the bar. Bringing it to his nose, he sniffed. "Liquor, Celia? You're only 18!"

"It's mine." The words were out of Corrado's mouth instantly. Celia's eyes widened in shock, but she straightened her expression out as her father glanced between the two of them again.

He didn't believe it. That was clear from the narrowing of eyes, the thin line of his lips. Antonio held the glass out to him. "Drink up, then."

Corrado took the glass and brought it to his lips, pausing to take a deep breath, before throwing it back. It felt like rubbing alcohol scorched his throat, tasteless and harsh, setting his chest on fire. He swallowed back bile as his body tried to force the liquor back out.

Eyes watering, he slammed the glass on the bar with a grunt.

"That's not right," Celia said, crossing her arms over her chest. "He's 18, too!"

"He's a man," Antonio said nonchalantly. "You're my little girl."

She huffed. "Double standards are a bitch."

Anger sparked in Antonio's eyes. "Language, young lady."

She grumbled, reaching over and snatching up Corrado's glass of water. "It's totally unfair. I can't do anything—you tell me what to drink, what to say, *who to date*."

She sneered the last part. Corrado tensed, whereas Antonio merely laughed. "I've never told you who to date."

"But you—" Corrado knocked his knee into hers and shook his head, warning her not to go there. Her mouth remained open as she considered it, but she conceded eventually. "Did you need something, Dad?"

"Just wanted to say goodbye," he said. "I have work to do."

He pulled her into a hug, nearly yanking her off the stool. Celia kissed his cheek, saying goodbye as he backed away. His gaze turned to Corrado then. "Moretti."

"Sir."

"A word, please."

Tensing, Corrado slid off the stool, avoiding Celia's concerned eyes as he followed the Boss. Antonio wandered a few feet away, to a pocket of empty dance floor. The enforcers followed, maintaining their distance, but their looming presence made Corrado's defenses prickle.

"Make sure my daughter gets home safe," Antonio said. "I know she's been drinking."

He hesitated for a fraction of a second. "Yes, sir."

Antonio cut his eyes at him. "That was honorable, what you did, but it was fucking stupid. You gotta let a woman fight her own battles."

"Yes, sir."

Slapping him on the back, Antonio nodded his goodbye and headed for the exit. The enforcers followed, moving around Corrado like he was a boulder in the middle of a rushing river. Corrado stood there for a moment before turning back. Celia sat halfway in her stool, halfway leaning across the bar as she yelled at the bartender. Corrado's brow furrowed as he approached, hearing her agitated voice. "Give me a break, man! It's just a drink!"

The bartender shook his head as he picked up a wet glass and dried it off. "Sorry."

"Come on!" she said. "You didn't say no before!"

"You've had your limit."

"But I didn't even get to drink the last one."

"Not my problem."

She groaned, the sound practically a feral growl. "Don't you know who I am? This is *my* party!"

Corrado slid back onto the stool beside her and motioned toward the bartender. "Vodka, straight up."

The man debated before pouring some vodka in a glass and sliding it down to him. Celia glowered at him as she settled back into her stool. "Such crap."

Corrado pushed the glass toward her, offering the drink. Without hesitation, she picked it up, smiling radiantly.

He couldn't help it. He smiled back.

He'd let her fight her own battles, sure, but it wouldn't stop him from doing all he could for her.

"Watch this!"

Corrado's footsteps abruptly stopped at those words. This wouldn't end well.

Celia kicked off her heels, one skidding along the sidewalk while the other struck a parked car in the street, but she was too preoccupied to notice. Corrado gaped at her, stunned as she broke into a sprint, throwing her hands out in front of herself. Every muscle in him seized as she flung her body over, her legs coming out from under her as she cartwheeled down the sidewalk.

Once. Twice.

Her dress rode up as she spun, bunching near her waist. Corrado caught a flash of her underwear on her third cartwheel, but he couldn't spare a second to dwell on it. She tried to land back on her feet but overshot it, skidding right onto her butt, her back landing flat on the sidewalk. Alarmed, Corrado jogged the few yards over to her.

Getting her home safe proved harder than he'd thought.

"Celia," he hollered, hunching over her. "Are you okay?"

Her arm shielded her eyes from him as she burst into laughter. "That hurt just a bit."

He scanned her as he reached out, assessing to make sure she wasn't harmed. Groaning, he tugged at her dress, yanking it down to cover more of her body. His frantic assessment only made her laugh harder as she swatted him away.

"If you want to feel me up, all you have to do is ask first."

"I'm not feeling you up." He scanned over her again, cringing when he realized his hand rested on her upper thigh. He withdrew it fast, feeling the heat of her flesh beneath his fingertips. Celia watched him with amusement, still deep in the throes of giggle fits.

"Come on," Corrado said, standing and reaching for her hand. "You're drunk."

She took his hand, her body like dead weight as he yanked her to her feet.

"I'm not drunk," she declared, staggering a bit once she stood. "Okay, just a little drunk."

He exhaled deeply once she was steady and tried to move away from her, his hand nearly sliding from hers. She gripped it at the last second, her fingers intertwining with his and squeezing. Blinking a few times, Corrado glanced at their connected hands in the darkness, seeing her shiny, milky white nail polish pressed against his tanned flesh. His hand dwarfed hers, momentarily making her seem fragile.

Corrado's eyes met Celia's. The amusement evaporated from her expression, replaced with an earnest vulnerability, a soft hint of yearning. Slowly, carefully, her free hand took his, lacing their other fingers together as she stepped closer to him. He stared down at her, the top of her head reaching his chin.

Teasingly, she licked her lips.

"Celia," he warned.

"Don't fight it," she whispered. "Please, Corrado. Don't fight it anymore."

"You're drunk," he rationalized.

"I'm sober enough."

"It's not right."

"It's not wrong either."

She rose up on her tiptoes, inching even closer. His heart hammered in his chest. *Don't do it*, his mind reeled. *Stop this. Stop it right now.*

But his body... his body didn't listen. The haze settled over him, detaching body from mind, the physical and mental disconnect urging him on. Celia pressed a light, barely-there kiss on his jawline. The tingle radiated from that spot, consuming his senses.

Leaning down, his lips found hers, soft at first, tender, but more eager when she let go of his hands. Her arms snaked around his neck, tugging him further down, her fingers running through the hair on the back of his head. Her tongue darted out, swiping across his lips before plunging inside.

And just like that, he was a goner.

Heat like he'd never experienced before rushed through his body, starting at the top of his head and extending to the tip of his toes. Frantic hands gripped her hips, pulling her flush against him, holding her there as he kissed her deeply. She fisted his hair, having just enough of a curl to get a good grip. Throbbing emanated from the spot, sending a quiver down his spine, pleasurable pain fueling him forward. His lips were frenzied, matching hers as she tried to devour him with a hard kiss.

"Celia," he murmured, pulling back long enough to take a deep breath.

"Your house," she panted, shoving against him, making him take a few awkward steps backward.

"What?"

"Your house," she repeated. "We can be alone there."

Her hands gripped him tighter, fingernails digging against his skin, as the harsh reality of her words struck him. Abruptly, he pushed away from her, breaking the kiss. "Slow down."

She stared at him incredulously, wide-eyed, her cheeks flushed as she panted. "I'm tired of waiting."

"You're drunk," he said. "Think about what you're saying."

"I have thought about it," she said, matter-of-fact, as she

reached up on her tiptoes, again pressing a light kiss on his jawline. She left a soft trail of kisses down along his chin. Despite himself, Corrado closed his eyes at the sensation, his hands relaxing on her hips. "I've thought about it… and thought about it… and thought about it. I'm tired of thinking about it. I want to *do* it."

Her words caused the blood to feverishly rush through him, his pulse racing from arousal. "With me?"

That simple question cracked the mood. Celia pulled away from him, her lips leaving his skin. *Thank God*, Corrado's mind screamed, while his body pleaded for the sensation back.

"No, not with you," she deadpanned. "With Johnny at the pizza place. You think I have a chance?"

He knew she was joking… he did… but it didn't stop the intense swell of rage that rushed through him. "I'll kill him."

Rolling her eyes, Celia stepped from his reach. "Way to ruin the moment, Corrado."

He ran his hands down his face, flustered. "It's for the best."

"How can you say that?"

"You're worth more than a *moment*, Celia," he said, reaching out and grabbing her hand again. "I'd rather give you a lifetime."

The flush on her cheeks deepened. "You're such an enigma, Corrado. How can someone like you—someone who says things like that—do what you do?"

"One has nothing to do with the other," he said. "I can't even compare the two."

"You have a twisted sense of morality."

"Thank you."

She laughed. "Not sure I meant that as a compliment."

He tugged her hand as he took a step. "Let's get you home. It's late. We don't want your father sending out a search team."

She put up no argument, walking in step with him as the two strolled down the street. Their fingers remained entwined until they approached the house at the end of Felton Drive. Corrado reluctantly pulled his hand from hers.

Wordlessly, she approached the front door as Corrado remained in the driveway. She grasped the knob, standing under the glowing porch light, and peered at him. "Promise me, Corrado."

"Promise what?"

"Promise you won't wake up tomorrow and forget tonight happened," she said quietly. "Promise you won't change your mind."

"I'll never change my mind about you," he said, "nor could I ever forget. You have my word."

She turned back to the door as it yanked open. They both froze, inhaling sharply, but Corrado managed to relax again when he spotted the familiar young face. Vincent stuck his head out, glancing between the two of them. "What are you guys doing out here?"

"Nothing," Celia said. "Corrado was just walking me home."

Vincent grimaced, waving his hand in front of his face. "Oh, gross. Why do you smell like a liquor bottle?"

Celia rolled her eyes, ducking past her brother. "Shut up."

Corrado started to leave when Vincent's voice called out again. "Corrado?"

He hesitated. "Yes?"

Vincent smirked. "You're a lot better than that last guy she went out with."

"We're not dating," Corrado said. "We're just… friends."

"I know," Vincent said. "I'm just saying, you know, she could do worse. She has done worse."

"I heard that," Celia yelled from the house. She reappeared, grabbing Vincent and yanking him inside. Glancing over, she gave Corrado a small wave as he retreated.

"Goodnight, Miss DeMarco."

"This is the worst card in the history of cards," she declared. "If this card were a drink, it would be cheap back alley moonshine."

"Like the stuff you drank last night?"

"That vodka wasn't cheap. Gave me more tingles than your card did."

Corrado's brow furrowed as he lounged on his couch. Early morning sunshine streamed through his open windows, a gentle breeze whisking in. The phone was tucked in the crook of his neck, pressed to his ear, as he shifted through the day's newspaper. "You know, I picked that card out myself."

"Then I hereby revoke your card-giving privileges."

"What was wrong with it?"

Celia dramatically cleared her throat on the line. "In all the things you undertake, may you meet with real success. And may all the years that are ahead be filled with happiness."

"Yeah?" He flipped the page of his newspaper. "What's wrong with that?"

"Really?" she exclaimed. "First of all, it's a second-rate rhyme. Happiness? Success?"

"They both end in –ess."

"Secondly," she continued as if he hadn't spoken, "could it be any more impersonal?"

"It had a rainbow on it, didn't it?"

"No, it had flowers," she said. "Sunflowers."

"Flowers, then. You like flowers, don't you?"

"Of course," she said. "I love flowers."

"Okay, then."

"You're missing the point."

"I think I am." He closed the newspaper, unable to focus on it, and shifted the phone to the other ear. "I thought all cards were the same. Didn't realize one could be more exciting than another."

"Well, had you *written* something in it, maybe it wouldn't have been so lame."

"I did," he said. "I signed my name."

"Yes, and that's it. It says 'Corrado' in tiny print. No 'congratulations'. No 'good luck'. Just 'Corrado'. I thought for sure you'd at least write something."

Closing his eyes, he grasped onto the phone and lay his head back against the couch. "I'm not much of a writer, Celia."

"I kind of figured that out back when I wrote you a letter and you never wrote back."

"You didn't ask me to."

"I shouldn't have had to."

Corrado laughed dryly to himself. "Why are you complaining about the card, anyway? I thought the gift was what mattered."

"Well, yes, sure... the money was nice... but that was a cop out, too. All you did was shove some cash in the envelope. Easy-peasy."

There was nothing easy about it. If she knew what he'd done to get his hands on that kind of money, she might have sung a different tune.

He started to say something, to joke around about how he accepted returns, when there was a slight commotion on the other end of the phone. He silenced when the Boss's voice rang out in the background. "Who are you talking to?"

"Angela," Celia said at once. "You know, my friend Angie?"

"Ah, yes," Antonio said. "Sure, I remember her. I need you to hang up, though. I need the phone."

"Okay, Dad," she said. "Just one second."

After a brief stint of silence, Celia blew out a long breath.

"So Angie, huh?" Corrado asked.

"Yeah, I just made that up. I drew a blank."

"Nice cover."

"Yeah." She sighed. "I guess I have to go."

"Okay," he said. "Goodbye, Celia."

"Bye, *Angie*."

Corrado set the phone down and reached for the newspaper, opening it to where he'd left off. He scanned half a page and started reading an article about some local break-ins when a loud ring once more shattered the silence. Balling the newspaper up, he tossed it aside and grabbed the phone. "Moretti speaking."

"Moretti." Antonio's voice was flat, all business. "You busy?"

"Not at all."

"Good. I have some work for you."

15

"Come on," Celia said, grabbing Corrado's hand. "It'll be fun."

He stood firmly in place, not budging. "I'm not going in there."

"Why?"

"Because I'm just not."

She pouted, poking her bottom lip out. "You sound like a petulant child, Corrado."

"You look like one."

She rolled her eyes, proving his point. "Oh, come on."

"No."

She tugged on his hand. "You're so ridiculous sometimes. We'll just stay for a little while."

"I'd rather not."

"Please? For me?"

He groaned. "Are you seriously begging?"

"Yes," she said. "What, do I need to get on my knees?"

She started to kneel in front of him, and he quickly grabbed her, yanking her back to her feet. He stared at her, horrified that she would do that. Did she not know what people would think? "You can't do that!"

She laughed.

He found nothing funny about it.

"Well, *I'm* going in," she said, letting go of him and walking away. "Stay here if you want."

Corrado flexed his empty hand, something about it feeling abnormal. He had gotten so used to her presence, their brief moments together filled with stolen embraces, that not touching her made his chest ache. He looked back at Celia, who casually strolled toward the entrance to the small fair, as if it didn't bother her at all. He debated, part of him stubbornly planted there, while another part yearned to go after her.

She glanced over her shoulder, the void intensifying.

What's she doing to me?

"This is absurd," he grumbled, starting toward her.

Celia paused at the ticket booth as he jogged to catch up to her. "One, please."

"Two," he corrected her, pulling out his wallet.

"I can pay for my own admission."

"Over my dead body," he said, handing some cash to the woman working. He turned to Celia after grabbing their tickets.

"Thank you," she said.

He shrugged. "It was only $5."

She smirked, satisfied with herself, and grabbed his hand again. "Not for paying," she said, leading him inside. "For conceding."

Conceding. He didn't do it often.

Squeezing her hand, he pulled her closer, their arms brushing against one another as they strolled through the fair. Celia's eyes lit up as she took in the chaos while Corrado just tried to endure the crowd. People gathered everywhere in masses, shouting and playing around, as whistles sounded and lights flashed.

He felt like he was back at the casino.

Celia's footsteps faltered when they reached a row of games.

"Oh, I want that!" she said, pointing at the large stuffed bear hanging at the very top of a display, a fat red bow around its neck.

"That thing?" he asked incredulously.

She shrugged. "It's cute. Can you get it for me?"

"Uh, I suppose," he replied, turning to the man standing behind the booth. He was massive, his forearms bulging, a blue bandanna on his head. "How much?"

"A dollar a dart," the guy said. "Pop one balloon, get a small prize, three gets a medium prize, and five for the big."

"So five dollars," he said, pulling out some cash again. He

held the five-dollar bill out to him and pointed at the giant bear. "That one."

"You gotta throw these and see how many balloons you pop," he said, counting out five plastic darts. "Then you see how many more you need."

"I won't need any more."

"Whatever you say, man. I've worked this booth for three years and never seen anyone hit five in a row."

He won't be able to say that after today. Picking up one of the darts, Corrado glanced at Celia. She wore a vibrant red sweater, accentuating the flush of her cheeks.

Red it was, then.

He turned to the booth and hurled the first dart, the plastic tip piercing the flimsy latex of a red balloon. Back-to-back, the next four darts flew through the air, striking red balloons dead center, every one bursting right away. The man stared at him with shock.

Corrado wasn't sure why. He told him that would happen.

"That one," he said, pointing at the massive stuffed bear again.

He grabbed it, pulling it down. "Man, you've got killer aim."

If he only knew…

Corrado took the prize from him and handed it off to Celia.

"So what now?" he asked, stepping away from the booth. "Anything else you want me to shoot or throw?"

"No, I'm good." She hugged the bear tightly, grinning. "How about we share a funnel cake?"

"A what?"

"You know, deep fried goodness smothered in powder sugar?"

"Never heard of it."

She looked horrified. "How can that even be? What do you eat at fairs?"

"Nothing," he replied. "This is the first time I've been to one."

She gasped. "You're shitting me?"

He laughed at her crass language. "No, I'm not *shitting* you. My mother wouldn't take us to these things."

"So you've never ridden a Ferris wheel?"

"No."

"Eaten cotton candy?"

"No."

"Bumper cars?"

"No."

A mischievous twinkle lit up her eyes. "I lied earlier. I think we'll stay a while. I'm popping your fair cherry."

As strange as it sounded, all Corrado could do was laugh again.

"I had fun," Celia said as they strolled toward her house hours later. She still lugged around that massive bear, picking at the last of her pink cotton candy. Corrado watched as she popped globs of it in her mouth, letting it melt on her tongue.

"I'm glad."

She glanced at him curiously. "Did you?"

"It was okay."

"That's not what I asked," she said. "Did you have even the tiniest bit of fun?"

He paused, half a block down from the DeMarco residence. She always asked him those things. Did he like it? Did he have fun?

Did it matter?

"I did," he replied honestly, "because you were there."

Her smile was radiant as she gazed at him. She stood up on her tiptoes, pressing her sugary lips to his. He never liked sweets before, but he suddenly craved more.

He deepened the kiss, and she moaned into his mouth, the sound giving him chills. He shivered, pulling back to take a breath, and a flash of something caught his attention the second he opened his eyes.

Corrado tried to react, to stop it before it started. There were two of them, the men dressed in dark clothing. One had dark skin, the other chalky pale, but their approach told him it wasn't personal. This was random. Unplanned. They were jumping on whomever they stumbled on.

Pity for them, that person was *him.*

The dark one grabbed Celia from behind, shoving his gun to her throat. "Cooperate and I won't hurt her."

Corrado immediately looked at Celia, assessing, seeing the terror in her eyes.

"Listen to them," she pleaded. "Please."

Corrado held up his hands in surrender. The second assailant grabbed him, and he gritted his teeth as the guy dug through his pants pockets, emptying them.

"Mercedes," he said as he eyed his keys. "Where's it parked?"

Corrado didn't answer right away. The man shoved the gun into Celia harder, making her yelp. It took every ounce of determination Corrado had to remain still, not wanting to get her hurt, but fire burned inside of him, giving way to that smoldering numbness.

"Down the street," Celia said, her voice frantic. "A block or so."

The man pocketed the keys, grinning. He'd scored a nice car and wouldn't even have to hotwire it.

"Give me the watch," he demanded, motioning toward Corrado's wrist. Reluctantly, he took it off and held it out to him as the second guy rifled through his wallet. He took out the cash and discarded the rest on the ground, not interested in any of it.

They snatched Celia's jewelry off her, relief flashing across her face when the man finally let her go. She grabbed a hold of Corrado, trembling as the man haphazardly aimed the weapon at them. The assailants backed away, satisfied, and for a brief second Corrado considered letting them go. Celia was safe, and that was what mattered. For her, he would have given them money and jewelry. She was more important than the car. But as one final act of defiance, they took the one thing he couldn't let them take.

The godforsaken teddy bear.

The moment it was ripped from Celia's hands, Corrado lost his composure. He almost felt it, the cracking inside of him as he separated from himself. Shoving Celia behind him, he reached into his coat and grabbed his gun.

The fools hadn't patted him down.

Shock froze them when Corrado pounced. Neither man stood

a chance. He didn't pull the trigger. He didn't even flip the safety off. He wouldn't kill them… at least, not *now*. But he beat both men unconscious, their bodies motionless by the time Celia dragged him away. His temper had gotten the best of him and controlled his every move.

Sirens wailed in the distance. Panicked, Celia gathered their things before grabbing him by the hand. He snatched up the stuffed bear as she yanked him down the street, not resisting. Instead of heading for the front door, she pulled him around the side of the DeMarco house, to a darkened area covered by tall trees.

As his senses came back to him, he waited for her to be horrified. He waited for her to be sickened by him. He expected fear. Anxiety. Disgust. He anticipated her anger. But never, in his wildest dreams, did he think he would see desire.

"Wow," Celia squeaked out, cheeks flushed. "That was… wow."

He couldn't even respond. He had no idea what to say.

"That was crazy," she said, pacing in front of him. "Seriously, that was just... wow... *crazy*."

"Are you okay?" he asked tentatively.

"Thanks to you. Jesus, Corrado, is it always like that?"

"Like what?"

"Like... *that*," she said again. "The adrenaline, the blood flowing, the pure craziness. My heart was in my throat. I felt like I was going to pass out, but I felt so high. I felt, I don't know, *alive*! Does it always feel that way?"

No, he thought. There had been a fleeting surge of anger, but there was usually nothing. No emotion. Numbness.

She wouldn't understand though, but he knew how she felt—it was how he felt with her.

"I know what you mean," he said quietly.

Celia smiled, and right there, right then, without any warning, she dropped to her knees.

This time he didn't stop her.

Falling back against the side of the house, his head rested against the cold brick. Now his adrenaline pumped. Now his heart raced. Now he felt high.

Now he felt *alive.*

The jingle of his belt buckle was magnified in the still night as Celia hastily unfastened it. Unbuttoning his pants, she yanked the zipper and let them fall down his muscular thighs. The night air swarmed him, cooling his skin, but inside of him a fire raged.

Reaching into his boxers, she grasped his erection. Her hand wrapped around the shaft, squeezing, stroking, exposing him to her, as he let out a low hiss. Eyes squeezed shut, he fought to block off his mind, the part of him opposed to this.

It's wrong. It's not right. It can't happen this way.

The voice of conscience screamed loud, but not convincing enough. Warmth enveloped him as she parted her lips, her tongue meeting his bare flesh. The feel of her for the first time, the slick heat as she took him in her mouth, wiped away all doubt lingering inside of him. Hormones surged. Pleasure exploded.

Nothing else mattered.

Nothing.

Corrado gasped, his hands drifting to her head, fingers running through her soft hair. He guided her, not forcing, not pushing, instead drowning in the sensations and losing himself in her touch. She didn't hesitate. She didn't falter. There was no second-guessing. No self-doubt. She sucked vigorously, stroking firmly, teeth lightly scraping.

He was losing his mind.

"Celia," he ground out through clenched teeth. "You're killing me."

It didn't take long, minutes at most. It built and built inside of him, filling him up until it had nowhere else to go. He threw his head back, smacking it against the unyielding brick. "I, uh... I, uh..."

I love you.

The words almost glided from his lips, but the explosion of pleasure rippling down his spine silenced him. Shuddering, his hands clenched into fists as orgasm rocked him. He convulsed, spilling down her throat. She kept going, taking in every drop. The pleasure faded into an intolerable tingle, his flesh sensitive from her touch. He pulled away, breathing deeply, and opened his eyes.

Celia remained on her knees, a seductive smirk twisting her glistening lips. A twinkle of satisfaction shined from her eyes as he fixed his pants. Corrado was vaguely aware of sirens still blaring in the distance, a subtle flashing of red and blue lights infiltrating the dark sky down the block.

He yanked Celia to her feet, wobbling a bit, his knees weak, his firm hands covering her cheeks, locking her in place as he kissed her hard. After a frozen moment of surprise, she kissed him back, lips moving feverishly against his. Celia wrapped her arms around his neck and shoved him back toward the house, slamming him against the rigid brick siding. Pain curled across Corrado's back, rippling down his spine, as a wave of pleasure washed through him. He grew aroused again, and Celia must've sensed it, because she pressed herself against the bulge in his pants.

"Stay," she gasped.

He shook his head, the movement barely registering, and forced out a response. "I can't."

"You can," she insisted, clawing the back of his neck as she tried to draw him closer. "I'll sneak you in."

"No."

The second he said the word, firm and final, a sharp pain shot through his bottom lip as Celia's teeth pierced the skin. He winced, the small gash throbbing as he ran his tongue along it, the familiar coppery taste of blood tingling his tongue. "You *bit* me."

She smiled guiltily as she backed up a few steps. "See you later, Corrado."

He caught her arm, clutching her wrist as she tried to walk away. "Tomorrow."

She cocked an eyebrow. "Tomorrow?"

He loosened his grip on her arm. "Tomorrow."

Hesitating, she stepped back in his direction, placing a small, chaste kiss on his lips. "See you tomorrow."

Corrado set off for home, strolling right by the idling police cruisers. Lights intermittently flashed, illuminating his downcast face. A small crowd had gathered, curious and anxious, but Corrado felt only contentment.

Just as he approached the scene, a blaring ambulance sped away, carrying at least one of the men in it. Corrado hazarded a glance across the street, spotting a few police officers hanging around.

No one looked at him. No one paid him any attention.

He continued on, walking the few blocks to his dark, empty house. Reaching into his pockets, he fumbled around for his keys but came up empty.

Cursing under his breath, he tried his coat, finding only his gun. No keys, no wallet, no watch.

He would have to remember to get it all back from Celia tomorrow.

Frustrated, Corrado walked around the outside of his house, shoving one of the cracked windows open the whole way to slip inside.

16

The sun outside had just risen when Corrado awoke to a string of knocks on the door. Groggily, he climbed to his feet, still dressed in yesterday's clothes. Grimy sweat made the stiff cloth cling to him. He tore off his jacket, tossing it on a nearby chair, as they knocked again.

Corrado headed to the front door, figuring it would probably be his father, maybe even Celia, or the Boss if he were set to have a bad day. Swinging it open, he braced himself, but he was unprepared for what he found.

Three men stood shoulder to shoulder on the porch. The one in the middle was dressed in a cheap gray suit, thick glasses on his face, his hair balding. Nothing substantial stood out about the man, but the guys flanking him gave it all away, wearing dark pants and bright powder blue button down shirts with Chicago Police Department patches sewn on the left arm. Dull badges were pinned to their hefty chests. Behind them, Corrado made out a set of police cars.

Sickness swam in his stomach. He didn't greet them.

"Corrado Moretti?" the middle one asked. "I'm Detective Walker. I was wondering if I could ask you a few questions."

Even before the detective reached into his pocket, Corrado knew he had made a terrible mistake. The fact was confirmed when the man held up a set of keys. "Do these look familiar?"

Corrado shrugged noncommittally.

The detective singled out the marked car key in the bunch.

"There's only one Mercedes parked on this street. We ran the VIN, and it came back to you. The key worked when we tried it."

Corrado stared at the man. Was that even legal?

"So?" the detective pressed, jingling the keys. "Familiar?"

Tense silence swarmed the air between them. He was torn on what to do. Lie and deny, hoping for the best? Or implicate himself in something inadvertently? He couldn't decide, so he did neither.

He just stood there in stone cold silence.

The detective lowered his hand, slipping the keys away. "We're going to need to take you downtown."

Corrado recognized the absurdity of his stubbornness, but cooperating was out of the question. The officer on the right whipped out a set of handcuffs as the other grabbed him and patted him down. Thank God he had taken off his coat.

The thick metal handcuffs, heavy on his wrists, dug into his skin as the officer secured his hands behind his back. Both officers snatched a hold of him, violently yanking him toward an idling cruiser.

"You have the right to remain silent," one officer started, reciting a set of words Corrado would come to hear over and over again. "Anything you say can and will be used against you in a court of law."

The right to remain silent... Corrado had every intention of following through with that.

Two counts of felony aggravated assault.

Corrado sat in a flimsy wooden chair beside Detective Walker's desk in the middle of the hectic Cook County police station. His left hand had been freed, but his right was secured to a locked drawer on the desk, keeping him fastened in place.

Officers huddled around in a small group, whispering conspiratorially, their eyes fixed on Corrado. He ignored it, avoiding their judgmental gazes, his mind spinning over his charges.

Two counts of felony aggravated assault. It had to be a joke.

"He isn't deaf, is he?" an officer asked, just loud enough for Corrado to overhear. "That secretary downstairs knows sign language, doesn't she? Maybe he doesn't understand what we're saying."

"No, he understands," another responded. "He's just a Moretti."

Despite himself, an amused smile tugged Corrado's lips. They clearly had been acquainted with his father.

The group of officers grumbled to themselves in unison, agreeing with the sentiment. They disbursed, shooting him sideways glares on their way to their desks, as Detective Walker made his way back over. Pulling out his handcuff key, he freed Corrado only to yank him to his feet and force his hands behind his back.

"Since you have nothing to say, we're gonna go ahead and book you," Detective Walker said, securing the handcuffs tightly on both wrists again. "Maybe a night in lockup will loosen your lips."

They transferred him to Cook County Jail and shuffled him around, from cell to cell, from room to room. He had no sense of time, but gathered it was well past dusk when they placed him in a dingy two-man cell. There were no windows, no view of the outside, but the chill of night hung in the air as if it had somehow seeped through the thick concrete slabs. Corrado stood still just inside the small space as the guard closed the bars, locking him in. He assessed his cellmate, a scrawny middle-aged man, and slipped into the unoccupied bottom bunk when he decided the man wasn't a threat.

He closed his eyes but didn't sleep, listening all night to the shriek of inmates and the clatter of metal in the darkness, acutely aware of every squeak of spring from the bed above him. Hours passed this way, tense and uncomfortable, before the jail came alive with daylight.

His hearing was that morning, in another grungy windowless room. He didn't speak, didn't address the court at all. He stood with his head held high as the gruff old man in a black robe read his charges in a scratchy voice. He banged the gavel, his gaze never once meeting Corrado. "Bail's set at ten thousand dollars."

Ten thousand.

Leaving the hearing, the guard escorted Corrado back out to the tier, releasing him from his handcuffs before showing him to a set of phones lining a wall. "Make your call."

Corrado grabbed the receiver of the only free phone and dialed one of the few numbers he had memorized—his father's.

It rang. And rang. And rang. Frustration brewed inside of him during the fourth ring, but it cut off when Vito's voice came on. "Yeah?"

"It's me," Corrado said. "I'm in jail."

"No shit?"

"No."

Sudden laughter rocked the line, so loud Corrado had to pull the phone from his ear.

"Your first arrest," Vito said. "I wondered when I'd see the day."

Corrado leaned against the wall, stretching the phone cord as far as it would go. "Bail's ten thousand."

Vito let out a low whistle. "Damn, kid, what did you do?"

He hesitated. "Nothing. I'm innocent."

"Of course you are."

"They charged me with felony assault," he said. "Two counts."

"Ah." Silence. "Thought I told you never to use your fists."

"I didn't."

"Right, right… innocent."

Corrado didn't correct his father, but that wasn't what he'd meant. He hadn't used his fists… he'd pistol-whipped them.

"Well, tough break, kid," Vito said. "Get up with me when you find a way out of this mess."

The line went dead.

Vito had hung up on him.

Corrado replaced the phone in the cradle and approached the guard. "I need to make another call."

"It'll cost you."

"What?"

"Only the first call's free. The rest you have to pay for."

Corrado stared at the guard with disbelief. "I have no money."

"Well, I guess you shouldn't have wasted your first call then."

Another day passed, then two more like it. Hunger and exhaustion ravaged Corrado as he lay in the filthy bunk, his arm draped over his eyes hour after hour, attuned to everything going on around him.

It was late on the fourth day when someone came for him. A guard pulled him out of his cell and led him out of the cellblock. Corrado walked leisurely, in no hurry to get anywhere, and was stunned when the guard led him back to intake. "I'm still not answering their ridiculous questions."

Are you angry? Do you want to hurt someone?

Corrado nearly laughed when they asked him that.

The guard chuckled under his breath. "You will if you want to get out of here."

He shot him a look of surprise. "I'm being released?"

The guard nodded. "Someone posted your bail."

Although he still said little, Corrado was much more cooperative on the way out. He couldn't believe his father had come around and bailed him out. He rubbed his wrists, sore from being handcuffed, and headed for the front door of the jail. He stepped outside, squinting from the late evening sunshine. Raising his hand to shield his eyes, he glanced across the parking lot, seeing the last person he had ever expected to see waiting.

Gia DeMarco.

She stood in front of Antonio's Cadillac Deville, rivaling Erika Moretti with her poise and stern expression. Corrado approached her, squaring his shoulders as he bowed his head. "Mrs. DeMarco."

"Enough of that," she said. "It's time you call me Gia."

"Gia."

She nodded in greeting. "Corrado."

"I'm surprised to see you here."

"Don't be," she said. "Nobody else is. As many times as I've had to spring my husband from this place, they ought to erect a statue for me out here in the parking lot."

"I thought my father—"

"Vito?" Gia scoffed, silencing Corrado right away. "They

would've let you stay in there forever to teach you a lesson. And I would've went along with it had I not spoken to my daughter."

Corrado's stomach knotted. "What did Celia tell you?"

Gia didn't respond, but her eyes told the answer: *everything.*

"Come." Gia walked around to the driver's side of the car. "I'd rather not linger."

Corrado climbed in the passenger seat, glancing around the DeVille as Gia drove. He'd never been in the Boss's car before. "Antonio lets you drive this?"

"*Lets* me?" Gia scoffed. "I may yield to my husband on occasion, but nobody lets me do anything, Corrado. If I needed his permission, you'd still be rotting in that cell... especially after what Celia told him."

Corrado stared straight ahead, gaze fixed through the spotty windshield, as words tumbled from his lips. "I'm dead."

"Dead?" Gia laughed. "Only if he's feeling merciful."

He said not another word as Gia navigated the streets of Chicago, driving right past Corrado's house without even slowing down. Corrado took a deep breath as they reached the end of Felton Drive, pulling right to the front of the brick mansion. He got out, tugging on the collar of his shirt. The days-old clothes were scratchy against his skin, smelling of sweat with just a hint of Celia's perfume still clinging to the fabric. He'd never been so unkempt in his life, his sockless feet sweating in the stiff leather shoes, his hair not brushed, everything wrinkled, as he walked into a house to face punishment.

He felt like abused cattle being herded to the slaughterhouse.

Gia's high heels clicked against the foyer floor, echoing through the downstairs. Corrado stepped in behind her and shut the front door, glancing around cautiously. His eyes drifted to the staircase when he heard footsteps, taking in the much-appreciated sight of Celia.

She made it halfway to the foyer when Gia stopped her. "I don't think so, young lady. Back upstairs."

Celia gaped at her. "But—"

Gia started to cut her off, but another sharp voice beat them both to speaking. "You heard your mother."

Corrado's eyes met Antonio's as the man stood in the doorway to the den. Vincent lurked behind him, watching the scene unfolding. Tension was thick, the air bordering suffocating.

"Ugh, so unfair," Celia growled, stomping back up to the second floor.

Shaking her head, Gia took off her coat and discarded it in the downstairs closet. "I swear, it's hard to remember that girl's an adult when she stomps around here like a twelve-year-old brat."

"She's not an adult," Antonio said sternly.

"She is," Gia argued. "She's eighteen."

"I don't care how old she is. She's still my little girl."

Giving up on bickering, Gia brushed past her husband into the den, snapping at Vincent as she passed. "You, too. Upstairs."

Unlike Celia, Vincent didn't argue. Sympathetic eyes regarded Corrado as the boy strode past, disappearing upstairs.

Antonio stood in the doorway, glaring at Corrado in the abandoned foyer, his lips a hard thin line of contempt. Breaking his stance, he strode down the hallway toward his office. He unlocked the door and pushed it open, pausing, casting Corrado a look that told him to follow.

Corrado made his way into the vast office, stopping right inside. Antonio stepped in behind him, the knots in Corrado's stomach tightening when he shut the door. He stayed in place as Antonio took his seat behind his desk, the man's vengeful eyes never leaving him.

It didn't take long for the silence to be broken. "I should kill you for this."

Corrado exhaled deeply, answering silently. *You should.*

"I don't take well to being ignored. When I speak, it's because I expect to be heard. You don't have to like it. I knew you *wouldn't* like it. But you had to listen."

"I know, sir."

"You *know*," Antonio said. "You know, but you ignored me anyway. That says something."

Corrado considered apologizing but thought better of it. Asking for forgiveness was akin to begging, and Antonio DeMarco had no respect for needless beggars. Besides, except for the fact that he'd disobeyed an order, he wasn't sorry. He didn't regret it. And lying came only second to snitching in the DeMarco guide to getting yourself killed.

After running his hands down his face in frustration, Antonio motioned toward an empty chair. "Sit."

Corrado sat down.

"She said you were robbed at gunpoint," Antonio said. "That some thug grabbed her and pressed a gun to her throat. That true?"

"Yes."

"Then I just have one question… why the fuck is he still breathing?"

The pure fury was clear in his voice.

Corrado cleared his throat. "That's only temporary."

"That so?"

He nodded. "I didn't want to kill anyone with her there."

"Didn't want her to see you as a monster?" Antonio asked. "Afraid she'd see what you really are and want nothing to do with you because of it?"

Corrado wanted to say no, to deny that with every fiber of his being, but he couldn't. Denying would be lying, and it wasn't until then that he realized that truth. He liked the way Celia regarded him with an unadulterated innocence, a raw vulnerability, like his presence was harmless. He didn't want to taint that.

"I saw pictures of the guys in the hospital," Antonio continued. "Killing them point-blank would've been the merciful thing to do. You didn't want her to see the monster? Hate to break it to you, but you showed her the most savage part of the beast."

"You're wrong."

Antonio cocked an eyebrow in disbelief. "Excuse me?"

"That wasn't the most savage," he said. "The most savage part wouldn't have cared if she were there."

Antonio stared at him in silence for a moment before his posture slightly relaxed, the hard line of his lips softening. "You're a great asset, Moretti. You have a lot of potential. I'd hate to have to lose you."

By losing him, he meant killing him. "I understand, sir. I'll stay away from Celia."

Antonio barked a sharp, bitter laugh. "Oh no, you won't."

Corrado blinked with surprise.

"Last time *I* broke her heart," Antonio continued. "But this time, it's on *you*. Despite my protests, you started something with my daughter, something she's expressed she wants to see through. And you know what happens when guys break my little girl's heart?"

"What?"

"I rip theirs out through their fucking throat."

Message received. "I hope to someday prove myself worthy."

"Worthy?" Antonio shook his head. "It was never a matter of you being unworthy."

"But I thought you didn't want us together because she was your daughter and I was... well... *me*."

Antonio's brow furrowed in contemplation before something seemed to strike him. "You thought it was because you're one of us? You thought I didn't want my daughter with our kind?"

"Yes."

"It wasn't because *you* weren't good enough," he said. "You're the best I've got. I know Celia, I know the hold she can have on people, and I didn't want her to soften you. I didn't want her to tame that beast. Because that beast? I *need* him a hell of a lot more than she needs the rest of you."

"She won't," he vowed. "If anything she'll make me harden."

As soon as the words slipped from his lips, he realized how it sounded. He hoped the Boss wouldn't catch it, but the raise of his eyebrow suggested differently. "Pun intended?"

"Not at all, sir."

Antonio relaxed back in his seat. "Of course not. Now that we're on the same page, ask me again. And do it quick before I change my mind, because there's a part of me that wants to. There's a part of me that wants to squeeze the life from you."

Corrado swallowed thickly, a small flare of nervousness making his throat dry. "I'd like to go out with Celia."

"That was a statement, not a question."

"Do I have your permission to go out with your daughter?"

Instead of answering, Antonio held out his hand, and Corrado took it, shaking firmly. Corrado tried to let go while Antonio squeezed, yanking him toward him. "If you break Celia's heart, I'll make you suffer. I don't care if I'm rotting in a grave somewhere. Hurting my children is hurting me."

"I understand. I swear on my life I won't hurt your family."

Antonio let go then. "Second floor, last room on the left."

"What?"

"Celia's bedroom," he clarified. "You asked me, now you have to ask her."

Corrado stood. "Yes, sir. Thank you."

He turned to leave when he heard Antonio mutter, "I should've just killed you, Corrado."

Treading lightly down the long carpeted hallway, Corrado slowed when he reached the last room on the left. The white wooden door was closed, soft, scratchy music filtering out from the cracks around it. Raising his hand, he rapped on it with his knuckles.

"Go away!"

Ignoring, he reached for the knob, grateful when it turned smoothly, and pushed open the door. A soft smile curved his lips when he saw her, lying on her back in the middle of a massive four-post bed. Her knees were bent, her feet flat against the multi-colored comforter, her arms spread out above her, her eyes closed. Lips moved softly, soundlessly, along to the lyrics of the unfamiliar Italian song streaming from the speaker of a nearby turntable. He let the lyrics wash through him, vaguely catching their meaning in English as her pale lips mimic the words.

Luna rossa, forgive me, luna rossa,
For the vows I made tonight that are untrue,
What else am I to do?

Reaching up, he tapped again on the open door. Celia stiffened, a loud groan vibrating her throat. "What part of 'go away' don't you fucking—" She pushed herself up, glaring toward the doorway, and paused mid-question. "—understand?"

He merely raised an eyebrow in response.

A soft blush coated her cheeks as her eyes brightened. "Oh, hey… it's you."

"Who did you think I was?"

Celia jumped off the bed. "Anyone other than you." She stopped right in front of him, her expression serious as her eyes scanned his face, studying every inch. "Are you okay?"

"Fine," he said.

"Are you sure?" Reaching up, she ran her hand through his disheveled hair before caressing his cheek, her fingertips leaving a trail of tingles along his skin. "I was worried about you."

He grabbed her wrist, stilling her hand as her fingers traced his bottom lip. "I'm fine, Celia."

Sighing, half out of exasperation, half with resignation, her eyes darted out to the hallway before focusing back on him. "It's not *tomorrow*, but better late than never."

She stood on her tiptoes to press her lips to his. Corrado blocked her, moving his head, so her mouth brushed against his warm cheek. "I'm not sneaking around anymore."

Celia's head darted back at the rebuff.

"No." She yanked her arm from his grip. "You promised."

Despite her objections as she tried to move out of his reach, he grabbed her wrist again and pulled her over to her bed. She flopped down on the edge of it, trying to pry herself from his grip. Not wanting to hold her against her will, he hesitantly let go. She stared down at her wrist, a frown on her lips, before returning her focus back on him.

"He could've killed me," Corrado said, his voice low as he stood in front of her. "Anyone else, any other guy, would be dead right now. You get that, don't you?"

"Yes, but—"

"There can't be any *buts* about it," he said, cutting her off. "I need you to understand. What I did was stupid."

"So, what, you came up here to let me down? Came to break your promise?"

"Of course not," he said. "I'll never break a promise to you."

"Then what?"

"I don't want just bits and pieces of you that I can steal away. I told you—you're worth more than being someone's secret."

"Yeah, well, it's not really a secret anymore," she declared.

"I know it isn't."

She groaned. "Then what, Corrado? What do you want?"

His strong hands cupped both of her cheeks as he leaned down toward her. He stared into her eyes, drinking in the devotion she—for some godforsaken reason—felt toward him. "I'm a greedy man, Celia. I want *everything*."

As soon as he spoke it, she wrapped her arms around his neck, dragging him toward her as she lay back on the bed. He hovered over her, their lips meeting in a fiery kiss that lasted a lifetime but ended in no time at all. The second she brought her legs up, wrapping them around Corrado's waist as she pressed herself against him, he pulled away. A small whimper of protest escaped her lips as she clung to him. "I thought you wanted everything."

"I do," he said. "But I'd also like to *live*."

She smiled sheepishly, loosening her grip on him so he could stand back up straight. She remained laying back, propping herself up on her elbows, eyes never leaving him as he glanced around her bedroom. The walls were a pale peach, blending in with the tan carpet, whereas the furniture was all white. Splashes of color were thrown everywhere, reds and greens and yellows and blues, but there wasn't a speck of pink to be seen. Posters covered the walls, some even torn straight out of magazines, the edges ripped, typing spattering the images. He scanned them, bewildered at the sight of so many scrawny, shirtless movie stars, before his eyes fell upon a Chicago Cubs poster near her bed. Over a dozen signatures covered it in black marker, right over the players' photos from the previous years roster. He scowled at it.

"Hey, don't hate," she said, noticing his reaction. "That was a gift from Daddy."

"Terrible present."

"Hell of a lot better than the card you gave me."

Corrado laughed, focusing his attention to the turntable. The song had ended, but the record continued to spin. Picking up the needle, he set it back down at the groove for the last song. It crackled and hissed, the music notes streaming through the speakers. "Favorite of yours?"

"How'd you know?"

"You were engrossed in it when I interrupted."

"It's pure poetry," she said. "Literally. De Crescenzo is an Italian poet."

Celia leaned her head back, her long dark hair fanning against the soft comforter as she closed her eyes, body writhing along to the rhythm of the music. Lips once more mouthed the poetic words, never missing a beat. For six minutes, he stared at her, watching, captivated, lost in the sway of her slender body, the curve of her hips and swell of her chest, the exposed flawless skin of her bare midriff as she breathed steadily.

He'd never seen anything so downright beautiful. A sense of peace fell over him, calming him, pacifying the always-tense nerves inside of him, and soothing his very soul. He wanted to take that moment, to capture it, and keep it forever.

The song came to an end, and Celia opened her eyes, once again smiling at him, but he didn't return her smile this time. Instead, his lips parted, mouthing the lone word, "*Bellissima.*"

17

Corrado bought a new suit.

Straight black and fitted, pants legs a hair's breadth above his polished shoes, shirt cuffs extending half an inch beyond his jacket. He had gone to Antonio's tailor and dropped a month's pay on the outfit. The heavy suit weighed him down as he fought to square his shoulders and sit up straight. The urge to fidget gnawed at him as anxiety crept through his bloodstream.

How was he going to survive the night if he could hardly make it through the first five minutes?

He sat across from Antonio in the dimly lit den at the DeMarco residence, as he waited for Celia to come downstairs. The man puffed on a cigar, the scent of smoke permeating the silent room as it wafted around them, making the air hazy. Corrado continually breathed it in, his lungs burning as it infiltrated his system. Even his eyes stung, but he said not a word.

He'd never been so nervous in the Boss's presence before.

The sound of footsteps reached his ears, and he was on his feet the second she stepped into the doorway. A dark blue strapless dress clung to her curvy figure, the bottom flaring out as it flowed down past her knees, a thick black belt looped around her waist. She'd curled her hair and pulled it up, exposing her neck.

She smiled sweetly at Corrado with gloss-coated lips before scrunching up her nose and waving her hand through the air. "Jesus, Daddy, did you have to smoke in here?"

"Watch your mouth, young lady," Antonio said. "It's my

house... I'll smoke where I want to."

"You told me you were going to quit."

"I will," he said. "Someday."

Rolling her eyes, she turned back to Corrado. "Ready?"

He nodded, starting toward her, and glanced at the Boss briefly on his way out of the room. "Sir."

"Corrado."

He offered Celia his arm, and she took it.

"Curfew," Antonio hollered as they headed to the front door. "Midnight sharp, not a second later."

"Two o'clock," Celia shouted back.

"Eleven-Thirty."

"Fine. One."

"Make it eleven."

She sighed dramatically. "Midnight, then."

Corrado was unsurprised at her failure to negotiate. Antonio DeMarco didn't compromise. It was his way or no way.

Celia's strappy black heels clicked against the porch when they stepped outside. Corrado closed the front door behind them, shoulders relaxing with relief, but his respite didn't last long. The moment he faced Celia, seeing her attentiveness as she stood back, meticulously scanning him from head to toe, he started sweating.

Her gaze reached his, her eyes sparkling as she seductively bit down on her bottom lip. "So where are we going? Your house?"

"We're going to dinner."

"Dinner." She nodded thoughtfully. "Then your house?"

"We'll see."

Her smile grew. "I'll take it."

Chuckling, Corrado led her to his car, opening the passenger door for her to slip inside. He shut it, tugging at his tie out of nervousness, before climbing behind the wheel. Celia fiddled with the radio as he drove north, filling the air with chatter. She seemed so calm and collect, so at ease around him, when he felt antsy enough to claw his way out of his own skin.

Corrado headed outside of the Chicago city limits, parking near a quaint corner restaurant in Evanston. Celia climbed out of the car—much to Corrado's displeasure, not waiting for him to open her door—and eyed the place. "Rita's."

"Ever been?"

"No," she said. "Daddy comes all the time, though."

"I know." It was how he'd discovered the place. Antonio had sent a message, asking Corrado to meet him at Rita's one evening for dinner. Corrado had been surprised to find out it was a small Italian-American eatery in the middle of a working-class neighborhood—not somewhere he'd expected a classy man like Antonio to frequent.

But after tasting the food, Corrado understood.

They were seated as soon as they stepped inside, the small table waiting for them under his name. The interior of the restaurant was as quaint as the outside, with its wooden paneled walls and red-checkered tablecloths.

He ordered water and spaghetti with meat sauce, while Celia indulged in chicken and Coca-Cola. She chatted away as they waited for their food to arrive. He listened, having no idea most of which she spoke about, but he relished in the sound of her voice. Their plates were eventually set in front of them, and Celia dove right in, having no qualms picking her chicken apart with her fingers and popping pieces in her mouth. She let out a throaty moan with her first bite, theatrically rolling her eyes into the back of her head. "Amazing."

The sound ghosted across Corrado's body, prickling his skin. He picked up his fork, shifting the spaghetti around before taking a small bite. The succulent flavor of the sauce hit his taste buds, rousing a vague long-ago memory of a woman with steel-gray eyes who cut his spaghetti into itty-bitty pieces so he wouldn't slurp it. Nothing seemed to annoy Erika Moretti as much as the way Corrado ate, and Zia did everything imaginable to shield him from his mother's wrath.

"So, out of curiosity, do you wear anything other than black?"

Corrado's brow furrowed. "What?"

"Every time I see you, you're wearing the same thing."

Instinctively, he glanced down at himself. "This is a new suit."

"Is it?" she asked with genuine curiosity. "It looks just like the rest of them. Always black, always fits you perfect. Don't you own anything else? Blue, maybe? *Please* tell me you own a blue suit."

His gaze shifted to her dress. "That wouldn't be your favorite color, would it?"

"Maybe."

Laughing, Corrado nodded. "I own one or two."

"Then why always black?"

He gave a slight shrug. "Frank Sinatra said a man should always wear black at night, and I don't often make it home before sundown."

"Hmmm." Picking up her glass, she swirled the drink around in contemplation. "So Ol' Blue Eyes, huh? What's your favorite song?"

"I like them all."

"Come on," she said, leaning closer. "You have to like one more than the others."

"Depends on my mood," he said. "*Luck be a Lady* when I'm having a good day. *My Kind of Town* when I'm feeling sentimental. *My Way* when I... well... work."

She stared at him peculiarly, taking a sip of her drink. "You didn't name any love songs."

He shrugged. "I like Summer Wind."

"Is that what you listen to when you, uh... entertain the ladies?"

The insinuation was clear in her voice.

"Couldn't say. It hasn't happened yet."

Surprise passed across her face. "Never?"

"Never."

"But... how?" She shook her head as she set her glass down. "You haven't, you know... with a girl?"

"No."

Her surprise turned to absolute astonishment. "You're a *virgin*?"

Corrado flinched at the word as she raised her voice, drawing the attention of some tables nearby. Couldn't she at least be *discreet*? "Celia, please..."

"Sorry, I just..." Her cheeks flushed as she dropped her voice low again. "How is that even possible? Girls had to have been throwing themselves at you."

"If they did, I never noticed."

"I don't believe that. Look at you, Corrado."

"What about me?"

"You're gorgeous."

Gorgeous. She'd called him cute once, months ago. Gorgeous was quite the step up.

"I just... unbelievable. Are you sure you've never...?"

"Positive." His expression fell. "You have."

She'd alluded to it before, but a part of Corrado remained in denial. It was clear, though, taking in her guilty expression, that she hadn't been kidding around.

She swallowed harshly, her throat muscles teasingly flexing as she nodded once, confirming it. "Does that bother you?"

Did it? *Absolutely.* The thought of another guy touching her, caressing her skin, kissing her soft lips, shoved him dangerously close to the brink. He dug his heels in, refusing to let it drag him over the edge. "Should it?"

She narrowed her eyes, wagging her finger at him. "You're not supposed to answer a question with a question."

He smiled lightly, remaining quiet.

"It wasn't a whole lot," she said. "Only happened twice."

"Same guy?"

Her silence answered that for him. Two different guys.

"The first was--"

"Stop," he said, holding up his hand. "I don't want to know."

"Are you sure? I'll tell you."

Not if you want them to live. "Your past is your past, and well… it's best if it stays there."

She shrugged, popping a piece of chicken in her mouth.

They finished dinner in comfortable silence, not as awkward as it could've been. Corrado ate a bit, his appetite vacant despite the delicious food, while Celia stuffed herself, eating all of hers before stealing bites straight off his plate. She ordered dessert, fresh tiramisu, and practically licked the plate clean. Corrado paid the bill while she excused herself to the washroom, leaving a sizable tip for the last-minute reservation.

He opened the door for Celia when they reached the car before climbing in beside her.

"Where to now?" she asked.

"Anywhere you want to go."

"Home."

The abrupt word was like a stab in the chest. She spoke with no hesitation. She wanted to go home?

"Home," he repeated quietly.

"Yes, home," she said, settling into the seat. "Yours, not mine."

The dim house stood still at ten o'clock at night. The faint sound of crickets chirping filtered in the open downstairs windows, a soft breeze flowing through, tempering the otherwise stuffy air.

"Would you like to sit down?" Corrado asked, motioning toward the living room. "I can get you something to drink. I don't have much besides water. Might have some orange juice or maybe some milk, but if that's not okay I can—"

"Corrado."

"Yes?"

"Stop rambling."

He blinked with surprise. "Yes, Miss DeMarco."

Celia laughed softly at his response and wrapped her arms around his neck. "You don't have to be nervous."

"I'm not."

She arched an eyebrow at him in challenge.

"Okay, maybe a little."

"Is it because you've never…? Because we don't have to if—"

"It's not sex that makes me nervous," he replied, shutting down that line of thought before she even ventured down that road.

"Then what is it?"

"You."

Her expression softened. "You don't have to try to impress me, you know. I'm already impressed. That day in North Carolina, when you stood up to my mother for Vincent, you won me over."

"It was the right thing to do."

"Yeah, but very few do that anymore. Everyone's so self-centered. They think about themselves, they worry about themselves, and the rest of the world comes second. But not you. You're the most honorable person I've ever met."

Slowly, he leaned down. "You're wrong." His voice dropped low as he chastely kissed her, again and again, whispering harsh words against her soft lips. "I'm a terrible person. Greedy. And angry. And vengeful. The most selfish man you'll ever meet. I'm *heartless.* I take what doesn't belong to me. I hurt anyone who gets in my way. And you want to know what the worst part is?"

"What?"

"I feel no remorse for *any* of it."

Her breath hitched. "I don't believe you."

"You should."

He pulled back, but her arms gripped him tighter, locking him in place. She kissed him then, a full-fledged kiss of passion, eliciting a soft groan from his chest.

She pulled away at the sound of it, putting space between the two of them. "So, uh, how about a tour?"

She wanted a *tour*? "You've been here before."

"I climbed in your window like a thief and got escorted right back out the front door," she said. "That hardly constitutes a visit."

"Fair enough," he conceded, waving down the hall. "After you."

He showed her the downstairs, flicking on lights in the different rooms, most of which she'd taken it upon herself to check out the day she'd broke in. He led her to the stairs. Celia walked in front of him, swaying her hips with each step, drawing his attention straight toward her backside. She stopped when she reached the top step, blocking him.

"How about that drink now?" she asked.

"Uh, sure."

"You got anything with alcohol in it?"

He shook his head. "I'm afraid not."

"Hmmm, just water then," she said, smiling. "Thanks."

He took a step back, eyeing her curiously, before heading downstairs. He went straight for the kitchen, flicking the light on before grabbing a small glass from the cupboard. He tossed a few ice cubes in and filled it with water before heading back out.

When he reached the stairs again, Celia was gone.

He started back up, figuring she'd look around on her own. It wouldn't take her long. Most of the upstairs was vacant, entire rooms full of nothing except space and squandered opportunity. He had no need for them. Besides the bathroom, the only other area he used was his bedroom, and it was scarcely furnished with the necessities—a bed, a dresser, and two nightstands.

The glow of the bedside lamp emanated from his room as he approached, the only door open on the second floor. Stepping into the doorway, he paused and blinked a few times to adjust his eyes.

And then every muscle in his body seized up.

Standing a few feet from him, the back of her legs pressed against the end of his bed, stood Celia. The blue dress lay rumpled in a pile by her feet, her shoes haphazardly kicked off on top of her clothing. All five-feet-seven of her slender figure was exposed, stark naked, not a single part of her hidden from his view. Impulsively, raptly, his eyes raked over her unclothed body, starting at her toes and working their way up, drinking in every drop of her bare flesh, savoring every last centimeter he could make out in the dim lighting. The curve of her hips, the striking hourglass shape leading to the swell of her perky breasts, mesmerized him.

His dry throat was scratchy when he reached her eyes, seeing a darkness lurking in them he'd never noticed before. Usually a warm brown, they now burned black, full of sin and secrets and surprises. They were the eyes of a predator, eyes that held an unadulterated hunger waiting to be satiated.

And this time, Corrado was the prey.

Without a shadow of a doubt, he threw up his white flag.

He surrendered.

Taking a deep breath, he brought the glass to his lips and

gulped down every drop of the water, trying to soothe his parched throat, but the real thirst he knew only she could quench.

Setting the glass down on the dresser, he pulled off his jacket and tossed it aside, not uttering a single word. His eyes raked down her body one more time as he approached, this time starting at the top and drifting down. Reaching out, he ran the back of his hand along her arm. She shivered at his soft touch, goosebumps pebbling her skin. His hand settled on her hip, pulling her toward him, as he leaned down and pressed a kiss to her throat. She tilted her head, moaning, as his lips trailed toward her collarbones.

Meeting her lips, he kissed her slowly, as she unfastened his black silk tie. She moved on to his shirt next, her hands trembling as she worked on the buttons.

Fear? Was she afraid?

Pulling back, he opened his eyes and scanned her face, trying to find any sign of distress, but he there was none. *Excitement*, he realized as she opened her eyes and bit down on her bottom lip, as if she were fighting to contain it all inside of her.

The blood furiously pumping through his system cleansed away every ounce of hesitation. Despite what he'd said to her, despite his warnings about what type of man he truly was, she offered herself to him. She was *giving* herself to him, all of her, and it was a gift he was more than happy to receive.

'Everything,' he'd said. He wanted *everything.*

And now he would take it.

Smashing his lips to hers again, he moved her hands out of the way and tore the rest of his shirt open before dropping it to the floor. He kicked his shoes off, discarding them, before fumbling with his belt. He had it unfastened, his pants unzipped and down around his ankles in a matter of seconds. Kicking them away, he pushed Celia onto the bed.

She broke the kiss, breathing heavily as she scooted back on it. He followed, hovering over her in his black boxers, and found her lips once more when she reached the pillows. Her body sunk into the comfortable bed, dwarfed by his six-foot-one broad frame.

Corrado grunted when her hand snaked into his boxers. She

gripped him firmly, stroking a few times, as her other hand shoved down the material. He reached to help her, pushing his boxers away and kicking them onto the floor with the rest of their clothes.

There was no talking, no contemplating. He kissed and caressed every inch of her, tasting her sensitive flesh, bringing her to the edge and shoving her over with nothing more than the tip of his tongue. Fingers tangled in his hair, she gripped tightly, tugging, as she arched her back and cried out. The sound of his name catching in her throat, the breathy, broken "Corrado" that escaped her lips, ignited a fire way down deep inside of him.

A fire he never knew always burned…

The first thrust, deep and hard, elicited another loud cry from Celia. He stilled, mid-stroke, and shattered his silence. "I didn't hurt you, did I?"

Her eyes, squeezed shut, never opened. "No more than I want you to."

"Are you sure?"

"Jesus," she panted, shifting her hips toward him to take more of him inside. "Don't stop. *Please.*"

"Please?" he whispered, leaning down to pepper kisses along her chest. He captured one of her nipples in his mouth and sucked on it.

"Please," she pleaded again, hands roaming his back, nails scraping his skin. "More."

He pushed into her slowly, sinking every inch of himself inside again. "Like that?"

"Harder," she demanded. "*Fuck* me, Corrado."

Those words were a lightning strike surging through his bones.

Pulling back, he thrust again hard, his hips slamming against her, and she gasped loudly, as if he'd knocked the breath right from her lungs. He did it again, and again, and again, finding her lips once more. She giggled into his mouth, gripping the back of his head. "Naughty boy, who knew you liked dirty talk?"

Apparently he did.

Celia continued teasing him, spurring him on as he gave her himself. He ravaged her body, pounding into her, every ounce of anger and frustration that had ever settled inside of him, making itself at home in the deep crevices of his soul, expelled through the force of his thrusts. Every time he thought he went too far, every time he tried to pull back, to reign it in, Celia would grip him tighter and claw at his skin, whispering words in his ear that could make a man as cold as steel turn to mush.

The sensation of being inside of her, their bodies connected, sent a chill down Corrado's spine that rivaled only the thrill he got from hearing her whimper and moan. *He* did that. *He* caused that. His hands—hands that roamed her flushed skin, hands that cupped her warm cheeks as he kissed her deeply—didn't just cause pain. Those hands didn't just brutalize. They were capable of pleasure, too, pleasure reserved for her.

His climax hit hard and ferocious. He lost his ability to speak, lost his ability to *think*, as he spilled inside of her. Grunting, he thrust a few more times before slowing to a stop, his weight pressing on her. She didn't protest as she held him, softly stroking his sweaty back.

Drawing back, Corrado stared down at her. His pointer finger—his trigger finger—gently glided across her bottom lip, pausing at the corner of her mouth, his thumb tilting her chin as he leaned down to kiss her. It was sweet, and innocent, and everything he never realized he was capable of being.

His nose rubbed against her jawline as he pulled away, breathing her in. She glowed from sweat, her body smelling like pure sex.

She smelled like *him*.

"No Sinatra," she mused when he rolled over in bed beside her. "Guess it wasn't Summer Wind, after all."

He pulled her into his arms. "No, you're the only music I need."

Corrado stood in the dark upstairs hall, leaning against the wall with his arms crossed over his chest, and watched Celia fix her hair in his small bathroom mirror. The curls had loosened, tendrils falling around her face as she tried to pin it in place. Her dress was back on, situated perfectly, shoes again strapped to her feet.

He, on the other hand, was slightly worse for wear. His wrinkled shirt was half tucked in, the top few buttons undone, exposing a hint of his chest. His hair was disheveled, wild from her fingers running through it.

There wasn't enough energy left in him to fix it.

"I'm ready," Celia said, shutting off the light and joining him.

Corrado motioned toward the stairs, grabbing his jacket before following behind her. They stepped outside into the cool Chicago night air as Corrado pulled out his keys. "I'll drive you."

"No, let's walk."

He glanced at his watch: a quarter till midnight.

Shrugging, he stepped off the porch, draping his jacket over her shoulders when she shivered. She shoved her arms in the holes to put it on, drowning in the oversized fabric.

Reaching over, she grabbed his hand, linking their fingers together as they strolled down the sidewalk in the direction of her house.

"Tonight was wonderful," she said. "Thank you."

His voice was quiet. "You don't have to thank me."

"Yes, I do. A few times, actually. I mean... wow."

"The pleasure was all mine."

She scoffed. "Hardly. Half of it was mine."

He squeezed her hand in lieu of a response.

They walked in silence as Corrado's thoughts drifted to the previous few hours, the night's events in a continuous loop in mind. Now that it was over, emotions tempered, common sense seeping back in, guilt nagged him, fueling the nervousness once again. He replayed it over and over, his stomach twisting.

About a block away, Celia stopped abruptly. Corrado only realized it when he met resistance from her hand. Footsteps faltering, he glanced back at her. "Everything okay?"

"I could ask you the same."

"What do you mean?"

"You're being quiet."

"Aren't I usually?"

"Yes, but not like this. You're usually quiet because you're so busy assessing your surroundings. But right now, you're so stuck in your head that you wouldn't notice a plane if it dropped out of the sky."

"I think I'd notice that."

"I don't know," she said. "You sure didn't notice the guy who whistled at me."

Brow furrowing, Corrado glanced past Celia, seeing a vague figure retreating down the block. A flurry of anger flared inside of him. What kind of man disrespected a woman like that?

What kind of idiot disrespected *him*?

"Corrado." Celia snapped her finger to hone his attention. "Seriously, what's gotten into you?"

He pulled his hand from hers and ran it anxiously through his hair. "I made a mistake."

"What kind of mistake?"

"I didn't use any protection."

Lost in the whirlwind, stunned by the sight of her naked in his bedroom, he hadn't given any thought to condoms. The subject had never come up between them.

She frowned. "I told you I've only been with two others. You don't have to worry... I don't have any..."

"It's not that," he interjected. "I trust you."

"Then what?" Her eyes widened when it seemed to strike her what he meant. "*Oh*."

"Yeah."

He expected shock. He expected terror. But he certainly didn't expect her to laugh.

"*That's* what's bothering you? The thought of having a baby?"

He flinched at her words, recoiling as if she'd struck him with a fist. The laughter died instantly, Celia's shock surfacing. "It really bothers you. Like, *really* bothers you."

He attempted to turn away, but she grabbed his arm.

"Corrado, relax, it's okay. I'm not going to get pregnant."

"You can't know that."

"I can," she said. "I'm on the pill."

His anxiety eased as disbelief set in. "You're taking *birth control*?"

"Yeah."

"You're Catholic, Celia."

"So are you."

"Your father would never approve of that."

She scoffed. "Like that man can talk with as much as *he* sins."

Corrado could only stare at her. He wasn't the perfect Catholic by any means. He sinned more than most others and never asked for forgiveness. He believed in God, of course, but he often wondered if God believed in him. It surprised him, though, that Celia would so blatantly ignore her beliefs for something so seedy.

He shouldn't have been surprised, given she had no qualms with premarital sex.

"Look, I'm no idiot," she said. "Better safe than sorry, right?"

He hesitated. "Right."

"And it's my body, right?"

No hesitation this time. "Right."

"Then no problem, right?"

"Right," he said. "No problem."

She linked their fingers once more and yanked on his arm. "Come on, I'm going to miss curfew."

They walked again, silence nearly taking over, but Celia's playful giggle kept him in the moment.

"What's so funny?" he asked.

"Just thinking about, well, you know." She blushed, nudging him with her arm. "There's *no* way you're a virgin."

"I am." He paused. "Or I was."

"Then how did you learn to do all that?" she whispered. "You made my toes curl."

"Uh, I don't know." He laughed awkwardly. "Just because I hadn't done it didn't mean I hadn't thought about it." *And thought about it... and thought about it some more.*

"I knew you'd be a natural, but wow."

"You knew I'd be a natural?"

"Like I said—you're always attentive to your surroundings," she said. "Makes sense that you'd be the same way with a woman."

Raising her hand in his, he pressed a soft kiss on the back of it.

"Only with you, *Bellissima*."

Corrado led Celia straight to her front door, letting go of her hand when they stepped on to the porch. He started to speak when the door swung open. Antonio stood there, a grim expression marring his face as he blocked the doorway. "You're late."

Corrado looked at his watch: eight minutes past midnight.

Celia rolled her eyes. "Give me a break. It's only a few minutes."

"A few? More like fifteen."

Corrado refrained from correcting the man, knowing it wouldn't make a difference. Even one minute late was equivalent to a lifetime.

"What are you going to do, ground me?"

Antonio stared at her for a moment before his eyes shifted to Corrado. The answer lay in his expression. He wouldn't ground her, but he had every intention of punishing *him*.

A slight sinister smile twisted the Boss's lips. "You seem to have lost your tie, Corrado."

Corrado glanced down at his disheveled appearance and wished he had spent more time tidying himself. "It got a bit suffocating."

"I bet it did." Antonio's eyes studied him. "Your socks seem to be missing, too."

"Yeah, my feet were, uh..." He eyed his ankles. "...suffocating."

"Well then," Antonio said. "I'm just glad you kept on the rest of your clothes."

"Daddy!" Celia hissed. "Can you *not*?"

"I haven't done anything."

"Can you give us some privacy?" she asked. "Please?"

It seemed even the Boss of *La Cosa Nostra* wasn't immune to the charms of Celia DeMarco. With the bat of her eyelashes, she could bring any man to his knees.

"Yeah, sure," he conceded, his eyes still focused on Corrado. "I'll be seeing *you* tomorrow."

"Yes, sir."

Antonio went back inside, and Corrado let out a sharp exhale. "Suffocating," he grumbled, feeling like an idiot. "He's going to suffocate *me* for that."

Smiling, Celia leaned up on her tiptoes and kissed him. She pulled back, pressing her hand flat against his chest. His heart thumped erratically against her palm.

"You're wrong about yourself," she said seriously. "You said you were heartless, but that's not true. I can feel it, Corrado. It's in there. And as long as it's beating, I know it's there, working overtime, and you'll *never* convince me otherwise."

After one last kiss, she stepped away, wrapping his jacket tightly around her. "I'm keeping the coat."

"Okay."

"I'm going to wear it to bed."

"Okay."

"With nothing on underneath it."

Winking, she slipped inside, leaving him on the porch with that mental image ringing through his head.

Corrado's punishment swiftly came the next morning in the form of a phone call from the Boss. He had just gotten to sleep, too wound tightly to relax right away, when the phone started incessantly ringing.

"Moretti speaking," he muttered, groggily plopping down on the couch in the living room.

"Breakfast."

The Boss's voice woke him up. "Excuse me, sir?"

"I want breakfast."

He hesitated. "Do you want me to meet you?"

"No, I want you to *deliver* it to me."

And Corrado did just that an hour later, showing up at the DeMarco residence juggling half a dozen containers of food from as many different restaurants. Antonio had rattled off an extensive list, from pancakes at a popular nearby diner to scrambled tofu from an obscure place outside the city limits. It was enough food to feed more than one family, but Antonio was the only one awake when Corrado arrived.

"Took you long enough," Antonio said, showing him inside. Corrado set the containers on the kitchen counter and stood back, waiting to be dismissed. Antonio opened them all, surveying the contents, before hastily throwing every last one right in the trashcan. "I'm not hungry anymore."

Contrary to his words, Antonio picked up an apple and bit into it, noisily chewing. "Since you're awake, Corrado, I got some errands that need ran."

"Errands?"

"Yeah, you know... dry cleaning to pick up, mail to deliver, bills to pay. Menial things that even someone like you could handle. Got a problem with that?"

Someone like you. Corrado grimaced. "No, sir."

Antonio fetched a sprawling list from his office desk and handed it to Corrado. "Off you go."

Corrado was out until after midnight handling everything, having barely had time to sit down and take a break all day. He collapsed on his couch, utterly exhausted, but by the time he dozed off his phone rang again.

It happened the next day. And the next day. And every day after that for the next two weeks. Antonio ran him ragged, treating him like he was dog shit on the bottom of his shoe—shit he wanted nothing more than to scrape away on the filthy sidewalk. Corrado blew through every penny he'd managed to save, always picking up the tab wherever he was sent, even being pushed so far as to having to pay the Boss's *goomah*'s rent.

The Boss… the man he respected more than anyone… had a mistress. That fact floored Corrado.

He only encountered Celia in passing during that time, sharing a few stray phone calls when she caught him at home. It tortured him, being forced to keep his distance after the intimate night they shared.

That was the point, Corrado realized.

Fifteen days of punishment for being fifteen minutes late.

Corrado still didn't tell him it was only eight.

Day fifteen finally came, and Corrado was awake and dressed by five in the morning. He'd no sooner sat down with the Sunday paper when his phone rang. "Moretti speaking."

"Good morning."

"Morning, sir."

"I'd like you to meet me at the church."

Before Corrado could even ask *when*, the line went dead.

Saint Mary's Catholic Church appeared deserted at that hour, even on a Sunday, the holiest day of the week. The Boss's car was already parked front and center when Corrado arrived, right in front of the large set of stairs leading to the wooden ornamental doors. Corrado parked his Mercedes behind the familiar DeVille and climbed out, taking a deep calming breath before heading inside.

The church was dim, only subtle lighting throughout the massive space, as the sun hadn't yet taken its rightful place in the sky. Corrado glanced around, trying to adjust his eyes, and spotted Antonio sitting in his usual spot in the front pew. Slowly, Corrado approached, his footsteps magnified in the silent building. Antonio didn't look at him, no visible acknowledgement as Corrado slid into the pew. His head remained bowed, his eyes closed, almost as if the man were fast asleep.

Out of respect, Corrado bowed his head as he waited.

It took a few minutes before Antonio even made a noise—a faintly audible sigh. Corrado peered over at the man, realizing he now stared straight ahead at the cross behind the pulpit.

"This is the only time I feel at peace," Antonio said. "Every day, my head is full of all these thoughts—who's doing what, who's doing who, where, when, how... I gotta worry about all these different people, all these different schemes, making sure everybody's happy so they don't go killing each other. But Sunday morning, when I step in here, I have nobody to worry about for a while but me."

"Do you come here every Sunday?"

Antonio shot him a look of admonishment. "Of course I do."

"I meant this early," he corrected himself. "Before services."

"That may be what you meant, but it isn't what you said. You should think about your words before you speak them."

"Yes, sir."

"And yes, I come here this early every Sunday... sometimes earlier, depends on how bad my week was. I like to sit and pray, you know... talk to God when there aren't so many others doing the same. Figure I have a better chance of him answering me that way."

"Has it worked?"

"Well... I'm not dead yet."

Corrado sat silently as he thought over that response. Was that what he prayed for? Survival?

"How long has this thing being going on between you and my daughter, Corrado?"

Corrado tensed at the shift in conversation. The Boss knew the answer to this question. "We had our first date two weeks ago."

"That's not what I asked. I want to know when it *started*."

When did it start? Such a loaded question. Was it a few months ago, when he'd stood in the foyer at the DeMarco house, convinced the sound of her voice would be the end of him? Or was it a week later when he'd gone to ask for the Boss's blessing, only to be shot down? Or maybe it was after that, the night of the fair, when that last part of him opened up and let her in.

Or maybe… maybe it was much, much earlier.

"I guess you can say it started when we were kids."

"So you've loved her for half your life."

Love. The word made his head swim. "Feels like my entire life."

"And how do you feel about that?"

Corrado cut his eyes at the Boss. "You're asking me about my feelings?"

Antonio laughed, relaxing in the pew. "Yeah, I guess I am."

Corrado remained silent, gazing around the quiet church. He understood why the Boss visited at this hour. There was something reassuring about being tucked inside the thick fortress walls and high vaulted ceiling. He felt so minuscule sitting there, a tiny fleck in a much bigger universe, unnoticed and maybe even overlooked. And while nobody truly wanted to be forgotten, an unseen man remained unscathed.

"Feels like a lifetime isn't near enough," he answered finally. "Especially *my* life."

Antonio nodded as if he'd expected that answer. "I was your age when Celia was born. I wasn't ready to be a father. Most days I think I'm still not ready. It's been eighteen years since then… so you can say I've loved that girl for half my life, too. I'm only thirty-six, Corrado, but when I wake up in the morning I feel old. I feel like I'm on the way out."

"You're one of the youngest bosses in history."

"Doesn't matter. Nobody stays in power for more than a few years. *Nobody.* I've been running things for a decade now. Maybe, if I'm lucky, I got another decade in me. If I'm damn lucky, I'll even live to see my fiftieth birthday. Any more than that? Well, there isn't enough luck in the universe to make that happen." Antonio laughed darkly. "I can have most anything I want in life. I have no problem stealing from others. But the one thing I want most, I can't take. You can't steal time. You can't rob God. And that pisses me off more than it should."

A hint of emotion cracked Antonio's voice.

"So every Sunday, I sit right here," Antonio continued. "I sit here, and I wait. I don't even know what I'm waiting on. Maybe I want Him to save me. Or maybe I just do it to fucking spite Him. But I'm here, because there's only one in this universe more powerful than me, and I'm not a coward. I'm going to face Him."

Those words brought up a memory, a conversation Corrado had with his father the first time he laid eyes on Antonio DeMarco at the casino in Las Vegas. Corrado had been shocked his father had a boss.

"We all got someone we answer to."

"Who does he answer to?"

"I don't know, kid. God, maybe?"

Antonio spoke again, pulling Corrado out of his mind with a question. "Have you told her?"

"Who?"

"My daughter," he said. "Have you told her you love her?"

"She knows."

"That's not what I asked. I asked if you *told* her."

"No."

"You ought to."

His voice was quiet as he mumbled, "I know."

A door across the church opened, a man appearing, his roman collar shining under the hint of morning sunshine sneaking through the stained glass windows. Antonio's expression brightened. "Father Alberto."

"How are you, my child?"

"Same as ever." Antonio slapped his arm around Corrado's shoulder. "You meet Corrado yet?"

Father Alberto approached. "I've seen his face in the crowd the days he graces us with his presence."

"Ah, well, I'm sure he'll be doing that more often now that he's dating my daughter."

Corrado tensed as both men eyed him with interest.

"Absolutely, sir." He glanced at the priest. "Father."

The priest walked away, motioning for Antonio to follow. The Boss stood. "Confession time." He paused, studying Corrado. "I'll love my daughter as long as I live, but I need to know someone will love her as long as *she* does. So if you ever decide to be that one… if you decide you want to marry her? You have my blessing… as long as you promise never to leave her behind."

Corrado was flabbergasted. "Thank you, sir."

Antonio shrugged it off, laughing as he turned around. "Just don't let her *suffocate* you too much."

18

"Here's the situation," the lawyer said, monotone voice nearly putting Corrado to sleep as he shifted through a file, the jacket of his brown suit bunching up around his frail shoulders. "The DA is offering probation for the lesser charge of simple assault."

"A plea bargain?"

"Yes."

"I'm not doing it."

The lawyer sighed impatiently. "It's a generous offer."

"I'm not pleading guilty."

"Look, Mr. Moretti. They charged you with two felonies. You're looking at years in prison and thousands of dollars in fines for this."

"No, you look, Mister..." Corrado had to peek at the nameplate on the desk to remember the public defender's name. "...Jackson. I'm not pleading guilty when I did nothing wrong."

"You pistol-whipped two men and left them for dead."

"They deserved it."

"And I'm sure the judge will *love* that defense."

Corrado didn't care what they thought. "I'll take my chances."

"I get it... you don't want to plead guilty... but it's in your best interest to avoid a trial."

"I agree."

"So we're on the same page?"

"Absolutely," Corrado said. "You're going to get them to drop the charges."

Corrado had been optimistic, but his hopes were dashed two weeks later when the judge ordered the case to trial. Studiously, he showed up to court the day of the proceedings, sitting beside his annoyed lawyer who wanted to be anywhere but there.

They selected a jury in less than four hours. The prosecution began, telling a tale of a violent boy who savagely beat two guys to the brink of death. They jumped right in, calling their first witness: the guy who had held a gun to Celia's head.

"You're going to have to testify," the lawyer muttered to Corrado, slouching in his chair as if he were trying to slink away. "Otherwise, their story is the only one the jury will hear."

"I'm not worried," Corrado said, watching as the man was sworn in. "It won't get that far."

The lawyer shrugged it off, turning his attention to the witness stand. The prosecutor stood—a stern woman with dull blonde hair—and approached the witness. "Marcel, can you tell me what happened the night of July 27th?"

Marcel Jones. Corrado knew his name, had memorized it the day the article ran in the newspaper.

"Yeah, uh, my friend and I were walking to the store, you know, for a drink..." He nervously cleared his throat. "...and we came upon this guy. He pulled out a gun and I thought he was gonna shoot us. We tried to fight back, but he overpowered us."

"And the man who attacked you," the prosecutor said. "Do you see him here in the courtroom today?"

Marcel cleared his throat, leaning closer to the microphone. "Nope."

A wave of murmurs flowed through the courtroom. Corrado stared straight ahead as Marcel spoke again. "I ain't never seen the defendant before. I don't know who he is."

The prosecutor requested a recess to regroup, but it was downhill from there. Their case ripped apart, every witness they called recanting, denying knowing anything.

It only took twenty minutes for the *not guilty* verdict to come in.

Corrado waited a few weeks, letting the hype die down, before he paid Marcel a visit. Under the cloak of darkness, while he slept in bed, Corrado broke into his house and slit his throat. The other man received a pass, a reprieve, but not Marcel. He had manhandled Celia.

Nobody would ever get away with doing that.

PART III

The Impossible Dream

19

The house appeared exactly the same.

The long dining room table was still cloaked with a thick white tablecloth, faint discolored splotches on the edges of it that bleach hadn't covered. The wall, despite countless scrubbings, still bore the faint orange tint of a plate of lasagna being hurled at it. A broken crystal vase sat on the mantle, a deep crack the whole way around it from where it had been haphazardly glued together.

A Moretti family heirloom.

Corrado hadn't ventured upstairs, but if he had, he knew he'd find claw marks on the banister leading to the hallway, ruts dug into the wooden floor outside of his childhood bedroom, telling tales of horror he kept mostly to himself.

He hadn't been to Las Vegas in about two years, hadn't stepped foot in this house or even heard his mother's voice. And yet, here he was, eating off the chipped china as her laughter echoed through the room, charming everyone around the table except for him.

He knew the true ugliness it disguised.

As if she sensed his thoughts, a small hand landed on his thigh, rubbing soothing circles along his slacks. Dropping his fork, not even the slightest bit hungry, he reached under the table and placed his hand on top of hers. He squeezed gently, showing his appreciation as his gaze drifted to the seat beside him.

Celia sat poised, an attentive expression on her face, but he saw the faded look in her eyes as she tuned out the conversation.

Glancing away from her, Corrado scanned the other seats. The DeMarco's sat across from them—Antonio and Gia, along with Vincent, who appeared to be little more than bored by the celebration, his elbow propped up on the table. To Corrado's left sat his sister, beside her an anxious Michael Antonelli. Unbeknownst to Corrado, who had taken no interest in his sister's life after moving, Katrina had started dating Michael, and the diamond ring gleaming from her left hand told him all he needed to know. It was modest, half a carat at most—nothing like the one Celia wore.

As the thought passed through his mind, Corrado absently toyed with the hand in his lap, fiddling with the ring on her finger. Six weeks after receiving Antonio's blessing, after making enough money to afford a ring, Corrado popped the question. He hadn't put much planning into it, merely took her to dinner and pulled the ring out over dessert.

Celia had been mid-story, rambling on about a friend of hers who Corrado couldn't even remember meeting, as she devoured a piece of tiramisu. She'd just shoved a forkful in her mouth when he flipped open the small black velvet box.

As soon as the five-carat diamond caught the light, Celia inhaled sharply… and started choking.

She dropped her fork, coughing viciously as her face turned bright red. Concern wiped away every ounce of nervousness as he jumped up. She held her hands up to stop him, getting herself under control as she grabbed his water and took a drink.

Once she seemed to be okay again, he retook his seat. The red in Celia's cheeks spread down her neck as blush overtook her skin.

"What are you doing?" she asked, the words barely audible.

Corrado glanced between her and the ring. "Asking you to marry me."

She gawked at him as he stared back, awaiting some kind of response. Tense moments passed of strained silence before she roared with laughter. "That's it? *That's* your proposal?"

He shrugged a shoulder.

She continued to laugh, shaking her head. Corrado's stomach

twisted. This wasn't going as well as he'd hoped. After a minute, she leaned toward him, her eyes fixated on the sparkling ring. "Why?"

Why. That godforsaken question. This time he had an answer.

"Because I love you."

As if some magical spell fell over her, Celia's expression softened, tears springing to her eyes.

She continued to stare at him.

Why wasn't she saying anything?

Looking away from her, he glanced down at the ring and closed the box when her hand shot out, covering it. "I love you, too, Corrado. *Of course* I'll marry you."

The date was set for July 15, a mere three weeks away. Everything was all ready, planned to Celia's liking. All that was left between now and then was surviving their current engagement party.

He tried to focus on the present as the sound of his mother's grating voice again tore through the room. He glanced at where she sat at the head of the table. She wouldn't even yield to Vito with the Boss present.

"And then," Erika said as she waved her glass, the red wine swirling around. Her third drink, maybe the fourth that Corrado saw, but that didn't account for what she drank before they arrived. He heard the slur of her words. She toed dangerously close to her limit. "That Samantha Mallory knocked on my front door, all three-feet of her little blonde self, and informed me that she was here to date Corrado. Can you believe it? This seven year old girl declaring her love for my teenage son."

Everyone around the table laughed with the exception of Corrado.

"It was a sight to behold," Erika continued. "I told her, 'honey, I get it, I know my Corrado's a handsome creature, but you're a little young for him'. And she cried—boy, did she cry! I hated having to break that girl's heart. But can you believe it? At seven? My kids didn't even know what love was at that age!"

Unable to take anymore, Corrado shoved his chair back, tossing his napkin over his plate.

Nobody said a word when he strode from the room. A stark

silence followed him as he made his way to the kitchen. The lights were on, something baking in the oven, but there wasn't a soul to be seen. Corrado walked over to the window.

A moment later he heard the clicking of high heels. He caught sight of Celia's distorted reflection in the glass, smelled her perfume as she approached. Wrapping her arms around him from behind, she laid her head against his back. "See? I knew you had girls throwing themselves at you."

He grasped her arms, pulling her to the front of him. He hugged her tightly, kissing the top of her head as he whispered, "it's all lies."

"What?"

"That never happened." He'd never heard of a Samantha Mallory. "She's lying."

"Why would she do that?"

"Who knows," he muttered. "Maybe she doesn't know the difference between fiction and reality."

"She seems so..." Celia paused as Corrado pondered the possibilities. *Horrible? Bitter? Deceitful?* "Normal."

A sharp laugh escaped his throat. If his mother were the definition, he wanted nothing to do with *normal.*

The two were still standing there, hugging in silence, Corrado's cheek resting against the top of her head, when the door to the kitchen ever so slightly opened, a frail form slipping in almost undetected. His eyes darted that way, sensing the movement, and caught a pair of startled green eyes.

The second their eyes connected, her gaze dropped to the floor.

Maura.

Two years had aged the young girl a lifetime. Signs of weariness showed on her face, the liveliness that had once twinkled in her hopeful eyes dimmed to a dull flicker. She had gotten taller, the dress that used to drag the ground now hovering high above her ankles. Her fiery red hair was tame, her clothes clean and skin bathed. Even makeup coated her face, hiding what Corrado assumed were remnants of bruises that his mother wouldn't want anyone to see.

"Sorry," Maura apologized. "I didn't know anyone was in here."

Celia withdrew from Corrado's arms at the sound of the female voice, spinning around to face the girl.

"I, uh…" Maura stammered, motioning toward the stove. "You know, before it burns."

He stepped away, not wanting to hinder her, and tried to drag Celia with him, but she wouldn't budge. Celia smiled brightly, instead taking a step toward Maura.

Corrado started to protest, but silenced his objections. Who was he to tell her what to do?

"I'm Celia," she said, holding out her hand. Maura gaped at it, wide-eyed, and Corrado grimaced when confusion took over Celia's face. As much as he didn't want to, he knew he'd have to explain.

'A helper', Vito had always called them. 'Sometimes you need a little help and there are people out there made for that.' He'd never come out and said it, choosing to stick to his lies of omission, but Erika had no qualms calling a spade a spade.

Slave.

She had spat the word so many times that even the venom lacing it had made her own flesh-and-blood flinch. Human trafficking was the underground worlds darkest secret. *La Cosa Nostra* didn't deal in it directly, but it was undeniable that some of the money filtering into the organization came from the slave trade. Antonio had a *'don't ask, don't tell'* policy.

If you don't see it happen, you can pretend it never did.

"Celia," Corrado said, wrapping his arm around her waist. "Maura."

"Hello." Maura's voice was meek, her eyes never quite meeting either of theirs.

Before Celia could respond, Maura sidestepped her extended hand and pulled a pie out of the oven, setting it on the counter before slipping right back out the kitchen door.

It took less than thirty seconds.

She had gotten good at evading.

Celia stared at the swaying door before facing Corrado, eyes narrowed suspiciously. "Who was that?"

"Maura."

"I got *that* much. Who is she?"

Lie by omission?

Or tell the ugly truth?

"She's a slave," Corrado said tentatively. He couldn't lie to her.

A vast array of emotions took over Celia's face, flashing in her expressive eyes. Shock. Disbelief. Dismay. Horror.

And then came the rage.

"You have a *slave*?" she hissed.

"My *mother* has one," he corrected her, but it did nothing to lessen her anger.

Her pointer finger shot out, jabbing him hard in his sternum. "What kind of sick, twisted bitch keeps a girl as a slave?"

Corrado grabbed her hand as she jabbed at him again. "Not so normal anymore, huh?"

After dinner, guests dispersed as others arrived, a steady flow of people streaming through the house—extended family, business associates, friends of friends. Everyone who was anyone made an appearance, coming out of respect.

The men gathered around with cigars later in the evening, half-full glasses of expensive liquor covering the table. The air became a haze of harsh smoke, constricting Corrado's view of his cards.

Wadded bills lay in heaps as the men played five-card draw. Bets were elevated to extraordinary heights as they bickered, throwing down cards and drawing more. Corrado played along, folding even when he held a winning hand.

His heart wasn't in it.

Vito raised the bet to $800. Antonio called the hand.

Corrado folded. He was done.

Picking up his glass, he swirled it around briefly before bringing it to his lips and taking a small sip. Not usually one to drink, he needed something to ease his nerves—nerves that had frayed the second he stepped back into this hellhole.

The faint trace of alcohol simmered in his bloodstream, relaxing his shoulders. The others drank heavily, a bottle continuously flowing, empty ones replaced. A few of the men grew belligerent, especially mouthy Michael Antonelli.

It pushed Corrado's thoughts toward his mother again. He hadn't seen her in a while, the women having excused themselves hours ago.

Corrado didn't bother waiting to find out who won the hand. He bowed out of the game, clutching his glass of scotch as he left the dining room. He strolled around, finding his mother and Gia chatting away in the living room, but there was no sign of Celia. He headed into the foyer, pausing and staring out the front door into the darkened yard, before glancing toward the second floor.

Leave it to Celia to make him go up there.

Hesitantly, he ascended the stairs, his free hand skimming along the rough banister, in no hurry as he strolled down the scuffed hallway. He paused when he reached his childhood bedroom and leaned against the splintered doorframe.

Celia stood inside, the dim bedside lamp emitting a soft orange glow across all of his old belongings.

"How did I know I'd find you up here?"

"Because I make it a habit to invite myself into your bedrooms?"

"This isn't my room," he said, holding his glass out to her. "Not anymore."

Her shoulders sagged with relief as she took the glass, throwing the liquor back. She shuddered at the burn and wiped her mouth as she gave the empty glass back.

She strolled over to a bookcase and ran her fingers along the spines of the books. "Your stuff is still here. It's so weird, like seeing another part of you. I didn't realize you loved reading."

"I don't," he said. "I stopped reading a long time ago."

Her eyes narrowed. "I recall you having *The Count of Monte Cristo.*"

"That's one book. It hardly counts."

"So it's your favorite?"

"There's a prison break, so it's more like research."

Celia moved away from the bookcase and ran her hand along the comforter on the bed. It was over a decade old, the batman symbol washed out and faded. "Superhero fan, huh?"

"Used to be."

"Not anymore?"

"Not since I realized *we* were the villains."

She laughed. "Yeah, yeah, yeah… you can say what you want, but I know that nerdy little Batman lover still exists inside of you."

"You're wrong," he said as she approached. "My mother murdered him."

"How?"

"Smothered him with a pillow. Right there in that bed."

"Then who are you?"

"His ghost."

He hadn't meant for it to unnerve her, but she trembled at those words.

Celia turned away, scrunching up her nose at the White Sox poster. "Does it bother you that I'm in your room?"

He opened his mouth to correct her, to once more stress it *wasn't* his room, but decided it was pointless. "I'm just glad you kept your clothes on this time."

Her eyes widened before a sly smile overtook her lips. Reaching up, she unbuttoned the top button on her blouse. "Hmmm, well…"

"Don't," he said, shaking his head. "I'll take you in the filthy basement tunnel at The Flamingo before I let you get naked *here*."

Her cheeks flushed as she whispered, "promise?"

A throat cleared in the hallway then. Celia's curious eyes tried to see around him, but Corrado didn't move. He didn't have to.

He'd heard her coming. "Katrina."

Celia made a face of annoyance, no longer trying to see.

"Mrs. DeMarco is looking for her daughter," Katrina said. "She's ready to leave."

Celia rolled her eyes but didn't argue. He ventured to guess she didn't like to be there any more than he did. She kissed Corrado. "See you back at the hotel?"

"Yes. I'll catch a ride later."

Celia strode out, not bothering to say goodbye to Katrina. Corrado listened to her high heels against the stairs and waited until she was gone before crossing the threshold into the bedroom. He walked over to his old desk, surprised everything remained exactly how he had left it. He had made enough money with his little schemes as a teen to afford to start over brand new. All he'd had when he arrived in Chicago were the clothes on his back and a single faded photograph of Celia. He had burned her letter, destroying her private words to keep them away from prying eyes, but he could never part with the picture. He carried it with him everywhere to keep it safe from destruction.

It was still tucked in his wallet.

He shut off the lamp to leave, eyeing his sister in the hallway. She scowled, arms crossed over her chest, head cocked to the side as she studied him with harsh eyes.

"Nice to see you, Kat. Congratulations on your, uh... engagement?"

She glanced down at her ring, her stance relaxing. "Thanks."

"Am I invited to the wedding?"

"Would you even come?"

"Probably not."

"Didn't think so."

"I wasn't aware you and Michael were close. I didn't think you liked him."

She scoffed. "He comes from a great family. His dad's going to nominate him for induction the next time the books open, you know. Michael's going places."

Corrado stared at her, surprised she knew so much about the process... although, he shouldn't have been. Michael Antonelli had always had a big mouth.

It was easy to be connected to the mob, but getting inducted was a rare privilege. They seldom opened the books, so to speak, to take nominations for men to join their ranks. Once you were inducted into *La Cosa Nostra* though, officially making you a made man, you were set for life. It was an honor reserved for the select few who had earned their place, who had time and again proven themselves worthy.

Something Michael Antonelli hadn't come close to doing. And knowing Michael like Corrado did? He never would.

"Congratulations, again," Corrado said, choosing not to broach that subject.

"I still don't like her," Katrina shouted as Corrado walked away. "And that brother of hers—ugh, he's even worse. I saw him outside earlier hanging out with the slave. Talk about pathetic."

Corrado's footsteps faltered for a brief second before he continued on, not letting her goad him into more conversation.

He headed back to the dining room and took his seat at the table beside the Boss. The game of poker was still going strong, more money surfacing during his absence. He refused when they tried to deal him in, instead pouring himself another glass of scotch to relax now that Celia was out of harm's way.

He sipped on his drink, glancing at the doorway to the room, and spotted Vincent lingering against the wall. Corrado watched the boy curiously as he listened to their conversation, standing on the sidelines because he hadn't been invited in.

Corrado had never quite been sure what to think of the boy.

"This is a good day," Antonio declared, folding on his current hand as he slapped Corrado hard on the back. "I'm proud. Hell, I'm *elated.* It's going to be an honor to be able to call you my son."

Those words struck Corrado hard, but his own gratification diminished when he noticed Vincent's reaction. He looked like someone had punched him as he hunched over, his face contorted with self-pity.

There was a commotion, a loud clattering in the kitchen, as the shattering of a glass cut through the air. Conversation ceased as Erika's slurred voice echoed through the downstairs. "What the hell's wrong with you?"

"Sorry, Mistress!" Maura gasped. "It won't happen again!"

"It better not, or so help me God, I'll make you wish you'd never been born."

Corrado shook his head, not surprised by the vicious threats.

Maura probably wished that every day. His eyes fell upon Vincent once more.

Vincent's back had stiffened, his hands clenched into fists. He wasn't feeling sorry for himself anymore.

And just like that, without uttering a single word, he told Corrado everything.

He'd never be a good made man. He didn't know how to bluff. Corrado saw right through him.

And for the first time, he truly sympathized with the boy.

The men attempted to return to their poker game, but the damage had been done. The lid holding the rage inside Erika Moretti had been unsealed faster than the cork was popped on a fresh bottle of wine.

Pop.

Shrieking ripped from the kitchen as Erika unleashed a verbal lashing, criticizing and cursing Maura's every move. The girl's cries only infuriated her more, words turning threatening before escalating to crashes and bangs, drawers slamming and things breaking, the kitchen engulfing in warfare.

All the while Vincent looked like he was going to be sick.

It went on and on for what seemed like forever until a telltale crack tore through the air, followed by a blood-curdling scream.

Erika was beating the girl.

"Vito," Antonio spat, slamming his cards down on the table. "You gonna do something about that?"

Vito froze. He was so used to ignoring it.

"Vito." Antonio's voice bordered on threatening as he growled his name again. "*Handle it.*"

"Yeah, uh..." Vito set his cards down and stood. "Excuse me, gentlemen."

Corrado sunk down in his chair and swallowed every last drop of liquor in his glass. He had lived in this house for most of his life. He knew what would happen next. Once his mother got started, she didn't stop until *she* decided it was over. Vito would make it worse.

The moment Vito appeared in the kitchen, Erika turned her rage on him. He begged her, humiliating himself within earshot of the Boss as he tried to diffuse the ticking time bomb, but his pleading fell on deaf ears. She was much too bitter, much too sinister, to let any common sense reign over her.

"Fuck you!" Erika spat. "You show up here and try to boss me around. You're nobody, Vito. *Nobody.* You think you're a fucking king, but you're not. You're nothing!"

"You shut your mouth," Vito snapped back, losing his cool. Erika wanted a fight, and Vito was always more than willing to oblige. "You *will* respect me in my own house."

"*Your* house?" She laughed maniacally. "You're never here! Your house is with that whore in Chicago. Tell me, Vito, does she fuck like me? Does she suck your puny dick? Does she do that for you? Huh?"

"Shut the fuck up," he yelled. "You don't talk about things you don't get. You have no goddamn right!"

"You're my husband! Mine, not hers. You belong to *me*!"

"Maybe if you'd start acting like a wife—"

"Fuck you! Don't blame me for this!"

"Who else is there to blame? After the shit you put our kids through—"

"Father of the fucking year right here," Erika shrieked. "Please, tell me more. Tell me how great of a father you were from a thousand miles away."

"I made mistakes, but *I'm* not the one wrecking our son's engagement party!"

"Oh, fuck him, too."

"What did you just say?"

"I said *fuck him.* He's nobody, too."

"Don't talk about my son that way, Erika."

"I'll talk about him any damn way I want to. I gave birth to that little bastard! He belongs to *me*."

"He's half mine."

She scoffed. "That's what you think."

Her words were like a bomb going off, the explosion tearing through the house. Vito snarled, "You bitch," seconds before violence erupted. Corrado heard the whack as Vito slammed Erika into the wall with so much force the photos in the dining room shook, a painting crashing to the floor.

"Vito, please!" Erika gasped. "Stop! Please!"

Now *her* pleading fell on deaf ears.

Antonio was on his feet, the rest of the men following suit when Erika's screams grew louder. They rushed out of the room, but Corrado remained standing there, astounded.

As much as they fought, his father had *never* hit his mother before.

Fighting continued, incoherent shouting coupled with glass shattering. Vito was dragged back into the dining room, kicking and screaming, finally calming down when the Boss stood between him and the doorway. He breathed heavily, his hat gone and hair a mess. "I can't fucking believe her."

"Watch yourself, Vito," Antonio warned.

"Did you hear what she said to me?"

Before anyone could make sense of the chaos, footsteps stomped their direction. Eyes darted to the doorway when Erika burst in, her eyes wild and chest heaving.

Vito glared at her, his anger flaring once more as he shoved past the Boss. "What the fuck—?"

Corrado saw nothing but the flash of silver as his mother spun around to face him. She raised her arms, both hands clutching a small handgun.

She aimed straight for his head.

Every muscle in Corrado's body seized up, locking him in place, as everyone else threw their hands up defensively. Men retreated, footsteps frantic, while a few ducked for cover.

Vito dove at Erika and struck her from the side the second she squeezed the trigger. The bang of the gunshot was loud, a small fiery explosion ripping from the end of the pistol as Vito threw her to the floor. The bullet zipped right past Corrado, crashing as it struck the mantle to his left. The vase shattered, exploding into dozens of fragments. Stinging tore through Corrado's cheek as a shard sliced his skin, but he didn't react.

He didn't even move.

The world was stricken by slow motion, the picture a haze, sounds diluted by a soft buzzing. Numbness coated Corrado like a bucket of ice water dumped over his head as he watched his mother struggle to break free, frivolously screaming. Vito pried the gun from her hands, shoving it across the room. It skidded along the floor, slamming into an adjacent wall, as she thrashed.

"You love him more than me!" she screamed, the words breaking through Corrado's fog. "You're supposed to love *me*!"

Vito yanked Erika off the floor, wrapping his arms around her, but she wouldn't be confined. Fists struck him hard as she escaped his grip, slapping him once across the face before storming away.

Corrado still just stood there.

20

There's no faster way to kill a celebration than by almost putting a bullet in the honoree. People fled the house, muttering goodbyes. In less than a minute the place became a ghost town, all the money still scattered along the table, forgotten as men made a hasty exit. Only a few enforcers remained, holding their post around the Boss until they were sure he was safe.

Vito tried to go after Erika, but Antonio shoved him back into the dining room. "You get that woman into rehab."

Vito blanched.

"You get her clean, and you get her sane," Antonio continued, "because if you don't, I'll kill her myself. You hear me?"

"Yes, sir."

"We came here because you said it would be fine. You broke your word, Vito. This isn't *fine*."

"Look, she's just—"

"Don't go sticking up for her now. We all saw what she did!"

"She wouldn't have really—"

"The *only* reason Corrado's alive right now is because you hit her when she squeezed the trigger!" Antonio clutched his hands into fists as he paced. "I knew something like this would happen. *Knew* it. I hoped it wouldn't; I wanted to have faith in you, but I guess I was wrong."

Vito's brow furrowed. "Huh?"

"If you can't control a woman, Vito, how can I trust you running a whole crew?"

Horror flashed in Vito's eyes, the sight of it drawing Corrado out of his fog. The Boss was the kind of man who held a grudge until it festered beyond reasoning. Being demoted meant you were dispensable, and that made you as good as dead.

Corrado inhaled sharply, the rush of dry air burning his chest, as he broke his stance. He suddenly became acutely aware of his stinging cheek, a slight ringing in his ears from the gunshot. Reaching up, he brushed his hand along his face, wincing at the small gash in his skin. Blood gathered along the wound, but nothing substantial. He'd survive. "No harm done."

Vito and Antonio both quieted when he spoke up.

"Your mother damn near killed you," Antonio said.

Corrado shrugged. Wasn't the first time.

Antonio groaned with irritation, glancing around the abandoned dining room at the leftover guests. It seemed to strike him then that his son was missing. "Vincent?"

No answer.

"Maybe he went outside," Vito suggested.

Corrado didn't contradict that. Vincent had slipped out when Vito headed to the kitchen to diffuse the situation, and Corrado had a sneaking suspicion where he'd find the boy now.

"He needs to go back to the hotel," Antonio said, gaze shifting to Corrado. "You mind finding him and taking him?"

"I'll need a car."

Antonio looked at Vito expectantly, and Vito's expression fell even more. He remained silent, never offering his Lincoln, so Antonio pulled out the keys to his DeVille. "Take mine. Vito and I have some more talking to do."

Corrado strode out of the room. He checked the hallway and kitchen, finding both empty, before begrudgingly taking the steps two at a time, heading for the dreaded second floor yet again.

This time he didn't stop.

He found another small staircase at the end of the hallway and headed up it, stopping only when he reached the dusty attic. The electricity didn't power the top of the house. The sweltering room was illuminated by the moonlight streaming through the old window, a missing pane of glass letting the stifling air cycle in and out.

Sitting right in front of the window, in a glowing patch of natural spotlight, was Maura, her legs tucked beneath her, her dress fanning out around her. In front of her, casting long shadows along the floor that nearly reached Corrado's immaculately shined shoes, stood Vincent, his fists shoved into his pockets.

Vincent stared down at her, his grievances soundlessly airing on his face, while Maura cried. She didn't look at the boy, almost as if she didn't see him, but her soft voice betrayed her oblivious appearance. "You know what I am."

"I don't care."

"You should."

"I don't."

Vincent was adamant, no uncertainty in his tone as he spoke those words: he didn't care. It surprised Corrado, hearing him sound so downright confident. Vincent's decisions were usually influenced by resentment, the rebellious streak of an insecure teenager, going left to prove a point whenever his father told him to go right.

A part of Corrado wondered if this were the same—did he seek out this girl, this little Irish slave, to spite his father? She was the complete opposite of everything Antonio would want for his son.

"Vincent," Corrado said, his level voice magnified in the vacant space, making the girl flinch.

Defensively, Vincent stepped in front of Maura. "What?"

"I'm supposed to take you back to the hotel."

Vincent stubbornly shook his head. "I'm not ready to go."

"Not your decision to make," Corrado said. "Antonio's orders."

Vincent's eyes narrowed, a flash of defiant anger stirring. "He can't make me go."

Corrado admired his tenacity—it rivaled Celia's, a DeMarco family trait. And much like his sister, he wouldn't win. Not against the head of the family. "Can't he?"

Vincent's expression softened at the question, subtle sadness washing away the rage. "Please don't make me leave."

"Not my decision either," Corrado said. "You know that."

"This is bullshit." Pleading hadn't helped. Back to rage. "I shouldn't have to leave if I don't want to."

"Why would you want to stay?" Corrado certainly didn't. "There's nothing here."

"Because I… I just do, okay? Is that so hard to understand?"

"Yes."

Groaning, the boy threw up his hands. "You people…"

"We people say it's time to go," Corrado stressed, getting irritated at having to stand there. "Don't make me drag you out of this house, because I will."

Vincent argued but cut off mid-word when Mara reached over and placed her hand on his leg. The simple touch, barely a graze against a pair of gray slacks, shocked Corrado into temporary awe.

"Go," Maura said. "You need to leave."

"What?""

"I don't want you here." Maura pulled her hand away from him. "So leave."

"But—"

"Please."

Maura's voice cracked when she squeezed out the word, her shoulders slumping as she folded into herself. Vincent stared down at her, but once again she refused to meet his gaze.

"I still don't care," Vincent ground out.

Maura didn't respond as she started crying again.

"Vincenzo," Corrado said, using the boy's real name, ignoring the fact that he grimaced at the sound of it. "Let's go before you make it worse than it already is."

Those words were the catalyst that finally forced Vincent to move. Grumbling to himself, he trudged past Corrado, shooting a longing look back at Maura before stomping down the stairs. Corrado gazed at the crying girl before turning his back to her and walking away.

Vincent waited for him in the foyer. Argumentative words seeped out from the dining room, Vito trying to defend himself while Antonio ripped into him. Corrado frowned, knowing he could do nothing to help his father, when there was a loud crash, the sound of something being thrown in the kitchen.

Vincent cringed at the noise.

"Go out to your father's car," Corrado said, gazing toward the doorway. "I'll be right there."

Vincent walked out, the screen door slamming behind him, as Corrado slipped into the kitchen. His mother grumbled to herself, a bottle of wine in one hand as she threw dishes into the empty sink with her other. She swayed as she took a step, drunkenly stumbling over her own feet. Instinctively, Corrado's hand shot out and caught her by her arm, keeping her upright. Erika snatched her arm away, nearly knocking herself over again.

"You're all worthless," she slurred. "There's a fucking mess, and that little bitch Maura is nowhere to be found. I don't even know why she's still here. She does nothing but eat my food and use my water and breathe my air. She's worse than even you. You never did anything but take up space, too."

He ignored the insult.

"I ought to get rid of her. Every slave I've had has been useless." Erika laughed bitterly. "Especially that first one… she deserved what happened to her."

Resentment brewed inside of Corrado as he glared at his mother. Smudged mascara lined her bloodshot eyes like day-old bruises, remnants of her red lipstick smeared around her mouth, the hue of fresh welts on a child's skin from a leather belt. Wrinkles marred her once pretty face, now covered with imperfections, her skin as wishy-washy as a corpse. Even from the distance Corrado smelled the sour scent of old alcohol seeping from her pores.

"What?" Erika spat, taking a sip of her wine. "Something you wanna say?"

There was something he wanted to say, all right.

Someday, you'll pay for everything you've done, and when that happens, I'll feel not an ounce of compassion. Because I can't. And it'll be your own fault, because you made me this way.

There was no threat to his thoughts. It was the simple truth as far as he was concerned. The sky was blue. The grass was green. And someday, Erika Moretti would pay for her sins.

"Goodbye, mother."

Turning away, he strode out of the house and climbed in the Boss's DeVille.

"And I thought *my* mom was bad," Vincent muttered.

Corrado didn't bother responding to that. Silence choked the car during the drive into the city limits. It wasn't until they'd reached The Flamingo and parked that Vincent forced more words from his lips. They came out strangled, like he'd tried his hardest to keep them inside, but they wouldn't be restrained. "What's going to happen to her?"

"My mother?"

"No. Maura."

Maura.

Corrado ran his hands down his face in frustration. "I don't know."

"You don't know?" Vincent asked doubtfully. "What do you mean you don't know?"

"I mean I don't know." What else could that possibly mean?

"But you're supposed to know," he argued. "I thought you knew everything."

Corrado glanced at him, expecting to find the boy sneering with bitter sarcasm, but sincerity shined from Vincent's eyes. "Look, kid—"

"Do *not* call me that," Vincent interjected. "I'm almost as old as you. I'll be a man soon."

"Being a man has nothing to do with age."

"Spare me the philosophy lesson," Vincent said. "I just want to know what's going to happen to Maura."

"You don't know the girl. Do you even care?"

"Yes."

There was that steadfast confidence.

"She'll die."

Vincent recoiled. "She'll *what*?"

"She'll die. We all will someday."

"Okay, *Socrates*. Thanks for nothing."

And there was the bitter sarcasm.

"I don't know what's going to happen to her," Corrado said again. "And I don't really care to know."

"But I *do*."

"You shouldn't."

Vincent groaned. "You sound just like her."

The conversation was going nowhere, and Corrado was getting a little exhausted with the meaningless back-and-forth. "Let me give you some advice that my father once gave me."

"Huh?"

"It's best you don't get attached."

Vincent glared at him. "That's terrible advice."

"It's worked for me."

Corrado stepped into the small lobby bar in The Flamingo and slipped onto an empty stool on the end. The bartender stopped in front of him. "What can I get you?"

He answered without even looking up. "Anything."

He'd drink piss warm moonshine right then to dull the memory of the night.

A minute later an orange and green aluminum can slid onto the bar in front of him. *Cactus Cooler.*

Brow furrowing, he glanced at the bartender. "Do I know you?"

"No, but I know you," he said. "Or, well, I know who you are. Management said you were coming and told us to stock that stuff, just in case you asked for it."

Corrado laughed to himself, picking up the can and studying it. "I haven't drank this in years."

"Oh. Well, if you'd prefer something else..."

"No, it'll do." Popping the top, he took a sip of the orange-pineapple soda and nodded at the bartender. "Thanks."

Clutching his drink, he strolled through the casino to the elevator, taking it to the top-floor. With the bulletproof windows and secret tunnels, the presidential suite was a mobster's dream... *literally.*

One had designed it.

Corrado unlocked the door and stepped inside, finding the bed empty. He made his way toward the dim bathroom, hearing the subtle sound of splashing water, and pushed open the door. Celia lay in the bathtub, lit candles surrounding her, a heap of bubbles covering her body. Leaning against the doorframe, he took a sip of his drink.

"Corrado Alphonse Moretti," she said playfully. "Are you drinking something *carbonated*?"

"Cactus Cooler."

"What the hell is that?"

He walked over and sat down on the edge of the tub as she sat up, sloshing water onto the floor. He handed her the can, and she sniffed it. "This isn't cactus juice, is it? Because it would be just like you to drink some healthy crap like that."

"Don't worry—it's right up your junk food alley."

She took a sip as she surveyed him in the dim lighting. "What happened to your face?"

"My mother happened."

"She hit you?"

"No," he said. "She shot at me."

She gasped, gaping at him, as he took the drink back.

"Needless to say," he continued, "I'm rescinding her invitation to the wedding."

Setting the can down, Corrado reached over and brushed some wayward hair from her face before cupping her chin, his thumb stroking her soft cheek. "You are far too beautiful to be marrying into my family, *Bellissima*."

Her expression softened. "Are you rescinding my invitation, too? Because if you try, I'll just crash the party."

"It wouldn't be a party without you," he said. "Just me in a suit, jacking off in a church like a chump."

She snorted. "Sounds like a good time to me."

Smiling, he leaned down to softly kiss her. He pulled back, but she grabbed his tie, locking him there. "You mentioned something earlier about a basement tunnel. How do you feel about making good on that?"

"So, about this Maura girl..."

Corrado closed his eyes, a long exaggerated blink of exasperation, before looking across the small table at his fiancée. Celia casually picked at a plate of bacon, a glass of fresh squeezed orange juice in her hand. "What about her?"

"What's going to happen to her?"

He frowned. "Have you been talking to your brother?"

"Huh? Why?"

"He asked me that same question."

"Did he?"

"Yes, and I'll tell you what I told him: I don't know."

"You don't?"

"No."

"Can you find out?"

He stared at her peculiarly. Why would he do that?

"Don't give me that look, Corrado," she said. "She's a fifteen year old girl."

"How do you know how old she is?"

"Vincent told me."

Sighing, Corrado closed his newspaper. She had talked to Vincent. "Did you lie to me?"

"No," she said. "I just avoided answering your question."

He wanted to be annoyed, but he was too impressed by her manipulation. Had she learned that from him?

"So?" she pressed. "Can you?"

"I *can*. Doesn't mean I will."

"Oh, you will," she said with certainty.

"How do you know?"

"Because I'm going to say *please*."

Tossing the newspaper aside, he stared at her, that irritation setting in. "I can afford to hire a maid. You don't need a slave."

She flinched, stopping eating. "How can you say that?"

"Say what?"

"What you just said." Anger laced her words. "She's a person.

A living, breathing, feeling *person.*"

"I know she is."

"Do you?"

"Of course."

He picked his newspaper back up, flipping to the place he'd left off minutes earlier. As soon as he started reading, Celia shoved her chair back and stood, snatching the top of the paper and shoving it down to look him in the eyes.

"Then act like it," she sneered.

Celia stormed off, slamming drawers as she changed into her one-piece bright blue bathing suit. She grabbed a towel and her sunglasses, not even acknowledging him again as she stormed out of the suite, slamming the door behind her as she went.

Frustrated, Corrado threw the paper aside, grabbing a muffin from the small basket in the center of the table before striding after her. He made his way to the lobby and out toward the pool, lingering at the side of the building as he watched her dive into the water.

"Corrado." The familiar voice of the Boss rang out behind him.

Corrado took in the sight of the husky man, bare-chested, wearing nothing but a pair of black swimming trunks. "Sir."

"You seen your father this morning?"

"Uh, no, sir."

"He's supposed to be around here," Antonio said. "You know, handling some things."

Antonio slapped him on the back before walking away, finding a spot to settle beside the pool near where his daughter swam.

Corrado slipped back inside the casino and gnawed on his muffin as he made his way through the lobby and to the office down the long hallway. He knocked on the door before stepping inside.

Vito sat behind the desk, surrounded by paperwork. Corrado sat down in the chair along the side—the same chair he'd taken up residence in day after day when coming to work with his father as a child.

"Your mother, uh… she's getting some help."

Corrado quietly ate his muffin.

"It's this outpatient thing," Vito said, "you know, at home."

Of course. It would take a miracle to get Erika Moretti to leave her house for *anything*.

"Doctor's gonna make house calls… so is the counselor."

"Counselor?"

"Yeah, like a drug counselor," he grumbled. "Not one of them crazy doctors. Your mother… the last thing she needs is some doctor fucking with that head of hers."

"You think it'll work?" Corrado asked.

"Of course, kid. She ain't *that* bad."

Corrado's opinion differed.

"She'll be fine," Vito said. Who was he trying to convince—Corrado or himself? "She's more pissed she has to do all the housework. That woman doesn't have a domestic bone in her body."

"She has help."

"Yeah, uh, not anymore," Vito said. "Can't have that girl in the house with those people coming by. Gotta be careful."

"What's going to happen to her?" Corrado mentally berated himself when he asked the question. Damn the DeMarco kids, putting those thoughts in his head. "You going to send her back wherever you got her?"

Seemed like a simple solution to him.

"Not possible," Vito said. "I lost twenty thousand getting that girl. You don't know anyone who could use some help, do you?"

"No."

"Celia couldn't use an extra set of hands? Maura's a good worker. Nice girl. Never caused any problems."

"You don't have to convince *me* of that. I was around her more than you were."

"Yeah, right, right… you're right. So? You want her? Maura?"

No. He stared at his father, that word echoing in his head, but Celia's concerns overshadowed it. "I'm sure Celia wouldn't be opposed to it."

"Great." Vito relaxed as if a weight had been lifted from his shoulders. "Call it a wedding present from your mother and me."

The pool area was packed when Corrado ventured back outside, scantily clad bodies everywhere. Corrado scanned the crowd, finding Antonio and Gia lounging in the bright sunshine, but no Celia to be found.

Heading back upstairs to the suite, he unlocked the door, his footsteps faltering. The sound of frantic crying reached his ears. Coldness swept through Corrado, every cell in his body on edge.

Celia sat at the foot of the bed, her head dropped low, her hands covering her face as her body shuddered.

"Celia?" he called, as he shut the door. "Sweetheart?"

She looked up at the sound of his voice, tears streaming from her blurry eyes, streaking her flushed cheeks. The crying stopped for a fraction of a second, just long enough for the universe to feel like someone had hit pause. The world had ceased to turn in that moment. Nothing existed—nothing mattered—except for Celia. He stared into her distraught eyes, vowing he'd destroy whatever made her feel that way. He'd kill whoever hurt the beautiful creature in front of him, whoever had been so callous and cruel as to make something so precious feel such pain.

He'd tear the world apart until he got vengeance.

But that moment faded when she covered her mouth to stifle a sob. Shutting the door, Corrado hurried over to her and grasped her hands, pulling them away from her face. Crouching down in front of her, he stared into her eyes. "Tell me what's wrong."

"We fought." The words came out as a strangled cry.

Fought? "You got in a fight?"

"We did."

"Who did?"

"Us," she gasped. "Me and you."

"What? When?"

"Earlier." She hiccupped as tears spilled down her cheeks. "I was so mad… and when I came back, you were gone. I didn't know where you went! I looked, and I couldn't find you, so I came back up here and you still weren't here, so I thought…"

He gaped at her, dumbfounded as she stammered on and on. "Celia, calm down."

"We're not even married yet," she cried. "We're already fighting!"

"We didn't fight," he insisted. "We *aren't* fighting."

Her crying slowed to a whimper as she caught her breath.

"My parents fight," he continued. "We just had a disagreement."

Celia sniffled, gazing at him. "What's the difference?"

"We're not always going to agree, Celia. It's impossible. You're a spitfire. You're going to have your opinions, and I can guarantee I'm not always going to approve of them."

"You should," she said, her voice cracking. "I'm always right."

"Like I said—we won't always agree." He cracked a smile. "But never, *never* will I fight with you. I'll never scream at you, I'll never throw things at you, and I'll *never* hit you. And if someone else ever does? I'll—"

"I get it," she said before he could elaborate. "I'm sorry."

"Don't apologize to me," he said, brushing her tears from her face. "Hearing you groveling will be worse than seeing you crying."

She rolled her eyes as she pulled herself together. "Where were you, anyway?"

"Talking to my father," he said, standing back up. "He's getting rid of Maura."

"What? What do you mean getting *rid* of her?"

"They can't keep her anymore. You asked what will happen to her, so I suppose that's up to you now, since she's yours."

"Mine? You *bought* her?"

"Of course not. He gave her to me as a wedding gift."

"*Gave* her to you?" Celia was on her feet. "She's a person!"

Why was she yelling again? "I thought you'd be happy about this, Celia."

"Happy? You thought enslaving a fifteen-year-old girl under my roof would make me happy? Clearly you don't know me."

For the second time that day, before the clock even struck noon, Celia stormed out and slammed the door behind her.

21

Saint Mary's Catholic Church was filled to the brim. Even Easter Sunday didn't pack so many bodies into those long wooden pews, an overflow loitering along the sides and in the back, standing stately, awaiting the service.

The Boss's daughter was getting married today.

No expense had been spared. Antonio insisted they marry at Saint Mary's, with Father Alberto heading the ceremony, but the rest was left up to Celia. Whatever she wanted, she'd get, Antonio swore, and Corrado had no intention of arguing. It was her day, after all… he was just honored she would share it with *him*.

So much to Antonio's displeasure, but more to Corrado's amusement, he stood at the front of the church wearing a simple royal blue suit. Nothing fancy. It had come straight out of his closet, hand picked by Celia.

No matter how much Antonio expressed his frustrations ('It's a Catholic wedding for God's sake—he's got to wear a tux!), Celia merely batted her eyelashes and reminded him, "you said whatever I want."

His get-up clashed with his groomsmen in their clean, classic tuxedos, even conflicted with the bridesmaids in their darker shade of navy blue, but no one seemed to notice. Attention focused on the father of the bride as he marched down the aisle with his daughter on his arm.

Celia wore a dress identical to the one her mother had been married in: white and flowing with long sleeve lace. As hard as she'd tried, her curvy figure couldn't fit into Gia's slim dress, so they'd improvised with a replica. Classic and elegant, a tiara in her hair, she looked like royalty.

Pricipessa della Mafia.

They stopped at the front as the music cut off. Antonio passed her off to Corrado with a simple nod that spoke volumes.

I'm giving you my pride and joy. You hurt her, I'll kill you.

Before Antonio made it to his seat—before the priest even spoke—Celia handed her bouquet off to a bridesmaid so she could fix Corrado's crooked tie for him.

The service wasn't elaborate, straight to the point with the usual Catholic vows recited by the priest. Up until they said, "I do," he still waited for her to change her mind about him.

But she didn't waver.

Father Alberto blessed their marriage, declaring them husband and wife without so much as a hiccup.

They sealed it with a simple peck on the lips that most would have missed in the time it took to blink.

Taking Celia's arm, he led her down the aisle, straight through the middle of the celebratory crowd. She beamed, brighter than the afternoon Chicago sunshine that blasted them when the doors opened and they stepped outside. A feeling of pure peace settled over Corrado that lasted about as long as it took him to glance toward the busy street.

Double-parked, blocking the limo with the streamers tied to it, 'Just Married' written on the back, was a beat-up brown Ford, two marked Chicago squad cars in the front and back of it. At the end of the steps, lingering on the sidewalk in front of them, stood a familiar man.

Detective Walker.

Not today. Corrado paused. *Whatever you do, don't say my name.*

His silent demand went unanswered.

"Corrado Moretti, you're under arrest... *again.*"

Obstruction of justice.

They had disrupted his wedding for a petty *misdemeanor.*

"You supplied false information during your previous arrest," the detective said during the drive to the jail. "You denied the car was yours."

Not true. He had simply evaded answering.

Furious, Corrado said nothing as they booked him. Threats were on the tip of his tongue—*promises* of vengeance he yearned to verbalize—but he wouldn't lower himself. He wouldn't give them the satisfaction.

All it would take was a few bitter words for them to slap him with another assault charge. It was what they wanted. These charges wouldn't stick. They were trying to instigate a reaction.

In less than two hours, Corrado was released on bail. He strode through the police station, finding Celia standing in the middle of the front lobby, hands on her hips. A single eyebrow arched at him. "Are we going to make a habit out of this?"

"Out of what?"

"You getting arrested."

"Probably."

A lesser woman would have been furious. Corrado wouldn't have blamed her—it was shameful. Locked up on their wedding day. But Celia, still clad in her wedding dress, burst into laughter at the absurdity of it.

A DeMarco party didn't stop for anyone—not even an absent bride and groom.

The reception was in full swing when Celia and Corrado made it to the mansion at the end of Felton Drive. Jazz music blared from the live band as guests danced the evening away in the elaborately decorated backyard. Dinner had been served, the cake even cut, people liquored up and borderline belligerent. Sacrilege for a formal Italian-American celebration, especially one for *La Cosa Nostra* royalty, but decorum had gone out the window when

Corrado had been put in handcuffs.

Hours later, the Boss remained hysterical.

"The nerve!" he spat, sitting behind his desk in his office, the shut door muffling the music to a dull murmur. Outside the music rang true with elation, but in here, locked away, it sounded like the strangled cry of trepidation. "How dare they interrupt today of all days! They show up at the church—*my* church, *my* sanctuary—and drag my son-in-law away in front of everyone!"

Corrado sat in the leather chair, rubbing his wrists, sore from the handcuffs. Salvatore and Sonny stood around the room, along with Vito. The men took in the Boss's every word—venom Corrado knew he'd been spewing since the incident.

"They did it to spite me," he declared. "To spite *us*! This blatant disrespect cannot be tolerated!"

"Whaddaya gonna do?" Sonny shrugged. "It's Chicago's Finest. They do these things."

"No, they don't," Antonio said. "Not anymore. Not on my watch. I've put up with their harassment for years. I took it all in stride. It's a part of the business. But this? *This* crosses the line. This was personal, and I'm not putting up with any more."

"What do you want to do?" Sal asked.

"That detective," Antonio said. "That, uh... whatshisname."

Corrado cleared his throat. "Walker."

"Detective Walker," Antonio said. "He needs taught a lesson."

Corrado and Celia didn't hang around their own reception. As soon as the meeting with the Boss ended, Corrado grabbed Celia's hand and pulled her away from the guests, taking her straight to his house.

Or *their* house, as it was now.

They snubbed tradition occasionally, giving in to temptation early in their relationship, but certain customs were inescapable. Up until their wedding day, Celia remained under her father's roof, sleeping in her bed every night. But now it was just the two of them, together, all alone. No need to worry about curfew. No need to worry about interruptions.

For tonight, anyway.

"*Bellissima*," he mumbled, rubbing her lace covered arms as he leaned toward her, standing in the living room. "How about we get you out of that dress?"

He kissed her passionately, their first real kiss of the day. Reaching behind her, he went for the zipper on her dress but she stopped him, breaking the kiss.

"Not yet," she said. "I have something for you first."

She darted into the hallway before returning with a present. Corrado's brow furrowed when she held it out to him. Flat as cardboard, perfectly square shape, covered in striped paper with a big blue bow on top.

"Where was this?" he asked.

"In the hallway closet."

"You hid a present in my house?"

"Yes."

How hadn't he noticed it?

It was strange, he supposed as he took it, but outside of the obligatory greeting cards from his father's associates over the years, nobody had given him a present before.

"But I didn't get you anything."

She rolled her eyes dramatically, shoving his hands that clutched the present. "Just open it."

His finger slid beneath the flap, ripping the tape on the end of the wrapping paper. He tore it off, discarding the paper on the couch. The orange cover on the LP vinyl was tattered around the edges, *Come Back to Sorrento* written along the top beneath the black bold Frank Sinatra.

"Sinatra," he said. "I haven't heard this one."

"Look at the fourth song."

Corrado scanned the track list along the side, stopping on track four. *Luna Rossa.*

Wordlessly, he walked over to his stereo as he pulled the record from the sleeve. Placing it on the turntable, he dropped the needle at the start of the fourth track before facing her.

He held out his hand. English, not Italian, but just as beautiful. "You never got your first dance, Miss DeMarco."

"You don't dance, remember?"

"I've decided to make an exception for you."

She took his hand, her cheeks flushing as he pulled her into his arms. "You can't call me that anymore. It's Mrs. Moretti now."

"Mrs. Moretti," he repeated.

"Mrs. *Corrado* Moretti."

"As much as I love the sound of that, how about we just call you Celia," he said, grinning as he pressed a soft kiss against her lips. "You're not a woman to be *kept*. You have your own identity."

"Well, well," she said playfully. "How very twentieth century of you, Mr. Moretti."

"Corrado," he corrected her, spinning her gently before pulling her back to him. He held her tightly against his chest, pressing his cheek against the top of her head as he closed his eyes, letting the music wash over him. The song was short, less than three minutes. Corrado stopped moving, his body going still as he let out a deep exhale of contentment, a pressure releasing from his chest.

"I found the one," he whispered into her hair.

"Favorite Sinatra song?"

"Yes," he replied. "But I meant *you*."

Corrado grabbed her, lifting her into his arms, and ignored her feeble protests as he carried her upstairs. He set her back on her feet right inside the bedroom, swinging her around so her back was to him. Slowly, methodically, he tugged the zipper down on her dress, his knuckles grazing her spine and pausing at the small of her back. He placed his hands on her shoulders and pushed the material down her arms as he caressed her skin.

Her dress dropped to her ankles.

He unfastened her bra, removing every last stitch of clothing from her body. Celia stood in place, allowing him to undress her, goosebumps coating her flesh wherever his hands touched.

Backing up, Corrado surveyed her. A blush tinged her bronzed skin as she wrapped her arms around herself. Corrado grasped her wrists, pulling her hands away when she tried to shield herself. He stared at her, stunned to see the uncertainty in her eyes.

"You're not nervous this time, are you?" he asked, half-teasingly, half honestly wanting to know. She'd been so confident, unwavering before.

"It's the way you're looking at me."

"How am I looking at you?"

"Like you look at the Taj Mahal. Or the Sistine Chapel. You're staring at me like you stare at the Mona Lisa."

"I've never seen those things."

"It's like you've never seen something so beautiful before."

"I haven't."

She shivered at his words. "*That's* the way you're looking at me."

"And that bothers you?"

"I can't live up to it," she said. "You can't put me on a pedestal. I'll only fall."

"You'll never fall," he said. "Not if I'm there to catch you."

A small smile infused her lips, despite the self-doubt still lurking in her eyes. "How do you do that?"

"Do what?"

"Say things so matter-of-fact and make people believe them?"

"It's not hard when what I say is true."

"There it is again."

He returned her smile, raising an eyebrow. "Do you believe me when I tell you there's nothing more beautiful in the world than you?"

She hesitated. "You make me want to."

"It's true," he continued. "You're the woman the Italians write their poetry about."

Her blush deepened. "You're exaggerating."

"I'm not," he said. "My life is ugly, Celia. *I'm* ugly."

"You're not," she insisted.

He ignored her. "I'll never deserve you, I'll never be good for you, but I'll spend the rest of my life trying to be *enough.* And the simple fact that you're letting me proves your beauty. Because your beauty, Celia, is more than skin deep." He let go of her wrists, the palm of his hand cupping her flushed cheek, his thumb brushing her lips, before running down her neck and across her chest. She sighed, her eyelids fluttering at his touch. "As beautiful as you are on the outside—and you are—it's what's beneath it that's the most beautiful of all."

"What's so special about me?"

He stared at her again. How could she even ask that?

"I've shown you parts of the monster inside of me."

"You're *not* a monster."

"I've shown you it," he said as if she hadn't interrupted, "and it doesn't terrify you. People look at me, and I can tell they're unnerved to be even breathing the same air as me, as if whatever's inside of me is contagious. But not you. You're not afraid to be with me. You're not afraid to let me inside of you. You're not afraid of catching my *disease*."

She grimaced at the way he spoke. "There's nothing wrong with you, Corrado."

She meant it. He could tell by the sincerity in her voice.

He hoped with everything that she always felt that way.

"Your light is the only thing in this world not tainted by my darkness," he said, his eyes leaving hers to rake down her flushed body. "The only effect I seem to have on it is to turn it a slight shade of pink."

"It's because you're still looking at me that way."

He laughed lightly, his focus returning to her face, noting her cheeks growing even redder. "*Luna Rossa*," he whispered. "My very own blushing moon."

He kissed her briefly before his lips left hers, trailing kisses along her jaw and to her neck. She tilted her head to the side as he made his way to her collarbones, before going lower.

Right there, in the middle of the bedroom, Corrado dropped to his knees. Celia stared down at him, breathing heavily, confusion in her eyes that faded at his wordless declaration of love. Her eyes closed, a shuddering breath escaping her parted lips, her hands gripping his hair as his lips found her body again, tasting her flesh.

She whimpered. Her knees trembled.

"I believe you," she said.

22

Very little made Corrado uncomfortable.

Although he had long ago learned to detach, he wasn't immune to feelings. He loved his wife—God, did he love her—and he loathed his mother more than anything. His emotions spanned the entire spectrum, but discomfort was one of those rare sensations that crept up on him.

And no moment, no situation, made him quite as uncomfortable as standing in the foyer of his house, clutching the door wide-open, with a young Maura on his front step. Vito stood beside her, frantically puffing on a thick cigar as his gaze darted around the neighborhood.

"Well, here you go, kid." Vito took a step back. "She's all yours."

"She's Celia's," Corrado clarified, but his father was already halfway to the idling Lincoln.

Corrado wasn't sure what to say. He stared at the girl, expecting her to do whatever she was supposed to do—whatever she *usually* did—but she just stood there, eyes downcast as if the grungy stone step were the most interesting thing she'd ever seen.

Maybe it was, Corrado thought. Maybe she wanted to clean it.

"Come inside," he said finally, growing impatient.

Maura stepped past him, into the house, and stopped in the foyer. She stared at the floor there, too, still not reacting. The wooden floor wasn't spotless, but it had been swept recently. What was so interesting about *it*?

Frowning, Corrado glanced outside as the Lincoln pulled away.

Something struck him…

He addressed Maura, who *still* wasn't moving. "Where are your belongings?"

Her low voice barely constituted a whisper. "What belongings?"

"Your things," he clarified. "Your clothes and… things."

"I have none."

His father had dropped her off with nothing except the clothes on her back.

Oh well.

He had come to Chicago with the same. He supposed she didn't need much. He surveyed her, assessing. Some clothes, certainly, and a new pair of shoes, as her sandals were at least half a size too small. She could have used a hairbrush, too. And a razor. And some soap. And probably some other sort of feminine things eventually.

He grimaced at the thought and shut the front door, harder than he intended. Maura recoiled at the slam, taking a few steps away from him, pressing her back flat against the wall.

At least she's doing *something now.*

"So, uh…" Where was Celia? She should have been home from the grocery store by now. "…I'll be in my office, but don't bother me unless it's an emergency."

He walked away, heading straight to the first floor office, and sat down behind his desk. He had no work to do—not that he even did much work in this room, anyway. His work was out in the streets, and there was no paperwork to be filed about it. He was still merely a street soldier, despite his coveted position on the Boss's personal payroll.

That would change soon, though. It was only a matter of time.

He mulled over that, scanning through the day's newspaper, when he heard movement around the house. Doors opened, drawers slammed, whispered voices filtering through the cracks. He continued to read until the office door flung open without so much as even a knock. On alert, Corrado's eyes darted over top of the paper, but the person who stood in front of him was hardly a threat.

Hardly a threat, but yet something in Celia's eyes made him tense. "What's wrong?"

"What's wrong?" she ground out, glancing out of the office before focusing back on him. "She was standing in the foyer with her head down."

"Still?"

"How long has she been there?"

He shrugged, glancing at the clock. "Thirty minutes, maybe."

"Just standing there."

"Yes."

"Alone."

"Yes."

"In the foyer."

"Yes."

She shook her head, throwing up her hands in disbelief. "Completely useless."

"She seems that way."

"I wasn't talking about *her*," Celia said, jabbing her finger in the air at him.

Dumbfounded, Corrado stared at the empty office doorway when his wife stomped back out. He folded up the newspaper and tossed it aside before following. Celia's voice sounded out from the kitchen, much more passive than it had just been. Corrado strolled that way, leaning against the doorframe. A dozen or so paper bags were scattered around, things lying on the counters as Celia put the groceries away. Maura helped, digging through the bags as Celia told her where everything went.

"Did you need help?" Corrado asked.

Maura flinched at the sound of his voice, green eyes meeting his for only a second. Celia, on the other hand, didn't even look his way. "I have help."

"Wonderful."

"*Wonderful*," she sneered, mimicking him. "Unbelievable, I swear."

Corrado ran his hands down his face in frustration. "I don't understand."

"I know you don't," Celia said, "and that's the problem."

He watched as his wife continued to put away the groceries, Maura working right along beside her. He wasn't sure what else to say, so he said nothing.

The phone rang after a minute, drawing Corrado into the living room. He picked up the receiver. "Moretti speaking."

"Corrado!" Antonio's voice greeted him. "You hungry?"

"No."

His curt response made Antonio laugh heartily. "Ever the honest one. How about you get hungry and meet me at Rita's? Thirty minutes."

The line went dead.

Hanging up, he headed upstairs and put on a tie, grabbing his jacket and revolver before heading back down. He paused at the kitchen again. "I'm leaving."

The anger melted away when Celia saw him dressed and ready to go. "Be careful."

He merely nodded. Careful was the name of the game.

It took a little over thirty minutes to make it to Evanston with traffic. Antonio was already seated at a table beside a young Sicilian guy named Amando Donati. The guys called him Manny, a sort of play off his name that doubled as a dig at his private life. Manny, a quiet masculine guy who always wore a short beard, had married an aging stripper, despite their ten year age difference. Manny took her in and supported her and her four kids, no questions asked. The guys jested him about it, calling him a nanny, but Manny took it in stride.

Corrado respected that—he didn't care about anyone's personal life as long as they kept it at home.

Manny worked as Antonio's chauffeur, a bodyguard whenever Antonio felt the need to travel with one. His presence told Corrado this was business, not pleasure.

Corrado slid into a chair across from the Boss, grateful not to be chastised for his tardiness, and ordered his usual: spaghetti with meat sauce. Antonio made small talk, joking all through the meal, the smell of the food not enough to spur Corrado's appetite to life. After they finished, Antonio cleared his throat and turned to Manny. "Amando, you mind giving me a minute with my son-in-law?"

"Of course not, Boss." Manny stood and walked out.

As soon as he was gone, the air around the table shifted, the relaxed atmosphere gripped by tension. Corrado eyed the Boss curiously, but Antonio carried on as if he couldn't sense the change. "How are things at home?"

A personal question. He hated these. "I have no complaints."

Antonio smiled, a strained sort of smile that carried no warmth. "Vito said he dropped your present off."

"Yes."

"How's that working out?"

"Again, no complaints."

"You never have any complaints," Antonio said, his expression more genuine now. "I'm just a little concerned, naturally. You already have heat on you from that detective. You don't need anymore trouble."

"I'll make sure she doesn't cause any."

"Good, good."

"Is that what this was about?" Corrado asked, wondering if he'd be called out of his house to talk about the girl.

"Of course not." Antonio reached into his coat pocket. He pulled out a small photograph and slipped it across the table to Corrado. It was a picture of a family, a man and his wife with their son. The older couple was strangers to Corrado, but the boy… he recognized him.

John Tarullo.

"You know them?" Antonio asked.

Corrado stared at the boy's face, an image flashing in his mind, those familiar eyes watching him from the door of Dolce Vita's the night he'd killed Luca. "I recognize the boy."

"Little Johnny," Antonio said. "Good kid, never a problem."

A weight lifted from Corrado's chest at the kindness in Antonio's voice. At least he wouldn't have to kill his wife's friend.

"His father, on the other hand…" Antonio let out a dry laugh that resulted in a cough. "He's got to go."

Corrado slipped the photo into his pocket with a subtle nod.

"Knew I could count on you," Antonio said, standing to leave.

He only made it a few steps before leaning down, close to Corrado, and added, "There will be another ten grand for this one if you make it hurt."

Make it hurt. He'd never requested that before. "Yes, sir."

Antonio slapped him on the back and left.

Corrado pulled out his wallet and tossed some cash on the table to cover the bill before walking out.

It was dark when Corrado left the restaurant. He strode down the block, bypassing his car, to the nearest phone booth. Stepping inside, he closed the door and grabbed the phone book, searching through it for the name Tarullo. He found half a dozen in the area and scanned the listings. Antonio hadn't told him the man's name.

He grabbed the picture from his pocket, flipping it over, but only found 'Tarullo' scribbled on the back. He shoved it away, returning to the phone book, and started at the top of the list.

Feeding coin after coin into the payphone, he dialed the numbers one by one, putting on his friendliest voice. "Is Johnny there?" he asked whenever someone answered. Again and again he heard he had the wrong number, no Johnny lived there. Maybe the man was smart enough to keep his number unlisted.

He reached the final one, simply listed as Tarullo, V. Corrado dialed the number, leaning against the booth as it rang.

A woman's voice answered, soft and polite. "Tarullo residence."

"Is Johnny there?" he asked.

"He's working tonight," she replied.

Ding, ding, ding.

"Working, huh? You know when he gets off?"

"I'm picking him up at ten o'clock."

Bingo. "Great."

"Can I take your name? I'll tell Johnny you called."

"No, it's all right. I'll get up with him later."

Corrado hung up and stared at the phonebook, noting the address. *19934 Barton Ave.*

Twenty-two minutes.

Corrado timed the distance between Dolce Vita's and the residence on Barton Avenue. Eleven minutes each direction. He would have less than a half hour to get in, get it done, and get back out again.

Plausible under normal circumstances. He had killed men in under a minute, dead in the blink of an eye from a single shot to the back of the head. But Antonio's words complicated matters.

Make it hurt.

The Boss wouldn't begrudge him if he stuck with a clean shot, quick and painless, but Corrado wasn't one to balk at a challenge.

A quarter after nine that night, Corrado parked his Mercedes down the block on Barton Avenue, just close enough to give him a clear view of the house. He sat in utter silence in the darkness, watching, and waiting, and watching some more.

At a quart till ten, a car in the driveway came to life and pulled away from the house. Corrado waited until it passed him before getting out, his glove-clad hands stuffed in his pockets so not to raise suspicion. The only hiccup in his plan would be if the man weren't home tonight, but those concerns were appeased when Corrado approached the house. The massive window to the living room was wide open, the blinds up, the curtains pulled aside. The man from the photograph sat on a recliner, snacking on a bowl of popcorn as he watched a movie.

So make it hurt... but don't let him scream.

And be invisible, so I'm not seen.

Corrado slipped around to the back door, finding it unlocked. He breathed deeply with relief as he stepped right inside the kitchen. He closed the door behind him and glanced around, still adjusting to the darkness. Stepping over to the counter, he pulled a chef's knife from the wooden block, gripping the handle, getting a feel for it. He had no time to waste.

Corrado slipped out of the kitchen, giving him a direct view of the living room. He glared at the back of the man's head, a mere few feet away, undetected. The itch to pull out his gun and put a bullet in his skull nagged at Corrado, but he swallowed it back.

The Boss would get what the Boss wanted.

Closing his eyes, he conjured up an image of the first death he'd ever witnessed. The brutality and hatred that surrounded him that day, the sheer horror he'd felt, and the heartbreak he'd been left with. He channeled it, letting it consume him, until the tips of his fingers tingled.

Opening his eyes again, he pounced, knife in hand.

The man caught a glimpse of Corrado in the reflection of the television and sat up straight, startled, but he wasn't fast enough to stop what was happening. Before he could speak—before he could *scream*—Corrado roughly grabbed a hold of the guys head, yanking it back toward the chair with his left hand, while he thrust the knife in the center of his throat with his right. The man flailed, gurgling, blood gushing from the wound as Corrado held it there, jamming the knife in deeper until he suffocated, choking on his own blood. The thick red ran down his chest, soaking his white undershirt. The bowl flew from his lap, hitting the floor, the pieces of popcorn coating the floor splattered with red.

In less than a minute, he stopped moving, his eyes glossing over as the flow of blood eased. His heart had quit. Corrado let go, leaving the knife wedged in his neck.

Quick, sure, but it had hurt.

Corrado's eyes shifted to the television at an equally grotesque scene. *The Exorcist.* He had to force himself to look back away.

As quickly as Corrado broke into the house, he slipped right back out. He took off his jacket and gloves, both soiled, and rolled them into a ball as he walked to his car under the cloak of darkness. He tossed them in a garbage bag in the trunk and tied it up before getting in the driver seat.

Starting the car up, he glanced at the time.

Five minutes to spare.

Without an ounce of hesitation, he drove away from Barton Avenue, heading back toward his neighborhood. He found a small store open that late at night and parked, avoiding the clerk as he headed into the little bathroom. Corrado scrubbed his hands before splashing water on his face.

The clerk eyed him peculiarly when he stepped back out. Corrado grabbed a box of raisins and a bottle of orange juice before approaching the counter. He pulled out some cash to pay but hesitated, spotting a display of fresh cut roses over by the door.

"How much for the flowers?"

"Three bucks."

"Give me some of those, too."

Corrado paid and picked up his things, grabbing some flowers on his way out the door.

Red, not pink.

Celia didn't like pink.

He made it home around eleven o'clock and walked inside, clutching the flowers, drink nestled in the crook of his arm as he popped raisins in his mouth, his appetite finally rearing its ugly head.

The house was dark, the quiet television in the living room emitting a soft glow. He walked that way, finding his wife sprawled out on the couch in a black nightgown.

Setting his drink on the coffee table, he sat down on the edge of the couch in front of her. His hand grazed her cheek, brushing her hair from her face. Her eyes opened. "Hey, you."

"Hey."

He held out the flowers, her expression brightening at the sight of them. "They're beautiful, Corrado. What are they for?"

"For being the light of my life."

She got up, darting from the living room, and returned with the flowers in a clear vase. She set them on the table as she sat back down. Corrado relaxed back on the couch and kicked off his shoes, munching on the raisins. "Want some?" he asked, offering the box to her.

She wrinkled her nose. "They're not smothered in chocolate."

"Why would they be?"

"To make them edible."

He laughed, shrugging, and finished off the box. As soon as he tossed his trash on the table, Celia snuggled against him. "What did you do tonight?"

"Went to dinner with your father."

"Really?"

He nodded. "What did you do?"

"Just hung out around here with Maura until she got tired."

"Where's she sleeping?"

She hesitated. "Our bed."

Corrado's eyes narrowed. "You're telling me the girl is asleep in *my* bed?"

"Our bed," she said again. "Where else was she going to sleep?"

"I don't know. I'm more concerned with where *I'm* going to sleep tonight."

"Well, I have no problem sleeping on the couch. And frankly, I didn't even know if you were coming home, so..."

Point taken.

He pulled her in front of him as he stretched out, snuggling against her on the couch. He draped his arm around her, hand stroking her thigh and hip before slipping beneath the hem of her nightgown. It worked its way higher, caressing her soft stomach, as his lips found her neck.

She hummed. "That feels so good."

Those words were all the encouragement he needed. He slid her underwear down, discarding it on the floor, before unzipping his pants. He throbbed in his palm as he stroked himself, hitching her leg around him. Slowly, he slid into her from behind, groaning as he filled her.

Corrado stroked her clit, rubbing the sensitive flesh, bringing her to orgasm quickly as he thrust into her. As soon as her pleasure subsided, she dropped her leg and moved away. Corrado started to protest, feeling the loss the moment he slipped out of her, but she turned around and silenced him with a kiss.

Shifting onto his back on the couch, Celia climbed on top of him. She sunk down on his lap, taking him deeply inside of her.

Shifting her hips, she rode him as his hands roamed her body over her nightgown, feeling her breasts, pinching her nipples through the flimsy fabric.

Celia grabbed his hands, pulling them away from her. She pressed them against the arm of the couch, holding them there. Corrado blinked a few times, glancing above him at their hands as she pinned him down.

He stared into her eyes, drinking in her serious expression. Anyone else and he would've killed them. Anyone else would be dead. But for her—and her alone—he offered a bit of control. He closed his eyes, letting her restrain him, letting her rock against him until he came inside of her.

23

The loud shriek echoed through the house, startling Corrado awake. He sat straight up on the couch, disoriented, as he heard frantic muttering coming from outside the living room.

"Oh no, oh God, this can't be. No… no… no… it can't be!"

"Celia," he called out, concerned as he climbed to his feet.

Celia bounded into the living room, clutching the morning newspaper. Her eyes were glassy with tears. He loathed the sight of them, vengeful at the thought of something hurting her. He'd kill whoever caused it.

"Tell me what's wrong."

She frantically held the paper up. As soon as he read the front-page headline, he knew what it was about.

Chicago Man Brutally Murdered in His Home

"Someone killed him," she cried. "They killed Daddy's best friend!"

Corrado had prepared for a lot of things. He wouldn't have even been surprised had she accused him of the crime. But those words astonished him. "Antonio's *best friend*?"

She nodded. "Daddy must be devastated! And Johnny... Oh God, Johnny! Remember Johnny from the pizzeria? This is his dad!"

Corrado stared at her as she shook the paper in his face, trying to process that information. He took the newspaper from her and stared down at it. "I thought Sal was your father's best friend. Or maybe Sonny..."

"They work with him," she said. "Virgil was different."

Virgil. So that was what the 'V' stood for.

"How was he different?"

"Daddy trusts Sal and Sonny. Daddy respects them. But Virgil? Daddy *loves* him. They're like brothers."

Love. Peculiar thing, the way Antonio DeMarco showed his love.

"They all grew up together," Celia continued. "Daddy, Sonny, Sal, Virgil. They went to the same schools, did everything together. Virgil decided to go his own way when the rest of them went into the business, but they stayed friends. Daddy's even godfather to his Johnny! Oh God, and now Virgil's dead…"

Celia grabbed the phone, still rambling, but Corrado knew the words weren't for him. Figuring she was calling her parents, he walked out to give her some privacy, heading upstairs to the bedroom to change. Yesterday's suit still clung to his body, soiled from sweat and sex, heavy with memories of sin and bloodshed.

He skimmed through the article as he walked. Virgil Tarullo, found dead in his home shortly before eleven o'clock by his wife and son. No sign of forced entry. No suspects. No one saw anything. Virgil was a picture-perfect family man who had no enemies.

He had a best friend instead.

He stepped in his bedroom, shutting the door, when a sharp intake of air caught his attention. Looking up, his eyes met Maura across the room, a horrified expression on her face. He'd shut them in together.

He tossed the paper down on the dresser and reopened the door. "I forgot you were here."

"I, uh… sorry."

He held his hand up to stop her apologies. His bed was stripped bare to the mattress, his sheets and blankets and pillows in a pile on the floor. "Did you do something to my bed?"

"I slept in it."

"And?"

"And I thought… well… I didn't think you'd want to use these sheets after…"

After she slept on them. She didn't finish, but he knew where that was going. "The washing machine is downstairs beside my office."

"Yes, sir."

She gathered it all up and lugged it from the room. He waited until she was gone before shutting the door again. After stripping out of his clothes, he headed into the bathroom to shower.

He stood under the hot spray, steam fogging the mirrors as the scalding water rained down upon him. His skin tinged pink as pins and needles crept across his back, the tingling burn seeping below the surface. He stood there, silent, stoic, letting the water wash away his sins.

A cool blast of air rushed through, chills sweeping over him. Celia climbed in the shower with him, a sharp scream piercing the air as she dodged the water. "Jesus, Corrado, that burns!"

Reaching over, he turned the knobs to cool the water down. Once it had chilled she stepped in front of him, into the spray. He wrapped his arms around her, letting the coldness soothe the burning of his flesh.

"I want to go see Daddy," Celia said. "Will you come with me?"

"Anything you want."

"I want Virgil back," she whispered. "I want him not to be *dead*."

"I can't give you that."

"I know," she said. "I know you would if you could, though."

He said nothing, continuing to hold her in silence for a moment, before finally letting go. He stepped out of the shower, leaving her to wash those thoughts away in peace.

A gloomy heaviness hung in every corner and walkway of the DeMarco residence, infiltrating Corrado's lungs with each breath he took. Antonio sat behind his desk as Sal and Sonny took their usual spots along the side of the office, sipping on scotch despite it being ten o'clock in the morning.

Antonio held a glass, too, not drinking it. He stared down at the golden colored liquid, swirling it around and around in his glass, lines of worry marking his troubled face. Distress was evident in all the men… never-ending frowns, bloodshot eyes, a silence that spoke louder than words could convey. Corrado stood in the doorway, unmoving, detaching, as he tried to make sense where no sense could be made.

Celia rushed toward her father, bolting around the desk. Sonny, usually on alert whenever anyone approached the Boss, barely even looked up. Antonio set his glass down as she wrapped her arms around his neck. "Oh, Daddy. I'm so, so sorry."

"Thank you, sweetheart." Antonio's voice was strained. "I can't believe it."

"I know," she said. "What his poor family must've seen!"

"They said it was gruesome," Antonio replied. "It's gonna take a fucking bulldozer to rid that house of that mess. Stabbed right in the throat, ten-inch knife. Said it pierced the chair behind him, like he was staked in the neck. Blood everywhere. Fucking ugly."

Celia let out a strangled cry. "God, who would do such a thing?"

Antonio's eyes subtly shifted to Corrado as he hugged his daughter, patting her back. "A savage."

"Is there anything I can do?" Celia asked. "Anything you need?"

Prying out of the hug, Antonio waved toward the doorway. "Your mother's making some food for the Tarullos… some lasagna and stuff that Ginny can heat up. Why don't you go ask her if she needs help?"

Gloom seemed to grow deeper when Celia left. Corrado remained there, unmoving, unwavering. He hadn't been invited to take a seat, but he hadn't been dismissed either. He scanned the men, trying to detect some sign of trouble, some indication of *anything* unusual, but their faces gave nothing away. The grief seemed genuine, tears gleaming in Antonio's eyes as he picked up his scotch once more.

"Sonny, Sal," Antonio said. "You mind giving me a minute with Moretti?"

"No problem, Boss," Sonny said, getting up and walking out. Sal lingered, finishing his drink before standing, eyes questionably scanning Corrado as he passed.

"Shut the door," Antonio instructed once the men were gone. Corrado obeyed before stepping further into the room. Antonio set his glass down and leaned back in his chair, his shoulders relaxing. He avoided Corrado's gaze as he pulled out a thick envelope. Tossing it on the desk in front of him, he nodded for Corrado to pick it up. "A hundred grand."

Corrado slipped the envelope into the inside pocket of his jacket. He had never been paid so much for a hit before—forty grand, fifty at most.

Antonio stared at him as a sly smile lifted the corner of his lips. "You're not going to ask any questions?"

He shook his head.

"This stays between you and me."

"Always."

Antonio's smile grew until a light, airy laugh left his lips. "Go on, get out of here."

Three days later, as autumn dawned, Virgil Tarullo was laid to rest in a small cemetery on the east side of the city. Corrado stood with his arm around his wife, holding her protectively.

Antonio stood beside them, with Gia and Vincent, Sonny and his wife to their right. Sal came alone, lingering off to the back, while Virgil's family took up the other side of the fresh grave.

They spoke ill of Corrado, calling him names, cursing him, damning him to Hell for what he had done… they just had no idea he was there to hear it. Their voices, their anger, their hatred washed over him, finding no way through his thick skin, unable to pierce his armor, as they grieved the man they had lost and condemned the one who had taken him away.

It had been a job, he told himself—a job that had paid for the black dress his wife wore, that had paid for the gas in the car that drove them, that had paid for the flowers Celia gave to the family before she hugged her friend, Johnny.

It was nothing personal.

Strictly business.

24

"Is it true?"

Out of breath, Vincent's chest heaved as he forced out those words, sweat dripping from his forehead, running down his flushed face. His dark eyes were wild, focused on Corrado, awaiting an answer.

Corrado stood at his front door, staring at the boy peculiarly. He had knocked feverishly, rousing Corrado from a light sleep on the couch. He had been up late working and in no mood for this. "You're panting."

"I ran here," Vincent said, raising his shirt to wipe the sweat from his brow. "So is it? Is it true?"

"Is what true?"

"Is she here?"

"No," Corrado replied. "Celia isn't home."

"Not my sister. I know *she's* not here."

"Then why are you?"

Vincent groaned with aggravation and tried to step into the house, but Corrado shifted to block his way. Vincent glared at him, his mouth set in a hard line of determination. *Gutsy.*

Corrado knew it straightaway, off the boy's stubborn expression. He had assured Antonio that Maura wouldn't cause any trouble, but trouble sought her in the form of a teenage boy.

"You should go home, Vincent."

Those eyes narrowed even more. "I don't want to."

"Then go somewhere else," Corrado said. "But you're not coming in here."

The door slammed right in Vincent's face.

Corrado turned around in the foyer, catching sight of Maura down the hallway. She stared past him, eyes fixed on the closed door. She was much more put together than she had been when Vito dropped her off. Celia bought the girl an entire wardrobe and more pairs of shoes than even Corrado owned. They furnished one of the spare rooms with a nice bed and dresser, but she still didn't seem comfortable.

In fact, she seemed more distressed now than when she had first arrived.

Maura blinked a few times as her frown deepened. She looked as if she had something to say, but instead her shoulders slumped, her sorrowful gaze going to her feet.

"Don't worry," Corrado reassured her. "He won't bother you."

Every muscle in Corrado's body felt weak, strained from overwork and lack of sleep. Exhausted, he trudged up the stairs to his bedroom and fell into the freshly made bed with relief. He snatched up a pillow, snuggling against it as he closed his eyes, and fell asleep on his stomach, still fully dressed.

His hair tousling woke him up, a tingle across his scalp that jolted him. Eyes wide, he pulled away from the extended hand and sat up, stunned to see Celia perched on the edge of the bed. Her hand remained mid-air as she eyed him with surprise. "Didn't mean to startle you."

"You didn't."

A smile played across her lips. "Liar."

"You did."

She laughed lightly. He couldn't lie to her, and they both knew it. He would skirt around the truth all day long, but blatant lies were a kind of cheating—betraying the trust she had placed in him.

He had no qualms cheating usually—he would cheat the law, cheat the government, cheat death—but he wouldn't cheat his wife.

Or her father, for that matter.

"You must've been sleeping hard. I rarely sneak up on you."

He rolled onto his back, folding his arms across his stomach. "I need a vacation."

"You do," she agreed, reaching out to stroke his hair again. "*We* do. We need two weeks of just you and me, away from everything and everyone."

Sounded nice, but getting away was practically impossible when you couldn't even get a full night's sleep without being dragged to a job.

"Soon," he promised. "As soon as I can get away, I'm yours."

The declaration wasn't even entirely from his lips when the phone downstairs rang. Corrado's eyes closed at the sound of it, a slight pounding starting deep in his head. "I should get that."

"Stay." Celia pressed a hand against his forehead before running it through his hair. "Rest."

He wouldn't argue.

He didn't have the energy.

She strode out, pausing in the hallway near the stairs. "Vincent! Get that, will you? Take a message."

A dull murmur of a response came from downstairs.

Before the ringing even stopped, Corrado was on his feet. He met Celia in the doorway when she tried to rejoin him. "Did you say Vincent?"

"Yes."

"He's here?"

"Yes."

"I told him to go home."

"He did."

"Then why is he here?"

She shrugged. "I brought him back."

Corrado stepped past her, bounding down the stairs. Celia followed right on his heels. "Corrado, wait."

He kept going.

"Corrado," she shouted. "Slow down!"

She grabbed him when he reached the bottom of the stairs, getting a tentative grasp on the back of his shirt. Her other hand grabbed his arm, yanking him toward her. "Dammit, stop!"

His footsteps faltered at the fury in her voice. He turned just in time for her to jab him in the chest with her pointer finger. Grabbing her hand, he held it there, raising an eyebrow at her. "What?"

"Leave them alone."

"He shouldn't be here," Corrado said. "I told her he wouldn't bother her."

"Does it sound like he's *bothering* her?"

No, it sounded like nothing. Soft subtle whispers, the words unintelligible—if they were even words at all. It was nothing more than humming to his ears. "That means nothing."

He let go of her hand when she dropped her voice low. "Please, Corrado."

"Don't beg," he growled.

"Please," she said again. "Just leave them alone. That's all I'm asking."

Laughter rang out from the living room, soft and feminine, entirely unfamiliar. A sound Corrado had never heard before. He walked to the living room, pausing in the doorway. Vincent and Maura sat on the couch, facing each other, an entire cushion of space between them, but something about the way they spoke softly felt startlingly intimate.

Maura lit up as she laughed again at something Vincent said, her eyes peering straight into the boy's. Corrado turned away from them, avoiding his wife as he headed for the stairs.

"She's enjoying herself," Celia said when he passed.

"If she wants fun, buy her some toys."

"Toys?" she asked incredulously. "She's not a *child*. She doesn't need dolls. She needs friends."

He said nothing in response as he went back upstairs. He stopped when he reached the top step, seeing Celia standing at the bottom, watching him.

"Your brother has until dusk," Corrado said. "If he's not out of my house when the streetlights come on, I'll *throw* him out."

He spoke matter-of-fact, a harsh edge to his voice, but Celia beamed with satisfaction, as if she'd won something with his words.

25

Even in the most chaotic times, things can grow monotonous if you become desensitized to the madness.

Day in and day out, Corrado did everything asked of him, going above and beyond the call of duty. He saw the gritty streets of Chicago more than he saw the inside of his home, running all hours of the night, helping Vito with jobs—robberies, hijacks, overseeing gambling rings, collecting taxes—as well as fielding extra work from the Boss directly.

It's only a matter of time, his father reminded him whenever the fatigue showed on his young face. *Only a matter of time before they put your name in the books, kid.*

With initiating would come a certain amount of freedom. Vowing yourself to them meant not having to constantly prove your worth… they already deemed you worthy. He'd be able to take a step back, be able to take a breath and relax.

But until then, he was at their beck and call, available anytime, day or night. He did it all without complaint, so accurately, so automatically, that it became as instinctual as breathing.

Corrado fought predictability, but he was a man of habit, finding little things that grounded him during the mayhem. He would stalk and eradicate, quick and easy, sometimes not as painless as others, and afterward, he'd stop by that same little store and buy flowers for his wife before coming home to her. It wasn't out of guilt—it was an act of balance.

A little of the good to even out all that bad.

He scarcely noticed after a while, as the tedium of it all kicked in, but he started bringing flowers home more and more. He never kept count, never kept a record, never even tried to remember, but the body count added up, the blood on his hands thicker and thicker.

Even at home he merely went through the motions some days. His small house dead center of Felton Drive fell into the trap, his once quiet sanctuary now anarchy.

He had underestimated Vincenzo DeMarco.

The boy was in and out of his house all hours of the night. Corrado would come home and find him there, making himself at home, after he had been told to stay away. Corrado would make him leave, sometimes physically forcing him out the front door, but without fail, the very next morning, he would be right back.

Corrado wasn't blind. He saw what was happening. He may not have understood—not completely—but he saw it. And he struggled against it. It was constant, round and round, over and over, another monotonous habit Corrado grew too numb to break. And while he clashed with Vincent, Celia grew distant, contradicting him every step of the way.

She would never condemn Corrado's life. She grew up in it. But she would never like it. She would never get used to his absences. When he came home at night, sometimes clutching a bouquet of flowers, she would give him a look of indecision.

"What did you do today?" she'd ask.

"Work," he would say, or, "ran errands for your father." He kept it vague, and she accepted his answers, but questions lingered in her eyes, the part of her that wanted details he couldn't bare the thought of giving.

"You know you can tell me anything," she would say. "I want us to be able to talk about everything."

He'd simply nod, grateful when she dropped the subject.

It neared the end of November and Corrado was out one night with his father, cleaning up from an underground gambling tournament. Corrado sat on top of one of the stained green poker tables, discarded chips splayed out all around him. Vito sat in a chair beside him, puffing on a cigar, tall stacks of cash piled up in front of him as he painstakingly counted every bill. It was late—two o'clock in the morning. Corrado glanced around, a small dim room beneath a local bar, a filthy concrete floor and faded brick walls, the air infused with the scent of piss and old beer.

You'd think the Mafia could find a better place to hang out in.

"Your mother's in the hospital."

The words came out of nowhere. Corrado's attention shifted to his father, all thoughts of the shabby hangout disappearing. "The hospital?"

"Yeah." He let out a deep sigh. "Doctor came out to the house and found her. Called an ambulance. She was having seizures."

"That's, uh…"

"Terrible," Vito said, finishing his sentence.

Corrado had been thinking something more like 'karma'.

"Anyway," Vito continued. "She's gonna be there for awhile, you know, getting real help now. I told her no more. She says she isn't drinking, that she just took too many of them pill the doctor gave her. An accident. But she agreed to stay in the hospital until they got her clean."

From booze to pills? He wasn't surprised. "Okay."

Vito stopped counting and looked at his son. "Your sister's coming to visit."

"Okay."

"She'll be here next week," he said. "I thought maybe we could have Thanksgiving together, you know, like old times."

Like old times. The way Vito said those words, with a sense of hopeful longing, irked Corrado. "I don't know. It would be nice to have a holiday for once where people don't throw things."

The smile playing on Vito's lips faded away. He stared at him hard for a moment before shrugging it off and counting the money.

Corrado jumped down from the table. "I need to get going. I have court in a few hours."

"Yeah? For what?"

"I'm not even sure."

Along with the uniformity had come repeated arrests, every few weeks like clockwork. He had seen Detective Walker's face enough the past month alone to last a lifetime.

Vito laughed. "Good luck with that."

Corrado slapped his father on the back, squeezing his shoulder as he passed. "I'll talk to Celia about Thanksgiving."

Vito didn't respond, but his smile returned.

"Fine."

Corrado stared at his wife skeptically when she shrugged and said that word. *Fine.* "You don't mean that."

"Why don't I?"

"Because that isn't what I thought you'd say."

Celia dug through the cabinets in the kitchen, pulling out everything to make dinner. "You thought I'd say no?"

"Yes." He paused. "You *did* hear what I said, right?"

She turned to him. "Your sister's coming to town, and your father wants us to spend Thanksgiving together."

"Yes."

"Then yes, I heard you."

"And your answer is 'fine'."

"What do you *want* me to say?"

"I don't know. I just thought you'd be more opposed."

"They're your family, Corrado. And yeah, I'm not your sister's biggest fan, but she wasn't too bad at our engagement party."

"That's because my mother monopolized the crazy."

"Come on. There has to be *something* redeeming about Katrina. You two shared a womb, after all."

"Celia." He pulled her to him. "The fact that I'm her brother *is* the only redeeming thing about her."

Celia laughed, wrapping her arms around his neck. "As right as you may be about that, I think we should give her a chance. Who knows? She might surprise us."

He conceded. "Fine."

"Fine," she repeated, pulling away from him to go back to her work. "We'll have dinner here. Maura and I can cook."

The following week, a rainy Thursday afternoon in the suburbs of Chicago, the Moretti family gathered for Thanksgiving dinner. Celia was polite, the perfect hostess, greeting their guests with warm smiles and cold drinks. As soon as Vito stepped in the door, he snatched a hold of Celia and whirled her around in a circle, dipping her playfully, before pulling her against him and planting a kiss right on her lips. Corrado stood at the bottom of his steps, leaning against the railing, a bit of tension receding from his body when his wife laughed. "Oh, Vito… maybe I married the wrong Moretti."

She cast Corrado a teasing look.

"No, you picked the right one," Vito said, slapping his son on the back. "I don't look nearly as good in a suit as this kid."

Corrado's eyes drifted to the open doorway when his sister appeared. Katrina stepped into the house, wearing a black sleeveless dress, shivering slightly, as Michael paused to put down an umbrella. Setting it aside, he stepped in the house behind her, his hand on her hip.

"Katrina," Celia said. "Nice to see you again."

"You, too." There was no warmth to his sister's voice but no hostility either. Indifference. "Nice house."

Celia's smile brightened. "Thank you."

Corrado greeted none of them verbally, offering slight polite nods instead as Celia led the family toward the dining room. Dinner was already prepared, piled along the long table. Corrado went to slip into a chair beside his wife when Vito shoved him out of the way to take that seat instead.

"Your house." Vito motioned toward the head of the table. "Your seat."

Instinctively, Corrado had yielded to Vito. After all, Vito wasn't just his father—he was his boss of sorts.

Corrado took the spot at the head of the table and grabbed the carving knife. He stared at the turkey before gripping the knife and jabbing it straight down the top of the bird. Something cracked, bones breaking away as the blade wedged into the rib cage. Celia cringed while Vito laughed heartily, putting his arm around her shoulder. "It's already dead, kid. You ain't gotta kill it."

Corrado sloppily carved the turkey, cutting away big slabs of meat. They dug in once he finished, piling their plates high with food. Friendly chatter filled the air, mostly from Vito as he bridged the conversation. Corrado didn't have much to say, only speaking when spoken to, but dinner held none of the strain he was used to with his family. It was friendly. It was happy.

Corrado didn't like it.

"So, Michael," Vito said, relaxing back in his chair, arm once again around his daughter-in-law as he sipped a glass of wine. "I'm glad you decided to make the trip to Chicago."

The words, casual on the surface, ran deeper in Corrado's mind.

"It's good to be here," Michael said. "I've always been interested in, uh… Chicago."

Definitely deeper.

"Good, good… you know, your father and me are good friends," Vito said. "It'll be nice to have Frankie's kid around. I'm sure Corrado wouldn't mind introducing you to the city."

Corrado stopped eating. He didn't like where this was going. "I'm busy."

His clipped tone caused the women at the table to glare at him, but Vito brushed it off. "Nah… you're never too busy for family, kid."

Corrado chose to remain silent then, dropping the subject, knowing he couldn't argue against that point without it coming back to haunt him.

After dinner, Katrina and Michael settled into the living room with Vito, while Celia grabbed everyone drinks in the kitchen. Maura sat at the small table along the side, as she quietly ate a plate of food Celia had set aside for her. Corrado helped his wife, growing aggravated by the animated voices ringing through his house. It was obvious to Corrado that dinner hadn't been out of some warped sense of nostalgia. It was little more than a dressed up, dragged out business meeting.

Frustrated, Corrado reached into the cabinet and slammed some glasses down on the counter. Maura flinched at the noise whereas Celia grabbed his arm to stop him. "What's gotten in to you?"

Laughter rang out from the doorway as Vito stepped into the kitchen. "He's pissed at me."

"You?" Celia turned to Vito. "Who could be mad at *you*?"

Vito shrugged, grinning. "My wife's always mad at me, and you know, he's got her blood in him."

Corrado slammed the cabinet door and picked up the bottle of scotch, filling one of the glasses to the brim. Picking it up, he guzzled the liquor.

"Might not be the *only* thing he got from her, either."

Resentment ran through Corrado. He clutched the glass tightly, struggling against the urge to throw it.

"Go on," Vito taunted. "Ain't a Moretti holiday unless something breaks, right?"

Corrado set the glass on the counter instead of launching it at him.

"What in the world is going on?" Celia asked, glancing between the men.

"Not a big deal," Vito said. "How about giving us a moment alone?"

Shaking her head, muttering to herself, Celia grabbed some drinks and walked out. Maura jumped to her feet then and tried to scurry out, but Vito stopped her, grabbing her abandoned plate from the table. "Whoa, sweetheart, don't forget your dinner."

She took it from him, wide-eyed, and muttered her thanks before leaving. Once the two of them were alone, Vito turned his attention back to his son. "Say your piece."

"I don't like him."

"You ain't got to, kid," Vito said shrugging. "But we do what we gotta do."

"And why do I have to?"

Vito raised his eyebrows. "You questioning an order?"

"Was it an order?"

"You know it was."

"Then you know I wouldn't question one."

Vito smirked at that. "Look, Frankie Antonelli's a made man. You know that. And when a made man needs a favor, we follow through for him. We ain't gotta like it. You ain't gotta like *him*. Hell, I don't like most people. But he's Frankie's kid."

"Frankie's kid." That was the second time Vito had called him that. "What happened to making our own name?"

"I told *you* to make your own name."

"What's the difference?"

"The difference is that moron ain't never gonna be anything better than just 'Frankie's kid'."

Despite Corrado's reluctance, he obeyed his father's order. He included Michael Antonelli on thefts and hijacks, showed him the bookmaking rings, took him to collect money and make deals. Any job Vito sent him on, he hauled Michael along, letting the boy ride his coattails for a way inside the crew. Michael would smirk, overconfident, as he introduced himself as Frankie Antonelli's son and Vito Moretti's son-in-law.

Corrado remained mute as Michael exploited those connections, garnering attention while he stood back in the shadows, doing what needed to be done. On the rare occasion someone acknowledged him, it was with a small nod of the head and a mere half-smile.

They knew who he was. They knew what he did.

They knew enough to recognize they didn't *want* to know any more about him.

26

A harsh winter set in almost overnight as a blizzard battered Chicago weeks before Christmas. Nearly two feet of snow covered the city in less than twenty-four hours, shutting down transit and clogging the streets. Life came to a proverbial standstill, iced over with a blanket of bitter frozen white.

But a little snow couldn't stop Corrado.

His phone had been ringing constantly for work—do this, do that, take this here, discard this there. He had been up all night as the white flakes fell from the darkened, cloudy sky, huddled under a thick coat, black leather gloves on his hands, making sure everything got where it needed to be. Made men were holed up in their homes, having no desire to brave the weather, which shifted even more onto Corrado's plate.

Dawn had just broken when Corrado drove home, navigating the frozen streets. He had called Michael hours earlier and told him to meet him at his house, but Corrado was running late. Exhausted, he pulled into his driveway, spotting Michael's Cadillac parked along the street, but seeing little else as he strode toward his front door. He rubbed his weary eyes as he stepped inside, hoping for some peace and quiet, but utter chaos met him at the door.

Before he had even shut the door, Vincent knocked right into him. Corrado snatched a hold of the boy's coat, shoving him roughly against the nearby wall. "Why are *you* here?"

Vincent stared at him, the force of the blow knocking the breath from his lungs.

"Let him go," Celia said, exasperated, as she stepped into the foyer and slipped on her coat. "He just came to get me."

"Get you for what?"

"Church," she said. "Since you clearly forgot it was Sunday."

Sunday. *Huh.*

"Anyway, I figured since you weren't here, you weren't coming. And then when your sister showed up…"

Corrado's brow furrowed. "Kat's here?"

She motioned toward the living room. "With Michael and some other guys. Not sure who they are."

"You're not sure who they are and you let them in my house?"

"*I* didn't let them in," she said, matter-of-fact, as she shoved him away from her brother. Corrado let go so the boy could slip outside. Celia paused there, her eyes scanning his face as she smiled. Softly, she kissed him, whispering against his lips, "Vincent did."

He let out a groan of irritation. "I'm going to kill that boy."

"No, you're not," she said, bumping against him as she skidded out the door. "You wouldn't dare hurt me that way."

He stood there after she was gone, listening to the voices in his living room. They were vaguely familiar, recognition striking him as he walked that way. Pascal Barone and Alex Como.

Capos.

More work.

Stepping into the doorway, Corrado addressed them. "Gentlemen."

"Moretti!" Pascal said. "About time you make it home."

"I was… working."

"Long night?" Alex asked.

Corrado shrugged nonchalantly as he sat down on the couch beside his sister, who flipped through one of Celia's girly magazines. "You could say that."

"Well... gonna be an even longer day." Pascal cast a sidelong glance at Katrina, assessing whether he should talk in front of her. To Pascal she probably looked like she wasn't listening, but Corrado knew she would absorb every word. "I won't bullshit you. Here's the deal. There's this shipment coming in this afternoon from Maine that we're going to hit. I don't need many guys, two or three at most. Simple job, quickest money ever made. I had some guys lined up, but with this weather..."

Corrado thought that over. "What's in the truck?"

Pascal laughed. "You wouldn't believe me if I told you."

"And it can't wait for the weather to break?"

"No, it's now or never."

Corrado was quiet for a moment. His father had a poker game set up in the hideout beneath the bar that needed cashed out, and he had a few loansharks to check in with, but the rest of the evening was wide-open. "You're hitting it tonight?"

Pascal shook his head. "Broad daylight."

"It's hard to push merchandise when the sun's up."

"Not what we're stealing."

"Okay." If the man said it, Corrado would believe it. Pascal was a capo, and he didn't have the influence to override him. "Just say when."

Corrado and Michael spent the morning handling Vito's business, running from place to place, meeting with some of the guys from the crew. A quarter till two they were in the car, heading to the docks out by Lake Michigan to meet up with Pascal and Alex. The men waited in an idling Chevy, the windows open a crack to let the smoke from their cigars filter out. Corrado parked beside them, cutting the engine and staring at the empty dock as they waited.

Nearly two thirty on the dot, a refrigerator truck crept up. Pascal and Alex got out, no hesitation. Corrado tossed his keys to Michael. "Don't wreck my car."

In. Out. Over. Corrado chanted those words in his head as he followed the men. Get in, get out, and get it over with. He reached into his coat, clutching his gun, as Pascal signaled for him to go around to the other side. He listened as Alex took up residence at the back of the truck, standing guard. Corrado ran around to the passenger side. It was a routine he had done so often he could manage it with his eyes closed.

He pressed himself against the truck and gripped the door handle. *Be unlocked.*

Within a matter of seconds, he heard the bang, something striking the back of the truck. His cue. Pulling the handle, he yanked it open and blocked the door with his body the same time the other door opened. The driver startled, yelping, and threw up his hands in panic when both men aimed guns at his head.

"Move over," Pascal demanded, cold voice leaving his lips in a bitter cloud of breath.

The driver slid over in the seat as Pascal and Corrado both climbed in, shoving the man in the center. Pascal started the truck, throwing it into gear and speeding away from the dock as Alex ran back to his idling Chevy.

They drove to a small, shabby motel in a remote part of the city, parking the truck behind the building. Pascal forced the driver out, the gun pressed to his side as he led him to the room on the end, rented under an obscure name. The driver sat down on the edge of the bed, sheer terror in his eyes as they darted from gun to gun, panicked pleading flying from his lips in stutters.

"Shut up," Pascal said. "Give up your wallet."

The driver slipped it from his pocket. "Take whatever you want. Anything. It's yours. Whatever you want."

Alex snatched it as Pascal hit the man, knocking him off the bed. "I said shut up!"

Alex pulled out the driver's license, throwing the rest of it on the floor. "Jason Marshall," he read aloud. "Center Street in Augusta, Maine."

"What you're gonna do, Jason Marshall," Pascal said, gun aimed at the man as he clicked on the television, "is sit here and watch something. And in an hour, you're gonna go out that door and walk about a mile back the way we came to the closest payphone to call a ride to pick you up. That's it. It's as easy as that."

The driver stared at him skeptically.

"But if you leave any sooner? I'm gonna have to kill you. And not just you—your whole family, too. I know where you live." He took the driver's license from Alex and slipped it in his pocket. "You see my face? Yeah? Well, take a good look at it. Because if you breathe a word to the cops, it'll be the last face you ever see. I guarantee it."

Pascal was out the door, no hesitation. Corrado followed, slowing when they reached the back of the building. Pascal stopped to lean against the corner, pulling a pack of cigarettes from his pocket.

"Are we leaving?" Alex asked.

"Go on ahead," Pascal told him. "Take the cars and meet us over at that steakhouse on Melrose."

"Sure thing," Alex said, him and Michael walking away.

Corrado stood there, coldness seeping through his clothes, wondering why they weren't leaving also. Time was of the essence in a hijack. But Pascal seemed to be in no rush, puffing away on a Newport.

Before Corrado had the chance to grow impatient, the motel room door opened and frantic footsteps crunched in the snow. Pascal let out an exaggerated groan as he stamped out his cigarette. "Couldn't even wait ten goddamn minutes."

His hand darted in his coat, whipping out his gun, as the truck driver scampered through the parking lot. Pascal stepped out from behind the building and fired, shot after shot, the echo bouncing off the trees. The driver fell into a snowdrift, bullets tearing into his back. He cried out, trying to drag himself through the lot, but Pascal was on top of him in no time. Squatting down, Pascal grabbed the man by the back of the hair and lifted his head up, pressing the gun to his temple.

A last shot exploded his skull.

Dropping him, Pascal slipped his gun away and strolled back over to Corrado. "*Now* we go."

They drove to the steakhouse, meeting the others behind the restaurant. Alex cracked the lock on the back of the truck and shoved the door open, laughing excitedly. "Jackpot!"

Corrado stared at the containers, reading the warning stamped onto them as he breathed in the sour smell of salt water. *Live Lobsters.*

They hijacked a truck of seafood.

"Ever stolen fish before?" Alex asked.

"They're crustaceans," Corrado replied.

Alex stared at him with disbelief. "Look at Mr. Encyclopedia-fucking-Britannica over here. They swim. We eat them. Same thing."

"Your wife swims," Pascal said. "You eat her, too, don't you, Alex? Doesn't make the bitch a fish."

"Fuck you," Alex said, his words betraying the humor in his voice. "She might be. She damn sure drinks like one."

Corrado's focus turned back to the lobsters. "No, I've never seen the point in stealing… *fish*."

"Watch and learn," Alex said.

Michael and Corrado got stuck doing most of the brunt work, taking them straight into the back door of the steakhouse. They jumped from restaurant to restaurant, each one associated to *La Cosa Nostra* someway, and sold the lobsters directly to the business owners for a fraction of their usual cost. The lobsters flew off the truck, the last one unpacked two hours later and taken into the backdoor of Rita's as the owner counted out a stack of cash and handed it to Pascal.

Corrado stood behind the truck, watching, no longer feeling the cold. He was drenched with sweat and melted snow, his toes numb, the water long ago seeping through his shoes. The stench of seafood clung to him. The more he sweat, the more he reeked. He wanted to rip off his skin and soak it in bleach.

It would take a week of scalding showers to wash this sin away.

They ditched the truck in a bad part of town and headed back to Corrado's, the four men gathering in the dining room as Pascal spread out their take. Twenties, fifties, hundreds… there had to be well over a hundred thousand dollars.

He watched Pascal count it when he heard movement in the kitchen. "Maura," he called, not moving.

A second later her meek voice rang out from the doorway behind him. "Yes, sir?"

The second she spoke, Pascal stopped counting and glanced over, his elated expression falling. He stared at her hard.

"Get my guests drinks," Corrado said. "The good scotch."

"Yes, sir."

Maura skidded back away, but Pascal's eyes remained on the doorway until she reappeared. Maura set empty glasses on the table beside the bottle of scotch, not bothering to pour any, before bolting out the door again.

Pascal's gaze shifted to Corrado, an incredulous look on his face. "She's fucking Irish."

"Yes."

He appeared awestruck, something on the tip of his tongue, but he swallowed it with a shot of scotch.

It neared dusk when the phone rang. Corrado excused himself from the dining room to answer it. He picked up the receiver, sitting down on the edge of the couch in front of his sister. Katrina remained in the living room, making herself at home on his couch, sprawled out watching television.

"Moretti speaking."

"Meet me at my house."

He closed his eyes at the sound of the Boss's voice. "Now?"

"Twenty minutes ago."

The line went dead. He had sensed anger in his voice.

Not good.

Corrado hung up, glancing back at Katrina when she shifted. Sensing his gaze, her eyes flicked from the television screen to him. She raised an eyebrow questioningly.

"I know you're up to something," he said to her, dropping his voice low so only she would hear. "Your act doesn't fool me, Kat."

She said nothing, turning back to the television.

Corrado excused himself, grabbing his coat and telling the men to make themselves at home while he dealt with some business. He left, opting to drive the few blocks so not to waste time trying to walk through the snow. Antonio stood in his driveway, leaning against the side of Manny's black sedan, while Manny sat behind the wheel of the idling car. Corrado parked and climbed out just as Antonio opened the back door to the sedan. "Get in."

Corrado slid into the back seat with no hesitation. Antonio got in beside him, the car pulling away before he even got the door closed.

They drove through town in silence. Corrado watched out the window, subconsciously memorizing the route. Twenty minutes later, they pulled into an alley beside a barbershop, and Manny cut the engine. Corrado followed the Boss, climbing out of the car and heading through a side door into the building. The place was dark and cold, growing drearier as they hit a set of side steps leading into a basement. A single swinging light bulb hung overhead, wires exposed, the light flickering as it cast a circular glow around a single wooden chair. Thick chains tied a man to it, circling his bloody, bare chest, as rope dug into his ankles and wrists. His face was swollen from being savagely beaten, Corrado ventured to guess from the baseball bat nearby on the floor.

Sonny and Salvatore stood in the basement, lurking as Antonio approached the guy. Corrado stopped in the shadows, not stepping into the light as Antonio pulled the gag from the man's mouth. He took an instant deep breath, a painful inhale that came back out in the form of a shriek of agony. Antonio silenced it instantly with a slap to the face, stunning the man into quiet sobs.

"Be a man!" Antonio spat.

"I'm sorry," he cried. "I'm so sorry. Please. Just… please."

Antonio's hands were around the man's neck, choking his words when he tried to plead again. "You're a coward. A fucking *cockroach.*"

He let go, shoving against him so hard the chair shifted. The man painfully gasped again as Antonio snatched the bat from the grimy floor.

"Confess."

The word, spoken so coolly, caused the man to sob harder.

"Confess," Antonio said again.

"I didn't—"

The swing of the bat was a blur to Corrado's eyes as it collided with the man's chest, cutting him off mid-sentence.

"Confess."

"Please, please, I'm *begging* you."

Another crack to chest resulting in incoherent screaming.

"Confess."

Strike after strike with the bat, bones audibly cracking as the man shrieked, followed simply by that lone word. *Confess.* Antonio savagely beat him, taking no mercy on the man as he cried and begged. Corrado forced himself to watch, but every blink brought on flashes of memory, the vision of Zia dying in front of him.

"Confess."

Antonio raised the bat again when the man let out a strangled breath. "Okay!"

Antonio paused, waiting.

"Just, please, stop," the man cried. "No more. I can't take anymore."

Antonio lowered the bat. "Say it."

"I did it. It was me."

"Did *what?*"

"I killed him." The man's voice cracked. "I killed Virgil Tarullo."

That garnered Corrado's attention. He blinked a few times, staring at the man in the chair.

"Tell me what you did."

"Please," the man pleaded. "I can't do this."

Another swift crack from the bat changed his mind.

"I broke into his house," he cried. "I took a knife, and I stabbed him. I stabbed him in the neck. I just… I did it. I killed him. Just please stop. No more. I can't take any more."

Antonio threw the bat aside, the crash of the wood against the concrete echoing through the barren basement. The man wheezed, barely able to breathe. It grew eerily silent, nobody moving, nobody speaking, before Antonio walked away.

"Get rid of him," he said to Corrado. "Send a message that they don't cross the DeMarco family. Let them know we're watching."

Let them know we're watching.

Corrado pulled out his gun when Antonio walked out. Sonny followed right behind, while Sal lingered. He strode across the room, stopping in front of the man in the chair, glaring at him before spitting right in his face. "I'd kill you myself, but your blood isn't worth dirtying my hands."

Once Sal was gone, Corrado stepped over to the man.

"Please," he pleaded. "Please. I didn't do this. I *didn't.*"

"I know," Corrado said as he raised the gun, aiming straight for his eye, and pulled the trigger, instantly silencing his cries, the force of the shot knocking the chair over. "I did."

Manny's car still idled in the alley when Corrado made it out of the building. Corrado opened the back door and slid in. Manny started driving right away.

"You're quiet," Antonio remarked on the drive.

"I have nothing to say..." Corrado paused before adding, "sir."

"You know, I don't often tolerate people questioning me."

Corrado rubbed his temple at the onset of a headache. "I'm not questioning you."

"I know you aren't," he replied. "But Salvatore did."

Corrado's brow furrowed. Sal?

"He wanted to know why we weren't acting. He wanted to know why Virgil's killer wasn't dead. Why we weren't out there, hunting down whoever did it. Reasonable questions, but I didn't like it. I don't like being questioned."

"Sal doesn't seem like the type to question things."

Antonio laughed at that. "He's a fucking salamander. Sneaky. *Slimy.* He gets into trouble? He drops his tail and runs. No sweat to him, he'll just grow another. He doesn't understand the concept of loyalty."

Corrado was flabbergasted. Salvatore was second in command.

"Virgil, he made a mistake. A *big* mistake. I try to be a fair man... I don't tell men what to do on their own time. Prostitution, slavery... I hold my tongue. I'm not the moral police. What a man does with a woman is his own business. I don't have to like it. But when you put drugs out on *my* streets, when you sell them to *my* people? Then you cross a line.

"I warned him. I *warned* Virgil. But he didn't stop. So I stopped him myself. And I don't regret that. I gave him a second chance. I don't do that. You fuck me once? You fuck nobody else ever again. But I let him fuck me twice. The man was my friend, and he thought that made him immune to the rules. *Nobody* is immune to the rules."

Corrado said nothing as the Boss ranted.

"Sal wanted blood, so I gave him blood," he continued. "It didn't matter whose it was. Sal would've had his own fucking mother killed just to make it even. He doesn't give a shit who the tail is that got dropped."

"Why's he your underboss then?"

Antonio glanced at Corrado when he broke his silence with a question. "Now you're questioning me."

"I'm merely curious."

"Curiosity killed the cat. It'll kill you, too."

Corrado nodded, understanding, and turned back to the window.

"It should've been his brother-in-law," Antonio said, answering despite his rebuke. "Luigi was set to step up into the position; he was set to take over from me. But then somebody killed him. Sal wanted it—wanted the responsibility. Wanted to honor his sister, honor his family. And I figured, you know, if I couldn't have a Russo, a Capozzi was the next best thing. But Sal wanted blood then, too. Never found who killed them, but I gave Sal blood, anyway. I started a fucking war for him. You wouldn't know about that, though. You were just a kid."

Corrado knew. It was how he had met Celia. It was the reason Vito sent them into hiding.

"It'll be a cold day when that salamander succeeds me. This organization needs ran by somebody made of steel. Not a fucking little lizard I could stomp on with my boot."

Manny pulled onto Felton Drive, coming to a stop in front of Corrado's house. Antonio waved him away. "You can come pick up your car tomorrow."

"Yes, sir." Corrado opened the door and climbed out, barely getting to shut the door again before the car pulled away.

Turning to his house, Corrado noted Michael's car still parked out front. He hoped for some peace finally, but that dented old Cadillac suggested otherwise.

He strode inside, slipping along the icy, snow covered path. The television was still on in the living room, but nobody watched it. Voices rang out from the dining room, animated slurring words. Corrado headed that way, finding Michael and Alex still drinking. The money had been cleared away. In its place on the table sat Katrina, feet dangling off the edge as she drank straight from the nearly empty bottle.

"Corrado," she said with a mischievous smile, holding out the bottle of liquor. "Want some?"

"No."

She shrugged, taking a swig. "More for me."

He glared at her. She reminded him of his mother right then.

Trying not to dwell on that, he focused on the others. "Pascal go home?"

Alex rubbed his neck, half-shrugging, while Michael sat frozen. A flush stained Alex's cheeks, the collar of his shirt misshapen. Michael just appeared terrified.

Something inside of Corrado jolted.

"Where's Pascal?" he asked, glancing between the men before again looking to his sister. Subtly, slyly, her eyes darted toward the ceiling as if by some visceral reaction.

It was all Corrado needed.

He took the stairs two at a time as he headed to the second floor, his insides twisting into knots when he heard the noises.

Bang. Bang. Bang.

Corrado strode past his bedroom, following the sound, and froze in the doorway to the guest room.

Maura's room.

Maura lay on her stomach, her body pressed into the bed, head roughly forced to the side with a thick, calloused hand wrapped around her neck. Pascal's sweaty, heaving body covered her frail form, each thrust slamming the headboard into the wall.

Bang. Bang. Bang.

Tears coated Maura's face, strangled cries on her lips dulled to a whimper by the hand choking her. Pascal whispered something in her ear, something Corrado couldn't hear, but the words fueled the girl's tears. Her eyes met Corrado's in the doorway, the emerald green diluted by terror.

Bang. Bang. Bang.

Corrado snapped.

He was in the room, ripping Pascal off of Maura before the man even realized anyone was there. Corrado threw him against the wall, his fist pummeling him as Pascal shouted for him to stop.

The spineless begging only spurred Corrado on.

He ruthlessly beat Pascal until his screams were whines, his body huddling on the floor, bloody and battered. Maura shrieked, terrified, so loud it made Corrado's ears ring, but he hardly registered her through his fog. Corrado's hand throbbed, his knuckles bruising and swelling, as he reached into his coat and pulled out his gun. He pressed it to Pascal's temple.

"You can't kill me." Pascal spit blood on the floor. "I'm *made*."

Corrado stared at him, finger hovering on the trigger. "Bang."

Pascal flinched at the word.

Pushing himself up, Pascal staggered, half naked with blood streaming down his face. Corrado grabbed his arm and dragged him out of the room, shoving him down the stairs. Opening the front door, he forced Pascal outside into the bitter cold before turning to the others as they gathered in the foyer.

Raising his gun, he aimed it at Alex. "Did you touch her?"

His eyes flashed with fear.

It was the only answer Corrado needed.

He moved on to Michael. "Did *you*?"

Michael threw his hands up. "I didn't, I swear!"

Corrado eyed him skeptically. "I don't believe you."

"I didn't!" Michael yelled. "Ask Katrina!"

He glanced at his sister but asking was pointless. "She lies."

"I didn't," Michael swore, pointing at Alex to deflect the attention. "He did, though!"

"Shut the fuck up!" Alex hissed.

"He was first," Michael said. "It was his idea!"

"You dumb fuck!" Alex spat. "You were gonna do her, too! As soon as your girl passed out."

"I wasn't! I swear!" Michael seemed even more terrified now as he looked at Katrina. "I *wouldn't.*"

Out of the three, Michael was the only one not made—the only one Corrado could get away with killing—but even that pushed it. He was the son of a made man. Corrado glared between the men, bitter about that fact. It wasn't the first time he had found Michael in this situation, wrapped up in something but somehow managing to remain guiltless. *Coward.*

"Relax, Corrado," Katrina muttered. "You're overreacting."

"Get out," he demanded. "All of you. Get out of my house and *never* come back."

Alex didn't have to be told twice. He darted outside, cursing. Corrado turned toward the doorway to ensure he was gone and spotted the red and blue lights flashing along the curb. He lowered the gun, quickly slipping it back into his coat as a pair of officers approached the house. One stopped beside the porch, gazing down at Pascal sitting in the snow, shirtless, pants still unzipped, while the other stepped into the open door.

"We got a call of a disturbance here," the officer said, eyeing him curiously, his gaze lingering on his battered hand. He glanced behind him at Pascal before turning to Corrado again. "What's your name?"

He said nothing.

"Corrado Moretti," Katrina chimed in, arms crossed over her chest.

"Ah," the officer said. "Moretti."

It didn't take a genius to know what would happen next. The second the officer reached for his handcuffs, Corrado knew he was in trouble.

Serious trouble.

"You're under arrest for assault," he said, forcing Corrado's hands behind his back, securing the handcuffs around his wrists as he read him his rights.

"I want them out of my house," Corrado demanded, glaring at his sister and Michael.

"You're not in any position to be making demands," the

officer scoffed, patting Corrado down, whipping the gun out from his coat. "Whoa, score!"

"This is all just a big misunderstanding," Pascal called from outside, climbing to his feet. Red-tinted snow clung to his pants. "Moretti and I just had a little fight, man-to-man. No big deal."

The officer pocketed the gun. "You're wrong. This is a big deal."

"Corrado? Oh, God! Corrado!"

Corrado's stomach dropped when he heard Celia's voice calling out for him. Could this get any worse? He glanced around in the darkness, watching her hasty approach from down the street. The second officer tried to stop her, stepping in her path, but she dodged around him, slipping on a patch of ice, frantic to reach him.

"Celia, go inside," Corrado said as the officer dragged him toward the idling cruiser. "Go there, and stay there."

"But what about you?" she asked. "Do I need to come down to the station?"

"Don't worry about me," he said. " I need you to stay here. It's important."

She didn't understand, but he wouldn't explain it. He *couldn't.* She'd find out soon enough… as soon as she walked in the house and found the petrified girl upstairs.

The officer opened the door to the squad car and tried to force him inside, but he resisted, still watching his wife. "Make them leave, Celia. I don't want them in my house."

He couldn't delay it anymore without adding a resisting arrest charge. The officer shoved him into the car and slammed the door.

One count simple assault.
One count unlawful possession of a weapon.

Both misdemeanors.

Corrado was booked into the system, his bail automatically set for three thousand dollars. No sooner he changed into the grungy orange jail jumpsuit, a correctional officer led him right back to booking.

"Must be your lucky day. Someone already posted your bail."

"I haven't even called anyone yet."

"Guess whoever it is knew how much it would be."

He was processed right back out, in less than an hour walking through the front doors, temporarily a free man. He froze when he stepped out into the cold parking lot, being greeted by the battered smiling face of Pascal. A cigarette hung from the corner of his mouth. He hadn't even bothered to wash off any of the blood.

"You?" Corrado asked incredulously.

Pascal shrugged. "You shouldn't have been arrested."

Corrado just glared at him.

"Like I told the cop, no big deal." Pascal took a deep drag from his cigarette before tossing it into a snowdrift. "We good?"

He offered no response. No, they weren't good.

"Okay, well, don't worry about paying me back," Pascal continued, shrugging off Corrado's silence as he walked away. "We'll chalk it up to your share from today's job."

No car. No ride. Not enough money on him to call a cab.

He didn't even know where to find a payphone.

Corrado was screwed.

He walked a mile in the cold to the closest bus stop before realizing public transit was suspended due to the weather. Frustrated, he sat down on the icy bench, wetness seeping through his clothes as he ran his hands down his face in frustration.

Closing his eyes, he dropped his head low and pulled his jacket tighter around him, grimacing at the stench still clinging to his clothes. He hadn't even showered yet. Home was over ten miles away.

A car pulled up as he sat there. His eyes opened when he heard the rumble of the engine, seeing the brown Ford coming to a stop right in front of him. The window rolled down, Detective Walker staring at him from the driver's seat. "Didn't take you for the bus type."

Corrado stared at the front fender of the car, not giving the man the satisfaction of a response.

"It isn't coming," the detective said. "But if you need a ride…"

Corrado's eyes drifted to the man then. "I'd rather walk than get in a car with you again."

"That'll be a rather long walk, Mr. Moretti."

"I suppose it will be," he said, standing and brushing snow from his clothes. "I ought to get started."

He walked away, shoving his hands in his pockets, refusing to respond when the detective shouted his name.

Five hours.

It took Corrado five hours, trudging through snow and slipping on ice, to make it home. His legs were numb, his feet aching. Every inch of his body felt frozen, pins and needles viciously rippling across his flushed skin as he shook, shivering, teeth chattering. He couldn't feel his fingers. They were like spikes—strands of ice that nearly snapped when he dared to make a fist to pound on the front door.

The house was locked. He had no key.

He was about to give up—about to kick in his own door—when he heard movement inside. The locks clicked, the chain jingling, before the front door yanked open. Celia stood there, her blue robe tightly wrapped around her, a scowl on her face.

Corrado wasted no time with a greeting, stepping into the house and going straight for the living room… into the warmth. He shivered again as the heat from the fireplace wafted across his skin, the bitter cold not wanting to loosen its grip on him.

Celia shut the door and joined him, lingering by the doorway. "I want to know what happened."

He shrugged off his coat, tossing it on the coffee table beside the vase of flowers. The red roses were drooping, brown around the edges. His eyes locked on them as a thought passed through his mind: he owed her a lot flowers for the man he killed in the barbershop basement.

"The girl didn't tell you?"

"She told me what she could between sobs," Celia said. "She told me those men *raped* her."

"They did," he replied. "That's what happened."

The flames from the fireplace cast ominous shadows around Celia's face as something flared in her eyes—rage. "Where the hell were you when this was happening?"

"Working."

"Working? Running errands, right? That's what you're always doing, Corrado. Always *working*."

"It's true."

"It's *bullshit*." Celia pointed at him as she took a few steps his way. He had never seen her quite so mad before, her body slinking like a panther, wanting to strike. "I want to know what you did today… what was so damn important that you left that girl here unprotected around those monsters!"

"They work for your father," Corrado reminded her. "They're just like me."

"Don't do that," she spat. "Don't try that old 'I'm a monster, too' bit again to try to distract me. I asked you a question, and I want an answer. You couldn't even go to church with me. So what did you do that was *so* important you had to leave her defenseless on top of it?"

"Work."

She closed the distance between them. "Not good enough!"

He shook his head. "You don't want to know."

"I *do* want to know," she said. "I want an answer."

"No, you don't."

Her eyes narrowed as she jabbed him in the chest. "What the hell did you do today?"

He snatched a hold of her hand before she jabbed him again. Her fingers hardly hurt, but it aggravated him when she did it. "I'm warning you. Don't ask me that."

"I already asked," she sneered, grounding out every word like a venomous curse.

"Fine, you want to know what I did?" He pulled her closer to him, his voice dangerously low as he stared her in the eyes. "I spent all night running errands for your father. Yes, *running errands*. And when I came home there were people in my house… people *your* brother let in. I wanted to go to bed, I would've even rather gone to church, but I couldn't. Instead, I had to do my father's work. Yes, *work*. It's what I do."

His words came out as a growl as he pinned her there, clutching her wrist, feeling her pulse frantically racing beneath his fingertips.

"I cashed out a gambling tournament, robbing men of their life savings because they were stupid enough to play one of our games. And then, because your brother let those *monsters* in my house, I had to hijack a lobster truck. A *lobster* truck, Celia. If you ever try to cook seafood in this house again after what I went through today, I swear to God, I'll lose it. And to top it all off, I watched two men take their last breaths… not one, *two*. One was executed because he couldn't follow a simple order, but the other…"

He shook his head, pausing, still staring at her. "I watched your father beat him half to death before I put him out of his misery, and all for something he didn't do. I killed him for a murder he didn't commit, and I *know* he didn't commit it, because *I* did, Celia. I did it. So *that's* what I did today. *That's* why I wasn't here. And the worst part… the part that's pissing me off most right now… is that I haven't been able to take a shower. I *stink*." He let go of her. "Is *that* a good enough answer?"

Celia took an immediate step back and clutched her wrist, blinking a few times. Her jaw hung slack, and while she said not a word, Corrado knew everything she wanted to say. It was there, plain as day in her expression—she finally saw the man he warned her about.

And those eyes—those warm brown eyes, always so welcoming, always full of compassion—glimmered with alarm.

He had to look away.

"Don't ask questions," he said quietly, sitting down on the couch as he ran his hands down his face. "For both of our sakes, don't do it anymore."

27

The steps creaked beneath Corrado's bare feet as he headed downstairs, drops of water hitting the wood as they dripped from his damp hair, streaming down the ridges of his exposed back. His skin itched, spattered red in patches from the singeing water.

His fourth scalding shower in twelve hours.

He smelled nothing except the stark, clean scent of soap, no trace of yesterday leftover, but he still felt filthy. Sleep had been evasive as he lay in his bed alone, staring up at the bland white ceiling and listening to the crying in the next room over. He heard his wife's soft voice, her soothing words not meant for him.

No, she had nothing to say to him. Celia had made that clear when she marched out of the living room without uttering a single word about what he had said.

He understood her anger. He took on her fear. He even endured her sadness. He would survive whatever she threw at him, but her silence was too much. He couldn't handle being shut out.

Stepping into the foyer, he unlocked the front door and opened it, finding his newspaper wrapped in plastic on the front porch. He carried it inside, shaking the snow off before slipping it from the packaging. His feet hit the stairs again as he headed back up, but he'd only made it two steps when the door behind him flew open. His head swung around when it slammed, his heart racing, on alert. He wasn't even wearing a shirt, much less carrying a gun.

Not that he even had a gun… the police had confiscated his.

No sooner he'd turned, someone knocked into him as they

stormed past him up the stairs. *Vincent.* Corrado reached out, grabbing the back of Vincent's coat to stop him, but the boy merely slipped his arms out of it with an irate groan, letting him tear it off as he kept on going.

Furious, Corrado followed, reaching him as he opened Maura's bedroom door and burst inside, breathing heavily. Maura's soft cries morphed to full-blown sobs when she spotted Vincent.

Vincent's footsteps faltered as he blinked rapidly.

"You have some nerve," Corrado growled, grabbing Vincent's arm. He was about to yank him back out when Celia got between them, shoving Corrado into the hallway.

She stood in the doorway, eyes narrowed. "Don't."

Corrado watched Vincent climb up on the bed with Maura before his attention drifted to his wife. "You're speaking to me now?"

"Don't," she said again.

"She's traumatized enough," Corrado said. "She doesn't need Vincent bothering her on top of it."

Celia shook her head, glancing back at her brother as he held Maura, stroking her untidy red hair. She turned back to Corrado, a fierce determination in her eyes as she pushed against him, knocking him back a few steps, and shut the bedroom door to give them some privacy. Her body blocked it protectively. "You know, Corrado Moretti… for being such a sharp man, you sure can be a *fool* sometimes."

He blanched. "Excuse me?"

"I've told you before—he's not bothering her," Celia continued. "He loves her, and she loves him. They're in love. The only one who seems to be bothered here is *you*!"

"That's absurd," he said. "They hardly know each other."

Her eyebrows rose in challenge. "Absurd? Tell me… when did you fall in love with me? Because I loved you the first time I heard your voice, and I don't think *that's* absurd."

"This isn't about us."

"Exactly. This is about them, so why are you making it about you?"

"I'm not. But she's—"

"But she's what? A slave? What, he can't love a slave?"

"I was going to say she's Irish."

"Oh, who gives a crap?"

"Your parents."

"Screw my parents. My father didn't want us together, either, but we sure didn't listen, did we? We can't help who we fall for, Corrado. Believe me. If we could, well…" She laughed bitterly, dropping her gaze, and he knew his words from last night were running through her mind, the sins he had divulged out of anger, things he never wanted her to hear. "Just… leave them alone. Please."

He closed his eyes as she resorted to pleading. "It won't end well, Celia."

"At least let them try," she said quietly. Corrado opened his eyes when she touched him. Her hand ran across his chest before grazing down the trail of hair to his stomach, her fingertips tracing his abs. "Don't they deserve happiness, too? Especially after what that girl has gone through? She grew up under Erika Moretti's roof, too, you know. You and her aren't that different."

Corrado pulled her hand away from him when her fingertips grazed the band around his boxers. "We're nothing alike."

"You'd be surprised."

"Nothing will surprise me anymore. Your brother's in love with a—"

"Girl," Celia said, cutting him off. "He's in love with a girl who was hurt last night in the worst way, in ways even that wicked witch of a mother of yours could never hurt her."

"Wicked witch?"

"That's what Maura calls her."

"She talks to you about that stuff?"

"Yeah. She talks a lot."

"She doesn't talk to me. She won't even come near me."

"You terrify her."

"I seem to have that effect on everybody."

Not me. Corrado stared at his wife, wishing she would say those words, wishing she would rebuke him, but she merely frowned, her eyes drifting toward his stomach.

"Come on," she said softly, tugging his hand as she stepped away from Maura's door. "Let's do something about your dry skin."

He didn't resist, letting her pull him into their bedroom. He plopped down on the bed, utterly exhausted, and stared up at the ceiling as Celia grabbed a bottle of lotion and squirted some onto his chest. His eyes drifted closed when she rubbed it in.

He didn't even protest the sickly sweet smell.

"How do you know he loves her?" Corrado asked after awhile. "How do you know it isn't rebellion?"

"I just do."

A door down the hallway opened and Corrado opened his eyes, sitting up when Vincent stepped into their room.

"She fell asleep," he said quietly, his voice cracking.

Celia patted the bed beside her. Vincent didn't hesitate. He walked over and plopped down beside his sister as he ran his hands through his hair. He dropped his head down low, gripping his hair tightly, as Celia rubbed his back.

"How could this happen?" Vincent asked, the words strained, spoken to nobody in particular. "She didn't deserve this."

"I know," Celia whispered. "It's gonna be okay."

The moment she said it, Vincent's body shook with sobs. He cried inconsolably, letting his sister pull him into her arms. She smoothed his hair, glancing overtop of his head at Corrado, that *'I told you so'* look in her eyes.

Corrado stood, uncomfortable with the emotional outburst, feeling like he was imposing. He nodded at Celia, acknowledging that, before he walked out.

28

The Mercedes roared to life, rumbling along the curb. Corrado flipped on the defroster, cranking it the whole way. He lounged back in the driver's seat, watching as the windshield slowly thawed, the layer of thin ice melting away, clearing his view of Felton Drive.

He glanced at his watch. He had an hour to get to Evanston to meet the Boss. He would be early today.

Putting the car in gear, his glove-clad hands gripped the steering wheel as he pulled away from the curb. He made sure the road was clear before swinging the car around to go the other direction. His attention on the road wavered as he fiddled with the heater, his breath still coming out as a fog, the temperature below freezing.

Christmas Eve. It was supposed to snow again.

He clicked on the radio, smiling to himself as Frank Sinatra crooned from the speakers. He turned it all the way up and glanced back out of the windshield. He approached an intersection, prepared to speed right through it, when cars came flying out in front of him. Corrado slammed his brakes, the Mercedes skidding and nearly hitting a parked car as it came to a stop sideways in the middle of the street. Red and blue lights flashed all around, reflecting off the rearview mirror as police cars descended upon him. In a blink the officers were out, surrounding him, guns drawn.

Heart racing, Corrado put the car in park and moved his foot off the brake. Slowly, he raised his hands in the air, to show he wasn't armed. No sooner his hands hit the roof, someone yanked his door open and snatched a hold of him, dragging him out of the car. He groaned when he slammed the ice-coated road on his stomach, his face scraping against the grainy asphalt. He felt the burn along his cheek when it tore the skin, a knee in his back as his arms were yanked behind his back. Handcuffs went on, digging into his wrists, before he was jerked to his feet by the metal chain linking his hands.

As soon as he was upright, his eyes met a familiar face. Detective Walker. "Corrado Moretti, you're under arrest for the murder of Miguel Pace."

Corrado's brow furrowed. "Who?"

This question had been genuine, out of surprise, but nobody clued him in. Instead, they read him his rights as they dragged him to the closest police cruiser, forcing him in the backseat. He laid his head against the cage in front of him, closing his eyes. He still heard the music rattling from his car speakers through the open door. *Miguel Pace.* Corrado tried to place the name.

Who the hell is Miguel Pace?

The question was answered when they took him to an interrogation room at the police station. Detective Walker sat down across from Corrado, another man beside him. Corrado had been released from the handcuffs and given a bandage for the scrape on his cheek, but he tossed it on the table, ignoring the injury.

"Miguel Pace," Detective Walker said, sliding a gruesome photograph across the table to Corrado. *Barbershop basement guy.* "Look familiar?"

"Hard to say," Corrado said. "I can't make out his face."

"That's because someone beat him with a baseball bat." The detective laid out some other crime scene photos, including a picture of the bat Antonio had discarded on the basement floor. "And that was before they put a bullet in his head. What do you have to say about that?"

"I'd say somebody wanted him dead."

"You?" the detective asked. "Did you want him dead?"

"I have no reason to want him dead. I'm not even sure who he is."

"He's Miguel Pace," the detective stressed before launching

into a biography about the man's life, making him sound like a picture-perfect citizen, but Corrado knew a faultless man would never even cross Antonio's path, much less be tied up in a basement by him.

"Why am I here?" Corrado asked, interrupting the detective. "What makes you think *I* did this?"

"Ah, the million dollar question." The detective sorted through a stack of papers before pulling out another photograph and setting it on top of the others. Corrado stared at it, recognizing his revolver. "Now does *this* look familiar?"

Corrado didn't answer that.

"It should," he said. "It was taken off your person by one of our officers the same night Miguel Pace was murdered. We processed the gun, just routine testing, and I'm sure you can guess what we found."

The detective stared at him, as if he actually expected Corrado to guess.

"We found blood splatter on it consistent with Miguel's blood type," he replied. "A ballistics test confirmed the bullet found in Miguel was consistent with the test-fire from this gun."

"That's a lot of consistency I hear," Corrado said. "And not a lot of certainty."

The detective glared at him. "Cut the shit, Mr. Moretti."

"I'd like to speak to a lawyer now. I don't appreciate profanity."

The detective stood, shoving his chair back roughly, and slammed his hands down on the stack of photos. "What, murder doesn't seem to fucking bother you, but foul language does?"

Corrado stared at the man, refusing to react.

One count of first-degree murder

Half a day had passed by the time Corrado was issued a jumpsuit. The heavy orange material hung from his body, scratchy against his skin. He was led to a phone and grabbed the receiver, ignoring the corrections officer as he tried to instruct him. He knew the deal. He had been here before.

He dialed the number from memory and leaned against the wall beside the phone, blocking his mouth for some privacy. It rang, and rang, and rang some more, before the curt female voice answered. "DeMarco residence."

"Gia," Corrado said politely. "Can I speak with Antonio?"

She laughed dryly. "You sure you want to? He's been on it for the past few hours. You must've done something wrong."

Corrado missed an appointment with the Boss. There wasn't much worse than that. "The sooner I speak with him, the better."

"Yeah, sure," she said. "Hold on."

A minute of rustling, of muffled arguing passed, before the phone was picked back up, Antonio's gruff voice on the line. He launched right into it, not even giving Corrado a chance to explain. "I told you to be at Rita's at 8 o'clock. I told you it was important. I don't fucking say these things for my health. I say them because I mean them."

"I know, sir."

"Then why weren't you there? I don't even get the courtesy of a call? I don't get a note? Nothing? You just leave me high and dry?"

He ranted on and on, his voice so loud Corrado was sure everyone around heard. He remained quiet, absorbing the Boss's anger, but after four minutes had passed he knew he couldn't take any more. The phone would cut off soon. "Sir."

Antonio stalled mid-sentence. "You have the audacity to interrupt me now?"

"I'm sorry, sir, but—"

"And now you're apologizing? You're just pissing me off more and more. You know what? I'm done with this conversation. I expect you at my house in ten minutes so we can discuss what we're going to do about this."

"I can't."

"You can't?"

"No, sir, I can't." He took a deep breath. "I'm tied up."

"With *what*?"

His eyes drifted toward the corrections officer, waiting to

escort him to a cell. "Handcuffs, momentarily."

There was a long pause. "You're in jail?"

"Yes."

"And you called me? You know these calls are monitored, and you fucking call my house? And you don't even warn me I'm being recorded?"

"I just wanted to tell you I wouldn't be at the meeting."

"I got that, Moretti. I got it when you didn't show up!"

He pushed away from the wall. "It'll never happen again."

"It better not. And don't ever call me from that place."

A second before the voice came on informing Corrado that time was over, Antonio ended the call.

Bail was set at half a million dollars.

Corrado remained in jail as Christmas passed, December slowly fading away. He lay in the bottom bunk of his cell, staring at the bed above him night after night, exhausted and irritated. He kept mulling over every word the detective had said to him. How would he get out of this?

New Years Eve rolled around when a corrections officer came to get him from his cell. "You're being released, Moretti."

Corrado sat up in the bed. "Someone bailed me out?"

"So it seems."

Half a million dollars… who would put up *that* much money?

He was processed out of the system and given his clothes back. After haphazardly dressing and collecting his things, he stepped into the lobby of the jail to find his wife sitting in one of the hard plastic chairs by the window, gazing out into the parking lot. Sighing, he strolled toward her as her eyes drifted his way, a frown tainting her soft face. "*Bellissima.*"

There was always a brief moment whenever Corrado came face-to-face with his wife after being away that it felt like he was seeing her for the first time all over again.

His chest tightened, and the air was suddenly thick, making it impossible to breathe. He was suspended in time, nothing existing except for them. There was no anger or hatred, no violence, no pain. No worry about the future or what would happen tomorrow. It was only then and there, and it was only *them*.

His heart stalled then, when their eyes connected, before pounding so hard that he felt the blood surging under his skin. He grew dizzy, his vision blurring from the intensity as his body flushed. He worried for a split second that he was going to pass out, every ounce of strength and resolve he fought so hard to maintain disintegrating. He was weak, vulnerable, with his chest cracked open, leaving him completely exposed.

All because of her.

It hurt, more than he ever expected such a thing to hurt. It felt like his body was giving out. Rebelling. Revolting. Like he was dying.

He never felt more *alive*.

But it was only for a moment. A simple moment where, for once, he felt normal, like maybe the world wasn't so horrible.

Pity it couldn't last.

Celia stood slowly, smoothing her dress, her expression unreadable. Without uttering a word, she walked away. Corrado followed, shoving his hands in his pockets as the cold air gnawed at his skin. He saw every single exhale from his wife's lips, the cloud of shaky breath speaking enough for her as she marched toward her father's DeVille in the parking lot.

He stopped in front of the vehicle. "You didn't drive my car?"

"It was impounded."

"You didn't get it out?"

Her eyebrows rose. "I was too busy trying to get *you* out."

"How did you?" he asked. "We don't have that kind of cash just laying around."

"I borrowed it."

"From where?"

She avoided his eyes, hesitating. His suspicion skyrocketed.

"Celia," he growled. "Tell me you did *not* go to a loan shark."

"What else was I supposed to do?"

"Get a loan from a *bank*."

"With what credit?" she asked. "I don't even have a job. I have *nothing* in my name. I couldn't even get a bondsman to work with me because of it!"

"Then you should've left me in there."

"I refuse," she said, narrowing her eyes as she pointed at him. "You belong at home, with me. I'm not leaving you to rot in some stinking jail cell when I can do something about it."

A rush of anger surged through Corrado, but he clenched his hands into fists, forcing it back. He wouldn't yell at her. This was his fault, not hers. "What were the terms?"

"Five points a week," she replied. "For five-hundred thousand."

He stared at her as he did the math in his head. Five percent interest was an extra $25,000 a week. "Who did you get it from?"

"It doesn't matter."

"Answer me," he demanded. "Who gave you those terms?"

"Pascal Barone."

That was the last name he had expected to hear. "You asked him for money? *Him*?"

"Nobody else had that much on hand."

Corrado's voice came out with broken, ragged breaths. "You know better than this, Celia. There's no way I can pay that much back anytime soon. I'm in his debt now."

"No, you're not," she said. "*I* am."

She climbed in the car, slamming the door, and started the engine. She sat there, clutching the steering wheel, glaring at him through the windshield. Corrado shook his head as he climbed into the passenger seat, not saying a word as she drove to her parent's house. The mansion on Felton Drive was lit up, surrounded by dozens of cars, as music and loud voices rattled the windows.

New Years Eve.

"I'd rather go home," Corrado said, staring at the house.

"Yeah, me, too," Celia grumbled. "Too bad we can't."

She got out, slamming the door again, and headed for the house without him. Corrado once again followed, blindly tying his tie in the darkness, attempting to pull himself together to face the Boss.

Once Celia stepped into the house, her expression shifted, a forced smile straining her lips. She greeted people, offering hugs and handshakes, as Corrado trailed behind, reaching out to grasp her hip.

When they neared the den, Corrado glanced inside, seeing the Boss gathered with the usual made men. Pascal was present, puffing on a cigar, relaxed, not a care in the world.

Fire raged beneath Corrado's skin.

Antonio caught Corrado's eye. The man said something to those gathered around as he stood, carrying his glass of scotch. He walked out, merely casting Corrado a pointed glare, as he headed straight for his office.

Corrado pulled Celia closer to him and pressed a soft kiss on her forehead before letting go. Concern shined from her eyes, but she said nothing as he followed her father.

Corrado stepped into the office behind Antonio and shut the door as the man took his seat behind his desk. He opened a drawer and pulled out a cigar, clipping the end and lighting it.

"So, murder, huh?" Antonio said casually, his voice betraying his hard expression. "Do they have any evidence?"

"They have the gun."

"How'd they get it?"

"It was on me the night it happened," he said, "when I was arrested."

"Ah, I heard about that," Antonio said. "You assaulted a made man. Why was that?"

"He's a rapist."

Antonio stared at him blankly. Unaffected. "He's also a murderer and a thief, but you don't see me beating him up for it, do you?"

"If he did it in your home, yes, I think you would."

"Do you?" Antonio asked. "Do you *think* so, Moretti?"

"Yes, sir."

"You think you know me?"

"Yes, sir."

"Then tell me... what am I thinking now?" he asked, sitting forward. "What do I want to do now?"

He hesitated. "I don't know."

"Well, I'll tell you," Antonio said. "I'm thinking about how I'd like nothing more than to skin you alive, how I want to cut your balls off and shove them down your fucking throat for fooling me."

Corrado blanched. *Fooling him*?

"I gave you my blessing to marry my daughter under the assumption that you wouldn't ever leave her. And here you are, facing twenty to life for murder because you let your pesky little feelings cloud your judgment, and you got careless. I don't like careless, Corrado. I don't let careless in my family. I'd rather my daughter be a widow at nineteen than spend her days with a *jamook*. And right now, that's how you look, fighting a made man like you're the fucking morality police."

Corrado remained silent. The Boss hadn't asked a question, so he wasn't going to speak.

"Sit down." Antonio waved at the empty chair. "I want to ask you something."

Corrado carefully sat down.

"What do you think about my son?"

That wasn't the question Corrado expected. "Vincent?"

"Yes, Vincenzo," Antonio said. "He *is* my only son."

Something about the way he said that made Corrado bristle defensively. "He's a good kid."

"A good kid," Antonio repeated, his lips twisting contemplatively as he puffed his cigar. "He concerns me more than my daughter, and she's the one always finding trouble. That girl got detention in school, broke curfew, talked back to me, fell in love with *you*..." He let out a dry laugh. "My son, though. He worries me. I asked him the other day, I said, 'Vincenzo, what do you want to do with your life?' And you know what he said?"

"What?"

"Be a doctor." Antonio shook his head. "He wants to go to medical school."

"That's honorable."

"What did *you* want to do?"

"I'm doing it."

"Before you knew about the life?"

"I wanted to be like my father, so I guess I wanted to do it before I even knew what it was."

"Now *that*, to me, is honorable," Antonio said. "That's how I was. I followed in my father's footsteps, too. So what's wrong with me? What's wrong with *my* footsteps to make my boy want to go to medical school instead?"

Corrado had no answer. He scarcely understood Vincent.

Antonio put out his cigar and downed the rest of his scotch in one large gulp. "Go thank Pascal for saving your ass again, since he funded your release, and then you're free to do what you want with your night."

"Yes, sir."

He stood to leave, heading straight for the den. Pouring himself a drink, he threw it back, letting the burn soothe his nerves, before approaching Pascal. "I appreciate you helping my wife."

Pascal glanced at him. "I know you're good for it."

Corrado extended his hand to shake Pascal's. He let go just as Vito walked over to him, throwing an arm over his shoulder, forcing another glass of scotch on Corrado.

"Murder in the first," Vito said. "I'm not sure if I wanna laugh or lecture you, so I'll just have a drink with you instead."

Corrado took the glass, clinking it to his father's, before downing the bitter, golden liquid. Shuddering, he set the glass down. He hardly felt like celebrating tonight. "If you'll excuse me, I haven't spent any time with my wife in days, and well..."

Vito waved him away. "Don't let me hold you up. You take care of your business, kid."

Corrado strode away, mingling through the crowd as he searched for Celia. He found Vincent sitting out back alone, drinking from a glass. Vincent grimaced, shivering with disgust as he took a swallow. *Alcohol.*

"I'm not twenty-one yet," Corrado said, "so I *know* you're not."

Vincent's back stiffened. "I saw you drinking."

"True." Hesitating, Corrado sat down on the step beside the boy. "I figured someone who wanted to be a doctor would be more law-abiding."

Vincent laughed dryly. "I see you've been talking to my dad."

"Yes."

"You going to mock me, too?"

"No," he said. "I don't believe your father mocked you either."

"He was offended," Vincent said. "Like I'm not allowed to have my own life."

"He just can't understand you."

"He doesn't even *try*."

"Antonio's a good man," Corrado said. "You're fortunate to have him as a father."

"You're only saying that because he's not your dad."

"Look, maybe you don't want to be like him, but you should appreciate having a father who cares what kind of man you'll be."

"He thinks being a doctor is stupid."

"No, he doesn't. He just can't stand you thinking *he* is." Corrado stood back up. "You seen your sister?"

"She's upstairs." Corrado started to walk away when Vincent spoke again. "You're not gonna tell on me for drinking, are you?"

"I'm not a rat, Vincent. Never have been, never will be."

Corrado headed upstairs, wandering down the quiet hall to the old bedroom Celia used to occupy. She sat on the end of the bed in the room, staring at nothing in the darkness. He faltered in the doorway, taking in the sight of her frown, her shoulders slumped. "You're angry at me."

Celia's eyes drifted to him as he approached. "I'm not."

"Then what's wrong?"

"I'm scared."

He stopped right in front of her and brushed some wayward hair from her face before grasping her chin and tilting her head up. Genuine fear glistened in her dark eyes. It made his chest tighten. "Don't be."

She grasped his hand. "I can't lose you, Corrado."

"You won't."

She didn't believe him. It was written all over her face.

"I love you," he said. "I'll do whatever it takes to make this go away."

29

Whatever it takes.

The beginning of 1982 found Corrado doing just that.

Every waking minute was spent working, doing every job imaginable for a bit of extra cash. Hundreds of thousands poured in every month but went back out as fast as he made it. He passed money along to the organization in exchange for help from connections. He hired the best criminal defense team in the city, financed lab work from the smartest scientists, paid the most respected expert witnesses to stand in his corner, hoping to discredit the prosecution and make the murder case go away. The assault charge from the fight had been dropped when Pascal refused to cooperate, so the lawyers argued his arrest was unfounded, therefore anything found on him that night had been seized illegally. But given he had no permit to carry a weapon, the evidence stuck.

When going legit didn't help, he called in favors, making deals in the dark as his wife slept soundly beside him. So peaceful, so trusting… he had told her she wouldn't lose him, and he was determined to make it so.

The trial started in early spring of that year. As soon as the jury was seated, Corrado calculated how to sway the verdict in his favor. The trial flew by, deliberations taking longer than the testimony. Every day that passed, every hour that dragged by, every tick of the clock found him more on edge. Celia paced the house, bordering on tears every time the phone rang or someone knocked on the door.

A week later, the jury deadlocked. A mistrial.

The prosecution immediately filed to retry him, the process starting all over again. He worked even harder this time around, hemorrhaging money, the trial slowly bleeding him dry. He could barely afford to make the interest payments to Pascal, much less pay off the loan. Every week that passed, every dollar he shelled out, found him just as much in the man's debt as before. Pascal knew it, too, and continually took it upon himself to call all hours of the night for menial jobs.

Corrado's resentment grew. He would stand in Pascal's living room, glaring at the man as he lounged on the couch, his arm draped over the shoulder of a young girl—a new one every time. Pascal would fondle her, make her go down on him as they discussed business, and Corrado—the good little soldier he knew he needed to be—would stare him square in the eye as it happened, unflinching. He waited him out, let him push him around, swearing one day he would see justice. As soon as he earned his place in the organization, as soon as Antonio *made* him, his first order of business would be formally requesting he be allowed to blow the cockroach's brains out. *Soon.*

The second trial, like the first, fizzled out with a hung jury.

"Well?" the judge said. "How does the prosecution plan to proceed?"

The district attorney conferred with his associates, heated whispers swaddling the courtroom. Corrado spotted Detective Walker in the gallery, glaring at him. A smile threatened to tug Corrado's lips as he nodded in greeting, only looking away when the DA stood up to speak.

"Your honor, the prosecution isn't prepared to make a decision at this time. We're going to need some time to assess whether or not to retry the defendant."

"Think long and hard," the judge said, his voice with an edge of aggravation. "Because if this happens again, I'm in the right mind to grant a full dismissal. This has gone on long enough."

Corrado stared at the judge when he banged his gavel. The judge, mid-sixties with graying hair and drooping eyes, leaned back in his chair and ran his hands down his face in exhaustion. He was clearly fed up with his job, out of patience and bordering losing respect for the process.

Maybe I shouldn't have bothered with the jury. Maybe I should've gone after the judge instead.

The Omen.

Corrado stood in the doorway to the living room, staring at the glowing television as the movie played. He watched, transfixed, only vaguely aware of the quiet murmuring from the couch nearby. It was the middle of the night—midnight, maybe one o'clock—and he had just got home from collecting money for his father.

"Sweet, huh?"

Celia wrapped her arms around Corrado, laying her head against his chest. Corrado hugged her, his eyes remaining on the television.

"It's a horror film," Corrado said. "Most people find that scary."

"I'm not talking about the movie. I meant *them*."

Corrado glanced down at his wife, following her gaze over to where Vincent and Maura sat together, whispering in the darkness. Vincent's arm was draped over her shoulder as she snuggled against him. "They're hogging my couch and not even watching the movie."

"You're such a hopeless romantic, Corrado Moretti," she deadpanned. "It's amazing more women don't swoon over you."

He shrugged a shoulder as his gaze shifted back to the television. The nanny stood on the ledge at the birthday party. Celia shifted around in Corrado's arms, glancing at the television when the woman jumped.

Celia gasped, her body tensing. Horror rocked the characters on the screen before shifting to a close up of the little boy's passive, unaffected face. "What the hell's wrong with him?"

Corrado pulled her closer to him. "Maybe he's a Moretti."

"I'm serious."

"So am I," Corrado muttered, moving her hair aside to kiss near her ear. "I'm pretty sure he's supposed to be the anti-Christ."

"That little boy?" Celia shuddered. "He's awfully cute to be evil."

"That's supposed to be what makes it so terrifying."

"Supposed to be?" Celia asked. "Come on, that kid doesn't scare you?"

Corrado couldn't restrain his amusement at her sincere question. She honestly thought he might be scared. "No more than every other kid does."

Celia jabbed him in the ribs as he chuckled. He laid his head on top of hers and closed his eyes as he inhaled, breathing in the scent of her perfume.

"You'd make a good father, you know," she said, the words barely audible as she whispered them into his chest. He opened his eyes, still holding her there, but didn't respond.

What could he say?

Soft giggles sounded out from the couch as Corrado turned his attention back to the television. Celia, realizing he wasn't going to respond, loosened from his hold. "Do you think they'll be okay together?"

"I think the anti-Christ plans to kill them."

Celia laughed. "Again, not about the movie."

Corrado pulled Celia away from the living room, into the hallway, out of earshot of Maura and Vincent. They hadn't been paying them any attention, too wrapped up in their own little world on the couch, but he didn't want to take a chance of them overhearing what he had to say.

"Well?" Celia asked, hands on her hips.

"She knows too much."

"What do you mean?"

"Exactly what I said—she knows too much. She's seen too much, been around for too long."

Confusion lined Celia's eyes. "What?"

"They won't forget that."

"Who?"

"The people who make sure we keep our mouths shut."

"Huh?"

He shook his head. "Don't make me spell it out for you, Celia."

She stared at him, confusion melting away. "Are you suggesting the Mafia won't let her have a life because she knows some of their secrets?"

"That's what I said."

"That's *not* what you said," she declared. "You were talking in riddles like this is some game, when it's not."

"I know it's not," he replied. "But it's also none of our concern."

"None of our concern?" She scoffed. "She lives with us! I can let her go free if I want, and maybe I want to, okay? Who's going to stop me?"

He admired her determination, even if it were gravely naïve. "You're playing with fire. Your father—"

"I can handle him," she said, matter-of-fact.

She was being absurd, but he said nothing. He had to let her fight her own battles.

Denying her would only make it worse.

The next afternoon, Corrado sat in the DeMarco den as Celia ranted and raved in front of her father. Antonio relaxed in his favorite chair, swirling a glass of scotch around, the ice clinking against the sides. His eyes focused intently on his daughter, emotionless, as he absorbed every word from her animated voice.

"And Maura's such a nice girl," Celia said, smiling brightly. "I've never met someone as sweet as her before. She's trustworthy, too. So just… *loyal.*"

She quieted, batting her eyelashes. Antonio stared at her for a moment before the loudest, most boisterous laughter burst from him. He slammed his glass down on the table beside him, spilling some of the liquor, as he waved her off, unable to contain himself.

Corrado's stomach twisted in knots for Celia.

Expression falling, Celia gaped at her father. "What's so funny?"

"You're talking about that slave girl. She's Irish, Celia. *Irish*!"

"So?"

Wrong thing to say. As soon as the word came out of her mouth, every ounce of amusement sucked out of the room. Antonio's laughter cut off like a needle ripped from a turntable, his eyes darkening. "Those people killed my parents… *your* grandparents. And you call her *loyal*?"

"She's not like them."

"They're all the same," Antonio said. "Every one of them."

"You're wrong," Celia said. "You don't know her."

"And I don't want to."

"But I like her," Celia argued. "She's my friend. Doesn't that matter at all?"

Antonio tapped his fingers against the arm of his chair. He stared at his daughter like he would stare at a stranger who walked into his home unwelcome. His voice was low when he spoke again, a bitter edge as he ground out the words. "You're spoiled, Celia Marie. I spoiled you, and based on the fact that Corrado let you come here, that he let you say all this to me, I'd say your husband spoils you, too."

Celia's eyes narrowed. "I don't need his permission. *Or* yours."

Antonio wasn't dissuaded by her declaration. "This here? This isn't happening. Whatever plans you're conceiving in your head stop now. You're my daughter, and I love you, but this isn't happening."

"But—"

"That's final."

He left no room for argument. Celia gaped at him before her face clouded with anger. She stormed out of the room, heading straight for the front door, slamming it behind her as she stomped outside. Corrado didn't move, remaining in his seat as Antonio's eye shifted to him. "You said that girl wouldn't be any trouble."

"I guess I underestimated your kids."

Corrado nodded at Antonio as he stood to leave. He barely made it to the doorway when the man spoke again. "*Kids*?"

Corrado's footsteps faltered.

"You said kids," Antonio said, stressing the 's' on the end. "What don't I know, Corrado?"

"What do you mean, sir?"

Antonio studied him for a moment before standing. "My office. Now."

Corrado's stomach sunk.

He slowly followed him into the office, begrudgingly shutting the door. Corrado could keep secrets from his father-in-law, could have a private life, could come and go as he pleased, but the Boss held his life in his hands.

"Sit down," Antonio ordered. "And tell me what you know."

Corrado carefully sat in the chair but said nothing. Antonio stared at him expectantly.

"This isn't the fucking police department," Antonio barked. "You don't have the right to remain silent with me."

He still said nothing.

Furious, Antonio stormed back across the room. Corrado tensed, half expecting the man to hit him, to physically force him to respond, but instead he flung open the door and stepped out into the hall.

"Vincenzo Roman!" he hollered, so loud Corrado grimaced. "Get down here, now!"

Antonio retook his seat, leaving the door wide-open. Minutes of strained silence passed before hesitant footsteps neared the office. Vincent appeared, faltering in the doorway, his gaze darting between his father and Corrado with alarm. "Yes?"

"Sit down," Antonio ordered, pointing at the chair Corrado sat in. He took that as his cue to get to his feet. Stepping aside, he lingered in the office, as Vincent shut the door and plopped down in the chair.

"Is something wrong?" Vincent asked.

"You tell me. Is there something I ought to know?"

Vincent slowly shook his head.

"Huh." Antonio feigned nonchalance as he grabbed a cigar. He didn't light it, instead rolling it between his fingers as he stared at his son. "You sure you don't want to talk about Maura?"

The color drained from Vincent's face as he swung around in the chair, wide eyes piercing through Corrado. "You *told*?"

Antonio slammed his hands down on his desk, drawing everyone's attention right back to him. "No, he didn't, but *you* just did. And you're going to tell me everything, Vincenzo."

Corrado's heart pounded rapidly. He didn't want to be there. It was none of his concern.

Vincent stammered, struggling for words. "I just... I like her. She's a nice girl."

"And she's loyal and trustworthy, right?" Antonio asked. "Sweetest person you've ever met?"

"Well... yes."

"She's *Irish*."

"So?"

Corrado cringed. Same thing Celia had said.

Antonio narrowed his eyes. "You're not to go near her ever again! I want you to stay away from that girl."

"That's not fair!"

"Get over it. It's time for you to grow up. You're not a child anymore!"

"Then stop treating me like one!" Vincent said. "Why do you keep trying to make me do what *you* want me to do? Why can't I do what *I* want to do?"

"Because I know what's best for you!"

"How can you? You don't even *know* me! You keep trying to turn me into you, but I'm not you! I don't care that she's Irish! I like her. No, I *love* her, okay?"

"You don't."

"I do!" Vincent said, jumping up from his chair. "I love her!"

"You're just saying that to spite me."

"You would think that," Vincent spat. "But it has nothing to do with you, Dad. I love her. *Her*. I don't care what you think. I don't even like you!"

"Take that back," Antonio spat, clenching his hands into fists, breaking the cigar in half.

"Fine," Vincent ground out. "I *hate* you, then."

Vincent stormed out, not waiting to be dismissed, his feet stomping down the hallway. Corrado stood still as Antonio stared at the empty doorway, a shell-shocked expression Corrado had never seen on his face before.

Heartbreak.

"He doesn't really hate you," Corrado said.

Antonio's expression shifted, the despair morphing straight to fury, while his eyes sought out Corrado as if just remembering he was there. "Did I ask for your opinion?"

Corrado squared his shoulders. No, he hadn't.

Throwing the broken cigar down on the desk, Antonio leaned back in his chair. "How do you know?"

"Because Celia said the same thing when you forbid us from being together."

"My daughter said she hated me?"

"Yes."

"Maybe she does."

"She doesn't," Corrado said. "She loves you. She respects you. She just doesn't agree with you."

"Or listen to me," Antonio muttered. "*Neither* of you listened to me. A lot of good forbidding you did. I control hundreds of men. They do what I want, when I want it. But my own fucking kids…"

"They're just like you," Corrado said. "You wouldn't let anyone stop you from having what you want, either."

"There you go, thinking you know me again." Antonio rolled the broken cigar around on his desk, deep in thought. "Get out of here, Corrado, before I decide to punish you for speaking out of turn again."

The first week of June, the District Attorney filed to retry Corrado for the murder of Miguel Pace. Corrado went through the motions again, blowing every cent he earned trying to ensure he would walk away a free man.

When the third jury was seated weeks later, he used his father's crew to bribe and intimidate as many of them as possible.

But he didn't stop there.

No, this time he got to the judge, too.

A week later, the third jury came back deadlocked. The judge declared a mistrial, banging his gavel as he spoke the words Corrado waited for: "Case is dismissed with prejudice."

He couldn't be tried again.

It took a few weeks, but the judge got a long-awaited appointment to Federal court… two days after Corrado's revolver was mysteriously returned to him.

30

"Here, kid, here's your take for the week."

Vito tossed an envelope at Corrado as he sat on top of one of the old casino tables in the basement hangout. Corrado caught it, opening the envelope as his father stuffed the rest of the gambling cash into the safe beneath the bar.

Corrado skimmed through the stack, flimsier than usual. "There's only twenty thousand here."

Vito shrugged. "Slow week."

Corrado had been running himself ragged for his father, hardly seeing his wife all week long. "I need the whole twenty-five."

"I need a lot of things, kid," Vito said. "You don't see me complaining."

Corrado shot his father a pointed look. "I owe Pascal that twenty-five. I'm supposed to drop it off tonight on my way home."

He barely made a dent in the loan, taking a few thousand off here and there, but the interest payments alone were bleeding him dry.

Vito flopped down in a chair. "Tough break."

Tough break. Shaking his head, Corrado stuffed the cash back into the envelope and stuck it in his pocket. He didn't bother saying goodbye as he strode out.

He drove to Pascal's, arriving in the middle of a party. The house was filled with people, music blasting, alcohol and smoke all around. He was ushered to the living room by someone from Pascal's crew. Pascal sat on the couch with two scantily clad girls snuggled up against him.

Corrado held the envelope out to him. Pascal pulled away from the girls and snatched a hold of it. "Kind of scarce this week."

"It's a bit short," he admitted.

"A bit?" Pascal asked. "A bit short is twenty, thirty, fifty bucks, not thousands."

"Slow week."

"Tell me something, Moretti. What would you do if someone owed you money and didn't come through?"

Kill them. He stared at Pascal, not answering. He didn't have to.

A slight smile curved Pascal's lips. "Got a job for you, if you're interested."

"What is it?"

He leaned closer. "Got a man that needs taught a lesson... a permanent one."

The hair on Corrado's nape bristled. *A hit.* He hadn't done one in months. "How much?"

Pascal held up the envelope. "How much are you short?"

"Five."

"Five then."

Five thousand? Blood on his hands was worth much more than that. "I'll pass."

"You'll pass?" Pascal asked, surprised.

"Yes."

Pascal tapped the envelope against the table. "It's ten-thirty. That means you have an hour and a half to bring me the rest of the money you said you'd have for me."

So it was going to be that way. "Yes, sir."

Corrado headed out to his car and climbed behind the wheel. Ninety minutes to make five thousand dollars.

He headed uptown and cruised the streets, shaking down a few people who owed him to get a few bucks. He stopped by stores, collecting early payments, hoarding every penny he got his hands on. Twenty minutes until midnight and he still needed a thousand. He stared at the clock as a few minutes ticked away, before driving home. His house was silent, completely dark. He strolled through the downstairs before heading up to his empty bedroom.

No sign of Celia anywhere.

Relief settled through him. She must have gone out somewhere with Maura. At least she wouldn't be there to see this.

He rifled through drawers, pulling out all the hidden cash, and still ended up short. Pausing beside the bed, he stared over at Celia's jewelry box, nestled between the legs of her gigantic stuffed bear, gleaming under the moonlight streaming through the open window.

The phone ringing downstairs shattered his train of thought. Sighing, he looked away. He would give the man his last breath before he ever stole from Celia.

Striding downstairs, he snatched up the phone. "Moretti speaking."

"Tell me my son is there."

Corrado hesitated at the sound of the Boss's raised voice. "Do you want me to say that or would you rather me tell the truth?"

"The truth, Corrado. Is he there?"

"No."

"Where the hell is he?"

"I don't know."

"If you find out, you make him come home. You hear me?"

"Yes, sir."

Corrado set the receiver down just as the front door opened. He stepped into the foyer, catching a glimpse of Celia. "Hey, have you seen your brother?"

Celia froze, holding open the door, wide-eyed as she turned to him.

"Did you hear me?" he asked, brow furrowing, as he glanced past her. "Where's Maura?"

She still didn't speak. She didn't move. Was she even breathing?

Coldness ran through him. "Answer me."

No response.

"Celia!" he growled, stepping toward her. "Where's your brother?"

Her lack of a response told him all he needed to know.

Grabbing her arm, he pulled her to him. "Tell me where they are."

"No."

No.

She finally speaks and she tells me no?

"I'm your husband, Celia. Tell me."

"No."

She tried to pull away, but he gripped tighter.

"This isn't the way," Corrado said. "Whatever you did, I can still undo it. Just tell me where they are before it's too late."

"I can't."

"You *can.*"

"Just let them go, Corrado. Let them be. *Please.*"

Any other time 'please' would have won him over, but not now. Not this.

"Your father already called here for Vincent," he said. "Trust me when I say you'd rather me find him than Antonio. So tell me where they are, Celia. While I can still do something about it."

Frowning, she yanked away from him. "I dropped them off at the bus station, okay?"

The bus station. *Unbelievable.*

Corrado rushed out the door, ignoring her protests, everything else forgotten. He jumped in the car and sped away from the house, straight to the Greyhound terminal across town.

He found them as soon as he arrived, sitting on a bench along the side, holding hands, a single black duffle bag on the floor by Vincent's feet. As Corrado approached, a lady came over the loudspeaker, announcing boarding for a bus to New York City. Vincent jumped to his feet, pulling Maura with him as he snatched up the bag. Smiles lit up both their faces as Vincent leaned down to kiss her.

The kiss was soft, but sensual. A kiss full of hope. A kiss for their future. Vincent pulled back, gazing into her eyes for a moment, before his attention shifted past her. And Corrado saw it there, in the boy's eyes, as his hope was doused in gasoline, his future going up in flames.

Busted.

Vincent yanked Maura to him protectively, his eyes darting

around the terminal for others, but Corrado had come alone. Slowly, Corrado stepped toward them.

"Go get on the bus, Maura," Vincent urged, his voice a frantic whisper. "I'll be right there."

The girl moved, listening to Vincent without so much as questioning why, but Corrado's stern voice stalled her. "I wouldn't if I were you."

Maura swung around, her fear palpable. A soft gasp escaped her parted lips. She obeyed him instead, remaining planted in spot.

Vincent groaned. "Look, Corrado, I—"

Corrado silenced him with a raise of the hand that made Maura flinch. Realizing it wouldn't help to argue, Vincent decided to act instead. Tugging on Maura's hand, he started toward the boarding passengers. "We're leaving."

"The only place you're going is home."

"That's the *last* place I'm going."

"Vincent," Corrado warned. "Stop."

"Make me."

The childish words set Corrado off. Snatching Vincent by the back of the collar, he dragged him through the terminal toward the exit, ignoring the looks tossed at him by the crowd. The boy tried to fight, but Corrado was undeterred. A punch landed against Corrado's jaw as he forced Vincent out to the parking lot. Corrado let go of him, adrenaline surging through his bloodstream, numbness coating his nerves as his jaw stung.

Vincent tried to hit him again, but Corrado blocked the blow, instinctively tempering the boy with a punch to his face. Corrado's fist, strong, clenched tightly, hit Vincent straight in the right eye. The boy grunted as a shriek rang out behind them. *Maura.*

"Vincent," she cried. "Oh God!"

Distracted, Corrado glanced at Maura, giving Vincent the upper hand. He lunged at him, knocking right into him, swinging his fists with fury like a cat backed into a corner, fighting for a way out.

He gave a valiant effort, trying to ward Corrado off, landing a few blows, but it only took a minute for Corrado to subdue him. Forcing Vincent's arm behind his back, he slammed him against the side of the Mercedes so hard it left a dent.

"I don't want to hurt you, Vincent."

The boy's breaths were ragged, his voice strained. "Fuck you."

The profanity did nothing but enrage Corrado further.

Corrado forced him in the passenger seat before tossing his bag in the trunk. "Get in the car, Maura."

Maura didn't argue. Corrado's voice, terse and edgy, left no room for argument. Even Vincent surrendered, slouching in the seat as he grumbled under his breath.

Corrado drove straight home, pulling up to his house and glancing in the rearview mirror at a sobbing Maura. "Go inside and stay there."

Again, she didn't argue.

As soon as she was inside, he sped down Felton Drive to the DeMarcos. He pulled up in front of the house and cut the engine. Vincent remained in the seat, staring out the side window. "It's not fair. I *love* her, Corrado. What else am I supposed to do?"

"You want my advice?"

"Yes."

"Find somebody else to love."

Vincent scoffed. "Gee, great, thanks. A lot of help you are."

"Until you grow up, Vincent, there is no helping you," Corrado said. "Running away isn't the solution."

"What *is* the solution?"

"Facing it head on."

Corrado got out and walked around to the passenger side, opening the door and motioning for him to get out of his car. Huffing, Vincent obliged, heading inside. Antonio stepped out of the den when they reached the foyer, his expression alternating between relief and confusion when he took in both of their faces, battered, bruising from the scuffle. "What the hell happened?"

Vincent flicked his tongue out, licking his split lip. Neither one answered the question.

Before Antonio pried any further, Vincent stomped upstairs.

Antonio gazed at Corrado once his son departed, questions in his eyes, but he didn't ask.

Somehow, he knew.

"Thank you, Corrado."

It wasn't until Corrado was on the way home that he discovered the money still stuffed in his pockets.

Pascal.

He drove straight past his house and headed across town, knocking on Pascal's front door.

Nearly two hours late.

A woman opened, eyes bloodshot, hair a mess. She eyed him peculiarly. "Pascal has been looking for you."

Of course he has.

Corrado followed her to the living room, where Pascal lay passed out on the couch, snoring, wearing nothing but a pair of silk boxers. She shook him awake. "Passy, that guy's here."

Pascal rubbed his eyes, his voice cracking as he said, "about fucking time."

Corrado pulled out the cash and laid it out on the coffee table, hesitating before pulling off his watch and setting it on top. He was still short a few dollars. The watch was worth enough to cover it.

"Ten thousand?" Pascal asked skeptically.

"I owed five."

"You're late, so it's doubled."

Corrado glared at him. He had struggled coming up with five. There was no way he could get ten.

Pascal laughed as he grabbed a cigarette. "Guess you'll be doing that work for me after all, huh?"

"Yeah." Corrado eyed the man with distaste. "Guess so."

It was much later, after nightfall the next evening, when Corrado finally worked off his debt for the week. He headed home to face his wife, knowing a man who had been unlucky enough to cross Pascal would never again face another living soul… not after what Corrado had put him through.

"Make him suffer," Pascal had said. Unlike when Antonio

expressed the same desire, he knew Pascal wouldn't have accepted it any other way. He still heard the man's screams rattling around in his sleep-deprived brain, a haunting tune he had single handedly produced.

Sweat beaded along his forehead as his tie hung loose, his shirt grimy and wrinkled. He felt repulsive. Pascal had trailed along, watching the entire thing play out with a sickening smirk. He got off on the carnage.

His expression was an image Corrado wanted to purge from his memory.

As soon as Corrado pushed his front door open at a quarter after ten, the first thing he encountered were his wife's brown eyes. Staring into them, everything else faded away. Her expression was blank, her face a mask of indifference, but those eyes told a different story. Her worry gave way to relief. He drank it in from across the room, the sight of her easing the melody of misery.

"You didn't come home last night. You didn't even call."

"Sorry." Sorry wasn't a word he said often, and certainly not one he took lightly. There was very little he allowed himself to feel remorse for, but upsetting the one person who loved him was where he drew the line. She deserved that much from him. "I didn't mean to worry you."

"But you did," she said, frowning. "I had no idea what happened. You could've been hurt, or dead..."

"Not tonight, Celia," he said, shaking his head as he shut the front door. "I can't do this right now."

She sighed, but otherwise remained quiet as he held out a dozen red roses he had picked up on the way home. She grasped them, her eyes boring into him, studying, surveying, suspicious. He looked away from her at the flicker of disappointment, unable to deal with it. He hated being bad for the only good thing in his life.

His feet were like concrete slabs against the wooden stairs when he headed to the bedroom and pulled off his jacket, tossing it in the hamper as he slid out of his shoes. Celia appeared and stood in the doorway behind him, watching as he undressed. She was already ready for bed, wearing a blue nightgown with her hair pulled back. The tension radiating from her was palpable and made the hairs on his neck stand up, uneasiness in the pit of his stomach.

He unbuttoned his shirt as he faced her. "It's been a long day."

"You're telling me."

"I really am sorry."

For every moment of heartache I cause you.

"I know you are, Corrado." Her voice was softer as she held her hand out. "Give the shirt to me."

He glanced at it, confused, before spotting the bright red blood splatter on the cuff. He hesitated too long for her liking, and she snatched it from his hand, muttering as she walked out.

He unzipped his pants as she paused in the doorway, her forehead wrinkled. She eyed the shirt cautiously, and he knew what was coming next before it even happened. "This isn't my brother's blood, is it?"

"No, *Bellissima*, it's not."

He was pretty sure it wasn't, anyway.

"Thank God," she whispered, disappearing into the hallway.

'Thank God' was right. He sincerely hoped a day never came where he had to answer yes to that.

He showered and put on fresh clothes before heading back downstairs, finding Celia in the living room. She stood in front of the fireplace, the fire just starting to come alive. He made out his shirt tucked in among the flames, the fabric burning to ash, disintegrating in front of his eyes.

He focused on Celia when the last bit of it faded away, watching her as she watched the fire, the flickering flames casting shadows upon her frowning face. He wondered if she understood what she was doing. Helping him cover his tracks, destroying evidence, made her an accomplice, an accessory after the fact. It sickened him to think he involved her in his world, but Celia was not the type of woman you shielded from things.

If he ever tried to protect her from something for her own good, he likely would need someone to protect him from her.

31

Cigar smoke permeated the air of the den as men packed the room, football blaring from the television.

The Chicago Bears—the one sports team the men agreed on. The Cubs and the Sox rivalry ran deep, instigating fights to the point that Antonio had banned baseball from being watched when they gathered.

The Boss was a Cubs fan. His only flaw, Corrado surmised.

So they gathered nearly every week, uniting, watching the Bears play. Most of the men had money riding on the game, always betting on the home team, no matter how terrible of a season they were having.

Today, the Bears were dominating the Lions—the first game after the NFL strike came to an end. Spirits were high, the underground betting world back on track with money flowing in again, lining all of their pockets a little thicker, but something in the atmosphere overshadowed the joy, an overwrought sensation of stifling air.

It seemed to hover around the Boss in his chair, his alcohol untouched as he puffed on cigar after cigar, lighting another as soon as one burned down too far. The smoke surrounded him like an ominous fog, his piercing gaze cutting through it as he stared at the doorway.

At Vincent.

The boy stood on the outskirts, his focus on the men and not on the game. He didn't notice his father's attention. No, nothing existed except for Pascal. Vincent's cyes regarded the man with a sheer hatred that Corrado had never seen the boy possess before, the warm brown of his eyes—eyes he shared with his sister—burning as black as coal.

Another fight brewed. Corrado sensed it, and he knew, from Antonio's rigid posture, that he did, too. It was only a matter of time before the boy lurking in the doorway, building with intensity, exploded.

The first half of the game came to a close. The men relaxed, pouring more drinks as they chatted, unaware of the impending eruption until it happened. Pascal laughed, saying something about a new girl he was seeing, the words igniting the bomb. Vincent pushed away from the wall, his nostrils flaring. "You're sick!"

"Vincenzo!" Antonio's grave voice struck hard. "Enough!"

"It's *not* enough!" Vincent yelled back, stopping right in front of his father. "How can it be enough when you did *nothing*?"

Silence swept through the room. The men stared, appalled, as Vincent talked back to the Boss, challenging him… *questioning* him.

"It's none of your concern," Antonio said. "You'd do well to mind your own business."

"She *is* my business," Vincent replied. "I *made* her my business."

"I told you that was over."

"And I told you I love her! I *love* Maura. How many times do I have to say it?"

Based on Antonio's expression, at least a few more times.

"Get out," Antonio barked, his eyes never leaving his son's, but it was clear the order was intended for everyone else. At once, the men scattered. Corrado trailed the rest of them, stepping out into the hallway. Most went right for the front door, taking it as a final dismissal, but Corrado lingered, catching sight of his wife down the hallway within earshot.

He strolled over to her. "Let me guess… you had something to do with this."

"Nope, not me. Apparently *somebody* told him to face the problem head on, and well, seems he's taking that advice."

His brow furrowed. "Who?"

"You, Corrado," Celia said. "*You* did."

He ran his hands down his face in frustration. He had.

The arguing in the den continued, voices raising before dropping low again, bitter words spat back and forth, only half of it reaching Corrado's ears. Antonio's refusal was steadfast, but Vincent put up a fight, deflecting everything his father said, throwing it right back in his face. Anyone else and Antonio would have had them killed on the spot.

It pays to be a DeMarco.

"I'm sorry you feel that way, Dad, but it changes nothing," Vincent said, his words with a sharp edge to them although his voice had leveled out. "I want to be with her."

"You're spoiled," Antonio chided, pulling out the same argument he had used against Celia. "You've had the entire world handed to you. I won't give this to you."

"I don't expect you to. I've never even asked you for anything before. But her… I love her."

"Then earn her. You want this girl? Prove it, Vincenzo."

"I will," he swore. "I'll do anything. Just name it."

"Corrado!"

Corrado cringed when the Boss yelled his name and walked to the doorway of the den. "Yes, sir?"

"This slave of yours… whatshername."

"Maura."

"Maura," he repeated, his face contorting at the Irish sounding name. "How much do you want for her?"

Corrado stared at him blankly. How much did he want?

"Just throw out a number," Antonio said, waving toward him. "Name your price."

Vincent responded before Corrado could, an angry growl about how she was nobody's property, but Antonio raised a hand to silence him, his eyes fixed on Corrado.

"Well?" Antonio said. "I'm waiting."

"I didn't pay anything for her," he said. "I don't expect payment."

"I don't care what you expect," Antonio said. "I told you to name a price. Vincent is interested in the girl, and we're certainly not going to just *hand* her to him."

Vincent couldn't be silenced then. "I don't want to *buy* her!"

Antonio's gaze shifted to his son. "You said you'd do anything… or have you changed your mind?"

Vincent shook his head. "I'm not changing my mind."

"So?" Antonio looked back at Corrado. "How much is the going rate for a little Irish slave?"

Vincent inhaled sharply, on the verge of speaking out again, but Corrado responded before the boy made it any worse. The Boss was testing them.

"Twenty thousand," he replied. "That's how much my father said he gave for her."

"And that was years ago." Antonio lit yet another cigar. "She's a bit more used up now."

Corrado fought a grimace at those words, keeping his expression straight, but Vincent couldn't stop the emotion from twisting his face.

"So taking into account depreciation, I'd say she's valued at about half that now." Antonio glanced at his son. "Ten grand, and the girl's yours."

Vincent's eyes narrowed. "I don't have the money, and you know it."

"Ah, well, I'm sure Corrado can find a way for you to make it," Antonio replied. "Isn't that right?"

Corrado stared straight ahead, expressionless. He couldn't say no, as much as he wanted to. "Yes, sir."

"It's settled then," Antonio said, standing up as the second half of the game started. "You come to me, Vincenzo, when you have your money, and we'll negotiate the terms of her sale."

Antonio walked out but hesitated in the hallway near Corrado.

"I expect him to earn it," Antonio said quietly. "The easier you take it on him, the harder I'm going to be on you. *Capice*?"

Corrado nodded stiffly. *Message received.*

Yet again, Corrado found himself being shadowed by someone as he went about his daily business. Unlike cocky Michael Antonelli, Vincent seemed to be a ball of frayed nerves, edgy and disgruntled, wanting to be anywhere in the world but on the streets with Corrado.

Corrado couldn't blame him. He didn't want him there, either.

He straddled a fine line between taking it easy on Vincent and putting him through Hell, doing just enough to make him sweat, to make him earn what little money flowed his way, but he found himself safeguarding the boy from real danger. Every time he looked at him, every time they headed to a job, all Corrado saw was Celia's little brother, the one she fiercely protected, the one she detrimentally tried to help.

The boy who wanted to be a doctor.

Corrado took him on a few of the easier hijacks, letting him stay in the shadows and watch, acting as their lookout. He forked over a few bucks here and there—more than he would have paid anyone else—but it wasn't enough to satiate the boy.

"This is really all you do?" Vincent asked one night as they sat in the room beneath the bar, cashing out the gambling game. Corrado had done it so much in his father's place it felt like a tedious chore.

"What did you expect?" Corrado asked, keeping his eye on the cash as he counted. "Pandemonium?"

"I don't know," Vincent replied. "I think I expected more glamour."

Glamour? "I don't do this for excitement, Vincent."

"Then why do you do it?"

"Because I can't imagine not doing it."

"Why?"

Corrado lost track of his counting when that word echoed around him. *Why*? "You ask as many questions as your sister."

"It's a legitimate question," Vincent said. "Why would you do something that doesn't excite you?"

"Because life isn't a game," he said, hesitating before changing his mind. "Actually, no, it is. This life *is* a game. It's a perpetual game of *Simon Says.* And I do this, because Simon says so."

"I'm guessing my father is Simon?"

"Yes, and I'd like to stay in the game, so I do what Simon says."

"That doesn't explain why you started playing in the first place."

"Because my father played the game."

"So?"

Corrado tossed the stack of money down. Lost count again. "This may come as a surprise to you, Vincent, but not all of us despise our fathers. Mine isn't perfect, but he's an honorable man."

"Honorable?" Vincent asked. "They're *criminals.*"

Corrado refrained from pointing out that, over the past week, Vincent had broken more laws than most people would their entire lives. "You define honorable as someone who follows society's rules. I define it as someone who makes their own rules. Honor isn't being a follower… it's being a leader."

"Yet you follow my father's every order," he pointed out.

"I suppose I'm not a man of honor yet."

Man of honor. Vincent didn't get the double meaning of those words, but Corrado felt it when he spoke them. Made men were called men of honor, and someday soon… *very soon*… Corrado would get that title.

"So this is it," Vincent said, surveying the grungy room. "You spend your days lugging boxes off trucks and catering to gamblers."

"Not as *glamorous* as being a doctor," Corrado said, emphasizing the word, "but it's a job."

"Well, what can *I* do?" Vincent asked. "At this rate, it'll take me a year to make enough. There has to be something more."

"You don't know what you're asking for, kid."

Vincent sneered at the word *kid.* "I'll be eighteen soon. Whatever it is, I can handle it. Besides, the sooner I get the money, the sooner I can walk away from all of this."

It was a good concept, walking away, but implausible. Once the life had you, it had you for life. Maybe Vincent didn't yet see that, but Antonio knew what he was doing.

He had shoved Vincent right into his footsteps by dangling the girl in the path in front of him.

"Fine," Corrado said. "You want more? It's yours."

He took him to stick-ups, took him to assaults, and took him to robberies, anything to make a few extra bucks. Vincent earned the money in less than two weeks—two weeks that found Corrado more and more in debt. He skimped on his own pay, his interest bill to Pascal going unpaid.

Corrado drove Vincent home that final night, the boy's pockets loaded with wads of cash, all ten thousand dollars. Corrado followed him into the house, lingering behind, as Vincent headed straight to the office. Vincent's steps were steadfast, a fierce determination in his expression.

This wouldn't end well.

Vincent shoved open the office door without knocking and stepped right inside as Corrado lingered in the hallway. Antonio sat behind his desk, rage brewing in his eyes. "Get out!"

Vincent's steps stalled, his hands in his pockets, prepared to pull out the money. "What?"

"Get out," Antonio said again. "You knock on that door and wait for permission before you walk in this room. You hear me?"

Vincent nodded slowly. "Sorry."

"Don't apologize," Antonio said. "Get the hell out and knock."

The boy hesitated before striding back out of the office, shutting the door as he went. Sighing dramatically, he knocked on the door, waiting for acknowledgment, but no response came.

"You gotta be kidding me," Vincent muttered, knocking again.

Corrado struggled against the urge to laugh. It wasn't that he got pleasure from Vincent's frustration, but… well… it was nice to see someone else being hassled.

Vincent knocked twice more before Antonio called out, "who is it?"

Closing his eyes, Vincent leaned his forehead against the door in annoyance. "It's me… Vincent."

"Who?"

He groaned. "Vincenzo."

"It's open."

"Of course it is," Vincent muttered, opening the door.

Antonio relaxed back in his chair, gazing at his son when he entered. "What can I do for you?"

"I have your money."

Surprised passed across Antonio's face. "*My* money?"

"The ten thousand."

"Oh, Vincenzo, that's Corrado's money." Antonio waved toward the hallway. "Come on in, Corrado. Join us."

Slowly, Corrado stepped into the room as Vincent pulled money from his pocket and set it on his father's desk. Antonio watched, curiosity in his eyes, as they boy splayed it all out.

"That's all of it," Vincent said. "That's it."

Antonio snatched up the cash, arranging it all in a thick stack before shoving it in an envelope. "That may be all of the money, but that's certainly not *it*."

Vincent's eyes narrowed. "What?"

"I said get the money, Vincenzo, and we'd negotiate."

"Negotiate," Vincent repeated. "What does that even mean?"

"It means there are terms to this sale," Antonio replied, his expression serious. "You might not like them, but your purchase requires a warranty."

32

January 21, 1983, on the evening of his eighteenth birthday, Vincenzo Roman DeMarco was inducted into *La Cosa Nostra.*

His initiation broke tradition. He hadn't earned his place. He hadn't worked in a crew. He hadn't proven himself. His hands were spotlessly clean. He was inducted based solely upon his family name, and he did it to be with the girl he loved.

Corrado hadn't been there—he wasn't a made man, so he hadn't been invited to the sacred initiation—but he heard the story. Nobody had questioned it. Nobody had objected. Another DeMarco, embraced with open arms, welcomed and wanted.

Loved.

While it happened, Corrado had been across town, sticking up a jewelry store with some other guys in his father's crew. Guys who had robbed, and murdered, and extorted. Guys who had earned their place time and again. Guys who, as usual, were disregarded.

Corrado seldom fell victim to the cardinal sins—greed, maybe, and occasionally pride—but a rare one simmered in his veins, tainting his bloodstream like spiked punch… one the DeMarco kids seemed to bring out of him too much for his liking. *Envy.*

It should have been *him.*

Why wasn't it him?

The question nagged him, again and again, over and over, for days following Vincent's initiation. A few men had been brought in, nominated for membership, and the books were set to close again. It would be months, maybe years before they reopened.

Hadn't he earned it?

It was a question he wouldn't ask out loud. He *couldn't.*

A week later, after the last scheduled man had been inducted, they found themselves at Rita's, gathering around plates of food and bottles of expensive wine.

Celebrating, Antonio had said.

Commiserating, Celia called it.

Corrado leaned toward agreeing with her. He remained ill-tempered, but he showed up as expected. The Boss's son-in-law. Antonio greeted him as soon as he walked in, pride on his face as he slapped him on the back. "How's my favorite son-in-law?"

"I'm your only son-in-law," Corrado replied.

He had moved past being Vito's kid and unknowingly stepped right into another shadow... a bigger one, this one with no blood to fuel the bond. He was family, technically, but not literally. He was nothing more than a title by marriage, given to him by the woman on his arm.

The bitter reality was like gasoline sloshing through his veins.

Vincent sat quietly through dinner, him and Maura across from Corrado and Celia. Maura's first outing with the DeMarcos. Corrado could tell she didn't want to be there any more than some of the others wanted her there. She had been included at Vincent's insistence… a fact that made the boy's own mother refuse to attend.

If they thought Antonio had been hard to crack, Gia was impossible. No son of hers would lower himself to be with someone like Maura, she had said. And if Vincent chose to slum, she wouldn't stand around and watch.

Corrado stared at Vincent the entire dinner, studying him, as the boy tampered with the wound on his right hand. The jagged slice across his palm started to heal, red and somewhat inflamed. Painful, Corrado gathered, from the grimace on Vincent's face whenever he closed his hand into a fist.

Corrado felt no sympathy.

Vincent believed he had fought to get there, sacrificed, but Corrado saw it different. Once again, the boy had it all handed to him... freely given what Corrado had worked hard for but got denied.

The sting of rejection ran deep.

"You're quiet, Corrado," Antonio said, gazing at him from his seat at the end of the table as dinner wound down.

"I'm fine," Corrado said.

"You don't seem fine."

"I am."

He swirled the spaghetti around on his plate. He hadn't eaten a single bite. He wasn't hungry.

"How's business?"

"Fine."

"You pay off your debt yet?"

Corrado's eyes cut down the table to where Pascal sat beside the Boss, relaxed, smirking, drinking a glass of wine. He had—for some reason—been invited to Vincent's celebration, forcing Vincent to sit at the same table, beside the woman he loved, near the man who had raped her. A cruel test of will power. "No."

"No?" Antonio raised his eyebrows. "Why haven't you made good on your loan?"

"*My* loan," Celia chimed in. "I borrowed the money."

"Quiet, honey," Antonio chided. "The men are talking."

Celia narrowed her eyes at her father, muttering "asshole" under her breath, barely audible, but Antonio heard it, based on the amused smile curving his lips.

"Well?" Antonio continued. "Why haven't you paid it off?"

"I'm working on it, sir."

"Apparently not hard enough."

"It's a lot of money."

"That sounds a hell of a lot like an excuse." Antonio turned to Pascal. "How much does he still owe?"

"Five hundred and seventeen thousand."

All hints of amusement died from Antonio's eyes. "That's more than he borrowed."

"*I* borrowed," Celia muttered.

"Interest," Pascal explained. "He was short a few weeks, missed some all together."

Antonio tensed, his muscles rigid as a sharp edge accented his words. "How many points was the loan?"

"Five."

"Generous," Antonio said. "Most would've charged ten."

Pascal shrugged, taking a sip of his drink. "I'm just that kinda guy, you know? I help out when I can."

Vincent scoffed under his breath.

"You need to work harder, Corrado," Antonio said. "This isn't acceptable."

"Yes, sir."

The subject seemed to be dropped, all men turning back to their food, but Celia's harsh laughter ignited it again. "Work harder? You know what's not acceptable, Dad? The fact that all my husband does is work. That's it! That's all he ever does!"

"Celia," Corrado warned, his voice low. "Don't."

"Listen to your husband," Antonio said, sipping his wine. "He doesn't need you fighting his battles."

"Of course he doesn't," she continued. "But he respects you, so he'd never go against you, even though sometimes *someone* needs to."

"That's why I married your mother."

"Whatever," Celia said. "Mom's the president of your fucking fan club."

Corrado cringed at her profanity-laced outburst as Antonio set his glass down, glaring at his daughter. "You don't speak like that, young lady."

"You say worse all the time."

"That's because I'm a man," he said.

"Oh, stop with the double standards already," she spat, jumping up from her chair, wagging a finger. "I'm an adult. I can speak any way I want."

Antonio slammed a hand down on the table, shoving his chair back to stand. "Not in front of me!"

Their back-and-forth bickering went on, neither backing down. Corrado glanced across the table at Vincent again. The boy sat so close to Maura their arms brushed together, both staring down at their plates. Corrado turned away from him, too, his eyes drifting to the vast glass window covering the entire wall of the restaurant.

As his eyes adjusted to the darkness outside, he caught sight of the black Ford creeping to a stop in the street, the faint glow of the streetlight illuminating the side of it.

Corrado's heart stalled for a fraction of a second. He didn't move, didn't blink, didn't *breathe* as he stared at the car, the world around him falling into slow motion. Adrenaline spiked his blood, intoxicating his senses, as numbness coated his skin.

The passenger side window slowly rolled down.

The flash of the gun muzzle sent the world into fast forward.

Corrado's pulse kicked into high gear, his heart thumping so hard, so erratically, he barely heard the arguing anymore. The abrupt eruption of gunfire shattered the window, as the noise ripped through the air. Antonio turned toward the street, barely having a chance to react, when bullets tore into his chest, knocking him backward over his chair.

Celia screamed, the high-pitched shriek making Corrado's blood run cold. Quickly, he snatched a hold of his wife and threw her to the ground, forcing her to safety. People ducked for cover, crying, as they dove beneath the table. Corrado didn't hesitate, didn't second-guess. His body reacted, as instinctual as taking air into his lungs. He was on his feet, reaching into his coat for his gun, as Celia screamed for her father, crawling over to him.

Corrado's feet moved, carrying him to the broken window, as he squeezed the trigger, back to back. The shots struck the lingering car, tearing through the metal and shattering glass, as bullets whizzed by him, so close he felt the rush of air. His ears rang mercilessly as he expelled every bullet from his gun.

He squeezed the trigger again and again, scarcely aware that nothing happened but the subtle click of an empty gun. The car tires squealed, smoke filtering around the back of it as it fled the scene. Before it disappeared into the darkness, Corrado noticed the flash of green on the back windshield, a sticker affixed to the corner.

A shamrock.

Corrado slipped the gun back into his coat as he turned to their table. Chaos reigned, men scattering and running for the door, as Corrado's eyes scanned the room, seeking out his wife. He rushed to her as she hovered over her father, sobbing. "Daddy! Oh God, Daddy!"

Corrado's blood ran cold, the image of the bullets striking Antonio flashing in his mind. He fell to his knees beside them, pulling Celia away from her father, expecting the two of them to be covered with blood, but there was none. Celia struggled against him, but Corrado overpowered her, pinning her arms against her sides as Antonio took in a deep inhale. His eyes opened, blinking rapidly as if stunted.

"Don't move, Daddy!" Celia cried, scanning the restaurant. "Somebody call 911!"

"Nonsense," Antonio ground out, his voice strained as he tried to push himself up. "I'm fine."

"You were *shot*!"

"Don't be ridiculous," Antonio said as he sat up.

Corrado loosened his hold on Celia enough for her to slip away. She reached for her father, tugging at his shirt, ripping it open. Buttons popped off, flying around them, as Celia exposed his black-clad chest… a bulletproof vest.

"Really?" Celia shoved her father. "I thought you were *hurt*!"

"I am." He winced, reaching up to grasp his chest over his heart. "I'm just not dead."

Corrado stood, relieved, and glanced around at everyone else. Vincent peeked out from under the table, his body pinning a shaking Maura beneath him. Vincent's eyes were glazed over, his mouth hanging open, as he stared at Corrado with awe.

"It's safe now," Corrado said. *As safe as it will ever be, anyway.*

"How did you…?" Vincent shook his head and pulled Maura into his arms. "You just walked right into the line of fire. They could've killed you!"

"They didn't."

"That's because they shoot worse than fucking storm troopers," he grumbled, shaking his head. "Bullets flew all around you. Jesus, it was like watching a bad movie."

Vincent pulled Maura tighter against him, leaning down to

whisper to her, consoling her, reassuring her, although the boy looked anything but comforted himself. Corrado turned back to his wife as she clung to her father, refusing to let go, despite him being safe.

Antonio hugged her, his gaze drifting to Corrado. "You saved my life."

"The Kevlar saved you."

Antonio stared at him. "I think I'd rather have you."

Corrado moseyed downstairs, rubbing his tired eyes as he headed for the front door. The morning breeze hit his bare skin, sending a small chill down his spine as he glanced out, wearing nothing but a pair of black boxers. He scanned the porch, his vision blurry, and came up empty.

"Celia?" he called out, shutting the door again. It was shortly after dawn, a soft orange glow touching the wooden floors as sunlight streamed in the windows.

"In here." Her soft voice reached him from the living room. He had woken up to an empty bed, no sign she had even slept beside him last night.

Strolling that way, he rubbed his stomach. He never ate anything the night before, slight hunger pangs gripping his sides. They got stuck at the restaurant for hours having to give interviews after the police arrived. Antonio had been smart enough to make Vincent and Maura leave, not wanting the girl to speak with the authorities, sending Celia away with them, despite her arguing she needed to stay. It was only after Corrado slipped her his gun, asking her to sneak it away, that she had gone willingly.

Accessory after the fact yet again.

He stepped in the doorway to the living room, seeing her on the couch. "Did you get this morning's paper?"

Wordlessly, she raised her arms, clutching the newspaper in the air with both hands. He stepped toward her, yawning, his eyes scanning the front page.

Reading the top headline, he froze.

The Kevlar Killer?

A grainy color photo was right below it, covering the left side of the page, of him leaning back against a police cruiser, arms crossed over his chest, as Detective Walker grilled him. The man had wanted to arrest him—had been dead-set on charging him for discharging a weapon—but his superiors overrode him. They had little more than witness accounts, total contradictions, and not to mention no weapons.

Stalking forward, Corrado grabbed the newspaper from her hands, suddenly wide-awake. He scanned the accompanying article.

Rita's was lit up in a hail of gunfire Saturday night as rival gangs came head-to-head at the popular Italian eatery. Witnesses say the DeMarco crime family was having dinner when a car pulled up out front and unleashed a spray of bullets on the diners. Antonio DeMarco, reputed boss of La Cosa Nostra, survived the attack, thanks to the quick reaction by one of his men.

Sources say Corrado Moretti retaliated with gunfire, scaring off the assailants and ending the attack as soon as it began. Moretti, a rising figure in Chicago's mob, is the son-in-law of DeMarco. At only twenty-years-old, he is rumored to be one of the Mafia's top earners, having already accumulated quite an arrest record that includes weapons charges, felony assault, and first-degree murder.

Corrado stopped reading after that line. "Unbelievable."

Celia shifted around on the couch to face him, the movement drawing Corrado's attention. None of the disgust he expected to see from her shone. Instead, amusement twinkled in her eyes. "You made the front page."

He stared at her, surprised by the humor in her voice. "This isn't funny, Celia."

"It kind of is. They even gave you a nickname."

He groaned, glancing back at the headline. "It's absurd."

"It's catchy," she said. "*The Kevlar Killer*. Rolls off the tongue."

"It makes no sense," he said.

"Oh keep reading… they explain it."

Shaking his head, he glanced back down at the page.

Sources say Moretti is notorious for coming out of situations unscathed. "Antonio DeMarco equates him to Kevlar," an anonymous witness tells us, "stronger than steel and just as defensive as a bullet-proof vest."

Corrado's eyes narrowed at those words. "That's not what your father said at all."

"Close enough," Celia replied. "Someone clearly heard him."

"Yeah," Corrado grumbled, "and ratted."

He stared at the photo, feeling more exposed than ever before. His crimes had always been anonymous, even his arrests and trials barely making a blurb in the crime section in a city overwrought with violence, but this was front page.

"You'd think the attempted assassination of your father would be their focus. I'm nobody."

"Oh, you're somebody, alright," she said. "You're the Kevlar Killer."

A fit of giggles erupted from her as she mock-whispered the nickname. Groaning, Corrado walked around to face her. "Not funny."

"Oh, come on." She lay back on the couch, grinning. "It is."

"It's not. My picture on the front page isn't staying out of the limelight or flying under the radar. At this rate, I'll never be made."

She laughed again, grabbing him and pulling him down to her. She captured his lips with hers, kissing him, nipping his bottom lip as she pulled away. Her face grazed against the stubble along his jaw before bringing her lips to his ear. "Kevlar."

Corrado pulled away, rolling the newspaper up and playfully swatting her with it. "You're enjoying this, aren't you?"

"I am," she admitted. "Look, this is one of those situations where you either have to laugh or cry about it, and I've done enough crying. Some men tried to kill my father last night. They *almost* killed him. They could've killed my husband, too!"

"They wouldn't have killed me."

"Why? Because you're made of Kevlar?"

She choked back another laugh as he cut his eyes at her. "Because they weren't aiming for me."

"Maybe not," she said, "but that doesn't matter. Christ, Corrado, you walked straight toward them! You could have died right in front of me! Do you know what that would do to a person? To have to watch someone you love die?"

"You'll never have to see that."

She rolled her eyes, sitting up again. "The point is, this entire situation sucks, so it's easier to find some humor and focus on it than to worry about the might-have-been and might-someday-be."

He tapped the newspaper on top of her head. "When did you get to be so smart?"

"I was born this way."

"Where were those smarts when I asked you to marry me? You should've run the other way."

"I was blinded by your ruggedly handsome good looks."

He leaned down and pressed a soft kiss to her lips before strolling across the room and tossing the newspaper into the fireplace on top of the kindling. Grabbing the lighter from the mantle, he flicked it, as Celia jumped up. "Wait!"

He hesitated, the flame going out, as she darted toward him. She snatched the newspaper out of the fireplace and ripped the front page apart, tearing out the article, before discarding the rest in the fireplace. Celia strolled out of the room, grinning, clutching the article to her chest.

Lighting the kindling, the remaining newspaper went up in flames. He watched it burn, the pages curling as they disintegrated, when the phone rang. He backed up a few steps, eyes still on the fire, and grabbed the phone. "Moretti speaking."

"Meet me at the church."

"Yes, sir."

He hung up, looking away from the fire, and headed upstairs to get dressed for the day.

The church was empty when he arrived a few hours before Sunday Mass. Corrado strolled down the aisle, glancing at the stained glass windows casting vibrant colors along the golden-toned pews. He strolled to the front, slipping into the same seat he had sat in last time he met the Boss here, and waited.

Minutes of peaceful silence passed before the door in the back of the church opened and someone approached. Corrado smelled the subtle scent of cigar smoke as the Boss slid into the pew beside him, making the sign of the cross and bowing his head. Corrado remained silent, letting the man pray in peace.

When Antonio raised his head again, he let out a deep exhale and slouched back in the seat, cringing. He reached up, rubbing his chest over his heart. "Got one hell of a bruise."

"Bet it hurts."

"Not as bad as it could've," Antonio replied.

"You sound like Celia."

Antonio smiled. "She sure didn't get that from her mother."

Corrado nodded and remained silent, unsure of what to say or why he had been called there.

"Look, I'll get to the point," Antonio said. "I need a favor."

"Okay."

"I need someone to look after my boy," Antonio said. "I know that's asking a lot, because I already entrusted you to take care of my daughter, but my kids… my kids are everything to me. Vincent, he isn't prepared for this life. I'll do whatever I can to mold him, but I can only do so much. He needs someone else."

"And you think that someone is me."

"I know it is. I knew it from the beginning. You're tough, Corrado. Dare I say as tough as Kevlar?"

Corrado cut his eyes at the Boss, seeing the amused smirk tugging his lips. *Just like his daughter.* "You saw the paper."

"Of course I did," he said. "My daughter see it?"

"Yes."

"She keep the article?"

He hesitated. "Yes."

Antonio roared with laughter, working himself into a coughing fit.

"You're a good man, Corrado. That's why I trust you with my family. I know you'll look out for them, and well, I know they need looking out for. Vincent's in deep with this girl, and I don't like it, but it's what he wants. He's willing to fight for it, for her, but I'm telling you… it's going to end badly. They say she's a nice girl, and maybe she is, but it isn't about her. It isn't about either of them. It isn't even about *me.* It goes way back. The Italian and the Irish… putting us together is like throwing water on a grease fire. You know what happens when you do that?"

"No."

"It gets too hot and explodes, and *everything* goes up in flames. Oil and water don't mix. And the Irish and the Italians, we're oil and water. My son's playing with fire."

Corrado knew the history between the groups in Chicago, knew about the bad blood that went back to Prohibition. Just the night before, he had watched an Irish car try to gun them down as they ate dinner. But he couldn't fathom how this girl… a girl not even a part of that life… could make it any worse.

"In that case, sir, wouldn't it be better if they were *away* from all of this?" Corrado asked.

"Are you questioning me?"

"I'm just trying to understand."

"Your father tell you where he got the girl?"

"No."

"We had this problem with this guy down on the south side… he ran betting games in our territory, set up this loansharking business right under our noses. We couldn't have that, you know, so Vito went in and took him out. When he raided his house, he found her in the basement… the girl. She was locked in a fucking dog cage. He called me, asked what he was supposed to do about that. I said it was up to him—take her or leave her."

"So he took her."

"He did," Antonio said. "Good thing, too, because Sal sent a crew out to burn the house down. Your father saved her life."

"I thought he bought her."

"He did," he continued. "In a way. He told me not to pay him for the job, you know, the contract. So I kept the money, and he got the girl."

"Twenty thousand," Corrado mumbled. Twenty grand for a hit.

Antonio glanced at him. "Not everyone's worth as much as *you*."

Those words stunned him.

"The point is, we got one of theirs locked up, Corrado. Well, we *had* one locked up. And it's easier to keep her close to the chest, you know, and control things, then to let her go all willy-nilly. If they find out who she is, what she was… all Hell could break loose."

A throat cleared behind them. Corrado turned around, on edge, seeing Father Alberto standing in the aisle. Antonio greeted him without even looking. "Father."

"When he opened the Abyss, smoke rose from it like the smoke from a gigantic furnace," the priest said. "The sun and sky were darkened by the smoke from the Abyss."

"The book of Revelations," Antonio said, chuckling to himself. "When Hell breaks loose… literally."

The priest smiled. "During those days men will seek death, but will not find it; they will long to die, but death will elude them."

"Sounds about right," Antonio said.

"Shall I alert the congregation that the locusts are soon coming?" the priest asked, a playful hint to his voice.

"Not yet," Antonio said. "The star hasn't fallen from the sky."

"Good." Father Alberto shifted his gaze to Corrado. "Mr. Moretti, quite the cameo you made in this morning's newspaper."

Corrado stared at the priest as Antonio laughed. He threw his arm over Corrado's shoulder. "Ah, Father, you'd be better off reading one of my daughter's gossip rags than the Chicago Times if you want the truth."

"If I want the truth, I come to the source," Father Alberto said. "Speaking of… are you ready for Confession?"

Antonio stood. "Of course."

Father Alberto nodded in acknowledgement, turning to Corrado again. "Hopefully someday you'll also join me in Confession?"

"Someday," Corrado agreed.

"He will," Antonio chimed in. "The day Corrado feels true remorse for something, he'll be banging down your door."

"No need to bang," the priest said. "The door is always open."

Father Alberto walked off, leaving them alone once more. Antonio glanced down at Corrado in the pew and hesitated. "Mark my words… my son's blood with be on that girl's hands someday."

"How are you so sure?"

"Because if someone did to one of ours what we let happen to one of theirs, I wouldn't hesitate to annihilate them."

33

The small, square card lay on top of a ripped envelope on the coffee table, beside the empty crystal vase. A few scraggly wilted rose petals surrounded it that Celia hadn't bothered to pick up when discarding the weeks old roses that morning.

Corrado sat down on the edge of the couch in the darkened, quiet living room, as the fire picked up steam in the fireplace. Sighing, he grabbed the card and stared at the front of it. White bells tied together with ribbon graced the cover, surrounding by a drab tan background, the words 'you're invited' beneath it in cursive.

He flipped it open, seeing the generic fill-in-the-black text, messy scribble covering the lines.

Vincent and *Maura* request the pleasure of your company on *February 14* at *7 o'clock* for their wedding at *home*. The RSVP line was left blank, as was any information about a reception. There wouldn't be one. It could hardly even be called a wedding. It was just Vincent and Maura, along with the priest, and whatever witnesses they could get to attend.

Corrado hadn't been one of them.

Closing the card, he eyed the front again before his gaze drifted to his watch on his wrist. A quarter after nine. The nuptials were long over.

The knob jingled, the front door shoved open as he sat there. High heels clicked against the wooden floor as Celia strolled down the hallway. She stepped into the living room, the smell of her perfume entering a fraction of a second before she appeared in front of Corrado. His eyes moved from the card in his hand to her, starting at the tips of her toes and working their way up to her face. She wore the tallest pair of heels she owned, making her legs look long and deadly as they jutted out from a form fitting, strapless blue dress.

Her best dress… she had worn it on their first date.

Her hair was pulled up, wispy curls falling loose. Celia's gaze settled on the invitation in his hand. "Regretting not coming?"

He shook his head. It had been the right decision. "They shouldn't start their life with someone like me hanging around."

Smiling sadly, Celia squeezed between him and the coffee table, knocking the vase over as she sat down in front of him. She set a foil-covered plate beside her. "Vincent wanted you there."

"Maura didn't."

"She never said that."

"She didn't have to."

Celia reached over and took the invitation from his hands, running her fingers across the image on the front. "It was a nice wedding, simple and sweet. Maura wore a white dress and had a bouquet of fresh lilies. They said their vows in the living room. Vincent was so nervous… he was convinced Maura would change her mind about him."

"She should."

Celia kicked his leg, her heel striking his calf. He grimaced, reaching down to rub it, as she laughed. "They make each other happy."

"I'm happy for their happiness," Corrado said. "Doesn't change the fact that your brother is a made man."

"And, what? Made men aren't worthy of being loved?"

He shrugged, sitting back on the couch as he gazed at her. "It's debatable."

Celia didn't entertain that with a response when she turned back to the invitation. "Daddy showed up. We didn't think he was coming. Father Alberto had already started the ceremony when he waltzed in. He said, *'you couldn't wait for me, Father?'* Father Alberto said, *'I would think you, of all men, would know the importance of being on time.'* "

Corrado smirked. "I bet your father liked that."

"He laughed," she replied. "Lightened the mood a bit. He didn't stick around after the ceremony… said his congratulations to Vincent and then left. Didn't speak to Maura at all, but at least he came."

"Yeah," Corrado muttered. "At least there's that."

Celia stared at him for a moment before standing up, motioning toward the plate on the coffee table. "I brought you some cake."

"I don't eat cake."

"You can eat *this* cake," she said. "Maura made it for the wedding. It's Italian Cream cake. You'll like it."

She spoke pointedly, her eyes piercing him as if imploring him to argue. He knew he wouldn't win this one. "Fine, I'll eat it."

Celia kicked off her shoes right there in the living room before strolling to the kitchen to grab some forks. She returned, snuggling up against him on the couch, as they shared the plate of cake. The icing was rich, not too sweet, and melted in his mouth every bite he took. After finishing, he tossed the plate back down on the coffee table and pulled her into his arms, kissing the top of her head.

"Do you have anything for me?" she asked quietly.

He glanced down at her. "Like what?"

"I don't know," she said. "Jewelry? Chocolate? Something?"

"No."

"Nothing?"

"Nothing."

"Not even flowers?"

He eyed the knocked over vase. "Why would I give you flowers?"

"Because it's Valentine's Day."

Oops. Corrado shifted around to face Celia as she sat up, eyeing him expectantly. Reaching out, he brushed the back of his hand along her warm cheek before trailing his fingertips down her neck and around her collarbones. "It should be illegal."

"What?" she asked.

"You going out of the house looking so beautiful."

A small smile tugged the corner of her lips, but she suppressed it. "Are you trying to distract me?"

Leaning over, Corrado kissed her neck. "Depends."

"On what?"

"On whether or not it's working."

She wrapped her arms around him as she lay back, pulling him on top of her. His hand grasped her hip, shoving her dress up as he pressed himself between her legs.

She let out a soft moan as he nipped at her jawline with his teeth. "It's not working."

He kissed her lips. "Didn't think it would."

Celia laughed when he pulled away. "You gave it a good try."

"I do what I can." Corrado stood, picking the vase up from the floor, and set it on the table beside the invitation. "It's such a generic invitation."

"Still better than that graduation card you gave me."

Corrado pulled his car to a stop at the top of the DeMarcos driveway, parking adjacent to the porch. He didn't get out, didn't blow the horn or make a move. He sat there, waiting, staring straight ahead.

After a moment, someone exited the house and opened the car door to slip inside. Corrado spared a glance at the passenger side as Vincent settled into the seat, not bothering with a seatbelt, not saying a word. Corrado eyed him curiously. The Boss had called, ordering him to pick up Vincent. No explanation, no further instruction—just pick the boy up.

"Where to?" Corrado asked.

Vincent shrugged a shoulder, mumbling, "wherever."

"Where are you supposed to go?"

"Wherever you go."

Vincent seemed on edge, head down, eyes fixed out the window as he fidgeted. The sight of his obvious nervousness stirred up the same within Corrado. He didn't like it.

"Wherever I go," Corrado repeated. Shadowing him again.

Corrado went about his usual nightly business—checking on the betting games and collecting *La Cosa Nostra* taxes. Vincent remained quiet, never relaxing, as the hours wore on. Corrado watched him curiously, knowing the boy was up to something. He was a made man now… there was no reason for him to be following *anyone*. He had propelled right past him and hundreds of others.

Vincent should be forming his own crew, leading others, enforcing rules… not tagging along on menial tasks on a Saturday night.

Corrado pulled up in front of the grungy bar on the south side. He climbed out, needing to cash the game out for his father, but Vincent made no move to follow. He remained still in the passenger seat, staring out the side window at the old building.

"Come on," Corrado said.

"I'll wait here," Vincent replied.

Corrado wanted to object, to tell Vincent to get the hell out of the car, but he couldn't order around a made man… not while he was still a peon. Slamming the car door, Corrado headed inside the bar and went straight down to the basement. He hastily broke up the game, cashing out the chips and sending men on their way with nothing more than a brusque wave.

Once the last guy left, Corrado counted the rest of the cash, dividing it up and putting it in the safe for his father. He grabbed his take, skimming through it—twenty-five thousand—before locking up and heading out.

He slowly approached his car, his footsteps faltering when he glanced in the open passenger side window. Vincent stared down at his lap. In his hands, he fiddled with a small .22 caliber handgun. Corrado's heart stalled. Definitely up to something.

On guard, Corrado climbed in the driver's seat, itching to grab his own weapon. He cast Vincent a wary glance as the boy tucked the gun away.

"Are you feeling okay, Vincent?" Corrado asked.

"Yeah, fine."

His voice betrayed him, the hitch in the words telling Corrado he was anything but fine.

"How about we call it a night?" Corrado suggested. "I just need to drop by Pascal's quick."

"Yeah," Vincent said, "sounds great."

Corrado drove across town to Pascal's, relieved to find the house quiet, the usual Saturday night party not waging. He got out, not oblivious to the fact that Vincent followed this time. Pascal swung the door open, doing a double take as he glanced between them. He wore a black three-piece suit, the smell of his cologne powerful.

"Corrado," he greeted him, his breath smelling of mint and not the usual alcohol. *Peculiar.* Pascal's gaze drifted past him to Vincent. "Junior. I'm surprised to see you here. I was just heading out."

Corrado reached into his pocket, pulling out the envelope of cash. "Just dropping off what I owe this week."

"Ah." Pascal relaxed a bit, motioning with his head for them to come in. They walked into the house, waiting as Pascal closed the door, before following him into the living room. The man took the envelope and skimmed through the cash. "Just the twenty-five."

"Yes, sir."

"You still owe over five-hundred," Pascal said. "You know that's unacceptable."

"I know."

"Anyone else and I would've sent my guys out to bust your fucking kneecaps by now," Pascal continued, hastily shoving the money back into the envelope. "I can't keep letting this go on. If you can't make good on your wife's deal, I'll have to go to her and make *her* make good on it."

It was a fine line Pascal walked, subtly threatening the Boss's only daughter. He would never hurt her—couldn't hurt her—without unleashing Antonio's rage. But the insinuation was there. Five hundred thousand was *a lot* of money, maybe worth causing a mutiny.

Pascal threw the envelope down on the table as he turned to face them. He opened his mouth as if to speak, his gaze darting over Corrado's shoulder. Something flashed in his eyes—a reflection, maybe, or a blast of passion, the man's steel blue eyes darkening to gray, as if the color had been sucked from them, frightened and withdrawing, running away.

Fear. Corrado saw terror.

"What—?"

The deafening explosion tore through the living room, the flash of gunfire like a grenade detonating behind Corrado. The world spun around him. Corrado watched, shocked, when a single bullet ripped through Pascal's chest, right over his heart. Pascal flew backward, straight into the table, before collapsing to the floor. Blood oozed from the wound out onto his white button-down shirt as horrid gurgling noises erupted from his throat. His chest heaved, his body struggling to breathe, but consciousness faded before he even hit the floor. Blood streamed from his nose, staining his chapped lips and dripping from his chin.

Pascal was a dead man.

Defensively, Corrado reached into his coat, reacting impulsively, and pulled out his gun. He swung around, aiming at the boy in the doorway. Vincent scarcely noticed, the pistol clenched between both hands, still aimed at Pascal with his finger on the trigger. Vincent stood still, unblinking, unresponsive. Sheer fury unlike anything Corrado had ever seen before was frozen on Vincent's face. This wasn't Celia's little brother anymore. This was someone else.

This was a man of honor.

A *vengeful* man of honor, out for blood.

"Vincent!" Corrado stepped toward him, aiming right for his head. "Put down the gun!"

The sound of Corrado's voice brought Vincent back to awareness. All at once his hands shook, violently rattling the gun before letting it clatter to the floor. He turned to Corrado, rage melting into shock. Tears welled in his eyes as he stared down the barrel of Corrado's gun.

"What have you done?" Corrado ground out, heart pounding like a steel drum against his ribcage.

Vincent's eyes drifted back across the room to Pascal. "What he ordered me to do."

"What *who* ordered you to do?"

Vincent stared at Pascal, not speaking, no longer responding.

Seconds ticked away, lasting a lifetime yet no time at all. Corrado's ears rang, buzzing from the gunfire. Realizing he wasn't going to get an answer, he lowered his gun. "We need to get out of here, Vincent."

No response.

"Vincent," he said again, grabbing the boy. "Did you hear me? We need to leave."

He nodded slowly, reaching down and grabbing his gun again. The sight of it in his hand put Corrado on edge, but the boy slipped it into his pocket, putting it away. Vincent turned, keeping his head down as he stalked toward the front door.

Corrado remained right on his heels, jogging to the car and speeding away before Vincent even got the door closed. His mind raced as fast as his heart as he tried to sort through what had happened, trying to decide what to do next.

"We need to call your father," Corrado said. "We have to tell him."

"He already knows."

He already knows. Those words washed through Corrado, soothing his nerves, as they answered the question of who ordered it.

Antonio.

He was the only one with the authority to sanction the murder of a made man. "Why didn't you tell me? *Warn* me?"

"I, uh… I didn't want you to do it instead."

Corrado laughed bitterly under his breath, checking his mirrors, making sure nobody followed them. He wouldn't have killed Pascal. He couldn't have. He had wanted to, so many times, but he hadn't been given permission. And without permission, he, too, would have been as good as dead.

He drove toward home. Vincent sat in the passenger seat, staring out the window, his hands still shaking. His first hit. Corrado remembered how he felt the first time he murdered someone.

Charlie Klein.

"Eighty-nine seconds," Vincent whispered, pulling Corrado from the memory before he fell into it. "It took him eighty-nine seconds to die."

Corrado shot him a peculiar look. "You *counted*?"

"Eighty-nine seconds," he said again. "Doesn't seem long enough after what he did. *That* lasted longer than eighty-nine seconds. She suffered more than him."

Corrado had no idea what to say.

"Did he feel it?" Vincent asked. "Did it even hurt him?"

Corrado hesitated. "Until he lost consciousness."

"How long was that?"

"A few seconds."

Vincent wiped a wayward tear from his eye. "That's it?"

Corrado nodded once. "It was a good shot."

"I wanted him to *suffer.*"

"He suffered. If you saw what I saw, you'd know it."

"What did you see?"

"I saw his life flash before his eyes," Corrado said. "Maybe his death didn't hurt so bad, but realizing he lived for nothing? That he accomplished nothing with his life? That he ended up *being* nothing? He suffered, Vincent. Dying senselessly is the worst way to go."

It's the way most of us will go.

Vincent wiped his eyes again. "It's still not enough."

"No," Corrado agreed, "it never is."

Corrado drove toward Felton Drive, slowing in front of the house Vincent had recently rented for him and Maura, but Vincent waved him on. "We need to go to my father's."

He sped up again, driving to the mansion at the end of the street. He slowed the car, about to pull into the driveway, but slammed the breaks when he nearly rear-ended another Mercedes sticking out into the street. The entire driveway was covered, the overflow along the street. Corrado's eyes scanned the area, counting at least a dozen familiar cars.

He considered dropping Vincent off and leaving, but one glance at Vincent told him that was out of the question. Something was happening, and the boy beside him could barely keep himself together. The nervousness had returned, maybe even worse than it had been to start with.

Antonio had asked him to look out for Vincent, and well… a job was a job.

Throwing the car in reverse, he flew backward down the street to the closest parking spot. He flung the Mercedes into it and got out. Corrado's footsteps were confident, quick, as he fiddled with his tie, trying to straighten it. He reached into his coat, wrapping his fingers around his gun for reassurance, as he strode past the cars in the darkness, leading to the front door.

Antonio stood on the porch in the shadows, dressed in all black, puffing on a cigar all alone. Corrado slowed as he neared the man, coming to a halt in the yard in front of the porch, as Vincent stepped around him. Antonio eyed his son. "Is it done?"

"Yes, sir."

Pride gleamed in his eyes that he suffocated as quick as it surfaced. "Go on inside, son. Give me a moment with Corrado."

Vincent said not another word as he dodged past his father. Antonio strolled closer, stopping at the edge of the porch, and stared down at him. "He do good?"

Corrado nodded stiffly. "Clean shot through the heart."

"Instant?"

"No," he replied. "About a minute and a half."

Eighty-nine seconds, Corrado recalled.

Antonio took a long drag from his cigar before putting it out on the porch banister and discarding it there. His stern eyes studied Corrado, scanning him, as his lips twisted contemplatively. "Give me your gun."

Corrado didn't hesitate, his hand still gripping it. He handed it over to the Boss.

Antonio took the gun, holding it in both hands as he stared down at the silver revolver. "Nice. Where'd you get it?"

"Took it off a guy when I was seventeen."

"Robbery?"

"Yes." Corrado hesitated before explaining. "He tried to rob me, anyway."

"And this was his gun?"

"Yes. I disarmed him… shot him."

Antonio raised an eyebrow. "First kill?"

He nodded.

"Did you know him?"

Another nod.

"How?"

"He was my friend."

"A friend, eh?" Antonio glanced up, his eyes locking with Corrado's. "How would you like some more of those?"

"Friends?"

Antonio cracked a smile. "You ready to join us, son?"

The stagnant air fell deathly silent. Men lined the room, standing shoulder to shoulder, backs pressed against the walls. None of them moved. None of them spoke. The fortress of criminals locked Corrado in.

A row of lit candles ran right down the center of the dining room table, the dim lighting casting dancing shadows along the floor. Not so much as a peep could be heard, not a breeze felt, the air warm and muggy. It slithered across Corrado's skin as sweat gathered along his brow.

Antonio sat at the head of the table, surrounded by the top earners who had worked hard to warrant receiving a seat. Sal and Sonny flanked the Boss, while Vito sat at the other end. A lone chair, dead center of the table remained vacant.

Pascal.

No one greeted Corrado or even acknowledged his presence, like he wasn't worthy of their recognition.

It was about as welcoming as a firing squad.

But Corrado stood out-of-the-way in the room, his shoulders squared and head held high, not the least bit intimidated. He eyed the weapons on the table in front of the Boss: a silver seven-inch folding knife with a serrated blade, a cross etched into the handle, and the revolver that had been taken from him.

"Corrado Alphonse Moretti," Sonny said, drawing Corrado's attention. "You know why you're here?"

His voice seemed amplified in the room. "Yes, sir."

"And you walked in of your own free will?"

"Yes."

"Then lets get to it," Sonny said. "Is your father alive and well?"

Corrado's eyes drifted down the table to where his father sat, expressionless. "Yes, he is."

"Your mother?"

"She's still breathing."

"Do you have any siblings?"

"A sister."

"Let's say I came to you and told you one of them was a rat, and I asked you to kill them. Could you do that for me?"

"Absolutely." He paused. "Do you want me to?"

A wave of murmurs flowed through the room, smiles cracking the hardest expressions. Even Vito let out a light laugh, unable to keep a straight face.

Corrado hadn't intended for that to be funny.

"I don't think that'll be necessary," Antonio chimed in, raising his hand and demanding silence.

"I have to ask, Moretti, and I need you to say it," Sonny continued. "This thing of ours, *La Cosa Nostra*, will be a life of Heaven for you. It's the greatest thing in the world, but if you want to be part of it, you need to understand it's for as long as you live. There's only one way in and one way out. You walked in on your own two feet, but you'll be carried out in a box. You understand that?"

"I understand."

Sonny nodded. "Good luck."

It came time for the blood oath and Corrado repeated it in effortless Italian. *Thank God for Vito's lessons.*

"And you swear never to betray our secrets," Antonio asked, "to obey with love and *Omertà*, the Sicilian code of silence?"

"I do."

It was a pledge he took as serious as his wedding vows. He would no sooner betray the man in front of him than he would his own wife, and he would rather die than ever harm her.

"Which finger do use to pull the trigger?" Antonio asked.

Corrado held up his right hand, wiggling his pointer finger.

Antonio motioned for him to step closer as he turned his focus to the other men in the room. "Does anyone have any objections to my bringing of Corrado Moretti into the fold? Any grievances they would like to air?"

Corrado's chest tightened at the question, but silence met his ears.

"Speak now or take it to the grave," Antonio warned them.

Still, nobody spoke.

Picking the knife up from the table, Antonio grabbed Corrado's right hand, yanking him closer. He bent his fingers back, almost painfully so, forcing his palm further into the air. Antonio took the knife, carving diagonally across his entire palm, from the end of his trigger finger the whole way down to his thick wrist.

Corrado clenched his jaw, swallowing back an agonizing hiss, as the jagged blade shredded his skin. It cut deep, nothing gentle about the motion, thick red blood oozing to the surface and rushing out, coating his palm. Antonio dropped the knife to the table and flipped Corrado's hand over, blood splattering a holy card of St. Jude.

Antonio picked up the card and held it above the nearest candle, igniting it. “Repeat after me: as burns this saint so will burn my soul."

Corrado repeated the words as Antonio handed him the card, engulfing in flames. He juggled it from hand to hand, trying not to burn his flesh. He felt the heat, like hot candle wax scorching his skin, overshadowing the pain throbbing from his open wound. The card extinguished quickly, disintegrating to ash in his palm.

"It's done." Antonio's eyes scanned the room. "This meeting is over. Leave me alone with my son-in-law."

All at once, a hoard of bodies moved, men stepping away from the wall as chairs were shoved backward. The silence was stolen away with a wave of chatter as men converged on Corrado, congratulating him on their way out the door. He remained silent as he dropped his hands to his side. Blood streamed down his fingers, drops splattering onto the floor. He clenched his hand into a fist to stop it, gritting his teeth at the fierce pain rippling up his arm.

Someone threw an arm over his shoulder. Corrado looked

over, surprised, as his father beamed. His thick hand grasped his chin, pulling him toward him, and kissed his cheek. "What did I tell you, kid? It was only a matter of time."

Before Corrado could react to the display of affection, Vito let go and disappeared from the room. The men left, Vincent being the last remaining, lingering along the wall before slipping out the door.

He still appeared frazzled.

Corrado stared at the doorway, knowing how the boy must feel, when Antonio cleared his throat. The moment Corrado looked back at the Boss, he pointed toward the nearby chair… the one that had remained vacant all night. "Take your seat."

He hesitated. "My seat?"

Antonio nodded. "It's reserved for you."

Corrado blinked a few times, his gaze on the chair. So simple in theory, his seat, but the underlying meaning overwhelmed him. Even Vincent had been made to stand along the sidelines. The men at the table were all veterans, men who had lived the life for decades, struggling and proving themselves again and again.

Corrado had only just been invited into the fray. Yet… he had a seat.

"Sit," Antonio ordered again, his voice not as gentle as before. Impatient. Corrado slid into the chair as the Boss exited the room. He returned with a towel and two glasses, a bottle of scotch in the crook of his arm. He tossed the small towel to Corrado. "For your hand."

"I'm fine, sir."

"I only just got you initiated," he said. "If you bleed out on my floor and I lose you already, I'm going to be pissed."

Corrado grabbed the towel, wrapping it around his hand to stop the incessant bleeding. Antonio poured two glasses of scotch, sliding one down the table to Corrado before retaking his seat, sipping from his glass. The stony silence returned briefly as Corrado's mind drifted, the alcohol going down smooth as the burning intoxication diluted the throbbing in his hand.

"Saint Jude," Antonio said, eyeing the remnants of the card

that had fallen from Corrado's hand. "You know why I chose that saint for you?"

"No."

"He's the patron saint of the impossible," he replied. "People invoke him when times get rough. When people lose hope, when it feels like a lost cause, they appeal to Saint Jude, and he comes through for them. He does the impossible. And that's why I chose him. Because you're my own real-life Saint Jude."

Stunned, Corrado set down his drink.

"Jude was at the last supper," Antonio continued. "He was given a seat, and at that table, he looked to Jesus, and he asked him why he wouldn't just manifest himself to the whole world after his resurrection. He *questioned* him. And well, I'm just gonna say, sometimes, some people get away with asking questions others would never have the guts to ask, because some questions deserve answers. So just this once, if you ask, I'll answer."

Corrado took in the Boss's severe expression in the candlelight as he parted his lips, the lone word escaping. "Why?"

He didn't elaborate. Just… *why*?

Antonio seemed to know what he was asking, though. He nodded, unsurprised by the question, and picked up Corrado's pistol. "When the books opened, your name was the first one out of my mouth… the *only* one. Nominations have to be seconded before they proceed, and I knew your father would vouch for you. But before Vito even had the chance, Pascal spoke up."

Corrado's stomach sunk. "He objected."

"Oh, no. Not at all." Antonio laughed. "He seconded it. Rather enthusiastically, at that. And that was when I knew it… if I proceeded with the nomination, you were as good as dead."

Corrado's brow furrowed. *How*?

"You know what the gun is for in an initiation, Corrado?"

"No."

"Once you walk in this room, you either walk out a made man or you don't walk out at all," Antonio explained. "Pascal was eager to get you here. And I knew, as soon as he seconded your nomination, exactly why. You see, you would've stood up here, and when I asked if there were any objections, Pascal would've raised his hand."

"Because I owed him money," Corrado muttered.

"Oh, that would certainly be his excuse," Antonio said. "You owed him *a lot* of money. And it's a valid objection, one we wouldn't have been able to disregard. You wouldn't have walked out of here a made man."

"I would've been taken out."

"I would've had to kill you with your own gun," Antonio agreed, tinkering with the weapon. "Rules are rules, after all. So I dropped your nomination and put up my own son instead. Threw Pascal for a loop. He didn't second that one.

"Other than maybe you, Vincent's the only person I knew that hated Pascal. So the night he got married, I gave him a gift—revenge. I gave him the contract. Because as valid as Pascal's grievance was with you? Vincent's was even greater. Then, as soon as the contract went out, I nominated you again. And guess what Pascal did?"

"Seconded it."

"Exactly," Antonio replied. "He thought he was coming here tonight for your initiation… for your *death*. He never suspected the seat I was opening up for you would be his."

Corrado sat quietly, considering those words. "That still doesn't answer my question. *Why*?"

Antonio set the gun down to pour himself another glass of scotch. "I gave you your answer weeks ago, Corrado… not everyone is worth as much as you."

PART IV

A Long Night

34

The Mafia worked like every other lucrative business. There were processes they went through, protocol that was followed, to ensure things ran smoothly. Everything was meticulously planned down to the smallest detail, very little left to chance.

They called it *organized crime* for a reason.

Everyone played a role. The more specialized you were, the more valuable, and the more you profited from your work. Corrado propelled straight to *Capo*, forming his own crew, overseeing hijacks instead of doing the brunt work, setting up his own betting games instead of cashing out his father's. The money flowed in, a steady stream of green piling up around him, but he never forgot where he came from.

He still killed for Antonio, never once turning down a contract from the Boss. Everyone was good at something. Some people painted. Others played music. Corrado just happened to be good at murder. He accepted that. Embraced it. That was who he was.

The Kevlar Killer.

The nickname graced the pages of the Chicago Times a few times as the years passed. Being *made* hadn't made life perfect. It hadn't even really made life better. It merely made every moment worthwhile for him. Chaos still surrounded him, bloodshed still fueled him, but he seized whatever shreds of peace he could get out of it all.

He lived for those moments—between the arrests, outside of the trials, away from the streets—when it was just Celia and him. He tried to be what she wanted, what she needed: a supportive husband, an involved family man. He found himself growing wiser as he approached his mid-twenties, slicker and more proficient at compartmentalizing. He would never be able to separate her from his lifestyle, but he managed to keep a part of himself untainted for her.

The 1983 black Ford LTD was parked in the driveway of the suburban two-story house on the west side of the city. The shamrock sticker affixed to the back corner had faded to the color of olives, no longer the vibrant emerald it had been glowing amid the gunfire, but there was no mistaking it.

This was the same car.

It had been nearly impossible to track down. The Ford LTD was one of the best selling vehicles in the early eighties, so there seemed to be one parked on every corner in Chicago. There were reports of it popping up around the city through the years, calls to the Boss with license plate numbers that turned out, every time, to be stolen. Their connections at the DMV were of little help, but finally—after four years—their contacts at the police department had come through for them.

An officer on patrol spotted the car, noticing the sticker in the corner. The word had gone out long ago that Antonio DeMarco was looking for that car. So instead of calling it in to the station, the officer called the DeMarco residence. Corrado had been there, having dinner, when the phone rang.

He jumped in his car, dragging Vincent along, and drove straight to the address.

The officer would be compensated handsomely for the tip.

"What do you think?" Vincent asked, slouching in the passenger seat as he gazed at the house, heavy bags beneath his eyes. The past few years hadn't been easy for Vincent as he struggled to accept his position in the organization. A bit of that rebellious boy still survived, resenting being a part of the life, struggling against conformity. He hadn't wanted to give up on his dreams, had been adamant that he could still have the life *he* wanted. Corrado thought he was naïve to entertain normalcy, but Vincent fought hard, enrolling in college after high school. During the day, he took classes; at night, he ran the streets. In a mere few weeks, he would graduate from the University of Chicago.

Pre-med.

The boy *still* wanted to be a doctor.

It amused Corrado, in a way, considering it was he who had paid for Vincent's schooling. Once they received the refund from the state of Illinois for his bail, Corrado had signed the check straight over to Vincent.

Corrado owed a debt, and it wasn't going unpaid.

Vincent used the money to buy the house they lived in, the rest paying for his college and being donated to a local rape crisis center where Maura now volunteered.

Admirable, Corrado had to admit.

"We aren't paid to *think*, Vincent," Corrado muttered, still surveying the car. "We're paid to act."

"Then why are we just sitting there?"

Good point. The shamrock led him to believe the car belonged to the Irish, but it was parked dead center of Ukrainian Village. The bulk of the mob lived further north or south, along the city borders.

What would the Irish be doing *here*?

"Why's it parked in *this* neighborhood?" Vincent asked, his train of thought going the same way.

"I don't know," Corrado said, reaching into his coat, ensuring he had his gun. "Let's go find out."

He got out, no hesitation in his footsteps as he strode right for the house. The sound of a closing car door alerted him to Vincent's trailing. Corrado stepped up to the front door, leaning close as he listened inside for noises.

Nothing.

Peeking around to the window, he glanced into the living room, seeing the glow of a television, the volume so low he couldn't hear it. A man sat alone on the couch.

Stepping back to the door, Corrado reached for the knob

and turned. Unlocked. He pushed it open, motioning for Vincent to follow him as he walked inside. He tiptoed to the living room, taking a deep breath as he drew his weapon and aimed straight for the man.

Vincent flanked him, also pointing a gun. The man jumped up, frenzied, and tried to scamper away. There was nowhere to go, no other exit. Panicked, he leaped up on the couch, hands in the air as he pressed his back to the wall. "Don't shoot! I haven't done anything!"

"Is that your car outside?" Corrado asked.

"Yes."

"Then you did something."

Fear flashed in the man's eyes... a dull green, bloodshot, almost the same shade as his red hair. Definitely Irish.

"Please," he pleaded, frantically shaking his head, his hands trembling as he raised them higher in surrender. "I swear, I didn't do *anything*. You have to believe me!"

"I don't have to do anything," Corrado said. "That car was used in a shooting."

"I just bought it," he said. "Two weeks ago!"

"I don't believe you."

He ran a hand through his hair, gripping tightly to the locks. His expression brightened. "There's no tag on it. You can check. I haven't gotten one yet. I haven't had a chance to register it."

There hadn't been a tag on it. Corrado noticed that.

"Please," the man pleaded again. "Just... put down the gun."

Corrado stared at him as he fidgeted. This wasn't all fear. No, he was paranoid. "Are you alone?"

"Yes."

"Check the house," he told Vincent. "Make sure it's clear."

"It is!" the man said. "You don't have to look."

Vincent ignored the guy's declaration and set off through the house, scanning rooms on the first floor before heading upstairs. Corrado kept his gun aimed at the twitching man, his nervousness growing even more as his gaze darted toward the staircase.

Waiting for something.

Preparing.

He wasn't alone.

As soon as that registered with Corrado, he heard a door being kicked in upstairs, followed by the sound of a high-pitched yelp.

Corrado snatched a hold of the guy and dragged him toward the steps. The guy pleaded the entire way, barely able to stay on his feet as Corrado lugged him to the second floor. Vincent stood in the hallway outside of a darkened room, his gun aimed at the floor, his eyes wide. Corrado threw the guy on his knees on the floor, aiming the revolver at the back of his head as he peered into the room.

Surprise ran through Corrado, making the gun dip briefly. A young girl huddled in the corner of the filthy room, crying as she clutched her swollen stomach. There was nothing in the room except for an old bed, the rusty metal frame barely holding together with a threadbare mattress on top of it.

"Jesus Christ," Vincent mumbled beside him.

Corrado shoved the gun against the man harder as he peered down at him. "I almost believed this was a misunderstanding."

"It is," he begged. "I swear!"

"You can't expect me to believe you now," Corrado replied. "You already lied to me once."

"She, well… it's not what you think."

The guy stammered, his body shaking.

"I want to know who you work for," Corrado said. "Are you one of O'Bannon's men?"

"Who?"

"Seamus O'Bannon," he said. "Are you in the Irish mob?"

"No, I swear!"

Corrado slammed the back of his head with the gun, knocking him flat against the floor. "I don't like men who swear needlessly."

Corrado squeezed the trigger, the gunshot explosive in the hallway as the single bullet tore through the back of the guy's head. Vincent jumped, startled, as the girl let out a frightened shriek.

"Warn me next time you're going to do that," Vincent spat, grasping his chest.

Slipping his gun away, Corrado cast his brother-in-law a

disbelieving look. He had a lot of nerve even thinking those words after what he had done with Pascal Barone.

Corrado's attention turned into the bedroom at the cowering girl, tears flowing down her cheeks as she pulled her knees up, trying to shrink away. Slowly, Corrado approached her. They were in a predicament. Never leave a witness behind. But this was a girl… a young girl. Fourteen, maybe fifteen. They weren't supposed to harm children or the innocent.

He squatted down in front of her and grasped her chin, keeping a tight grip on it when she tried to pull away. Her half-open eyes were black… so very black… nothing but dilated pupil surrounded by broken blood vessels, the white tinted pink. She was strung out. While *pregnant.*

He could kill her just for that.

"Ivan," she whimpered. "Ivan Volkov."

He cocked his head to the side. The gun perched in his hand pointed at the floor between his knees. "Who's Ivan Volkov?"

"The man he worked for."

"Volkov."

"Yes."

"Ukrainian, right?"

"Russian."

"That fucking Russian immigrant tried to have me killed?"

Corrado stared across the dim office at the Boss, taking in his look of astonishment. "Seems that way."

Antonio ran his pointer finger around the rim of his glass as he chewed on a toothpick. Corrado had never heard of Volkov before the girl uttered his name, but the DeMarco family seemed to be well aware of the man's existence. Narcotics. Prostitution. Kidnapping. *Ruthless bastard makes a living hurting the innocent.*

Vincent had turned pale at the mention of him.

Before leaving the scene, Corrado had interrogated the girl, getting as much information as possible before she grew woozy.

Whatever she had taken was hitting her system, and she was worthless within a matter of minutes. Volkov was in his mid-forties and had only been in the country a few years, but he had already made a name for himself in the streets.

"We're not in competition," Antonio mused, "so either he's trying to expand or he's out for hire."

"Who?"

The sound of the shrill voice from the doorway made the hair on the back of Corrado's neck stand on end. Antonio glanced over, not appearing surprised as Salvatore strolled in the office.

"Ivan Volkov," Antonio said, taking a sip from his glass. "You know him?"

"Vaguely," he said, helping himself to a drink.

"Well, he's the one who tried to kill me."

Sal paused before facing them again. "I thought it was the Irish."

Antonio sighed. "So did I."

Sal's eyes shot to Corrado. "*You* said it was the Irish."

"I did," he said, "and it was an Irish guy… but he was working for Volkov, not O'Bannon."

"Nonsense," Sal said. "He *had* to be working for O'Bannon. He's the only one who wants the Boss dead."

Most of the underground world wanted Antonio DeMarco dead.

"You don't *really* think this Volkov thing is credible, do you?" Sal asked incredulously when nobody responded to him. "Where'd you even hear about it?"

"Some girl," Antonio replied. "Corrado and Vincent found her with the Irish who owned the car."

"So one of the Irish's whores points the finger at someone else and you believe her?" Sal shook his head. "She could have pointed the finger at one of us. Would you have believed her then?"

"Of course not," Antonio said tersely. "I'm just checking every avenue, Sal."

"And while you're doing that, O'Bannon's walking free," Sal responded. "I'm not questioning you, Boss. You say it's this other guy, and hey—I'll believe you. But I just think some people might be trying to lead you down the wrong path."

Corrado's back stiffened at the accusatory tone in Sal's voice. Antonio eyed him peculiarly as he stood up, motioning toward the door with his head. "I'll walk you out, Moretti."

Surprised, Corrado stood, nodding to the underboss. "Salvatore."

Corrado strode out with the Boss right on his heels the whole way to the front door. They paused on the porch as Antonio pulled the toothpick from his mouth and fiddled with it. "What did you do about the girl?"

"Dropped her off at that crisis center Maura works at," he replied. "Vincent said they'd find her shelter."

"Ah, yeah. That place." Antonio stuck the toothpick back in his mouth. "Ask around the streets for me, see what people know. I need to know if this was personal or business."

35

Corrado slouched down on the couch, arms crossed over his chest, feet propped up on the coffee table beside the crystal vase full of fresh red roses. His eyes were fixed on the television across the room.

Friday the 13th.

High heels clicked against wood, heading Corrado's direction, the sound only vaguely registering to his ears. His guard dropped at home around Celia, noises that would once send up red flags rolling right off his back. He trusted her implicitly… the only one he let himself be at ease around.

Ironic, really… the only person with the stealthy ability to kill him was the one he trusted never to try.

Her footsteps stalled briefly in the doorway to the living room before approaching him. "I didn't think you were going to make it."

"I told you I would," he replied, moving his head to see around her when she stopped in front of him. "I don't lie."

She let out a laugh of disbelief.

"To you," he clarified, tearing his gaze from the screen to look at her. "I don't lie to you."

A skin-tight black dress accentuated her curves, her hair falling in waves past her shoulders as she pushed it aside to put on her earrings. His eyes trailed the length of her body, drinking in every drop of her beautiful frame. She rolled her eyes at his appraisal, playfully kicking his leg with her black heel. She snatched one of the roses from the vase. "You brought home flowers."

"Yes."

"You're so sweet," she said, clutching it to her chest as she leaned down, lightly kissing his lips. "I'll finish getting ready."

When she walked away, he turned his attention back to the movie.

A few minutes passed before she returned, makeup on, hair pulled up. She stopped in front of him again. "I'm ready."

He surveyed her once more. "You should wear your hair down."

"Why?"

He shrugged, looking around her. "I like it better that way."

Celia stood there, and out of the corner of Corrado's eye, he caught sight of her pulling the pins from her hair, letting the waves fall loose. "So are you ready?"

"I want to finish watching this movie first," Corrado said, motioning toward the television.

"How much longer is it?"

"Not sure," he said. "I think it just started."

Celia let out another laugh, this one full of amusement, as she stalked over and shut off the television. "It's already after eight."

"So?"

"We're late."

"It's New Years Eve, Celia. Late would be after midnight."

"Get up," she demanded. "We're going."

Resigned, Corrado rose to his feet. "Yes, ma'am."

A smile of satisfaction touched her red lips.

They grabbed their coats before heading out. Celia kept up with him as they walked down the block toward the modest white house. Corrado stepped up on the porch and rang the doorbell beside the red door, hearing the chime. It tugged open after a moment, Maura appearing, snickering at something. She halted mid-laugh as her sparkling green eyes caught Corrado's gaze. Her pale skin, splashed with freckles, seemed to go unnaturally white at the sight of him.

It was the same look she gave him every time he came around.

"Hey, Maura!" Celia said, wrapping herself around Corrado's arm, leaning her head against his shoulder.

The color returned to Maura's cheeks. "Hey, Celia."

A greeting for him never came from her lips.

Maura showed them in, taking their coats despite Celia's insistence she needn't do that. The girl had changed quite a bit over the years, growing more outgoing, more relaxed in society, more comfortable in her own skin, but certain traits never faded.

Like her insistence of helping others.

Like her desire for order in life.

Like her distress whenever a Moretti came near.

He had long since moved past being simply Vito's kid, but to her, he would forever be the one who stood by and watched as she suffered.

Over and over again.

They strolled through the downstairs, mingling with the other guests, most of which Corrado didn't know. There were no other made men, none of his kind. They were couples, happy and agreeable, the kind of normal people who held nine to five jobs, who slept soundly at night, believing monsters weren't real.

A few minutes after they made it to the party, another guest arrived—a young girl, carrying a small baby in her arms, a blue blanket loosely draped over it. A tiny arm jutted out the side, the hand balled into a fist. Corrado watched the girl as she weaved through the crowd, finding a seat off to the side alone. She scanned the others, speaking to nobody, her eyes catching Corrado's.

He recognized her: the drugged girl who told him about Volkov.

She had changed, her body more sturdy, but it was the same girl. She wasn't on anything that he could tell. Something in her expression, though, the vacant stare in her eyes alarmed him. She was a shell.

"I need a drink," Corrado muttered.

"Get me one, too," Celia said, letting go of his arm.

He strode off to the kitchen, bypassing the other guests, and nearly ran into Maura in the doorway. She gasped, backing up a few steps to let him walk in. She shifted away, keeping space between the two of them, not saying a word. He headed straight for the alcohol on the table, pouring two glasses of champagne as Maura skidded out of sight.

He shook his head as he took a sip. *This is going to be a long night.*

Hours dragged by, each excruciating second ticking slowly. Celia infused herself into the crowd, getting to know everyone, while Corrado stood along the wall in the living room, out of the way, watching his wife as she charmed every soul she encountered.

And watching the girl as she stared blankly at her baby when it cried.

After a while, Corrado strolled over to the girl, casting a glance around the room before sitting beside her. "I want to talk to you about Ivan Volkov."

She blanched. "What about him?"

"How well do you know him?"

The girl answered quietly, a longing look on her face as she glanced at the child. "I thought I knew him well."

"You know anything about his business?"

She hesitated. "Some."

"If I wanted him to do something for me, take care of someone, would he?"

"If you had enough money, there wasn't much he wouldn't do. That's mostly *all* he does."

"And that guy who was at the house, the one who drove the Ford... what did he do for Volkov?"

"Anything he asked him to," she replied. "People came to Volkov to have jobs done. He did business with a lot of different people."

"Any Italians?"

"Not that I saw, but..." She hesitated. "...he talked a lot about them."

"What about us?"

"Volkov didn't trust Italians. He said you were the quickest to turn on your own, that he saw it firsthand."

Interesting. Corrado could tell she was uncomfortable and didn't want to press the issue. Standing up again, he nodded. "Thank you."

"You're welcome," she mumbled. "I wasn't much help."

Oh, she had been plenty of help. She told Corrado what he needed to know. It may have been business with Volkov, but it had been personal for someone else.

Murder by hire.

The sound of tapping glass hushed the room. All eyes shifted to Vincent as he stood in the front, his arm around Maura. "Before midnight comes, we wanted to thank you for coming tonight. It means a lot to us."

Maura nudged him. "Tell them."

"Tell us what?" someone shouted.

A smile lit up Vincent's face, his eyes brighter than Corrado had seen in a while. Vincent reached over, pressing his hand to Maura's stomach. Without uttering a single word, he told them everything.

"No way!" Celia shrieked, wide-eyed, shoving past people to get closer to her brother.

"Yes, way," Vincent replied.

Maura's face flushed, her eyes darting to the floor as the crowd cheered. Celia squealed, rushing at them, wrapping her arms around the two of them in a tight hug.

"I'm going to be an aunt!" Celia said, swinging around, moving out of the way so others could congratulate the couple. She scanned the room, her gaze settling on Corrado as tears sprung to her eyes. The baby near him cried, drawing Corrado's attention away. The girl just sat there, ignoring her child, and stared at Maura instead.

He recognized the look on her face.

Envy.

Celia rushed over to Corrado, wrapping her arms around his neck and forcing his attention back on her as midnight crept up on them. The room erupted in shouts as people counted down the seconds.

Ten

Nine

Corrado reached up, brushing the tears from Celia's cheeks as they smeared her mascara. He hated seeing her cry.

Eight

Seven

Celia leaned into his touch, sighing as he caressed her soft skin.

Six

Five

He cupped her chin, tilting her face up so she would look at him.

Four

Three

Lurking in her warm brown eyes, beneath the happiness, was a deep yearning, sadness she fought against. She did her best to squelch the ache, to deny it so he wouldn't know it existed, but he saw it. He knew her too well. She couldn't hide anything from him.

Two

One

Celia didn't want to be an aunt. Celia wanted to be a *mommy*.

Horns went off, people celebrating, singing along to the song on the television. Corrado stared into his wife's eyes, drinking in her longing, her thirst, wishing more than anything that he had it in him to quench it.

"I love you," he said. It was all he could offer. Would it ever be enough?

"I love you, too," she said, the sadness fading away. "More than anything."

Yes, maybe love would be enough. *Maybe*.

She reached up on her tiptoes, her eyelids fluttering closed as she kissed him deeply, passion in the movement of her lips. Corrado forgot about everything, blocking out the outside world as he gave her what he could of him.

She pulled back, breathless, a small laugh escaping as she brushed her fingertips across his lips, wiping away her lipstick. "Happy New Year, Corrado."

1988.

Detective Walker stood along the curb, leaning against the fender of the dirty brown unmarked police car as he stared at the brick house on Felton Drive.

Corrado Moretti's house, to be precise.

Corrado stepped out to get his morning paper. He stopped

there, tapping the rolled up newspaper against his hand as he stared at the graying detective staring at him. He remembered once, long ago, when Celia had stood in that exact spot.

He much rather preferred her.

"Detective," he said politely.

The man just glared at him.

Corrado turned to go back inside.

All day long the detective remained there, sometimes sitting in the car, sometimes standing outside. He read magazines, listened to the radio, and stared at the front door of the house for hours on end. Around dusk, the car drove away as Corrado stood at his window, watching.

After nightfall, Corrado dressed and set out walking toward the end of the street. He strolled, in no hurry. Antonio had just told him to come by whenever he could make it.

It was a cool night, a soft breeze rustling the leaves on the trees. People roamed as cars sped by.

The start of the weekend.

The start of a new year.

He reached the DeMarco residence and stepped into the driveway when he heard some movement behind him. He turned his head, alert, and squinted in the darkness. The man stepped out from around some trees, the familiar face shining beneath the corner streetlight. Detective Walker.

"Following me, detective?"

"I was here first."

"This is private property," Corrado said. "You know you need a warrant."

The detective waved at the sidewalk around his feet. "Your boss doesn't own the street."

"My father-in-law, you mean."

He grinned. "Same thing."

"You know this is harassment," Corrado said. "I haven't done anything wrong."

"You beat two men unconscious," Detective Walker said. "You assaulted another the same night you murdered a man. If that's not *wrong*, I don't know what is."

Corrado studied the man. He rocked on his heels, his hands in his pockets, not an ounce of fear. *Ballsy.*

"Goodnight, detective," Corrado said.

"I'll see you tomorrow," he replied as Corrado walked away. "And the next day. And the next day. And every day after that. This is the year, Mr. Moretti. The year we stop playing this game."

Corrado walked to the porch and raised his hand to knock, but the door opened before he could. Antonio stood there, his gaze fixated past him at the street.

"Friend of yours?" he asked, motioning toward the loitering man.

"More like a thorn in my side," Corrado muttered. "He's determined to nail me for something."

"That's that detective?" Antonio asked. "Uh, whatshisname."

"Walker."

"He still giving you grief?"

He had been giving him grief for half a decade now. "Nothing I can't handle."

"Handle, huh?" Antonio stared out at the sidewalk. "Yeah, it'll be handled, but not by you."

Corrado nodded as those words sunk in. He would be the first they suspected if anything bad happened to the man. The entire Chicago Police force was aware the detective had made it his mission to bring him down.

"I owe him, you know, for that stunt he pulled at my daughter's wedding." Antonio's gaze shifted back to Corrado. "Speaking of which, you never took her on a honeymoon, did you?"

"I haven't had the time."

"You're supposed to *make* the time," Antonio stressed.

"Yeah, well, my boss is sort of a hard ass."

Antonio clapped him on the back as he led him inside. "Well, I have it on good authority he'll be giving you some time off soon."

Antonio led Corrado straight back to his office. *Business.* At the Boss's command, he took a seat, declining a drink.

"We need to deal with our enemies," he said straightaway, not beating around the bush at all. "I've been trying to take the high road, you know, the Capone way… this city being big enough for all of us… but they're pressing their luck now."

"Sir, they've been pressing their luck for years, since they put three bullets in your chest."

"In my vest, you mean," Antonio corrected him. "And frankly, maybe they were pressing it before then. Sal still thinks most of our problems lead back to the Irish."

"Is that what *you* think?" The only opinion that mattered to Corrado was the Boss's.

"I don't know," he replied. "Sal says maybe they were the ones who killed his family. And maybe they are—I wouldn't put it past them. They kept one of their own in a fucking cage, you know? What kind of savage does that?"

"The kind that needs taken out."

"Exactly," Antonio said. "But I can't stop thinking about this Russian guy and how he factors in."

"I believe someone hired him, sir."

"The Irish?"

"Most likely." The alternate was unfathomable to Corrado. One of their own? He couldn't believe it.

"Which is why they need taught a lesson."

"And you want me to do that?"

"First I want you to do something else."

"What's that?"

"Take my daughter on her long overdue honeymoon."

The next few weeks the detective followed Corrado everywhere, popping up all hours of the night. Corrado went about his days, ignoring the man, but he made it impossible to get any work done.

February rolled around, winter fading from Chicago. Corrado drove across town to Dolce Vita Pizzeria and strolled into the restaurant, forgoing his usual table to approach the register. John stood there, ringing someone up. After he cashed them out, his gaze shifted to Corrado, his smile falling. "What can I get you?"

"Large deep dish, extra pepperoni," he replied, pulling out his wallet. "To go."

John rung him up, and Corrado handed him some cash, refusing his change, instead stuffing it in a jar on the counter for a tip. He moved off to the side as John turned to the next customer. "What can I get you?"

"I don't know," the familiar voice said. "What do you recommend, Mr. Moretti?"

Corrado closed his eyes briefly before facing the detective. "I heard the place across the street has good orange chicken."

John seemed almost offended, but the detective laughed. He ordered a small Stromboli and paid before stepping aside also.

"You eat across the street often?" the detective asked.

"You tell me," Corrado said. "You've got my schedule memorized by now."

He had been meticulous the past few weeks, keeping to the most boring routine possible.

"Peculiar schedule you have, by the way," Detective Walker said. "Neither you or your wife hold down a job, yet you seem to have a never-ending cash flow."

"Family money," he replied.

"You should do something with that," the detective said. "Something legitimate. Invest it or something."

Corrado glanced at the man. "Huh, you know, that's not such a bad idea."

His pizza was up shortly. Corrado took it and headed to leave.

"I'll be seeing you around, Mr. Moretti."

Corrado pushed open the door and paused. "Yeah, we'll see."

He headed home with the pizza, finding his wife sprawled out on the couch, flipping through channels with the remote. Corrado set the pizza on the coffee table in front of her as she sat up to make room for him.

"What's on it?" she asked, flipping the top up to eye the pizza.

She smiled when she saw the entire pie covered in pepperoni, so thick you couldn't even see the cheese. "Johnny loves me."

Corrado sat down beside her. "*I* bought it."

"But he made it."

"How do you know?"

"Because he knows how I like it."

Corrado's eyes narrowed as she grabbed a slice and shifted sideways on the couch to face him.

"Jealous?" she asked, taking a bite, teasingly.

"Should I be?"

"If you love me."

"Then yes," he said. "I'm burning with envy."

She laughed, shoving him playfully. "I see how it is. Johnny wouldn't mock me that way."

"John wouldn't do anything to you," he replied. "Not if John wanted to live."

Celia rolled her eyes. She didn't laugh. Despite his playful tone, she knew he wasn't joking. "So what did I do to deserve extra pepperoni? I know you prefer eating it with all that other crap."

He shrugged, grabbing a slice.

Celia stared at him in silence, eating her pizza, assessing him. "What's going on, Corrado?"

"What do you mean?"

"I mean I know you," she said. "You're buttering me up for something."

"I am."

"Why?"

He let out a dramatic exhale. "I have to go away."

She shifted position, sitting straight up. "What? Where?"

"Italy."

She gaped at him. "Italy? Like Italy-Italy?"

"Is there another Italy?"

"Little Italy."

"That's just across town."

"Exactly!" Her voice rose. "That's why I'm hoping you're going there. You can come home at night when you go to Little Italy!"

"I'm not going to Little Italy," he said.

"But… Italy's so far away."

"It is," he agreed. "Far, far away."

"No." She threw her pizza down. "You're not going."

"You're telling me what I can do?"

"Yes."

He stared at her, stunned. "I'll go if I want to go, Celia."

"No, you won't," she said, matter-of-fact. "Not without me."

"Ah." Corrado reached into his jacket, pulling out the envelope and holding it out to her. "Good thing you're invited, then."

All traces of anger melted away as she snatched the envelope from him. "I'm invited?"

"Yeah," he said, shrugging. "Wouldn't be a honeymoon without you."

She tore open the envelope holding the plane tickets and gasped. "We're going to Italy?"

"We are."

"Italy-Italy?"

"The one and only."

She jumped on him, tackling him to the couch as she punched him in the chest, harder than he expected. "I can't believe you did that to me! You made me think you were leaving me!"

Laughing, he grasped her hands. "I'll never leave you."

"Promise?"

"I'll never leave you," he said again, linking their fingers together. "Not if I can help it."

Three days later, the two of them departed for Italy, spending two weeks traveling the country and soaking up the culture. They watched an opera at La Scala in Milan, made love on a balcony in Verona, and soaked up the sun floating along the Venice canals. Their time in Florence was filled with architecture, churches and museums, leftover ancient ruins, before they headed further south to Rome.

Rome was the heart of the trip. They spent days immersed in

the city, life back in the states a blurry memory.

For the first time in their marriage, it was truly just *them.*

When Corrado awoke their last morning in Rome, sunlight streamed through the glass doors leading outside of the small villa. He lay in bed, stark naked, a flimsy white sheet loosely draped across him. The ceiling fan above him spun round and round, his eyes following the dizzying movement.

Celia was fast asleep beside him.

A knock sounded from the door. Corrado stood up, wrapping the sheet around his waist to cover himself. They knocked again just as Corrado reached the door. Opening it, he came face to face with a middle-aged Italian man.

"*Signore,*" the man said. "You, uh, Moretti?"

"Corrado Moretti, yes."

"You on phone needed," he said in broken English, mimicking holding a phone to his ear. "*L'America.*"

Corrado's stomach sunk. A call from America? "Who is it?"

"*Emergenza.*"

Emergency.

The man waved impatiently, urging him to follow. Corrado was out of the room without a second thought, not bothering to wake Celia. He clutched the sheet around him as he followed the man to the front office and snatched the phone off the desk where it lay. "Moretti speaking."

"Corrado." Salvatore's high-pitched voice greeted him. "Hope I'm not interrupting, but we have a situation."

"What?"

"It's your father," he said. "He's been arrested."

His father? Arrested? Wasn't the first time. It hardly constituted an emergency. "Yeah? What are they saying he did this time?"

"He killed that detective."

They caught Vito red-handed… *literally.* The gun was in his hand, blood splattering his skin, as he stood on the detective's porch in front of half a dozen police officers.

A silent alarm had been tripped when Vito broke into the house.

Corrado and Celia flew straight home to find officers waiting in front of their house for Corrado. They arrested him for suspicion of murder, but he wasn't surprised.

He expected to have the finger pointed at him.

Despite his airtight alibi, despite him being in an entirely different country when the murder occurred, they kept him locked up for forty-eight hours, grilling him intensively, trying to get him to turn, but he didn't.

He never would.

Begrudgingly, they released him, having no evidence to charge him. Another arrest that led to nothing.

Corrado never went to Vito's trial.

Day after day he'd get up early, just before the sun rose in the steely Chicago sky. He'd shower and get ready in silence, going through the motions, making sure his clothes were flawless, his tie as straight as he could possibly get it. He'd snatch the day's newspaper from the porch as he left his house, climbing into the driver's seat of his Mercedes and making the trek to the Cook County Criminal Court Building.

Most days he'd drive right by, not slowing down, and go somewhere else. Where didn't matter—a coffee shop, a diner, anywhere open at that hour, where he'd ask for a glass of ice water and he'd read the newspaper. But some days, rare moments, he'd find a parking spot and climb out of his car before strolling to the front entrance of the courthouse. He'd never go inside, never even step foot into the heated lobby, but he'd stand there, and he'd wait. What was he waiting for? A glimpse? A sign? He wasn't sure.

After a few minutes of nothing, an hour at most, he'd get back in his car and leave.

Celia never questioned it, never pried about what he did and where he went. He figured she liked to assume he went out of support for his father, so he kept the bitter truth to himself: he didn't want to see what went on in that courtroom.

He'd catch short segments on the news and see photographs on the front page of the paper, glimpses of his father's stoic face, his mother always front and center of the judgmental peanut gallery, but as for first-hand? *Not a chance.*

And he knew without a doubt, his father was grateful for it.

Corrado never witnessed the verdict, but he was there that day, sitting behind the wheel of his car. He stared out the side window from his parking spot, watching as the crowd spilled outside, some cheering, others appearing shell-shocked. He knew not the verdict, and his mother's face didn't give it away as she stepped out of the courthouse, a dark fur coat swallowing her petite frame. Her expression was stern, her steps steady.

Not drunk.

Another woman came out behind Erika Moretti, her feet wobbly in a pair of flats. She took a few steps before her legs gave out beneath her. Falling in a crumbled heap to the sidewalk, her face contorted with sobs. Others from the crowd grabbed her, pulling her back to her feet, carrying the burden of her weight as they struggled to help her walk. They moved closer, around Erika as she remained by the door, unmoving as if she posed herself to be a magnificent statue.

As the others approached, Corrado got a good glimpse of the distraught woman's face.

Vivian, his father's mistress.

He knew it then. *Guilty.*

Corrado slumped further in his seat as he vacantly stared at the steering wheel. Maybe only thirty seconds passed… maybe twenty minutes. But when Corrado's eyes slowly drifted back to the courthouse, the crowd had thinned, everyone moving on.

Everyone except for statuesque Erika Moretti.

Weeks later, Corrado skipped the sentencing hearing. He didn't even put on the façade of pretending he would go. He didn't have to. The mandatory sentence for what Vito had done was life without parole.

36

"Oh my God! *Oh my God*!"

Celia's shrieking echoed through the house, speeding up Corrado's footsteps as he descended the stairs and headed straight for the living room. He found her, phone clutched to her ear.

"Okay, okay… yes, I got it… we'll be right there!"

She slammed the receiver down as she let out a squeal. Her wide eyes met Corrado's. "It's time!"

He stood frozen. "Time for what?"

"The baby!"

The baby... "What about it?"

She clenched her hands into fists as she bounced on the balls of her feet, unable to contain her excitement. "Maura and Vincent are having the baby! *Right now*!"

Corrado refrained from pointing out only Maura was having a baby, unless he had missed something by dropping out of high school mid-Biology class, instead offering her a smile. Her happiness was at least infectious, even if he didn't share her enthusiasm.

"That's great news," he said, meaning it for the most part.

She reached up on her tiptoes, kissing him. "Let me grab my shoes and we can head to the hospital."

His expression didn't fall until she bound from the room. Sighing, he ran his hands down his face. It was going to be a long night.

They arrived at the hospital at nine o'clock that evening to a hectic waiting room in the labor and delivery ward. Despite the other dozen people waiting, nobody else had shown up for Vincent and Maura. They found seats off in a corner, and Celia skimmed through parenting magazines while Corrado sat with his head bowed. He closed his eyes, not praying, not sleeping... he just needed a moment of peace, a moment of darkness.

The bright lights of the hospital were giving him a headache.

As time wore on, the crowd thinned, quietness subduing the waiting room. Corrado opened his eyes, yawning as exhaustion set in. Celia seemed as bright eyed as she had been hours ago.

Glancing over, he saw her reading an article about how to create well-adjusted children with good emotional control. The very top tip: say 'I love you' every day.

Despite himself, he laughed at that.

"What's so funny?" she asked, laying a hand over the magazine article.

"Does it say anything about children whose parents *never* say those words?"

She gazed at him peculiarly. "Your parents never said it?"

"Never."

"Not even once?"

"No."

That threw her for a loop. "Has *anyone* ever said that to you?"

"You."

"Other than me."

He nodded. "Once. *Zia.*"

"An aunt?"

Close enough. "I was seven."

"What happened to her?"

"She died the next day."

"Oh." Celia seemed at a temporary loss for words. "Well, *I* love you, and I'll tell you every day of my life."

He reached over and grabbed her hand, squeezing it as she turned back to the magazine.

A few hours later, Vincent burst in, his eyes swimming with tears as he scanned the room. His gaze settled on them.

"What's wrong?" Celia asked, on her feet in seconds, rushing toward her brother.

"Nothing's wrong."

"Then what is it?"

"It's a boy," he whispered, his eyes widening as that knowledge seemed to sink in. "I have a son."

Celia squealed, throwing herself at her brother. "I have a nephew!"

"You do." Vincent laughed. "And he's *perfect*."

The boy had been born around dawn on the morning of June 3. They said the moment he came into the world, he inhaled sharply before letting out a blood-curdling scream. The doctors had been worried about his lungs because he was a few weeks ahead of schedule.

Clearly, they worried for nothing.

Corrado stood outside the nursery, peering through the thick glass at the cradle, a card affixed to it with all of his information. Eighteen inches long, six and a half pounds. *Carmine Marcello DeMarco.*

He was puny compared to the others.

Maura rested in recovery with Vincent at her side, while Celia had run off to find a phone to call her parents. Corrado had ventured through the halls, somehow ending up here, right in front of the child.

Another DeMarco.

"Congratulations."

Corrado turned his head, eyeing the blonde woman in a pair of pink scrubs. "Excuse me?"

"The baby," she said, motioning into the nursery. "Congratulations."

He let out a dry laugh, looking back at the boy. "It's not mine."

"Oh, my mistake. You had that look about you."

"What look?"

"That terrified look, like you wouldn't know what to do with one of those things if you had to take it home with you."

"I wouldn't," he admitted. "It's my wife's nephew."

"Your wife's nephew." She smiled. "Wouldn't that make him your nephew, too?"

Corrado shrugged. *Technically.*

"So then congratulations *are* in order," she said. "You've got a new family member."

The nurse wandered off right before Celia reappeared. She skipped to his side, wrapping herself around his arm. "God, look at him! Isn't he beautiful?"

Beautiful. Corrado stared at the boy. His head was misshapen from birth, dark hair covering it. His eyes were dark blue—the little bit of Biology class he remembered told him they'd likely change. His dry skin was more reddish than tan, broken out in rashes. The oversized clothes swam on him, his body scrunched up, his hands clenched into fists.

It looked more alien than human.

Pissed off alien, at that.

Even through the thick glass he heard the boy's angry screams.

"Whatever you say."

Corrado strolled through the hospital halls a few days later. He hadn't been back since that first night, swamped with work as he tried to cover for Vincent out in the streets. He had scarcely even seen his wife, but he had a bit of free time and he knew where he would find her. He paused at the nurse's station down the hall from the nursery, casually knocking on the desk to garner the nurse's attention. "Can you tell me what room I can find the DeMarcos in?"

The nurse on duty grinned at him. "Well, hello again, *uncle*."

His brow furrowed before recognition dawned... the same woman from the nursery. "Hello."

"They're in room 214, just up the hall and around the corner," she said, pointing in the direction. "Popular family you have there. I feel like I've given out those directions a dozen times today."

Corrado nodded, unsurprised. A made man would be inundated with attention at a time like this… especially one related to the man who controlled them all.

He strolled down the hall, following the nurse's directions. He stalled when he turned a corner, coming face-to-face with none other than the Boss. Antonio caught Corrado's eye. "Corrado."

"Sir."

Antonio grasped his shoulder. "Can you believe it? My boy has a boy."

He didn't say it, not in so many words, but it gleamed in the man's prideful eyes: *I'm a grandpa.*

"Have you seen the child?"

"Yeah, he's in the room," Antonio said, straightening out his expression as he let go. "Well, if you'll excuse me, I've got another patient to visit... one of Manny's kids is here. Needs a bone-marrow transplant."

"Send him my well-wishes."

"I will."

Antonio strode off as Corrado walked to the room. He stopped right outside, his footsteps faltering at the vision in front of him.

The curtains were wide open, the blinds pulled up. Sunlight streamed through the vast window and encased Celia in a warm spotlight as she leisurely paced the floor. Her hair was messy, pulled back in a braid, not a stitch of makeup on her face. She was dressed down, jeans and an oversized shirt.

A Chicago White Sox shirt.

His shirt.

She had never before been so beautiful.

The blue bundle in her arms squirmed as she rocked the baby and talked sweetly to him, her eyes bright, smile absolutely radiant.

Even without the sunshine, he knew she would still glow.

The baby cooed, not crying, wide-awake and staring up at her, as if just as captivated by the woman before him as Corrado was.

As he stood there, watching, taking in the sight of her, his chest tightened, something inside of him stirring. He inhaled sharply, too overwhelmed to remember how to breathe. And just for a moment, a fleeting moment, as her infectious joy swept through him, he allowed himself to imagine the what-could-have-been.

Her stomach, swollen with a child... *his* child, tucked beneath that White Sox shirt, straining the fabric. His hand pressed against it, feeling the baby kick his scarred palm. Celia in labor, smiling through the pain, crying tears of joy the first time she held the baby. *Their* baby. A little girl, so much like Celia.

Maybe she would be kindhearted like her mother.

Maybe she wouldn't be a monster like him.

He imagined Celia holding *that* baby in her arms, clutching the bundle tight to her chest, feeding her and singing to her. Long dark hair, tanned skin, and the warmest brown eyes... her mother's eyes. They stared, lovingly, trusting. Eyes he would do anything for.

A lifetime flashed before him—recitals, dances, dates, and boyfriends. He'd kill anyone who hurt her, destroy anyone who crossed her, protect her for as long as he lived.

And just as that thought passed through his mind, the vision shifted and the happiness drained away. Violence and mayhem, death and bloodshed—*that* was his life, not those other things. The brief peaceful moment faded away, shattered in a hail of gunfire, dissolving into a pool of red, dying right in front of his eyes.

The never-would-be.

It couldn't happen.

He would do the world a great injustice by keeping Celia to himself, but he couldn't risk it. He couldn't infect an innocent kid with the ugliness that lived inside of him, with the anarchy that existed around him. Selfless or selfish? Honorable or a disgrace? He wasn't sure what that made him, besides a broken, tainted man.

A man unworthy of the vision in front of him, but he greedily drank it in anyway.

The baby whimpered, on the verge of crying. Celia tensed and headed for the bed. Laughing, Maura held her arms out, taking her child from Celia.

Vincent slouched in the nearby chair, eyes fixed on his wife and son, as if nothing else mattered. Corrado supposed, to him, nothing did. That was his world, the meaning of his existence. They gave his life purpose.

Corrado's gaze shifted back to his wife… his purpose… just as

Celia noticed him there. She smiled, a smile this time reserved for nobody but him. "Hey, you!"

"Hello."

She strolled over, fixing his tie as she gazed up at him. "I'm surprised to see you here."

"I had a few minutes, so I thought we'd grab some lunch."

"Sounds great," she said, glancing down at herself with a grimace. "Just let me freshen up a bit."

"You look fine," he said.

She ignored that with a roll of the eyes as she headed for the restroom.

Vincent stood up from his chair, brushing wrinkles from his clothes, as he approached Corrado. "Can I, uh… can we talk for a minute?"

Corrado nodded, stepping out into the hallway, as Vincent followed him. "If you're concerned about work, everything's right on track. I've made sure your crew stayed on task and—"

"No, no, it's not that." Vincent waved that off. "I just wanted to ask you a question… about my son."

Vincent's eyes lit up as he said that word. *Son.*

"What about him?"

He stammered a bit before just spitting it out. "Will you be his godfather?"

Corrado froze. *Godfather*. "Me?"

"Yes. Maura and I… well…"

"Have you brought this up to my wife?"

"Not yet."

"Don't."

Vincent blanched.

"Look, Vincent, I'm honored you'd ask, but I have to decline."

"But—"

"You might die someday, and when you do, you won't want *me* to be responsible for that boy."

Vincent appeared genuinely stunned but shrugged it off. "Since you brought up business, I should make some calls," he muttered, walking away. "Thanks, anyway."

Corrado watched his brother-in-law leave before turning back to the hospital room. Maura sat up in bed, rocking her whimpering baby. She brushed her fingertips along his cheek. "Don't cry, *sole*. It'll all be okay."

Sole. Sun.

Feeling as if he were imposing, that tightening returning to his chest, he walked away. He strolled down the halls, hoping Celia would find him whenever she was ready, and happened upon the nursery again. Standing in front of the glass, staring at the children was the last person Corrado expected to see. "Gia."

She didn't move as he paused beside her. She stood poised, her gaze glued to the empty cradle affixed with the DeMarco name.

Gia hadn't been accepting of her son's choices, hadn't approved of the relationship, and hadn't wanted anything to do with the marriage. Adding a child on top of it hadn't improved things.

"He's in the room," Corrado said, motioning toward the empty cradle. "If you'd like to see him."

"I saw him." Her voice was curt, bitterness spewing with the words. "He's tan and has dark hair."

"He does," Corrado agreed. Her assessment of the baby was about his emotional as his had been.

Gia broke her stance, looking at Corrado, her eyes piercing. "Maybe nobody will know."

"Know what?"

"That he came from an Irish cunt."

Corrado couldn't refrain from grimacing. Staring at her, seeing no compassion in her eyes, sensing no love in her voice, she reminded him startlingly of his own mother.

37

Too bright fluorescent lights shined down on the grimy visitation room, illuminating the puke green colored tables filling every inch of the suffocating space. A rank odor hung in the air, reminding Corrado of the scent of blood coating the filthy floor of an abandoned mold-infested warehouse.

That was a smell he had become acquainted with over time.

He sat calmly in the flimsy chair, feeling it bow a little with each shift of his body weight. He wondered how much blood had been spilled in this room. Sure, guards stood on watch at all the exits, but the visitors and prisoners outnumbered them five to one. It would take little effort to coordinate an attack, the chair he sat in alone enough to knock an unsuspecting guard unconscious. He could take two, maybe three guards all on his own, and he was sure his father could knock a few out, even handcuffed and shackled. In a matter of minutes, they could be out the door, slipping away from the correctional institute and disappearing in broad daylight.

He mulled it over, envisioning it, as he absently rubbed the tip of his trigger finger and thumb together. Bad habit… one he knew he needed to break.

It was his only tell, giving away that something bothered him. His expression remained passive, but his fingers were frenzied.

A buzzer sounded, a door nearby popping open. Before he even entered, Corrado sensed his father. Flanked by two guards, Vito strolled into the room, confidence in his steps. His eyes darted around before settling on Corrado.

Wordlessly, he sauntered over, dragging out the chair across from him. His arms and legs were free of restraints. *Even easier for an escape.*

Corrado glanced at the guards briefly before focusing on his father. He didn't move, didn't grab a chair or attack. He stayed put, pushing the dangerous thoughts from his mind.

Vito relaxed back in the rickety seat, the chair creaking. They stared at each other. Neither said anything. Corrado had wondered what he'd see when he came. Distress? Anger? Fear? Would he smile, happy to see his son? Would he be dejected, broken down?

But there was none of that. His father's calm demeanor remained.

"I thought I taught you better than this, kid."

Vito spoke first.

"You taught me well."

"Couldn't have, since you're here. You know better. You don't do this; you don't visit these places. They told me you were here, asking to see me, and I couldn't believe my ears. My kid, willingly walking into a prison? No fucking way he's that stupid. But here you are."

Corrado wasn't surprised. As many times as he'd been arrested, as many times as he'd found himself in lockup, his father had never once gone to see him. "Here I am."

The question was in Vito's eyes. Why? He didn't ask it, though, and Corrado didn't respond. He wasn't sure he had an answer anyway.

Vito stretched his legs out under the table, his gaze never leaving Corrado's. "You shouldn't be here."

"Neither should you."

Vito's restrained expression turned into a full-blown grin. "Your lips to God's ears."

"You have appeals," Corrado said. "Retrials."

"Doesn't matter," Vito said. "They could try me a hundred times, and the verdict would be the same. No amount of appealing is gonna take the gun out of my hand."

A tinge of guilt stirred inside of Corrado. He opened his mouth to verbalize it, but Vito cut him off.

"Don't you dare fucking say it," Vito declared, a hard edge to his voice as he sat up straighter. "Don't you apologize like some little pussy boy. You don't *ever* apologize, even when you're wrong."

Those words took him back a decade. Instinctively, the response slipped from Corrado's lips. "Yes, sir."

Vito relaxed again, his gaze leaving his son as he glanced around the room. Corrado wondered what he was thinking… if maybe he were concocting the same escape plan. But after a moment Vito turned right back to him, no conspiratorially glint in his eyes.

"This ain't the first time I had to do time, you know."

Corrado's brow furrowed. As far as he knew, his father's record was clean. He'd been arrested, and suspected… but there weren't convictions. No prison sentences until now.

"1969, I got drafted. Vietnam was happening, and they had that lottery… picked my fucking birthday first. September 14." Vito laughed humorlessly as Corrado stared at him with shock. *Military*? "Most of the guys didn't even turn in their draft cards. I thought they were idiots. What were the odds, you know? So I filled mine out when I turned eighteen, thinking it would keep me out of trouble. Guess *I* was the idiot there."

"I was seven then." Corrado didn't recall much from his younger years, but his first clear memory was from seven years old.

"Yeah, they did it right after Thanksgiving. I came home for Christmas that year, and I knew… I knew I was gonna be getting draft papers. I don't know if you remember that Christmas. It was—"

"A nightmare."

"You do remember."

"It was impossible to forget."

"Yeah, I guess so," Vito said. "After what happened that year, I knew I couldn't go. Not that I wanted to or anything to begin with, but I couldn't leave you kids in that *nightmare* to go fight someone else's war."

He'd used Corrado's word—nightmare—intentionally, a peculiar look in his eyes as he spoke it. Corrado stared back at him, refraining from speaking the truth.

Vito may not have gone to war, but he'd left them anyway.

"Got my papers the next spring and burned them. Took the government about six months to catch up to me. Arrested me for draft evasion… took the jury ten minutes to convict. Sentenced me to five years in prison."

"How?" Corrado's eyes narrowed. His father had never been gone for five years.

"Appeals," he said. "Thought I'd get out of it since I had young kids, but they said that would only work if your mother was dead. It was tempting sometimes, you know. Killing Erika would've solved it all."

It should've sickened Corrado to hear his father say that in such a serious voice, but he felt nothing.

"Last appeal reduced my sentence. I had to do six months—that was it. Antonio came to the casino when he got the news. You were there, I don't know if you remember it. He told me to go do my time and hurry back, because he'd need me. There was a war brewing at home, he'd said. A war I *would* have to fight." Vito shook his head. "So I left while you kids slept, turned myself in."

"I never knew," Corrado said.

"Of course you didn't," he responded. "I was back home before anyone even knew to miss me."

Corrado *had* missed him… missed him when he had woken up to his father disappearing again.

"The point is, I've done time before," Vito continued, motioning around the room. "And compared to those six months, this is nothing."

"You got more than six months this time," Corrado pointed out. "You got even more than five years."

Vito shrugged him off. "It ain't about the length of time, kid. I did those six months as punishment for being a fucking coward. Every day I woke up in that cell, knowing I was there because I was too spineless to do my duty. But now? Now I can look myself in the mirror, because I did what was expected of me. And that's what matters. I don't regret what I did to get me here, kid. But dodging the draft? Even I'm disgusted with myself there."

Corrado didn't know what to say. So many of his classmate's

families had been disrupted, fathers and older brothers sent off to war, a lot of them never coming back. He hadn't shown much in the way of sympathy, since his family hadn't been affected. But it could've been him... it could've been his father.

He couldn't imagine how different his life would've been.

Corrado surveyed the visiting room, watching the other prisoners as they affectionately embraced their visitors. None of that warmth surrounded his table.

"They're so relaxed about visits," Corrado said. "I came here expecting to have to look at you behind a sheet of glass."

"I ain't done nothing to piss them off yet, so they still got me in general population."

"Is that smart?" Corrado asked, raising an eyebrow in curiosity. He imagined his father had plenty of enemies roaming around, people who would kill him for the honor that came along with taking down a high-ranking member of *La Cosa Nostra*... even an incarcerated one.

"What are they going to do, kill me?" Vito asked coolly. "State of Illinois already took my life, kid."

"Yes, but—"

Vito sat up, moving toward Corrado so suddenly it caught the attention of the nearby guards. Automatically, Vito relaxed his posture so not to draw them to their table. "You afraid of death?"

His answer was instant. "No."

"Not at all?"

"No."

Vito shook his head. "When your mother got pregnant, I was ecstatic. I was gonna have my son. Vito Junior. I knew it in my soul. She had a hard labor. Real hard. I sat beside her bed, holding her hand, telling her how beautiful she was. And she was beautiful—no doubt about that. Two days later the doctors made her push... and push she did. Pushed, and pushed, and pushed.

"They didn't like fathers there for that back then, so I stood in the hallway and waited, waited for my son, waited to hear you cry. And I heard it... heard the loudest scream I'd ever heard in my life. And I heard some screams before, kid. But this scream was enough to make ears bleed. I shoved my way inside the delivery room, and there it was… Erika holding this shrieking baby.

"'My son?' I said. She shook her head. 'Your daughter.' *Daughter.* I ain't planned on having a daughter. Before I could say anything, Erika waved toward the other side of the room. 'Your son's over there,' she said."

"You weren't expecting twins," Corrado said. He'd known that… his mother had made it abundantly clear during one of her drunken rants.

"Didn't even think it was possible," Vito said. "I ran to the other side of the room, looking for my boy, my son… my Vito Junior. And I found him. But he wasn't crying. He wasn't screaming. No, he was *dead*."

Coldness swarmed Corrado, a shiver tearing down his spine that he tried to ignore, but he visibly shook.

"You were bluer than the night sky. They were just looking at you, and I couldn't figure out why. 'Why the fuck are you just standing there?' I asked, shoving the doctor. 'Save my boy.' He looked at me, and you know what he said?"

"What?"

"He said, 'your wife told us not to bother.'"

Those words hung thickly in the stifling air of the visiting room.

"That was the first time in my life I ever hated someone," Vito continued. "I never got over that. Life with Erika before that was beautiful, but after that?"

"Nightmare."

Vito nodded slowly. "The doctor, he tried to warn me… said if they revived you, you'd have all these problems. Said you'd be a shell. I said if he didn't save you, he'd be less than a shell by the time I was done. So they revived you, and you started breathing, but you didn't cry. They tried to make you cry, but you wouldn't. They took that as a sign you had problems, brain damage, but I knew. My boy was strong. My boy wasn't gonna bend for those motherfuckers who wished him dead." Vito's gaze settled intently on Corrado. "Proudest moment of my life, kid."

Corrado stared back as those words sunk in.

"Of course, your mother wasn't happy, having two babies to take care of. She named your sister Katrina... means *pure* or something, I don't know. Didn't care, either. But I named you Corrado... my wise, brave ruler."

"Why not Vito Junior?"

"Vito Junior died," he said, matter-of-fact. "You're the one who made his way back."

Corrado mulled that over, absently rubbing his fingers together again. "Why are you telling me this?"

"Because you ought to know," he said. "Everyone fears death one way or another, whether they wanna admit it or not. You don't fear your own death because you already died, but that doesn't mean you don't fear death at all."

"I don't."

"You do," Vito insisted, his voice dropping low. "I guarantee if someone stuck a gun to Celia's head and pulled the trigger in front of you, in that split second before she dropped, when you saw the horror in her eyes... the terror she has of death... you'd feel it, too. A fear like no other."

The image flashed in his mind: his wife, dead on the filthy ground, her blood spilling out around her, warm brown eyes ice cold and wide-open, terror lingering in her unseeing gaze long after the brain stopped registering the horror. He'd seen the look in the eyes of others. But on her, on Celia, he couldn't fathom it.

Strong hands clenched into fists of fury at the mental image alone. Vito remained slack in his chair, nodding without surprise at Corrado's visible distress.

"She's your one weakness, kid. And if you let them see that, they'll exploit it."

"She's my wife," Corrado said. "They already know."

"They know she's your wife, but they don't know she's your weakness," he said. "They never knew Erika was mine."

"But you said you hated her. You were never around. You cheated. You—"

"Made sure nobody knew," he said, cutting Corrado off. "That's love, kid. Love makes no fucking sense. As much as I sometimes hated your mother, I never stopped loving her. A few times I wanted to kill her myself, but I couldn't, because killing her would be killing me, and suicide's one hell of an unforgivable sin."

Corrado couldn't understand how his father loved someone so cruel, so vicious, so cold-blooded… but then again, somehow, Celia found it in her to love *him*.

"Speaking of weaknesses," Vito said. "Maura have that baby?"

"Yes," Corrado said. "They named him Carmine Marcello."

"Carmine Marcello," Vito echoed. "A nice Italian name for a half-Irish boy."

"Celia says he has the brightest green eyes now to show it."

"Celia says?" Vito raised his eyebrows. "You don't see him?"

"I keep my distance," Corrado said. "Vincent doesn't like seeing Maura upset, and well, it's hard for her not to be upset when I'm around."

"Can't say I'm surprised," Vito said. "She's Vincent's weakness. If he doesn't learn to control that, he'll get her killed."

"Antonio says it's the other way around."

"I don't often disagree with the Boss, but nah... her blood will be on Vincent's hands someday."

Vito's eyes drifted across the room, settling on something beyond Corrado's shoulder. Corrado turned around, looking at the big clock on the wall. Half past ten in the morning. Visitors were given two hours, and a mere thirty minutes had lapsed since Vito had been brought in.

An hour and a half to go.

Not much else was said, a few casual words here and there. Both men remained silent and passive, absorbing their surroundings as they'd been trained to do in life, as the clock ticked away. When the time had nearly elapsed, Vito let out a long sigh, the sound full of desolation, but his expression gave nothing away. Still the calmness. "I need a favor from you, Corrado."

Corrado. His father rarely called him by his name.

"I need you to look out for someone for me," he said.

His stomach sunk. "My mother?"

Vito shook his head. "Your mother will be fine. I made sure of it all these years. She doesn't need me around. Katrina will be fine, too. But Vivian… she's come to depend on me, and well… you know."

He couldn't be there for her anymore.

"What do you want me to do?"

"Just check in on her."

"You want me to keep you updated?"

Vito shook his head stiffly. "Absolutely not. In fact, I don't want you to come here ever again. I don't want *any* of you to come here. I'm letting the guards know—no visitors. Period. You're lucky I even came down here to see you. I had half a mind to turn you away, but…"

"You needed this from me."

"I did," he agreed.

"I'll check in on her then."

"Thanks," Vito said as the clock behind Corrado hit noon. Pushing his chair back, Vito stood. A small, wistful smile curved his lips as he momentarily gazed at his son. "How about those Sox, huh? You think they'll go the whole way?"

With no uncertainty, Corrado shook his head. "They haven't done it since 1917."

"Eh, it could be worse, kid." Vito took a step back as the guards approached. "You could be a Cubs fan."

The sound of Vito's laughter mixed with the buzz of the door as they led him away.

38

The air around the table was suffocating. Corrado hadn't experienced this much tension in the DeMarco's dining room since the night he had walked in to be initiated, and he was sure the men who lined the walls that night were a lot friendlier than the lady sitting across from him.

Gia.

The only words spoken had been the obligatory 'please' and 'thank you', 'yes, sir' and 'no, ma'am', but somehow, it was like they had all run out of things to say. Voices dried up along with all traces of warmth, dinner untouched as forks scraped needlessly against the fine china, everyone pushing the food around in an attempt to look busy.

Nobody was fooled. They all knew. It was only a matter of who would speak up first.

Definitely not Gia, with her bitter scowl focused on her son's wife. Maura held sleeping Carmine against her chest, tucked securely in a yellow baby carrier, one hand protectively over his back as if trying to shield him from the hostility. The chances of either of them speaking up were about as good as the odds of Corrado being the one to break the silence.

Not happening.

Celia sat beside him, her focus on the lasagna on her plate unwavering. She, like him, had no idea why a family dinner had been called. No, it would be one of the DeMarco men… whichever one grew fed up with the strain first.

If Corrado were a betting man, he would put his entire fortune on the Boss.

A minute passed, then another, and a few more, before an exasperated groan echoed through the room, a fork slammed down.

Corrado looked down the table with surprise. *Vincent.*

"She's my *wife*, mother," Vincent said sharply. "Get over it."

Gia glared at him as Antonio tossed his silverware down, not far behind his son in frustration. "Don't talk to your mother that way."

"Then tell her not to treat my wife this way."

"I have," Antonio said, picking up his glass to take a drink. "She doesn't listen to me."

"Then why should I?"

"Because you have no other choice. You *have* to listen to me."

"I didn't come here to have dinner with my boss," Vincent said. "I came here to see my father. He still lives here, doesn't he? Or am I wasting my time?"

Antonio waved his hand toward Vincent. "I'm right here. But if you came to see me, why are you so worried about what your mother's doing?"

"I hoped she would come around."

"She's sitting here, isn't she?" Antonio asked. "I'd say that's progress."

It was the first time all of them had been in a room together for anything, much less coming together voluntarily for dinner.

"Why don't you just say what you came to say, son?" Antonio suggested. "You wanted us here for a reason."

Vincent's gaze turned to his wife. She smiled reassuringly.

"Fine," Vincent said. "Maura and I, well… we're getting another son."

Just when Corrado thought it couldn't get any tenser, the entire table froze. Another son? It only lasted a few seconds before Celia let out a shriek of excitement. "I'll have *two* nephews?"

Vincent nodded.

"God, you guys..." Celia laughed. "You don't waste any time, do you? I mean, I'm happy for you, but… she *just* had a baby, Vincent. Can't you keep it in your pants for a minute?"

Maura's face turned bright red.

"Yeah, well, that's the thing." Vincent ran a hand through his hair nervously. "He's not really *ours*."

Celia's brow furrowed. "What?"

"He *will* be ours," Maura clarified, breaking her silence. "Soon."

"Very soon," Vincent agreed.

Celia blinked at them with confusion, but Corrado understood. Adoption. It was why they were so anxious tonight. Touchy subject among a circle of people who didn't trust outsiders and put emphasis on bloodlines.

"Who is he?" Antonio's voice was terse. "Or rather, *what* is he?"

"Daddy!" Celia admonished. "He's a baby! *Their* baby. Or he will be... as soon as they have him."

"They're not *having* him," Antonio said pointedly. "They're *getting* him. Learn to listen, Celia Marie, or keep your mouth shut."

Celia recoiled, struck by her father's callous words. Corrado cleared his throat. "Sir, with all due respect..."

"Don't 'with all due respect' me, Moretti. I'm addressing my children right now."

Corrado closed his mouth again. Their father might have been sitting at that table, but it was most certainly still Corrado's boss.

"Your father asked you a question, Vincenzo," Gia said. "Answer him."

"He's, uh… well, his mother has some Italian blood."

"Some?" Antonio asked. "What's she mixed with?"

"Irish."

Gia cringed.

"And the father?" Antonio asked, raising his eyebrows. "Italian?"

"No, he's, uh…" Vincent hesitated. *Not good.* "He's Russian."

"*Mio Dio*," Gia muttered, making the sign of the cross. She threw her napkin down on top of her plate and stomped out of the room.

"Russian," Antonio repeated, still clutching his glass. "You're taking this rebellion of yours a little far, aren't you?"

Anger flashed in Vincent's eyes. "It's not a rebellion. If you don't like it, if you don't want anything to do with it, fine. Don't.

But this is my life. Mine."

"Those people tried to kill me," Antonio said sharply.

"Those people?" Vincent shook his head, shoving his chair back. "Maura didn't try to kill you. My children didn't try to kill you. Those people have nothing to do with any of this!"

Vincent stood, fed up with trying to explain himself. It was the same argument Corrado had heard them have time and time again. Antonio set his glass down. "Sit back down, Vincent."

"I'm not going to sit here while you insult my family."

"Sit down," Antonio barked. The Boss was back in full effect. Vincent glared at him before hesitantly retaking his seat. Antonio waited until his son was planted in the chair before his attention turned to Maura. "I apologize if what I say offended you. It wasn't my intention."

She nodded. "It's okay."

"I don't understand it," Antonio said, turning back to his son. "But I raised you, so I have to trust you know what you're doing."

"I do," Vincent said. "We want this."

"Then congratulations." Antonio stood. "Stay and finish your dinner. I need to have another talk with my wife."

Corrado focused back on his plate of food when Antonio left, stabbing a piece of lasagna with his fork. "That went well."

"Tell me about it," Vincent muttered. "It was a nightmare."

Corrado shook his head. "I was being serious."

Nothing had been thrown. No guns were pulled. Nobody even cursed.

He ate his dinner now that the tension had lifted as Celia drilled them for information, her voice full of enthusiasm. "When do we get to meet him?"

"Actually, you already have," Maura said. "Remember the girl at our New Years Eve party with the newborn?"

"No way!" Celia squealed.

"She tried, but she's just so young and she just…" Maura trailed off. "She can't handle it."

"And you think you guys can?" Celia asked. "Two little ones?"

"Well, Carmine's such an easy baby," Maura said, gazing down at him adoringly as he slept. "And the other... well... he's almost one now. We've kept him here and there the past few months, and he's such a sweetheart. So outgoing and playful."

"What's his name?"

"We haven't given him one yet," Vincent said.

"He doesn't already have one?"

Maura's smile faded. "Not one that he recognizes."

"Well, I have faith you'll come up with the perfect name," Celia said, raising her glass to toast them. "I can't wait to spoil the hell out of him."

Dominic Angelo DeMarco

The adoption went through in early December of 1988, just a few weeks before the holidays. Christmas was an elaborate event that year, Corrado's bank account taking a hit as Celia splurged on gifts, more toys than he had ever even *seen* before piling up in his living room. He humored her, never once criticizing, not putting his foot down when she covered their house with frilly decorations.

He even helped her set up their first Christmas tree.

"You're kidding," she said, brushing hair from her face as it fell from her loose ponytail. "You're twenty-six years old, and you've never had a Christmas tree?"

"Does it look like I'm kidding?" he asked, stringing the colorful musical lights around the thick branches of the evergreen. She always seemed surprised when he shared those things with her, like she still believed he had a normal childhood.

"No." She pursed her lips. "Who doesn't get a Christmas tree?"

"We haven't," he pointed out. "Not until this year."

"That's because we haven't had a reason to get one before."

They still didn't have a reason as far as Corrado was concerned, but he continued to humor her even as it stirred up the rare guilt that existed inside of him. She would never have her own children because of him, so it was only fair, he figured, that he accept her splurging for her brother's kids.

"Had I know you hadn't had one before," Celia continued, "then we would've gotten one years ago."

Exactly why he hadn't mentioned it before. He plugged in the lights, the bulbs flashing to some high-pitched melody blaring from a speaker on the power box.

Celia squealed and clapped, jumping up and down, as the vibrant lights cast a colorful glow on her face. "Perfect! Now the garland! And tinsel! And bulbs! Oh, and can't forget the angel for on top!"

She sprinted from the room as Corrado kicked the button on the power box to turn off the obnoxious tune.

It was going to be a long Christmas.

Despite his worry, the holidays flew by, a blur of family and celebrations. Late in the evening of Christmas Eve they stopped by Vincent's house, dropping off dozens of wrapped gifts, before they all set off for the church for Midnight Mass. The place was packed to the rafters when they arrived, but the first pew on the left in the front remained empty.

Corrado and Celia sauntered down the long aisle, hand in hand, as Vincent and Maura followed them, carrying the boys. Rows of parishioners quieted when they passed, gaping at the family, before breaking out into hushed murmurs of gossip when they thought they were out of earshot.

Corrado heard, though. He heard their grumbling, the criticism they wouldn't dare say to any of their faces. He heard it, and ignored it.

Their opinions meant nothing to him.

He stopped at the front pew and slid down to the far end, as Celia took a seat beside him. Maura settled in beside her, clutching Carmine to her chest as he slept. Vincent sat beside his wife, Dominic on his lap, wide-awake, wide-eyed.

Although Vincent made it to church every Sunday, it was the first time his family had come with him.

They sat still, waiting, until Antonio arrived. The church fell into a stone cold silence the moment he stepped foot through the doors, his wife on his arm. There was no murmuring as he passed the rows, no disapproval, and no hostility. People bowed their heads as if God Himself had graced them with His presence. Antonio politely nodded as he passed acquaintances, pausing beside the front pew to survey his family. Corrado caught his eye, seeing the smile cracking his stern expression.

Antonio motioned to the bench, his gaze on his wife. She hesitated for a few seconds before sliding in beside her son... beside Dominic... as Antonio flanked the other end.

Corrado laughed to himself, drawing Celia's attention. "It's something, isn't it?" she whispered. "Mom's playing nice."

He draped his arm over her shoulder, pulling her closer. "It's a Christmas miracle."

They stood for the elaborate procession as the choir sang *Come All, Ye Faithful*, Celia belting the song out at the top of her lungs while Dominic enthusiastically clapped his hands, watching his aunt. Mid-song she reached over, snatching him from his father's arms. She sang to him, planting a kiss on his puffy cheek, leaving a smudge of red lipstick behind as he squealed with excitement.

"You're going to fit in wonderfully, kiddo," she whispered to the little boy. "Just keep that sense of humor. You're gonna need it."

Corrado smirked, standing with his hands clasped in front of him.

The passionate service flew by as Father Alberto poured his soul out through his words, never forgetting to urge them to respect, and cherish, and love one another. Celia held tightly to Dominic the whole time, giving Vincent a break, as Carmine slept through the entire Mass. After it was over, Corrado followed his family outside, hoping to avoid conversation, but Father Alberto caught him by the exit.

"Mr. Moretti," the priest said, grasping his arm when he attempted to slip by. Corrado glanced down at where the man's hand clutched his bicep before looking him in the eyes, surprised he would have such nerve, but the priest showed no apprehension. A small smile touched Father Alberto's lips at the incredulous look on Corrado's face. "I've had many men just like you walk through these doors and find asylum once inside. You don't have to be an exception."

Corrado stared at him. "Church sanctuary is a myth."

"But the seal of the confessional is real."

The man let go of Corrado's arm to address another worshiper.

Shaking his head, Corrado stepped outside into the cold Chicago night. His family stood on the steps, Dominic still in Celia's arms. He approached them as Celia's eyes lit up. She focused on her brother and Maura. "Can we keep him?"

Whoa. Corrado's footsteps faltered.

"Just for tonight," Celia said, wrapping her arms tightly around him, his head lying on her shoulder. He was still awake, for now, but heaviness accented every blink of his eyes. "We'll bring him home tomorrow."

Skepticism twisted Maura's expression as she pursed her lips. "I don't know."

Celia's expression fell. "If you're worried, you know, because of my husband—"

"No, no, that's not it," Maura said. "It's just that… it's Christmas."

"So?"

"So there's cookies, and stories, and I know they're still little now and won't understand, but…"

Corrado stepped up behind his wife, clearing his throat as he leaned down toward her. "She's saying Santa Claus doesn't come to our house."

Celia tensed a bit, realizing he had been listening. "He can."

"No, he can't."

"We have a chimney."

"If something comes down my chimney, I'm shooting it… *especially* a fat man wearing a suit."

Celia gasped, covering Dominic's ears, as Vincent let out a laugh.

"Fine," Celia conceded, handing the boy over to Vincent. "Another night then?"

"Another night," Maura assured her. "Any other time you want the boys, they're yours."

Corrado had never seen Celia so radiant.

Maura made good on her promise and let Celia keep both the boys on New Years Eve. Corrado made sure he had work to do all night as they slept soundly, safely, in his bed.

1989 dawned, life moving in a blur as January whittled away, Dominic and Carmine's christenings approaching. Carmine's ceremony was an event to rival that of Midnight Mass, elaborate, the pews packed with well-wishers, family and friends, all watching as the quiet little boy was christened. Salvatore Capozzi stood up at the front, superiority in his stance as he stood before the priest and agreed to be his godfather, committing to help raise the child in the Catholic faith.

The moment the priest anointed Carmine, splashing holy water on him, he let out a startled, piercing shriek that made Gia close her eyes and shake her head, muttering, "the devil's in that boy."

Dominic's christening, a week later, was more laid-back. Gia didn't even make the effort to show up. Sonny Evola quietly stood before the priest, his expression serious as he took on the role of godfather.

Vincent hadn't bothered asking Corrado.

When the priest anointed Dominic, the boy blinked rapidly, stunned, before squealing.

Happily.

39

Corrado parked his Mercedes in the packed lot, hesitating in the car, trying to convince himself he wasn't making a mistake being there. It felt absurd, traitorous in a way, for him to step foot on these premises. But he had made a promise… a promise he wouldn't break.

He climbed out, fixing his tie as he strode toward the crumbling apartment building. The buzzer was broken, the entire intercom hanging by wires, a cinderblock used as a makeshift doorstop. *Unsafe.*

Corrado stepped into the dingy building, grimacing at the stench of mildew streaming off the damp, dark carpet. The sky blue paint chipped, completely gone in places, exposing a filthy white under layer of plaster. He took the stairs, not trusting the elevator, and trekked up four flights to reach the right floor.

Apartment 42.

He strode down the hallway, hands in his pockets, the lights hanging from the ceiling flickering and buzzing like a scene from a low-budget horror flick. He reached the right door, staring at the numbers, the 4 hanging upside down by a lone screw.

Taking a deep breath, he tapped on the door.

It only took a minute for it to open a crack, a chain lock still connected as a pair of brown eyes peeked out at him. They studied him peculiarly before the door slammed right in his face, the chain jingling before the door flew open again.

Corrado tensed as Vivian launched herself at him. She

wrapped her arms around him, nuzzling in his neck as she cried, her body trembling. Corrado rubbed her back as he walked her into the apartment.

Once inside, he shut the door and pried her away from him. She let go, smiling sheepishly, tears streaming down her cheeks. "I'm sorry. It's just... it's like seeing Vito again."

He tried to ignore his discomfort. "How are you holding up?"

His question brought on another round of sobs. "I just wish I could see him. Wish I could talk to him. It hurts so much, and I feel like I can't breathe. I love him with everything inside of me. And he doesn't even care."

"He cares," Corrado insisted.

"Then why won't he let me visit?"

"He doesn't want you to see him that way, caged like an animal."

"That doesn't matter to me!"

"But it does to him. He needs to keep his pride. It's about the only thing he has."

"It's not fair," she cried. "I miss him."

"I know."

As much as Corrado didn't want to admit it, he missed him, too. There were months of his life where he went without hearing from his father, without seeing his face, but this was permanent.

Vivian told him to make himself at home and offered him something to drink. He asked for some water, his anxiety making him parched, as he sat down on the edge of her frayed couch. The apartment interior wasn't any better than the outside—grimy floors, chipped paint, and a slight foul odor she tried to conceal with an abundance of fragrant candles. It created a peculiar aroma that clung to the furniture, like wilting flowers in an old leaky vase.

It wasn't the kind of place he expected his father to house his mistress. He worried about infection just breathing the polluted air.

Vivian returned, handing him a fresh bottle of water. Thank God, because he wasn't sure he trusted a glass from her cabinets. Taking a drink, he scanned the room.

"I know what you're thinking," she said, sitting down beside him, so close their knees touched. Corrado wanted to move over, to get some personal space, but he was pinned right against the arm of the couch. "You're wondering why Vito would ever slum it with someone like me."

"Actually, I'm wondering why my father would let you live like this. I thought he was better than that."

"He is." Vivian frowned. "This place wasn't always this bad. I lived here when I met Vito, but I stayed with him so much that most of my stuff ended up at his house. I kept this apartment as Plan B, I guess. I knew he was married, so part of me always expected to end up back here. The building went to hell since then, but there isn't much I can do about it. Your mother took control of Vito's assets, and well, you see where that leaves me."

Corrado surveyed the squalor again, watching a bug scurry across the floor. He put the lid back on his water, no longer thirsty.

"I should be going," he said, standing up. "I just wanted to stop by and make sure you were okay."

"I am," she said, not sounding confident. "Or I will be, anyway."

Corrado headed toward the door, hesitating with his hand clutching the knob. Half a dozen locks aligned the splintered wooden door. "I'll see what I can do about getting you out of this place."

"You don't have to do that," she replied, standing right behind him. "I know it has to be awkward, being around me, knowing what I was to your father."

He shook his head, turning to her. She had warmth in her eyes, a softness to her face. He could see what Vito saw in her… *kindness.*

That he didn't get from Erika.

"No more awkward than being around my mother," he replied.

He opened the door to leave when her body slammed against his, her arms wrapping around his torso from behind. She buried her face against his shoulder as a fresh wave of sobs rocked her.

"Thank you," she whimpered. "You're a great man, so much like your father."

Corrado nodded, acknowledging the compliment, and slipped away before she cried anymore.

The stench from the building seemed to have embedded into the fabric of his clothes, infiltrating the fibers, pressing upon his skin. He drove home, breathing through his mouth to avoid smelling it any more than necessary.

Celia wasn't home when he arrived. Heading upstairs, he stripped out of his clothes, throwing them in the hamper. They needed a good soaking. Feeling the same about himself, he jumped in the shower, standing under the hot spray, scrubbing his skin.

Afterward, he threw on a pair of sweat pants and strolled downstairs, hearing noises in the kitchen. Celia worked studiously, putting away groceries. Corrado watched her for a bit, standing in the doorway until she spun around, catching him there.

"Hey!" she said. "I hoped to get to see you tonight."

"Here I am." He had missed dinner the night before, having to call and tell her he wouldn't be coming home. He had heard the disappointment in her voice, something that bothered him. He promised a night of just the two of them, no interruptions, a nice dinner where she didn't have to cook, and he planned to deliver.

"How long are you home for?"

"All night," he replied.

"You, not working on a Friday night? I don't think that's *ever* happened before."

He had bitten the bullet and entrusted the day-to-day operations to his crew. "I took a personal day."

"A personal day? Is that like paid vacation?"

"Something like that."

"So what did you do on your personal day?"

"Ran some errands."

"Ran errands," she echoed, putting away the last of the groceries before walking over to him. "Sounds like *work* to me."

He shrugged. Felt like work, too.

"So you're all mine tonight?" she asked, pressing her hand flat against his bare chest. "No one else's?"

"All yours," he replied, grabbing her hand, bringing it to his lips to press a kiss on the back of it.

"How about we order pizza and watch a movie?" she suggested. "We can watch one of those scary films you like."

"Whatever you want."

Poltergeist.

Corrado had seen it a few times, but he never got Celia to sit down and watch with him. He pulled the VHS off the shelf, waving it at her, chuckling at the apprehension on her face.

"Can't we get zombies or something instead?" she asked. "A little girl being kidnapped is bad enough. Adding evil spirits to it is unforgivable."

He glanced at the shelf again, scanning the titles. "Night of the Living Dead?"

"Sounds wretched," she said. "How about vampires?"

"Salem's Lot."

"Ugh." That one she sat through. "Werewolves?"

"The Howling."

"Do you have Teen Wolf?"

"That's a comedy."

"So? It's cute."

"I don't do *cute*."

"You do me," she argued. "I'm cute."

He glanced over at her. She leaned against the arm of the couch, her knees pulled up, arms wrapped around them. "You're beautiful, Celia. And that movie is terrible."

"Fine." She huffed, waving him away. "Put in the first one, then."

Corrado slid Poltergeist into the VCR and grabbed the remote before sitting down on the couch beside his wife. She shifted her body, snuggling up against him.

Despite her reluctance, it didn't take long for Celia to get engrossed in the movie, so much so that when the ring of the doorbell echoed through the downstairs, a high-pitched yelp tore from her lips. She jumped, her eyes darting around in shock. Corrado held back laughter, his arm draped over her shoulder.

Celia sat, frozen stiff, before logic seemed to return to her. "The delivery guy's here."

"Okay." Did she think he couldn't hear? He sensed her gaze as the doorbell rang again. Dragging his attention from the movie, he saw the expectant look. "What?"

She shook her head as she stood. "Don't worry, Corrado. *I'll* get the door."

"Okay," he said again.

"Sometimes I just don't know about you," she grumbled, grabbing her purse.

He smiled, watching her stomp out. If she wanted him to get it, all she had to do was ask.

She returned with the food and placed it on the coffee table before sitting back down on the couch. The plain box had an orange checkerboard pattern, *Pizza* written along the top. Dolce Vita Pizza had closed down the year before, the economic downturn taking a hit at businesses in the neighborhood, but the building hadn't stayed empty long. A mere two months later, a white Grand Opening banner flapped in the wind beneath the brand new sign reading *Tarullo's Pizzeria.*

Bought and paid for by John Tarullo with the money he received from his father's life insurance policy.

Corrado opened the lid, taking in the massive hoard of pepperoni piled on top of the pizza. Celia grabbed a slice, winking at him.

He took a piece. "This counts as your dinner rain check."

"No, it doesn't," she said. "We're not even sitting at the table."

"So? We said dinner; this is dinner."

"It doesn't count as a real dinner if we don't have plates or forks."

"Yes, it does."

"No, it doesn't."

"Then what is this, if not dinner?"

She shrugged. "Call it a snack for all I care. It doesn't count."

"Then what's for dinner tonight?"

"Nothing," she said. "We're not having dinner tonight."

"Who doesn't have dinner?"

"We don't," she said. "Not when we order pizza."

She was one of the most stubborn people he had ever encountered. "You're wrong."

"I'm right," she said, turning away to watch the movie again.

Before he could counter, the phone beside him rang. He

tensed at the sound and Celia laughed. "Okay, maybe I'm wrong, after all. The phone is interrupting, so it *must* be dinner."

Sometimes it seemed like she just enjoyed giving him a hard time. "I won't answer it."

"You will," she said. "What if it's important?"

"It can wait."

"What if it's my dad?"

"It's not."

"You won't know that until you answer it."

Knowing she wouldn't drop it, he snatched up the phone, eyes still on the television. "Moretti speaking."

"Corrado." Antonio's voice greeted him. "You busy tonight?"

He hesitated. "No, sir."

"Good," he said. "I got something that needs taken care of. Come to my house."

The line went dead. Without saying another word, Corrado hung up the phone and set his half-eaten slice of pizza back in the box.

As usual, she was right.

"Like I said…" Celia kicked her feet up on the couch, shifting away from him, her attention returning to the movie. "…this doesn't count as my rain check."

The house was pitch black when Corrado got back home in the wee hours of the morning. The cold, stale air hung eerily silent. Corrado walked to the living room to start a fire, not close to being tired, knowing Celia would be asleep at this hour.

He stepped into the room and reached for the light switch when movement on the couch caught his eye. He froze, heart thumping wildly, as he stared at the form in the darkness. The light from the window, a nearby streetlight, gave enough of a glow for him to make out her features. "Celia?"

"Who is she?"

Her tone was icier than the house.

"Who?"

"Don't do that," she said, a quiver in her voice. "Don't treat me that way, Corrado. Be a man and tell me."

"I don't know what you're talking about."

"Don't lie to me!"

He flicked the switch, wincing at the sudden bright light, as he stepped closer to the couch. Celia jumped up, her hair a mess, makeup wiped off. She didn't cry... no, not anymore... but she had. Her bloodshot eyes were puffy.

"I don't lie to you," he said, reaching out to her, but she smacked his hands away and took a step back.

"Don't touch me." Her eyes narrowed with disgust. "Don't even *look* at me."

Her irritation didn't deter him. He stared her straight in the eyes. "I don't know what you're talking about," he said again, voice calm despite his utter confusion.

"There's makeup on your shirt," she spat, snatching up a white button down shirt from the couch cushion where she had been sitting. "Lipstick on your collar!"

"It's yours," he said with disbelief. Why was she acting this way? It wasn't the first time his shirt had been stained by her makeup.

"It's not mine."

"You're mistaken."

"I'm not," she spat. "It's *pink*!"

"That's impossible," he said. "You don't wear pink."

She shook the shirt angrily, stepping toward him. There it was, the smear on the edge of the collar, another right on the shoulder, mixed with faint black smudges. Bright pink. There was no mistaking it.

Vivian.

He closed his eyes. *Not good.*

"Is that where you were?" she spat, shoving the shirt against his chest. He stumbled backward a step, surprised by her strength, and clutched the shirt. "Off with some whore? Is that why you were showered and changed in the middle of the afternoon? Huh? Is it?"

"It's not what you think," he said.

"Not what I think?" She let out a high-pitched laugh, the

mocking sound concealing what he knew to be real hurt. "I can smell it on the shirt. It reeks."

"It does," he agreed. He still faintly smelled the stench.

A flash of pain took over Celia's expression like she had been struck before the fire returned to her eyes, burning brighter than before. A switch had been flipped inside of her, setting her off.

She lunged at him.

Corrado was so caught off guard it took a moment for him to react, enough time for her fists to strike his chest. The force of the punch wasn't enough to take his breath away, not enough to leave a mark, but the damage it caused ran deep. He wouldn't do this with her. He wouldn't be this way. They wouldn't be *that* couple.

They wouldn't be his parents.

He responded by grabbing her, pinning her arms at her sides to stop her striking fists. He restrained her, blocking her blows, as he leaned down and growled in her ear. "We're not doing this. I'm not going to *fight* you."

"How could you?" The tears flowed down her cheeks now. "How could you do that to me?"

"I haven't done anything."

"I love you," she cried.

"And I love you," he said quietly. "Only you."

"Then why? Why would you? How could you?"

"I wouldn't," he swore. "I *didn't.* I would never touch another woman. You know me better than that."

"Do I?" she asked, trying to pry away from him. "Let me go!"

He hesitated before loosening his hold. He wouldn't keep her there against her will. She shoved away from him, stepping back, wiping her tears. The shirt dropped to the floor between them and she kicked it away, disgust twisting her face.

"You should," he said. "You should know me."

"I thought I did."

"That…" He motioned toward the shirt. "…meant nothing."

The flash of pain struck her again as she gasped.

This wasn't coming out right.

"Her name's Vivian," he explained. "She's—"

"A whore?" she spat, eyes widening. "It's true?"

Irritation swam beneath his skin. He tried to swallow it back, to remain calm, but she was pushing him. "She was my father's mistress. He wanted me to look out for her, since he can't anymore."

"And, what? You *fucked* her?"

He grimaced as she spat that word at him. "I didn't touch her."

"Then how did her lipstick get on your collar?"

"She was crying," he said. "She hugged me."

"She hugged you?" she asked with disbelief. "You expect me to believe that?"

"It's true," he said. "She cried into my shoulder. I didn't ask her to do it. I didn't *want* her to do it. I didn't even want her to touch me. But she did. That's not my fault."

"Not your fault? You shouldn't have even been there!"

"My father asked me to do it," he said. Why couldn't she grasp that? "What was I supposed to do?"

"Tell him no! She's his mistress, not his wife! She was sleeping with a married man! Whose to say she wouldn't try to sleep with you?" That fire flared in her eyes again. "Whose to say she *didn't* sleep with you?"

"*I* say she didn't," he yelled, raising his voice as he pointed at himself. "That should be enough for you."

It wasn't. He saw it in her eyes.

"I'm a lot of things, Celia DeMarco, but I'm not this. I'll cheat the law, I'll cheat on my taxes, I'll try my damnedest to cheat death, but never… *never…* will I cheat on you."

She stared at him, breathing heavily, tears still streaming down her cheeks. "Moretti," she ground out.

"Excuse me?"

"My last name is *Moretti*," she stressed. "You called me a DeMarco."

"Because you're acting like one."

She raised a sculpted eyebrow at him. "How exactly does a DeMarco act?"

"Emotional."

A sharp laugh of disbelief tore through the room. "Sorry I'm not *frigid* like the rest of you Morettis."

He glared at her, those words picking at him like little needles against his skin. "I'm not frigid."

"You feel nothing," she spat.

She was intentionally being spiteful. He didn't like it. *At all.*

"Come on." Corrado grasped her wrist and yanked. "Let's go."

He dragged her to the doorway before she pulled from his grasp and hissed, "I told you not to touch me."

"Then follow me on your own."

He strode outside, pulling out his keys. He left the front door wide open, not even glancing back as he climbed behind the wheel and started the car. A few seconds passed before the passenger side door opened, and Celia slid into the seat. She didn't speak as he pulled away from the curb, the sky lightening on the horizon.

She might have been angry, might have been hurt, but a part of her still implicitly trusted him.

He drove through town, bitter silence gripping the car until he pulled into the packed parking lot, not bothering to search for a spot, just skidding to a stop. He threw the car in park and cut the engine. "You don't believe me? I'll show you."

"What?"

The question was only half out of her mouth when he got out and slammed the door.

Celia climbed out behind him, hollering at him. "Corrado? Where are you going?"

"To prove to you I didn't lie."

Her footsteps stalled briefly before speeding up to reach him. "You brought me here? To the whore?"

"She's a decent woman."

"She was your father's dirty little secret."

"She wasn't much of a secret. Everyone knew about her."

"That makes it even worse! Where's her self-respect?"

He pulled on the front door of the building, holding it open for Celia. She stepped around the cinderblock and grimaced when she entered the building. "God, what died in here?"

He walked in behind her, the door slamming against the

cinderblock. He cut his eyes at his wife. "Maybe her dignity did."

"Funny," she sneered, following him to the stairs. She reached for the banister but hesitated, instead wiping her hand on her clothes, not wanting to touch anything.

They trekked to the fourth floor. Corrado knocked on the door of 42 and waited, knocking two more times before he heard movement inside the apartment. The door was pulled open, once again blocked by the chain, as the woman appeared in the crack. "Corrado?"

"Vivian," he greeted her. "I just need a moment of your time."

"Sure." The door closed again, the lock jingling, before it opened the whole way. Vivian eyed him apprehensively, noticing Celia. "Uh, hey."

Celia spoke hesitantly. "Hello."

"Well, come in," she said as she stepped aside. "Make yourselves at home."

Corrado stepped around her, pausing there as Celia walked in. "Vivian, this is my wife, Celia. Celia, Vivian."

"Nice to meet you," Vivian said at once, smiling. That kindness Corrado had sensed earlier surfaced full force. "I've heard a lot about you."

Celia's eyes cut to Corrado, subtle, swift, but Vivian noticed as she closed the door. "Actually, it was from Vito. He always talked about how lucky his son was to have married such a great woman."

"He is lucky," Celia agreed as she relaxed a bit. "*Very* lucky."

Corrado shook his head. "I don't believe in luck."

That earned him another look from Celia. "If you aren't lucky, what are you?"

"Persuasive."

She rolled her eyes as Vivian laughed. She offered the two of them something to drink, never once questioning why they were there at that hour or what they wanted. She was hospitable and chatty, complimenting Celia, engaging her in conversation about things that meant nothing to Corrado—clothes, and shoes, and hair-dos. He sat on the edge of her frayed couch once again as the two women traded stories for a bit, almost as if they were old friends. The sun had risen outside, taking its place high in the sky, when the words slowed to a trickle.

"We should be going," Corrado said, interrupting before they found something else to gossip about.

Celia stood, smoothing out her clothes before pulling Vivian into a hug. "It was great to meet you."

"You, too," Vivian whispered, tears springing to her eyes. "You're so kind."

Celia pulled away from her and strode to the door as Corrado followed. He nearly made it out before Vivian lunged at him, hugging him from behind. He tensed, back rigid, as she burst into tears.

"Sorry," she said, letting go as she wiped her eyes. "It's just, you know…"

"I know," he said. *Vito.*

He walked out into the hallway, shutting the door, when Celia descended upon him. She narrowed her eyes, poking him hard in the chest. "If you ever go near that woman again, I'll *kill* you."

Corrado blanched. "But you liked her."

"I did," she agreed. "And maybe she *is* a decent woman, but she's also a grieving woman… a woman grieving for a man you're a hell of a lot like."

His brow furrowed as he took her hand. "I don't look like Vito."

"You do," she insisted. "You carry yourself like him, too. And that woman in there isn't blind to that fact."

"You're being absurd."

"No, you're just a fool."

40

The ringing of the phone cut Celia off mid-sentence, tension falling over the table. They were having dinner together for the first time in a week.

She had cashed in on her rain check, and Corrado had promised this evening to her. There weren't to be any interruptions. No work tonight. No one was to stop by. His phone wasn't supposed to ring.

He should've known better.

He ignored it until Celia sighed. "Go ahead and get it."

"No," he replied. "They can wait."

The phone continued to ring.

"It could be important," she said.

"Nothing's more important than dinner with you."

She sighed. Again.

The ringing stopped, silence sweeping through the house for a few seconds, before it started up again.

Whoever it was called right back.

"Answer it," Celia said. "Before they show up here."

Corrado threw down his fork, tossing his napkin aside, before shoving his chair back. "Excuse me."

She merely waved him away as she continued to eat.

He strode to the living room, snatching up the receiver. "Moretti speaking."

"Mr. Moretti, it's Reverend Parker, the chaplain at Menard Correctional Center."

As soon as those words met Corrado's ears, he shook his head. *Vito.* "If you're calling about my father, I'm afraid I can't help you."

"Yes, well, it's important."

"There's nothing I can do."

"Unfortunately, sir, there's nothing any of us can do." The reverend's voice sounded hollow. "I'm sorry to inform you, Mr. Moretti, but your father passed away."

The man kept talking, very little registering as Corrado scratched absently at his jaw, coated in almost a weeks worth of scruff. He waited until the man paused before chiming in. "I appreciate the call."

"Of course," he said. "If you have questions, you can contact the warden at—"

Corrado hung up before he could rattle off the phone number. Speaking to the prison warden was as bad as dealing with the police.

Returning to the dining room, he retook his seat.

"Let me guess," Celia said. "You need to leave."

"No." He placed his napkin in his lap and picked up his fork.

Celia glanced at him with surprise. "No? Who was it?"

"The chaplain."

"You mean the priest?" she asked. "Father Alberto?"

"No, Reverend Parker, at the prison."

"Oh Lord," she said, picking up her drink to take a sip. "What's Vito up to now?"

"Nothing," he replied. "He's dead."

Celia froze, glass half way to her lips. "What did you say?"

"I said he's dead."

Celia gasped, her hand shaking as she set her glass down. "Vito?"

He nodded.

"How can that be?" she asked, her eyes glossing over with tears. "It has to be some sort of mistake, right? He can't really be… there's just no way."

"He is," Corrado replied, shoving the food around on his plate with his fork.

Celia jumped up, shaking her head frantically. "We have to do something. We have to call someone. *Something.*"

She bolted for the door, frenzied, but Corrado snatched a hold of her to stop her. Pushing his chair back, he pulled her into his lap, wrapping his arms around her when she started to cry. Hiccupping gasps rocked her chest, tears streaming down her cheeks as she clung to him.

Her hand grasped the back of his neck, fingernails digging into his skin. "I'm so, so sorry, Corrado."

She was trying to console him.

He held her tightly, laying his head against her as he rubbed soothing circles on her back, letting her cry. No tears streamed from his eyes, but he felt it deep in his chest, a tight knot of emotion as a lump in his throat made it hard to swallow, hard to breathe.

"He's dead," he whispered, stress audible in the strain of his voice as he rocked her in the chair. "My father's dead."

Convicted Cop Killer Murdered in Prison

It didn't even make the front page. Corrado found the article tucked in the newspaper a few pages in, wedged between an article about school budget cuts and reports of voter fraud.

A purported member of the Chicago Mafia has died at the Menard Correctional Facility, where he was serving a life sentence.

Officials say Vito Moretti was found dead around noon on Friday in the prison chapel, the victim of a fatal attack. Moretti, 44, had gone to the chapel for Reconciliation when he was stabbed multiple times in the neck and face. The weapon, suspected to be a sharpened pencil, was not found at the scene.

The prison was immediately put on a lockdown. Officials say the surveillance equipment in the chapel malfunctioned prior to the incident. They have no suspects, but believe it to be a fellow inmate.

Moretti was convicted of the murder of Chicago detective John Walker and had only recently been transferred to Menard. He had been placed in general population at his own request, despite prison officials' concerns about his numerous enemies.

Murdered in the prison chapel, found face down in a pool of blood. He had been praying… it was the only way someone would catch Vito off guard, the only reason he wouldn't fight back.

As a child, Corrado believed his father was invincible, ten feet tall and bulletproof. But he wasn't.

He never had been.

Brilliant James Bond walked right into the enemy's trap. Batman got exposed as a mere mortal. And Vito Moretti, resilient and fearless, got taken out with a harmless implement. *A pencil.*

The bigger they are, the harder they fall.

The reality of it was a slap to the face. Vito didn't get to go out in a blaze of glory. Vito went out on his knees, with his eyes closed, as he appealed to a God that wouldn't spare him.

A few days after the article ran, Corrado was scanning through the newspaper when he came upon another familiar name in the obituaries: Vivian Modella.

It didn't say what happened to her, but Corrado could guess. *Grief.* He burned the newspaper in the fireplace right away, before Celia happened upon it.

Bitterness festered inside of Corrado, his anger growing as days passed. Erika flew in from Nevada and claimed the body. Vito had been cremated overnight without Corrado even being informed, robbing him of his burial rites… robbing him of a Catholic funeral. By the time Corrado heard what his mother had done, she was already heading for home.

Never in his life had he wanted to kill someone as much as he did then. Killing, to Corrado, had always been a job. It was technical, methodic. It was never emotional. But thinking about his mother, thinking about how wronged his father had been, stirred up a suppressed need for retribution. The bloodthirsty sensations engulfed him, dragging him deeper into a darkness that he had only dove into a handful of times in his life.

The part of him, he guessed, that had died the day of his birth. The part of him that never got brought back to life. It was a part of him that knew nothing of sunshine, of happiness, of love, of compassion. His heart didn't beat. His lungs didn't breathe. He was a walking corpse.

The living dead.

The bright sun scorched Corrado's skin as it hovered high above in the hazy afternoon sky, not a single cloud anywhere to temper it. Despite it being the beginning of September, fast approaching autumn, the air still sweltered like the peak of summer. Mid-nineties, not a single breeze, very little shade around the dry, desert land. Corrado certainly hadn't missed that.

Somehow, over the years, he had learned to enjoy the cold.

He didn't want to be here. But a job was a job, and the Boss had personally ordered him to do it.

"You know all about that place," Antonio had said. "Take care of it for me."

On the contrary, Corrado knew nothing about it. Except for a few vague childhood memories, their operations around Nevada remained a mystery to him.

He, respectfully, pointed that out, but Antonio dismissed it. "Doesn't matter. You could use a vacation."

So Corrado stood beside his rental car in the desert, just over the border into California, surveying the barren ground, mulling over the Boss's words. Nothing to see for miles except cracked earth with a splash of occasional trees. That wasn't Corrado's idea of a vacation.

Who would ever come to this hellhole willingly?

A door opening drew his attention to the lone house in the vicinity. He had driven in circles around the abandoned town of Blackburn for over an hour before catching a gleam of something off in the distance. There was no mailbox, no sign, nothing to indicate anyone lived there, but as Corrado followed the narrow, worn path through the desert, he came upon the large ranch.

Frankie Antonelli stepped out onto the porch, his sleeves rolled up. "I see you found the place."

"Wasn't easy."

"That's the point. Hard to get in, even harder to get out." Frankie waved him forward. "Come on out of the heat."

Corrado stepped inside, expecting the man to lead him to his office, but instead he veered left to the living room. Corrado took a seat in the closest chair as Frankie plopped down on the couch, documents splayed out in front of him on the coffee table.

"Monica!" Frankie shouted. "Come here!"

Footsteps descended the adjacent stairs. In less than a minute a woman appeared, wearing a yellow summer dress, her dark hair pulled up. She stalled in the doorway, not coming any closer. "Yeah?"

Frankie glanced up at her before motioning to Corrado. "That's my wife, Monica. Monica, honey, this is Corrado Moretti."

His name sparked something in Monica's eyes. "Katrina's brother."

Corrado refused to humor that title with a response.

"Yeah," Frankie answered for him. "The in-laws."

"Well, it's nice to meet you, Corrado," Monica said.

He nodded. "You, too."

"Before you go back upstairs, get us something to drink." Frankie focused on the stacks of paper. "Bourbon for me and whatever Corrado here wants."

"Water," Corrado said.

Monica disappeared, returning with their drinks. She hesitated in the doorway again, holding them, not stepping any closer.

She knew better than to come near Frankie's work.

Seeing her conflicted expression, Corrado stood and stepped toward her, taking his water and Frankie's alcohol. He thanked her, seeing the relief in her eyes, while Frankie blatantly ignored her.

Corrado watched her curiously as she left. He couldn't imagine *ever* treating his wife so dismissively.

Over the next few hours, Frankie broke down the Vegas scheme for Corrado… things his father had never bothered to explain. The entire operation was being shifted to Frankie, territories Vito once controlled being turned over. Corrado helped him line up connections to make the takeover as smooth as possible, using his family to bridge the divide. Antonelli was a made man and had seniority, but he had never earned the clout in Vegas that the Moretti name carried.

After all, Vito Moretti was a legend in the streets.

It neared dusk when Corrado grew tired and hungry. He

smelled food cooking in the kitchen, the scent of simmering marinara. It seemed to be affecting Frankie too, because he closed a notebook and sat back. "How about we call it a night?"

Corrado nodded. He could use a long shower and some sleep.

"Wanna stay for dinner?" Frankie asked. "Monica makes a mean Chicken Parmesan."

"Not tonight," Corrado said.

"Tomorrow, then." Frankie reached out to shake his hand. "I won't take no for an answer."

Corrado stepped out of the living room just as Monica burst out of the kitchen, sweating, an apron shielding her dress.

"Leaving?" she asked.

"Yes, ma'am," Corrado said. "It was a pleasure to meet you."

She smiled sweetly as he left.

The moment Corrado stepped onto the porch, the heat blasted him again, nearly taking his breath away. He inhaled, blinking a few times to adjust to the dusty air, as he scanned the property. Out of the corner of his eye, he caught sight of a young woman along the nearby horse stables, her back to him. The screen door slamming behind him caught her attention, and she swung around, stunning Corrado with the swell of her stomach beneath her filthy white tank top. *Pregnant.*

Corrado's eyes narrowed as he scanned her. She was a small girl… young and naturally pretty, with a round, soft face. No more than sixteen, with rich sun-kissed skin, splashed with red along her cheeks. "I wasn't aware you had a daughter."

The Antonellis *didn't* have one. Michael was an only child. This girl… she wasn't theirs.

"Yeah, uh, no… she's not my child."

"Is she *carrying* your child?"

That thought was unfathomable to Corrado as the memory of Pascal invaded his mind. Not long after Vincent had killed Pascal, Alex had also been found dead. Corrado didn't ask who did it, didn't question it, but part of him wondered if Vincent had more blood on his hands.

"No," Frankie said. "I'd never touch the girl like that."

"But somebody did."

Corrado left it at that. The man remained silent, but shame shined from his eyes.

Not his child... his grandchild?

Michael Antonelli *was* that kind of person.

Corrado turned back to the girl, watching as she clutched her stomach and winced, hunching over as the pain registered on her face. It was brief, lasting a few seconds before she straightened back up.

Corrado stepped off the porch, motioning toward the girl. "She's going to have that baby soon."

"I know," Frankie grumbled. "I figure it's due in another two months or so."

"More like *days*," Corrado stressed, glancing back at the girl as another wave of pain hit her. "Or maybe even hours."

Early the next morning, Corrado arrived back at the Antonelli ranch to find a much somber atmosphere. Frankie sat on the couch, his voice barely a mutter as the two of them finished work.

Monica was nowhere to be found.

Frankie offered him a drink, getting up to get it himself. Corrado watched him skeptically when he got back to work. "It's peculiar that you have *help* around here, yet your wife does the cooking and you're serving."

Frankie paused, his eyes fixed on the table in front of him. He was silent for a moment before picking up where he left off. "Ever hear you sound like your father?"

"Occasionally."

"My son's nothing like me."

It didn't escape Corrado's notice that he deflected the attention instead of addressing it.

"I blame his mother," Frankie continued. "I'm guessing yours didn't coddle you."

"Unless coddling involves bruises and welts, no."

"Spare the rod, spoil the child," Frankie muttered. "I tried to teach Mikey right, but his mother made him think the world owes him. She spoiled him. And she's spoiling the girl, too."

Corrado's eyes narrowed suspiciously. Spoiling a slave?

"You were right," Frankie said. "The girl had that baby late last night. Monica found them, wanted to bring them in the house. She's always trying to do that."

"Does she have a name?"

"I don't know," he muttered. "I didn't ask about the bastard."

"I meant the girl."

"Oh. Yeah. We call her Miranda."

"And you're keeping..." *your granddaughter* "...the bastard?"

"She's here, isn't she?"

Frankie's voice turned defensive. Corrado dropped the subject, knowing better than to push him.

They finished their work mid-afternoon, and Corrado left, never once seeing Monica. There was no invitation for dinner.

He wouldn't have stayed, anyway.

He had other things to do.

The house was a disaster. A layer of dirt coated the wooden floor, a muddy carpet adorned with footprints. Glass shards splattered the short path, sunlight reflecting off of them like twinkling stars.

Corrado didn't knock. All hope of civility had gone out the window months ago. He had a purpose and it had nothing to do with playing nice.

The rotten stench of decay hung thickly, not an ounce of air flowing through the house. He closed the door behind him, blocking the natural light, everything falling into darkness.

It was eerily silent, not a single noise. No humming, no buzzing...

No electricity.

Some people never change.

Corrado strode through the downstairs, stopping in the living room. No sign of his mother.

He sat down on the couch, his shoes crunching in a pile of debris. Glancing beside him, he was surprised to see his father's face smiling back at him. The frame was broken, only a few jagged pieces of glass still connected to it. The picture had been scratched up, handled so much the faces were smudged with fingerprints.

The only family photo they ever took.

Corrado had been seven at the time and dressed in a suit that matched his father's perfectly—black, with a light blue button down and black silk tie. Vito was impeccable, as always, whereas Corrado's shirt was covered in wrinkles from playing, his tie crooked and loose from him fiddling with it all afternoon. Staring at the photo, glancing between him and his father, he noticed the resemblance for the first time. He had his father's strong jawline and deep, dark eyes, his curls and even the same cockeyed smirk. He never much noticed it growing up, but now, looking back, he saw what everyone else saw.

Looking at himself, he saw Vito.

His mother hadn't left him uncontaminated, though. Although he had learned to hide his feelings like his father, he shared a common anger with his mother… anger that churned deep inside of him when he heard the tromping on the floor above. The footsteps headed down the stairs. He heard her profanity laced muttering as she navigated her way to the kitchen, avoiding the jagged glass. Cabinets banging, things tossed around, the unmistakable sound of a bottle of wine being uncorked. Corrado remained silent, sitting back on the couch as he set the photo face down on the table.

Vito wouldn't want to see what was happening there today.

Reaching into his coat, he pulled out his revolver, spinning the cylinder nonchalantly. The subtle ticking reverberated through the air void of all other noises. The footsteps started back out of the kitchen as she headed his way.

He caught sight of her from his peripheral when she entered the dark room, a full glass of wine in one hand with the rest of the bottle in the other. "I'm surprised you bother with a glass at all."

The sound of his chilling voice stalled her footsteps and

shocked her so much she jumped. The glass slipped from her hand, shattering as soon as it hit the floor. She nearly lost her grasp on the bottle but caught it by the rim, clinging to it with a shaky hand. She stared at him, trying to pull herself together and hide her surprise, but even in the darkness, it was clear as day.

"I guess I won't be bothering now," she mumbled, glancing down at the glass before taking a drink straight from the bottle.

Shaking his head, Corrado spun the gun's cylinder once more before closing it. "Where is he?"

"Who?"

"My father."

She laughed as she took another drink. The fear faded, her posture relaxing. "You always were an idiot, Corrado, but I didn't think you were *delusional.* He's dead. Gone. Never coming back."

Corrado acted like she hadn't spoken as he asked again. "Where is he?"

"Go to Hell," she spat. "That's where you'll find him."

Corrado was on his feet, lunging at his mother before her diluted senses even realized he'd left the couch. He snatched a hold of her, his firm hand wrapping around her neck as he shoved her into the wall so hard everything around her shook. She gasped painfully, stunned, losing her grip on the bottle of wine. It clattered to the floor, tipping over, the red alcohol spilling out all around her bare feet.

He leaned in close, his voice dangerously low. "Tell me what you did with him."

The time for questions was over.

"I burned that bastard until he was nothing," she growled, struggling against him, but he was too strong and she was much, much too drunk.

"Give me his remains."

"Too late," she said. "They're gone."

"I need them."

She laughed again, the humor choked as he grasped her tighter, anger surging through him.

"There's nothing funny about this," he said. "My father deserves to be buried. He deserves a funeral."

"I gave your father *exactly* what he deserved. I made sure he was nothing more than dust in the wind."

"No."

"Yes. I dumped him on the ground and kicked him around until he blew away."

"You wouldn't."

"I did," she said. "He never wanted to be here, anyway. This time, he's gone for good."

Losing his composure, Corrado slammed her back against the wall again, so hard she lost her breath, as he pointed his gun to her temple.

"Do it," she taunted, tears streaming from the corner of her eyes, the sight of them stalling Corrado's finger as it hovered over the trigger. "Kill me."

He glowered at her, pinning her against the wall.

"Do it!" She spit right in his face. "I *dare* you!"

Corrado let go of her, stepping back as he lowered the gun. Hesitating, he slipped it back in his coat and wiped his face with his sleeve.

"You fucking coward!" she yelled, her tears coming on harder, choking her words as she shook. "You're just as chicken shit as he was!"

He pointed at her, trying to rein in his anger. "Killing you would be too merciful. Instead, I'll give you what you deserve… misery. You can stay here, all alone in your house, and drink yourself to death for all I care. Because you're already dead to me, mother."

"Fuck you!" She came toward him, but he turned his back to her and went for the front door. "You were dead to me the day you were born, Corrado! I never wanted you. Nobody did, and nobody ever will!"

He paused as he opened the front door, watching as she winced in the afternoon sunshine, backing away from the light as if allergic to it. "I used to believe you when you said that, but you're wrong. Somebody told me a long time ago that you were wrong about me, and I should've believed her. She was a better woman than you'll ever be."

"Who?"

"*Zia*," he said. "My *Zia*."

With that, he walked out, slamming the door behind him.

Vito's Lincoln was parked in the driveway, gleaming under the sun's rays. Every window had been shattered, the outside dented, scratches carved into the paint. Corrado ran his hand along the hood as he walked around it, the metal burning his fingertips. He let out a deep sigh, gazing at it, seeing his father's fedora on the driver's seat.

Reaching through the broken window, he grabbed the hat and placed it on his head, cockeyed. He gave one last look at the Lincoln before turning away.

"*Arrivederci*, Dad."

PART V

That's Life

41

"This is absurd," Corrado muttered, pulling the oversized black hoodie on overtop of his plain white t-shirt. The temperature outside hovered in the mid-sixties. Sweat already started building beneath the layers.

He grabbed the bulletproof vest from the bench as Celia groaned. "Now *that* is absurd. Do I have to wear it?"

"Absolutely."

He motioned for her to come closer and she begrudgingly shuffled his way, a pout on her lips. He pulled the heavy vest on over her fitted white tank top, securing it tightly, before handing her one of his long-sleeve black button down shirts. She put it on, buttoning it the whole way up. It hung loose on her frame, but not as loose as the camouflage cargo pants she wore. She *drowned* in them.

Vincent's pants, apparently.

"You don't have to wear a vest," she whined, tugging at her heavy clothes. "Why do I?"

"I'm made of Kevlar, remember?" he joked, pulling on his favorite black leather gloves. They clung to his hands like a second skin while Celia shoved her hands in a pair of enormous camouflage gloves.

Vincent's again.

She continued to pout as Corrado grabbed the black knit hat and put it on her, tugging it down around her ears. His hands grasped the sides of her head as he stared her in the eyes.

"You're fierce," he said, kissing her forehead as he concealed his smile. She was a mere house kitten trying to wander into a lion's den. "I don't know what possessed you to want to do this, though."

"Daddy thought it was a great idea."

Corrado tensed. The Boss. "He's not coming, is he?"

"No, he said his involvement would be unfair."

Thank God. "I can't believe he'd even *approve* of this."

She shrugged weakly, her shoulders bogged down from the armor. "He said it would be interesting."

Interesting, indeed, but still... *absurd.*

Corrado loosened his hold on her, gently smoothing her hair flowing out from beneath the hat, as he glanced around the dingy locker room. There were a dozen people besides the two of them. Corrado recognized them all—if not by name, by face. Nine men, including Vincent and Manny, the others just guys on his crew. The three women were less familiar... Sonny Evola's daughter, Manny's wife, and one of Celia's long-time friends.

Everyone was clad in layers of protective clothing and body armor. Corrado was probably the least prepared. "I'm just not sure about *us* doing this."

"Oh, come on," she said. "Don't ruin your party, Corrado. You've never had one before."

He regretted sharing that tidbit of information. "I'm not eleven, Celia. It's not a big deal."

"You're thirty," she said. "That makes it an even bigger deal."

She grabbed a protective mask and shoved it at him, raising her eyebrows, daring him to argue. Corrado took it, conceding. He still thought it was a terrible idea, but he wouldn't spoil her special day.

Even if it was *his* birthday.

He perched the mask on top of his head as he picked up the gun, getting a feel for it. *Paintball.*

"You know I'll kill anyone who shoots you," Corrado said, eyeing the weapon.

"You won't," she said playfully. "No murdering on your birthday."

"It's my party," he muttered. "I'll kill if I want to."

Celia laughed as an announcement came on, telling the players to report to the field. Corrado helped Celia secure her mask before situating her gun and ammo. Red paintballs. Of course.

He had chosen green.

"Be careful out there," he told her.

Through the mask, she grinned excitedly. "You, too."

"Always."

The playing field was three acres of terrain, adorned with paint-splattered structures and bunkers. Dozens of trees were scattered around, giving plenty of places for everyone to hide. Dusk neared, vibrant lights shining down along the edges of the outdoor range, creating an ominous glow.

The loud whistle blew, signaling the start of the session. People scattered, diving for cover, as Corrado ripped off the bulky mask and pulled his hood over his head. *Game on.*

The pops of gunfire were sporadic, targeted. These men were trained. They didn't waste ammunition or shoot blindly. Corrado pressed himself against the side of a shed. His eyes studiously scanned the area, spotting movement around structures, heads peeking out from behind trees. He popped off shots, striking some guys in his crew within minutes.

The men went down first. Corrado and Vincent took them out easily, diving behind buildings and sneaking up on men from behind until it was just the two of them and the women.

Vincent and Corrado seemed to realize that fact at the same moment. Corrado swung around to face him, spotting him hunched beside a tall tree. Both men instinctively fired at each other, popping off round after round, striking structures and barely missing their targets as they expertly ducked out of the way, shielding themselves.

Vincent was a better shot than Corrado recalled him being.

Practice makes perfect.

A shot from the slight right distracted Vincent, a bright red paintball splattering the building beside his head. *Celia.* The other women had chosen pink.

Vincent turned his gun to aim for Celia, but Corrado popped a shot off before he could even go for the trigger. A green paintball splattered his mask, obstructing his vision. The blast was so hard he jolted backward, dropping the gun.

Out.

Corrado didn't waste any time after that. Back-to-back he knocked out the other three women, shots that intentionally grazed them, not wanting to inflict any pain. They stomped off the field, leaving just two.

Corrado and Celia.

Corrado headed for a bunker to his left, pausing there as his eyes scanned the terrain. Celia had been off to the right of him before, but she was stealthy. He wouldn't underestimate her. He spun in a circle, watching, waiting for movement, finding none and hearing nothing.

Was she hiding?

No, that wasn't Celia's nature.

She would come for him.

The sky had darkened, the surrounding lights casting even deeper shadows along the playing field. He continually monitored the area, straining his ears to detect even the slightest movement.

He had plenty of practice at this.

A minute passed, maybe two, before he heard it: the subtle crunch of feet against the ground, the rustling of grass, the shift of airflow.

Celia was right behind him.

Corrado spotted her a few feet away in the shadows. He raised his weapon, his finger on the trigger, but froze when she looked at him.

For the first time in his life, Corrado hesitated.

Celia scrambled for her gun, squeezing the trigger repeatedly.

Pop. Pop. Pop.

Two paintballs flew right past him, but the third hit him straight in the chest, striking hard enough that he winced. The sting, like the snapping of a rubber band, lasted only a few seconds, but the burn ran deep as he lowered his gun.

She'd shot him.

Celia pushed up her mask as he touched his chest, feeling the red paint splattering his hoodie. "Did it hurt?"

"A little."

"Then why'd you let me do it?"

He raised his eyebrows. "Excuse me?"

"You had me," she said, matter-of-fact. "You could've shot me a dozen times before I even saw you."

"No, I couldn't have," he said. "I couldn't have shot you at all."

Smiling softly, realizing why he hadn't pulled the trigger, she strode over to him as she yanked off her gloves, tossing them to the ground. Her hand slipped beneath his shirts, running up his bare chest to where she'd struck him, eerily close to his heart.

The skin felt tender. Definitely going to bruise.

"I think you're actually made of spider silk, Corrado," she said quietly. "Tougher than Kevlar and so much more fascinating. I'm not sure the world could ever understand how complex you really are."

"Are you calling me Spider-Man?" he asked. "Because I have no plans to be anyone's superhero."

She reached up on her tiptoes to kiss him. "Maybe not, but you're *my* hero."

Laughing, he wrapped his arms around her. "Now you're being absurd again."

He hugged her, drinking in the scent of her perfume.

"Happy birthday," she whispered against his chest. "I hope you have so many more of them."

"I will," he promised. "And I'll spend every single one of them with you."

"What the hell?"

Frankie yelled as soon as he stepped inside his house. Something crunched beneath his shoes, tripping him as he leaped over an obstruction in the pathway. Corrado's brow furrowed as he stepped into the doorway, out of the intense heat and into the cool air.

A tiny little girl huddled away from Frankie's looming body. She sat on the floor, her back pressed against the bottom railing of the staircase, a slew of crayons spread out on the floor around a stack of paper.

"Miranda!" Frankie screamed, his face bright red with anger, the vein in his forehead throbbing. "Monica!"

He stormed off, straight out the back door, not giving Corrado another thought as he sought them out. Corrado remained in place, staring down at the child as she reached over and picked up the purple crayon, broken in half from Frankie stomping on it. She clutched both halves in her fists. "Am I in trouble?"

Corrado was thrown off-kilter when she asked him that question, her voice quiet but strong. His initial reaction had been to correct her terrible enunciation—trouble, not *twouble*—but he refrained. She dealt with enough grief.

His eyes turned toward the mess in front of her, the top page scribbled all over, colorful streaks on the wooden floor around it. She hadn't stayed in the confines of her paper. "Most likely, yes."

He turned back to the girl, surprised to find her looking at him. Her eyes caught his gaze, and she didn't look away. Something in her expression struck him as familiar. She had a soft, round face and wide brown eyes—eyes with way too much natural curiosity. Definitely an Antonelli.

He waited for her to plead, for her to apologize, but the girl said nothing. She frowned, turning to her picture as her hand slowly, carefully, reached for the paper. She picked up a few pieces, folding them a bunch of times, before sticking them in the pocket of her pants. She reached toward the crayons next, grabbing the green and red, sticking those in her pocket, too. The entire time she watched him from the corner of her eye, her motions so slow it was almost comical… as if she believed if she made no sudden movement, he wouldn't notice she was taking any of it.

The girl left the rest there, exactly as it had been, even returning the broken crayon to the floor. She didn't move again until the back door flung open and Miranda rushed in. She snatched a hold of her daughter, picking her up and holding her close.

"I'm so sorry," Miranda said. "Miss Monica took her from the stables when I was working. I didn't know… I didn't think… please, don't punish Haven."

Haven?

"Just get her out of here," Frankie growled.

"Yes, sir."

Miranda rushed toward the back door again as the girl wrapped her arms around her mother's neck, peeking over her shoulder. Her eyes caught Corrado's again. He stared back at her, feeling almost as if she were waiting for him to tell on her, like she was trying to intimidate him.

Good thing for her, he didn't rat out *anybody*.

Frankie grumbled when they disappeared, kicking the paper and crayons out of the center of the hallway. "Damn girl got marks all over my floor. Monica's always bringing her inside and letting her run wild, like she belongs in here."

"So you named her Haven," Corrado said, his hands in his pockets as he surveyed the mess shoved out of the way. How hadn't Frankie noticed the missing things?

"*I* didn't name her anything," Frankie said, heading for his office today. "Let's get this work finished so you can get out of here."

Frankie had trouble running their operations in Nevada. Antonio frequently sent men down to assist when he got overwhelmed. Usually it was Corrado, but occasionally he'd send Vincent or another *Capo* he trusted. It was in and out, a few hours sweating in the desert to set things straight for a few weeks. It was tedious bookwork, numbers and statistics, the things Corrado watched his father doing growing up.

They spent the next hour wrapping up some plans on a takeover of a small place north of the city. Frankie went to walk Corrado outside when they finished but stopped in the hallway, something again obstructing his path. Frankie groaned with frustration as he sagged against the wall.

Monica was on the floor, on her hands and knees, trying to scrub the crayon markings from the wood. Her eyes narrowed at her husband. "You blame *me* for this, Frank, not her."

"She knows better."

"She's just a kid," Monica said, sitting back on her knees. "She doesn't understand."

"The sooner she learns, the better," Frankie said. "She doesn't belong with us."

"She does," Monica argued. "I want her here."

Frankie pushed away from the wall, his frustration melting to vicious anger in a split second. He grabbed his wife's arm, yanking her from the floor, baring his teeth as he growled, "no."

No. A simple word, laced with more hostility that Corrado had heard from him when he scolded the slave.

Monica pulled away from him, tears in her eyes as she stomped upstairs. Frankie strode outside, throwing open the front door, reaching into his pocket for a pack of cigarettes. "That woman would let any stray in my house. It's the reason we left Chicago in the first place. I bring her out here to the middle of no-fucking-where, and she still pulls the same shit."

"We are who we are," Corrado muttered, stepping off the porch and heading for his rental car. His eyes scanned the property, his gaze stopping at the stables. There, standing in the wide-open entrance, was the little girl. She raised her hand, casually waving goodbye to him.

He didn't wave back, didn't acknowledge her, but he paused there, watching. A child, with no concept of what she was, of what she would someday be… with no concept of what kind of person her mother was, or how she had even been created. She had no idea what kind of man she was staring at, what kind of monster she so nonchalantly greeted.

In another life, in another world, she could have been different. She had enough Italian blood flowing through her veins to make her treasured. Maybe her parents weren't much of anything, but her grandfather was a *made man.*

If only he would admit who she was.

It took a moment for Miranda to yank her daughter into the stables, into the shadows, away from sight.

Corrado gave Frankie a polite nod. "I'll see you next time."

"Do they really have a girl?"

Corrado looked overtop of his morning newspaper at his wife

eating breakfast. A peculiar sense of déjà vu struck him. "You'll have to be more specific."

"The Antonellis."

Ah. "Yes."

"It's true?" she asked. "Who is she?"

"Nobody," Corrado said, turning back to his newspaper. "Just a girl."

"What? You mean like Maura?"

"Exactly like that."

Celia gasped, dropping her fork. "You're serious? She's like *that*?"

"It's more common than you think, Celia."

"But she's just a girl!" Celia said. "A *little* girl!"

"She's not that little."

She scoffed. "She's still a child."

Corrado realized then his wife didn't mean the woman, Miranda.

"My mistake," he said. "I thought you meant her mother."

"Her mother? So her mother's a, uh...?"

"Slave." He said it for her. He knew she hated that word. "Yes."

"And what does that make the little girl?"

"The daughter of one."

Celia picked up her napkin and launched it across the table at him, hitting his newspaper. "Don't start bullshitting me *now*, Corrado. We both know it makes her one, too."

"Why'd you ask if you already knew?"

"To get you to admit it."

"Fine." He closed the newspaper and tossed it aside. "It's true."

"And what's going to happen to her?"

Definitely familiar. "I don't know. And this time, Celia, I'm not going to find out."

She stared at him hard as if she wanted to argue. He expected her to argue, to get up and storm out. But instead she picked up her fork once more.

"How'd you even know about her?" Corrado asked suspiciously.

"Maura told me."

"How does she know?"

"She saw the girl the weekend Vincent took her to Vegas."

He took her to Vegas? "And where was I?"

"Who knows," Celia muttered. "I was here babysitting alone. You never came home."

"When was it?"

"Two weeks ago," she said. "Valentine's Day."

Out of everything they'd said the past few minutes, the barely restrained hostility tossed back at forth, those last words were what struck him hardest. He'd forgotten another Valentine's Day. "I'm sorry."

"Don't be," she said, tossing her fork down again, this time to stand up. "After twelve years of marriage, I'm used to it by now."

42

The dark brick building set back off the busy highway, surrounded on all sides by tall trees. It blended into the quiet south Chicago neighborhood, laid-back and low-key, as the modest tan sign above the entrance displayed the name in deep red cursive.

Luna Rossa

Below it, in sparkling gold, the sign bore the word 'lounge', so subtle it wasn't noticeable unless right up on it. It had been intentional, just like the absence of all neon signs and advertisements.

It wasn't intended to lure people off the street.

Corrado stood in the freshly paved parking lot, leaning back against the side of his Mercedes, his arms wrapped around his wife in front of him. Her hair smelled like cinnamon sugar as he inhaled, resting his chin lightly on top of her head.

"I love it," she said. "It's perfect."

He smirked, gazing at the building. Construction had completed the week before, a day ahead of schedule and right on budget. Corrado couldn't be happier.

The project was born one fall night when Corrado had a particularly rough evening. He arrived home close to midnight, the scent of mildew and old alcohol clinging to his clothes, overpowering the sweet fragrance from the bouquet of flowers in his hand. He had hoped to spend some time with his wife, hoped to purge the day's events from his thoughts, but instead he found an empty house with a hastily scribbled note on the table:

Helping Maura. Don't wait up.

Don't wait up.

How many times had he told her those exact words?

He didn't much like it in reverse.

She hadn't made it home until two in the morning. Corrado sat on the couch, his shirt unbuttoned and shoes kicked off as he flipped through channels on the television. The flowers lay on top of the note on the coffee table, already starting to wilt.

"I thought you'd be asleep," Celia said, running her hand through his hair, her fingernails scraping lightly against his scalp. The tickle shot down his spine, his eyelids drooping at the sensation.

Man, he was exhausted.

"You weren't home."

"I left a note," she said, sitting on the arm of the couch beside him as she massaged the back of his neck.

"I saw it."

"And you still waited up."

"Of course."

She gazed at him in the dark room, the glow from the muted television illuminating her face as she frowned. "I worry about you, Corrado. Don't you ever want more?"

He stared at her, those words making his stomach sink. "I have everything I need."

"Not need," she said. "*Want.*"

He answered honestly. "I don't know."

"You should have something that's yours," she said. "Something you pour your soul into."

"I have you."

She gripped the back of his neck. "Besides me."

"Wor—"

"Don't even say work."

Did he want more than that?

"You work hard," she said, not waiting for him to come up with an answer. "Harder than you need to."

She reached over, grasping his right hand, running her finger along the scar across his palm. Although she didn't elaborate, he knew what she meant. He had fought hard to be *made*, to earn his place, yet despite the title, he still did the brunt of the work himself.

Work others should be doing for him instead.

Corrado dwelled on that all night and the next day as he worked the streets, going in and out of grungy buildings around the city. Just once he wanted to step foot somewhere where he felt welcome, somewhere where he didn't have to fight the urge to gag.

For guys who prided themselves on being honorable, they sure frequented some disgraceful places.

He mentioned that in passing to Antonio, who laughed it off. "The only way you're going to get a classier hangout is if you open one yourself, Corrado."

He'd been joking, but Corrado took those words to heart.

Luna Rossa, every aspect built to his strict specifications. And standing in the parking lot beneath the warm spring sunshine, his wife in his arms, he felt almost as if he were seeing *himself.* It was an extension of him, a reflection of his personality. *Luna Rossa* was everything he loved in the world, translated into something legitimate, something to be proud of.

It was his and his alone, built from the ground up, his soul poured into it, just as his wife had suggested.

"Come on," Celia said, pulling out of his arms, a sparkle of excitement in her eyes. "Show me the inside."

"You don't want to wait for the others?"

"Nope."

Corrado pulled the keys from his pocket, shifting through them until he found the one for the main entrance. The door was steel reinforced, top of the line in security. He had done everything imaginable to make the place secure, to thwart break-in's and vandalism, even making the glass shatter-resistant.

Unlocking the door, he moved aside, motioning for her to go ahead of him. She paused in the dark walkway as he turned off the alarm and flicked the row of switches, one-by-one flipping on the lights. Celia looked around, her eyes wide with intrigue as she studied the place in the dim lighting. Everything was dark and wooden with deep red trim. Four tiers of shelves lined the mirrored wall behind the long bar, stacked with hundreds of bottles of the finest liquor and spirits, glowing red spotlights shining above them.

Dozens of booths and tables took up the back half of the building, the atmosphere darker the further back you walked. The vast area between the tables and the bar was wide open, the waxed floor sparkling beneath twinkling spotlights.

Celia gasped as she walked out onto the gold-tinted dance floor, her high heels clicking against the wood. She held her arms out and spun in circles, smiling radiantly as she gazed up at the lights. Her red dress, skin-tight on her chest but flowing from her waist, stopping near her knees, stood out strikingly as she twirled. "This is *beautiful.* Who knew you had it in you?"

Corrado stepped behind the bar and grabbed two small glasses. He poured vodka in both, adding a splash of cola to Celia's, before holding it out to her. She took the drink, shoving a stool out of the way as she climbed up on the black marble bar. Corrado shook his head, grinning, but said nothing as she made herself at home on top of it, her heels digging into the leather stool seat.

She sipped her drink, glancing around some more, as Corrado stepped out from the bar. He strode over to the Compact Disc jukebox along the edge of the room, gold and red with wooden paneling to match the rest of the club. There would be a DJ on staff most nights and occasionally live music, courtesy of the piano in the far back, but it was all he had then. He fed coins into the slot, choosing the same song for every selection: *Luna Rossa.*

Celia's eyes widened when Frank Sinatra's voice crooned from the speakers. "How'd you get this on CD?"

"I have my ways," he said. "There's nothing in this world I can't get."

"Huh." She shifted around on the bar to face him. "Nothing?"

"Nothing," he stressed, stopping right in front of her. He threw back the last of his liquor, feeling the burn in his chest as he set the empty glass down on the bar beside her. "If I want it bad enough, it's mine."

Sipping the last of her drink, she set her glass down beside his. A devilish smirk lifted the corner of her red lips. "Does that include me?"

"*Especially* you."

Corrado shoved his way between the two stools, stepping between her legs. He laid his hands on her knees and ran them up her thighs, pushing her dress the whole way up to her waist as her arms wrapped around his neck, her fingers running through the hair at the nape.

"I *always* want it, Celia," he said, his voice low and gritty, his words earnest. "I always want you."

Grasping the sides of her panties, he tugged, sliding them over the curve of her ass and down her thighs when she lifted off the bar. He threw them to the floor before yanking her closer to the edge of the bar. One hand slid up her inner thigh, her legs spreading for him, as his other hand gripped the back of her neck and pulled her face toward him. He kissed her hard, passionately, as he stroked her center, his thumb grazing her clitoris.

She was already ready for him.

Her breath caught as he pushed two fingers inside her, curving them upward, reaching for that spot he knew would drive her wild. He pumped them in and out, teasing her. His mouth moved from hers to her neck, his lips trailing along her collarbones, his teeth nipping at the hint of breast. She shivered, her hands gripping his hair as he bent down, his head dipping beneath her dress.

"Oh, fuck!" she gasped, the curse cracking as it lodged in her throat when his mouth came into contact with her sensitive flesh. He tasted her, licking and sucking, his fingers over and over grazing her sweet spots, as she writhed on the bar, leaning back on her elbows. Whimpers tore from her throat, louder and louder, as he brought her closer to climax.

It hit her hard, muscles seizing up, body going rigid seconds before the convulsions. She cried out, tossing her head back and nearly throwing herself right off the back of the bar. Corrado grabbed her just in time, standing up straight with surprise as she let out a sharp laugh. "That would've hurt."

"It would've," he agreed, letting go of her once she was steady. His hands went straight for his belt, the buckle clanging as he unfastened it.

Celia arched an eyebrow. "Not done yet?"

"I'm just getting started."

He unbuttoned his pants and reached into his boxers, grasping a hold of himself. His erection throbbed in his palm when he pulled it out, stroking a few times with his left hand as he grabbed her with his right. A startled yelp escaped her when he yanked her off the bar, pinning her back against the vinyl padding along the edge. She wrapped herself around him, her legs around his waist, her arms circling his neck.

He thrust hard, eliciting a hiss from Celia as he banged her back against the bar. "This might hurt, too."

"I hope so," she teased, holding on to him.

Perching her there, he pounded into her, her body wrapped around his. The pointy heels of her shoes dug into his ass like tiny daggers, the sharp stabs of pain spurring him on. He gave her all of himself, thrusting so hard she gasped loudly, the breath knocked from her lungs. Tingles shot down Corrado's spine as pressure built inside of him, the sounds of wet slapping skin mingling with the sultry music. He panted, gripping her hips, his face in the crook of her neck, inhaling the spicy combination of her perfume and her natural aroma, as he slammed against her a few times.

His orgasm hit, so strong he grunted, biting down on the skin along her shoulder blade as he spilled inside of her.

He stilled his movements, pinning her against the bar as he caught his breath. Celia ran her hands up his back, beneath his suit coat, and laughed when she grasped his gun, still tucked in place.

"You are so full of sin," she whispered against his skin.

Kissing her once, he set her on her feet and took a step back, smiling as she tugged her dress down. Her cheeks were rosy, her hair tousled. The imprint of his bite mark gleamed just north of her right collarbone, brighter than the flush of her skin.

Before he could point it out to her, bright sunshine streamed through the walkway into the club from outside as the door open. High-pitched cheery voices met his ears, the sound spurring Celia into a panic. Cursing, she shoved past him, frantically smoothing her dress and toying with her hair as she stepped that direction.

Corrado fixed his pants, tucking his shirt back in, and was securing his belt when Vincent appeared. Always intuitive, Vincent froze, his eyes wide as he snatched a hold of the waist-high little boys and pushed them behind him.

"Really, guys?" Vincent looked between Corrado and Celia. "You couldn't wait?"

Celia's cheeks burned brighter as she avoided the question, instead focusing on the boys. Vincent's eyes turned from her to Corrado. He finished situating his shirt before reaching down and snatching Celia's black silk panties from the floor, shoving them in his pocket with a slight shrug.

Did he expect him to apologize? He had no regrets. *None at all.*

"If it wasn't my sister, I might give you kudos," Vincent said, approaching him at the bar as Celia took off with Dominic and Carmine in tow, giving the excited boys a tour. "Nice place."

"Thanks," Corrado said. "No Maura?"

Vincent was silent, giving Corrado the only answer he needed. *No Maura.*

"It's not you," Vincent said. "It's just, you know… everyone else."

Corrado knew. Despite what Vincent said, it was him. Maybe not only him, but still… *him.* He turned away from his brother-in-law, watching as Dominic shrieked, tearing across the dance floor, his pale skin glowing white beneath the lights. "Yet you brought the kids."

"Yes."

"To a bar."

Vincent cut his eyes at him. "Judgment is the last thing you should be dishing out after what I can only imagine you just did to my poor sister on that bar."

"Not judging," Corrado said, slapping Vincent on the back and pulling him closer as he whispered, "and I fucked her so hard she could barely breathe."

"Ugh, disgusting!" Vincent shoved away from Corrado as he laughed. Corrado strode across the room as more sunlight filtered in, voices carrying through. "Jesus, what's gotten into you today?"

Corrado shrugged, turning to look at Vincent, taking a few steps backward as he replied, "I'm happy."

Vincent raised his eyebrows before addressing Celia. "Has that ever happened before?"

"What?" she asked.

"Your husband being happy."

She nearly lost her balance as Carmine wrapped himself around her waist. "Maybe once or twice."

Corrado turned away from them, glancing toward the entrance as a mass of guests emerged. Antonio and Gia; Salvatore; Sonny and his wife; Manny and his family… *more kids.*

Corrado welcomed his bosses personally. Nothing would ruin the high he felt tonight, nobody would dampen his mood, not even people of the three-feet-high variety.

Manny's kids ran past as Corrado greeted the man and his wife. "Amando," he said, before taking the wife's hand and pressing a kiss to the back of it. "Ma'am."

"Where's *my* hello?" the terse voice asked. He turned, coming face-to-face with Gia. She was dressed flawlessly, as usual, her expression stern.

Corrado reached out and took her hand. She had expected the same greeting as Manny's wife, but instead Corrado pulled her closer and kissed her cheeks. "How's my beautiful mother-in-law tonight?"

Gia's cold demeanor thawed the slightest bit as she raised an eyebrow at him. "Phenomenal, Corrado. How are you?"

"Great."

She patted his cheek. "I can tell."

"Grandpa!" The shrieking voice echoed through the room as soon as Antonio stepped out onto the dance floor. Antonio glanced around, a smile plastered on his face when Carmine shot through the club straight toward him, not slowing down. Antonio reached his arms down as the kid ran into them.

"Ah, there's my boy," Antonio said, pride in his voice as he held little Carmine with one arm. He was small for a six-year-old… or smaller than Dominic, anyway. Dominic ran over, receiving a less warm greeting, but Antonio looked down at him with genuine affection. "Hey, kiddo."

"Hey, grandpa," Dominic said as he hugged his waist.

Antonio patted Dominic's back before setting Carmine on his feet beside his brother. "You two being good for your father?"

"Yes," they both muttered.

He grabbed their chins, tilting their heads up. "Yes what?"

"Yes, sir."

The boys spoke in unison, earning a hearty laugh from Antonio that morphed into a coughing fit. He shook it off, clearing his throat, his voice strained as he said, "good boys."

He ruffled their hair before motioning for them to run off, both boys shrieking as they joined the other kids in a booth near the back of the club.

Others arrived, members of *La Cosa Nostra* invited with their families, while the staff came on duty for the first time. They had gone through orientation for days after a rigorous round of interviews where Corrado interrogated them and investigated them, making sure every single person he hired was dependable enough to be allowed through his doors. This was his last test… opening night wasn't for another week, but tonight was a trial run. If they carried themselves well in a room full of notorious criminals, they were officially hired.

And everyone who passed this test, who proved themselves to him, would have a job for life, as long as they didn't betray him or do anything to break his trust.

Because trust was something he didn't dish out easily, and if Celia had drilled anything into his head the past few months, it was that he would have to learn to give a little.

"You can't run it all by yourself," she'd said, "although, God knows, you'd damn sure try, wouldn't you?"

Old Rat Pack songs crooned from the speaker system all night long as the alcohol flowed freely. Round after round of shots were poured, two bartenders working hard to keep the drinks going out to the tables, the tip jars on the bar overflowing with wads of cash for their hard work. Energy ran high, people danced, celebrating, toasting, kids playing, while Corrado stood back, watching the whole thing.

Besides the drink he shared with his wife, he hadn't had a drop of alcohol all night.

Celia, on the other hand, was wasted. He kept a close eye on her as she danced, sure no one would be stupid enough to lay an inappropriate hand on her, but once again… trust didn't come easily.

Vincent approached a few hours later, pausing beside him along the edge of the dance floor, near where the kids played some sort of strange *Simon Says* dancing game. Vincent smiled as Dominic stood dead center, commanding the group.

"He acts the most like a DeMarco," Vincent said, watching them. "And he wasn't even born one."

Corrado surveyed the young boy. No, not a DeMarco… not genetically, anyway. Volkov blood ran through Dominic's veins. They never discussed it, never acknowledged it, but they all knew.

The kids had spent a few nights at his house with Celia, but much like their mother, they tended to keep their distance from Corrado. A learned trait, something not outright taught, but something they picked up intuitively from the world around them.

"It's not all about blood," Corrado said. "He's a DeMarco because he's emulating one."

"But my father barely has anything to do with Dominic."

"Not your father," Corrado said. "You."

"Me?"

Corrado looked at his brother-in-law, seeing skepticism in his eyes. "Don't be so surprised, Vincent. It took me a while to see it, but you're a DeMarco through and through."

He seemed taken aback. "Thanks."

"Don't thank me," Corrado said. "I didn't tell you that to boost your ego."

"Well, it did anyway, so thanks."

Corrado shook his head. "You're welcome."

"Carmine, on the other hand, is all Maura," Vincent said, looking around the club. "I don't even know where he ran off to."

There was no telling with Carmine. The entire *La Cosa Nostra* world prized the little boy, treating him like royalty, overlooking his obvious detriments… the splash of freckles on his nose and the blazing green eyes that spoke of his Irish blood.

"I'll find him for you," Corrado said, taking a step back from the dance floor. "I should do a round with the guests."

He strode off through the crowd, greeting newcomers, making sure nobody had any problems. He headed toward the back of the club, toward a booth where most of the ruckus came from. Antonio sat in the center, flanked by powerful men on both sides. Cigar smoke hung around the men like a thick, toxic cloud, everyone smoking except for the Boss. He chewed on a toothpick as he surveyed his men.

"You doing okay, sir?" Corrado asked.

Antonio glanced at him, beaming. "Never been better."

Corrado returned his smile as the Boss rubbed his chest. "You need anything?"

"You got any TUMS?" he asked with a grimace. "Got indigestion something fierce."

"I don't have any," Corrado replied, "but I can get you some."

"I'd appreciate it."

He caught a waitress's arm as she headed past. "I need you to run down the block and buy some TUMS."

"Yes, sir."

"And make it fast."

She scurried away as Corrado turned back to the men. "You guys seen Carmine?"

"Ah, my godson!" Sal grinned, a cigar between his lips. "*Principe* was here a minute ago."

Antonio's expression fell, concern shining through for a few seconds before he flashed another grin, but he hadn't been fast enough for it to escape Corrado's notice. Something was bothering the Boss.

Something to make his well-trained mask slip.

"Thank you," Corrado said, stepping back from the table. He would figure out what that was about later. "I'll find him."

He walked away, only making it a few steps before sharp notes struck his ears, contradictory to the smooth melody of Sinatra playing through the sound system. His gaze darted to the piano in the far back as he headed that way, finding the boy standing behind it in the shadows, his fingers running over the keys. He pressed down on a few black keys, making notes sound out, producing an off-key melody. Corrado paused at the corner beside the piano.

Carmine hadn't noticed him. He was concentrating. *Hard.*

"What song are you trying to play?"

Carmine snatched his hand away from the piano, backing up like the thing had burst into flames, his green eyes darting straight to Corrado with distress. "Sorry."

Corrado didn't move, not wanting to startle the child and make him flee. "What song was that?"

"I don't know," he said. "It was the black key threes notes."

Corrado cocked his head to the side. He sounded like he knew what he was talking about. "Are you taking piano lessons?"

He nodded enthusiastically.

"Do you know any songs?"

"No."

"Whenever you learn one, we'll have your father bring you here so you can play it for us."

His eyes lit up, the green sparkling. "Okay!"

Corrado motioned toward the dance floor. "Your father's looking for you. Go to him."

"Yes, sir."

Carmine ran off through the crowd with Corrado a few steps behind him. He stepped out onto the dance floor, hearing his wife's manic giggling, and found her just in time to see her stumble in her high heels. He grabbed her, pulling her into his arms. "Whoa there, *Bellissima.*"

She wrapped her arms around his neck. "You're handsome."

"You're drunk."

"I am," she admitted. "Doesn't mean you're not handsome."

He laughed at her logic, his hands resting on her hips as he pulled her protectively against him.

"Tonight was fun," she said, grinning as her gaze darted toward the bar. "We should do that again."

"I own the place," he replied. "We'll do it any time you want."

"Now?"

"Not now."

She giggled, kissing him sloppily. He tasted bitter liquor on her lips. "We can do it somewhere else then."

He pulled back, shaking his head. "You're insatiable."

"And you're handsome."

"Later," he promised. "But I have to handle some stuff here first."

She pouted, resisting when he tried to pull her off the dance floor. "I just…"

Sudden tears swam in her eyes, the sight of them alarming him. "Celia? What's wrong?"

She shook her head frantically, almost losing her balance.

Corrado stepped back to her, everything else forgotten. "Tell me what's wrong. What happened?"

"Nothing," she choked out, a tear streaming down her cheek. "I'm just so proud of you."

"You're crying because you're proud of me?"

"Yes," she said, wiping her eyes. "You're happy."

"You're drunk."

"Happiness looks good on you."

Drunk didn't look very good on her.

"Come on," he said, pulling her away from the crowd, over to where Vincent stood with the kids. Vincent's brow furrowed at his sister's tears, but Corrado shook his head, silently telling him not to ask.

"I should get going," Vincent said, pulling out his keys. "Gotta get the kids home for bed."

"Take your sister with you," Corrado said.

Celia objected, the pout back on her face, but Corrado kissed her deeply, silencing her words. All argument seemed to be forgotten when he pulled away.

"Don't try any cartwheels tonight," he whispered, just loud enough for her ears. "Your underwear is still in my pocket."

She tugged on his tie, grinning slyly as she slurred, "I'll see you at home."

"Goodnight." She would be passed out before he made it there. His gaze turned to his brother-in-law. "Vincent. Kids."

"Bye, Uncle Corrado," Dominic said, reaching for Celia's hand. She kicked off her heels, carrying them in her free hand, before leading the boy to the door.

"Congratulations," Vincent said, grabbing Carmine by the shoulder, pulling the boy away.

Corrado watched his family leave as the waitress approached with a roll of TUMS. Corrado took them, pulling out his wallet. "How much did they cost?"

"A buck and a quarter."

He pulled out a twenty. "Keep the change."

Corrado made his way back over to the booth, pulling up a chair beside it as he held out the roll of TUMS to the Boss. Antonio tore the wrapper and popped some in his mouth. "The family all leave?"

He nodded. "Vincent's making sure Celia gets home safely."

"Good."

Corrado let himself relax. Most of the families had cleared out, the wives and children gone, leaving the place full of made men. They chatted nonchalantly, occasionally slipping into talk about business. Antonio remained silent through most of it, popping TUMS like candy and listening.

After a while, Corrado excused himself from the table to check on his employees. He surveyed what was left of the crowd before sitting down at the bar and telling one of the bartenders to get him some water.

"Water?"

Corrado turned his head as the stool slid out beside him and Antonio took a seat.

"Yes," Corrado confirmed. "Water."

"You can't trust a man who drinks water at a bar," Antonio said. "He's there for the wrong reasons."

The bartender returned with the drink, hesitating in front of them. "Anything for you, sir?"

"Eh, I guess I'll have a water with my son-in-law."

The bartender moved away, getting a drink for Antonio, before hurrying to help someone else. Antonio picked up his glass and took a sip. "Is it because of your mother that you don't drink?"

Corrado tensed. "I drink."

"You been married to my daughter how many years now?"

"Over a dozen."

It was hard to believe.

"In a dozen years, I've seen you drink maybe a dozen times."

Corrado picked up his water. "I don't want to be anything like her."

"You're not," Antonio said. "I'm a good judge of character. I wouldn't have let my daughter marry someone like that."

"Why'd you let her marry me?"

"Because I trust you."

"Even after finding out I drink water at a bar?"

"For some people, the rules are meant to be bent," Antonio said seriously, reaching into his pocket and pulling out a knife… a familiar knife, the one that had been used at Corrado's initiation.

His palm itched at the sight of it.

"Here," Antonio said, setting it on the bar and pushing it toward Corrado. "Take it."

Corrado stared at it. "Why?"

"Come on now." Antonio shot him a pointed look. "Don't ask that damn question."

Silencing, Corrado picked up the knife, running his thumb along the elaborate engraving on the handle, wondering how many men had sworn allegiance to the man beside him before bleeding on this blade.

"You know, you'd make a good boss someday, Corrado," Antonio continued. "If you could get past the Salamander, anyway."

That apprehension was back on Antonio's face, but this time he wasn't as quick to conceal it.

"Is everything alright?" Corrado asked, concerned.

"Yeah, just this damn indigestion," Antonio grunted, shoving the stool back to stand up. "I think I need to go home and sleep it off. I'm not feeling so hot. You got plans tomorrow?"

"No."

"Come to my house in the morning," he said. "I got something I want to talk to you about. Something I might need you to do for me."

"What?"

"Not tonight," he said, squeezing Corrado's shoulder. "Tonight's special. Enjoy it."

Antonio walked away, grimacing as he rubbed his chest.

"I'm worried about you, sir."

"Don't worry about me," he replied, casting Corrado a genuine smile. "It's everyone else you should worry about, son."

Antonio strode toward the exit, his footsteps wavering as he reached the edge of the dance floor. His knees wobbled and he hunched over before his legs gave out on him. Corrado watched as the world fell in slow motion, the sound of Frank Sinatra's "My Way" ricocheting through his ears, drowning out everything else, and distorting his senses.

Horror filled him, bitter cold like ice, as the Boss dropped hard, face first to the wooden floor.

Boom.

Corrado was on his feet, rushing toward him, as others in the club took notice. Frantic murmuring filled the air, shouts for help, someone yelling for them to call 911. The world sped up again as Corrado dove at Antonio, grabbing him and pulling him onto his back.

The Boss laid there, his skin tingeing an icy tone of pale blue, foam forming on the corner of his mouth. Blood coated his face around his busted nose, but it wasn't flowing.

Corrado had witnessed enough death to know the man's heart wasn't beating anymore.

43

Antonio Dominic DeMarco

Antonio Dominic DeMarco, 50, of Felton Drive, Chicago, departed this life on Friday, May 6, 1994. Funeral will be held Wednesday, May 11, at Saint Mary's Catholic Church, with burial to follow in Hillside Cemetery.

Two sentences. That was it.

Despite the simplicity of the obituary, Corrado knew how hard Celia had worked to perfect it, stressing over every last syllable, trying to capture her father's legacy in a few short words. She had written out his entire life story in a notebook before balling up the paper and tossing it in the fireplace, going with *this* instead.

Antonio would have approved. He preferred things to the point.

Because it didn't matter what she wrote, what was printed in the obituaries about the honorable man they all revered. The world would believe what graced the front page instead.

Gluttony Kills Notorious Mob Boss

Gluttony. They found a way to make a massive coronary into a striking headline. They painted a picture of a wild, reckless man, hell-bent on destroying the world and everyone in it... himself included.

Corrado threw the paper in the fireplace that morning and lit it on fire. Celia didn't stop him. She had already torn out the simple obituary for her scrapbook.

It captured him better than the thousand-word front-page exposé.

The article had been laced with quotes from an anonymous source, detailing parts of the Boss's life in ugly detail... things people couldn't have known unless they were close to him. Someone was spilling their guts to reporters again, defiling Antonio's legacy with outrageous claims.

True outrageous claims. Even worse.

There was a rat amongst them.

The article spoke about a man who had his best friend murdered, a man who ordered hits at Rita's as casually as he ordered spaghetti.

Someone had been there, someone who had witnessed the secret meetings and knew about the murders. That bothered Corrado. Who would do that to a man like Antonio?

Corrado had never known the Boss's middle name. *Dominic.* He rolled the word around in his head as they stood beneath the dreary sky in the cemetery that Wednesday afternoon, his arm around his grieving wife as she leaned into him, letting him support her. It had been the most elaborate funeral the city had seen in years. Dozens of black cars, covered in flower wreaths, the church overflowing as people crammed in along the street. He was sure tomorrow's newspaper would cover it, sharing exciting details of all the famed guests as if they'd gathered for some celebration.

For the first time, Corrado considered burning a newspaper *before* reading it.

Nothing would be written about their sorrow, about the pain of loss. Corrado lost a friend; he lost a *mentor*. He lost a man who called him "son" with genuine intentions. Losing a boss meant little in comparison.

Maybe that went against *La Cosa Nostra* rules, something meaning more than the organization. But like Antonio had said: for the right people, rules were meant to be bent.

Died at the age of fifty of 'natural causes', just a few days shy of his birthday. Antonio always knew he wouldn't see fifty-one.

His old arch-nemesis God got him good.

Corrado sat on a bench in the back yard of the DeMarco mansion, absently spinning the wedding ring on his finger. Kids tore through the yard, playing chase, as some boys tossed a football back and forth. They were loud and rambunctious, as little kids often were. Usually inclined to avoid them, Corrado found them much more tolerable than what awaited him inside.

As much as Corrado respected the Boss, loved the Boss, would mourn the boss, the display of emotions made him uncomfortable. He felt like he was drowning in a sea of bodies, his chest wound tight in knots. He wanted to comfort his wife, wanted to take away her pain, but he was powerless.

At least outside he could think... he could *breathe.*

So he sat there, giving Celia space, fiddling with his ring, wondering if today was the day she would regret marrying a man like him.

He wouldn't blame her if she did.

His gaze distractedly scanned the yard, spotting Dominic and Carmine in the huddle of boys. They seemed at ease, like today was just another day, one like yesterday, just like tomorrow. Death seemed to have little effect on them.

When Corrado had been their age, the reality of death had devastated him. Was it because they hadn't been there? Could they possibly understand what they hadn't seen?

A subtle rustling from behind alerted Corrado to someone's approach. He didn't move, didn't even look, as Maura sat on the opposite end of the bench. A few feet separated the two of them, but it was closer than she had ever voluntarily come to him before.

She folded her hands in her lap as she crossed her legs, her eyes on her kids across the yard. Corrado suspected what she wanted as soon as she sat down, but he remained silent, hoping she would change her mind

Don't ask me that.

Whatever you do, don't come to me.

She cleared her throat, seeming to startle herself with the sound, and said the words he dreaded: "You have to help her."

Haven.

"I can't," he said, his voice calm. "It's not my place to intervene."

"Somebody needs to," she whispered, "before it's too late."

"She belongs to them. It may not be right, but that's how it is. There's nothing that can be done about it."

"But there *has* to be."

It was quiet for a moment before Corrado let go of his wedding ring and relaxed back on the bench. "She may not appear to be in the best of situations, but she's quite well taken care of, given the circumstances. She spends her days playing and she has her mother there."

"I know," she said. "But she deserves so much more."

"I won't argue that she seems to be a nice child, but that doesn't change the facts. She's a slave. She's *their* slave."

Maura closed her eyes. "She's me."

"She has it a lot better than you did."

"For how long?" Maura asked. "How long until she realizes the truth? How long until she gives up hope?"

"When did you?"

"I don't remember ever having any until I met Vincent."

"I admire you, Maura," Corrado said. "But you can't save them all."

"It's just her. Just one."

"What's so special about *her*?" he asked, genuinely curious. Why that girl?

"Have you ever spoken to her?"

Answering a question with a question.

"Once," he replied.

"And you don't see it? She has an innocence that takes my breath away, so pure and... *sweet*."

"She's a child," he responded. "All children are sweet."

"Was your sister?"

She had a point.

"It's more than her age—it's her soul. She needs someone to give her a chance."

"That someone's not me," he said, not budging. "I'll check on her when I visit Blackburn, but beyond that, it's not my place."

"I understand," she said quietly.

He could tell she didn't.

Corrado stood when someone called his name. He walked away, hesitating after a few steps. "You should watch who you talk to. Asking questions isn't smart, Maura. I would hate to see you hurt. It's not worth it."

He walked away, heading toward the house, as Maura mumbled, "it's worth it to me."

Vincent was standing in the doorway of the backdoor, his eyes following Corrado as he approached. "She ask what I think she did?"

Corrado paused, eyeing him curiously. "Depends on what you think she asked."

"Haven."

It surprised him how casually they all spoke of that child. "You knew she was going to ask me?"

He shrugged slightly, as if not sure of the answer himself. "I knew she wanted to help her. After we saw her, well… I asked—"

"You did not," Corrado said, cutting him off. "Tell me you didn't ask Frankie to give her to you."

"Not give," Vincent said. "Sell… but he turned me down."

Of course he did. Monica was attached to the child, even if Frankie wanted nothing to do with her.

"I can't help you, Vincent."

"I'm not asking you to," he replied. "I told her to drop it."

"You better hope she does."

"She will," he said. "You're the last person she would ever go to for help, and she went to you. It's over."

Shaking his head, Corrado walked away, encountering Manny in the hallway. He stood alone, his head down, his expression heavy. He had been close to the Boss, driving him to jobs, protecting him. Besides Corrado, he was probably most aware of what Antonio did off the record.

A frown tugged Corrado's lips when he considered that. "Amando."

Manny looked up quickly. "Corrado."

"How's your kid?" Bone marrow transplant, Corrado recalled. The kid had gotten one not long after Carmine had been born. The

Chicago Times sponsored a community drive to find a suitable donor. Took up part of the front page that day.

"Better."

"Good." Corrado paused, contemplating, before forcing out the next part. "You must be really grateful for the people at the newspaper."

Close to dusk, as the mourners cleared out, Corrado made his way through the house, strolling down the long downstairs hallway, his hands in his pockets, his black silk tie hanging loose. He strode by the Boss's office, pausing outside the closed door. Locked, he knew. The Boss always kept it locked, the key kept on his person at all times.

Would anyone ever go in there again?

He didn't have many fond memories of the room, as being called in there usually meant something critical, but he had learned many lessons sitting in the stiff leather chair in front of the man's desk. He had learned about life and family, honor and loyalty, morals he would carry with him until his last breath. Antonio's faith in him had made him incredibly wealthy at thirty-two, but the money would never amass to the love the man had passed onto him. It wasn't sentimental, or soft… it was tough love, love that sometimes hurt.

But love nonetheless.

He never said it, not once, but Antonio hadn't had to. He showed him instead by giving him the most precious thing the man had.

"Corrado?"

Corrado turned at the sound of his wife's shaky voice, surprised to find unshed tears burning his eyes. He blinked them back, opening his arms to her.

"Are you okay?" she asked.

"I should be asking *you* that."

"You're allowed to feel," she said, pulling back from his embrace. "You *are* human, after all."

He smiled softly at her. "That's supposed to be our little secret."

"I haven't told a soul," she said playfully, marking an '*X*' over her chest with her finger. "Cross my heart."

Corrado leaned down as he nudged her chin, tipping her head up to kiss her. "I have to get going, *Bellissima.*"

"Work?"

"Something like that."

"Be careful," she said, hugging him again before pulling away. "I'll meet you at home, okay?"

He nodded, watching her walk away, dreading he had to leave her at a time like this, but it was unavoidable. Taking a deep breath, shoving back the emotion that had bubbled up inside of him, he strode out back. He found his brother-in-law in the yard, the back porch light illuminating the grass around him as he tossed a football to his boys. Maura sat along the side, on the bench, watching.

"Vincent," he called. "We have to go."

Vincent stared at him, body rigid, not paying attention to his kids. Corrado caught the movement from the corner of his eye as Carmine pulled his arm back, using every ounce of force the little boy possessed to launch the football. It flew through the air, wobbling a bit as it spiraled, before slamming Vincent straight in the side of the head. The boys broke out in laughter as Vincent grabbed his ear.

"Shit," Vincent spat, stunned, as he turned to Corrado. "You distracted me."

Corrado shrugged. "The boy has decent aim."

Vincent scoffed under his breath, holding up a finger to tell Corrado to wait as he ran over to his wife and whispered something in her ear. She nodded as Vincent hollered to the boys. "Gotta go, kids. Mom's gonna take you home."

They whined, but the men didn't stick around to listen to it. Corrado trudged back through the house with Vincent right beside him, fixing his shirt and tightening his tie.

"You're not going to say goodbye to your mother?" Corrado asked as they stepped out front.

"Do you want to get there on time?" Vincent shot back.

"Are you getting smart with me?"

"Do you really want to argue about this?"

Corrado almost took the bait—nearly argued back—but he restrained himself. Vincent had gotten good at avoiding answering questions. And Corrado, well… he hated asking them.

"Let's go," he said, unlocking his car doors. "Can't be late."

Rita's had been chosen as the meeting place. 8 o'clock sharp. Corrado struggled finding a parking spot, having to swing his car in a lot a few blocks away. The closed sign hung in the door, the light inside dim, despite the hours listed on the glass stating they stayed open until midnight. Corrado opened the door with Vincent right behind him. Vincent stalled on the outskirts, remaining in the back, as Corrado slipped past the men gathered in a sort of obscure circle. He paused in the center, taking his place at the proverbial table, right where Antonio had told him he belonged.

They were the last to arrive. Sonny scanned the group of men, assessing, assuring they all belonged, before clearing his throat. "Nominations."

His voice was meek. The word had to be forced from his lips.

"Me."

All eyes shifted to Salvatore when he spoke, nominating himself.

Sonny scanned the men again, eyebrows rose as he waited for someone else to speak up, but nobody did.

"Seconded," Sonny said quietly. "Any objections?"

Once more, Sonny looked around, awaiting something, but nobody said a word.

"It's done," he said, frowning. "This never happened."

All at once, men shuffled out of the restaurant, some through the front door, most out the back. Corrado stood there, watching Sal as the man grinned smugly.

La Cosa Nostra had a new Boss… and Corrado wasn't sure how to feel about that.

'Don't worry about me,' Antonio had said. 'It's everyone else you should worry about, son.'

Those were his last words, the last spoken breath to escape his lips before death took him. Those words echoed through Corrado's head in the days that followed as he picked them apart, trying to find some hidden meaning… a cryptic message he was sure existed in the sentiment.

'It'll be a cold day when that salamander succeeds me,' Antonio had told him on the way back from the barbershop that day.

Had Antonio sensed this was coming?

Vincent grabbed his shoulder, drawing his attention away, as he motioned toward the exit. Corrado followed his brother-in-law to the door when Sal spoke behind him.

"We need to open the books again."

"Already?" Sonny asked.

"Yeah," Sal said. "I got just the guy to nominate."

"Who?"

"Carlo Abate," he replied. "You'd be hard-pressed to find a more loyal man than him."

The next morning, Corrado walked out onto his porch and grabbed the newspaper. He stepped into his foyer as he opened it, surveying the front page, coldness running through him when he read the headline.

Chicago Mafia Has a New Boss

Frowning, Corrado scanned the accompanying article, tripping over some words two paragraphs in.

Sources say the former Don was against Capozzi succeeding him. "Antonio believed it would be a cold day in Hell when that happened."

Corrado read those lines again and again as he let out a resigned sigh. Strolling to the living room, he threw the newspaper into the fireplace and dialed a number… one he hadn't called before.

Salvatore Capozzi.

"Yes?" Sal answered on the first ring.

"It's Corrado."

"Ah, what can I do for you?"

"I'd like to make a request, sir."

"Twenty minutes, my house."

Corrado hung up and headed upstairs to get dressed. Celia was still asleep when he slipped out of the house, driving to Lincoln Park where Salvatore lived. Corrado knew the address but had never been there before, never having much reason to visit. But he was the Boss now.

The Boss.

Corrado would never get used to it.

They met in Sal's den, the morning's newspaper laying in front of him, the headline glaring at the men as Corrado got right down to business. "I know who it is."

Sal regarded him curiously. "How?"

"I just do."

Pouring himself a drink, despite it being so early in the morning, Sal lounged in the chair, a mischievous glint in his eyes. "I know all about you, Corrado. I know how much trust Antonio put in you. If you say you know who it is, I'll believe you. The only question I have is what are you going to do about it?"

Corrado glanced down at the headline. "Permission to take out the rat?"

A small smirk overcame Sal's lips as he waved him away. "By all means, exterminate."

44

Corrado checked his mirrors as he drove, intentionally making wrong turns and weaving through traffic to ensure he wasn't being followed. It took him an hour to get to a run-down section of the city that should've taken half that time, maneuvering past abandoned factories that people barely noticed anymore. The jobs had been shipped overseas, given to foreigners willing to work for pennies on the dollar. The companies used to sustain the neighborhoods, but now unemployment forced people to steal to feed their families.

And the government claimed *they* ruined Chicago. They said *La Cosa Nostra* destroyed families, degraded the people and made it hard for others to make an honest living.

I think people in glass houses shouldn't throw stones.

He pulled his car in beside the large warehouse, concealing it between two buildings. He made his way inside, securing the door behind him.

The place was dark, the few windows boarded up. It smelled of mold and stale cigarettes, trash scattered throughout that had been there for years. Rats infested building, scurrying past, ducking away from sight, but there were more of them than there were hiding spots.

Corrado made his way to the back of the warehouse, to a sectioned off portion with no exit to the outside. It had once been a break room, the ceiling lower and the area enclosed.

The moment he stepped inside, two guys from his crew

greeted him. Corrado nodded, unsure of their names. Soldiers were soldiers. They weren't who he was there for, anyway.

Huddled in the corner, frightened, was Amando. He was disheveled, wearing only a pair of sweat pants. They had dragged him right out of bed. Although he cried, Corrado wasn't at all sympathetic. The truth was he hadn't endured real suffering yet.

"Manny, the man of the hour."

"Sir—"

Corrado cut him off before he got anything out. "That's not how this is going to work. You've done enough talking."

Manny stared at him with horror-filled eyes.

"Antonio was a big believer in penance," Corrado said. "So if you take your punishment and adequately repent, you'll be forgiven. It's as simple as that."

"I'll do anythi—"

Hauling his foot back, Corrado kicked him right in the face. Manny cried out, trying to block himself as he huddled further into the corner.

Corrado glanced around, seeking out supplies, as a soldier kicked a black duffel bag toward him.

'*Make it hurt.*' If Antonio were alive, Corrado knew he'd say those words. Manny had fucked him over again and again.

Tossing the bag on a worn wooden table, Corrado unzipped it to pull out a coil of rope. He motioned for the soldiers to pull Manny to his feet. Corrado stood behind him, tying his wrists together. He left no wiggle room, the rope digging into his flesh, the friction burning his skin. After ensuring the knots wouldn't budge, he dragged him to the center of the room.

Manny provided little resistance. Fighting meant certain death, whereas he still believed he was strong enough to survive.

Too bad Corrado had yet to meet a man who was.

Above their heads and along the walls of the enclosure, portions of the framework of the building were exposed, leaving an elaborate maze of steel beams. He took the loose end of the rope and threw it up over one beam above them so it dangled down on the other side. A soldier grabbed it, tugging just enough to tie the other end to a portion of steel along the wall.

"This might hurt," Corrado warned.

Panic flared in Manny's eyes as the soldiers yanked on the rope, wrapping it tighter. The more they pulled, the further Manny's arms were forced into the air behind him.

After a moment, he had nowhere to go but up.

Inch by inch his feet rose from the ground, his cries growing louder with every tug. The weight of his body was held by his wrists, most of the strain placed on his shoulders. The ropes, they called it. It had been used to torture many men over the years for information, the excruciating pain loosening tongues.

A few feet from the ground, Corrado ordered them to stop, the men breathing a sigh of relief as they secured the rope for the last time.

Not Manny, though.

There would be no relief for him.

Corrado pulled the knife out—Antonio's knife. "When you took your oath, you swore your loyalty. Do you remember the promises you made?"

Manny nodded, trying to remain silent despite the pain.

"So where was the loyalty when you went to the reporters? Where was the honor when you turned your back on family? Where was the love when you turned on the Boss?" Corrado sliced an 'X' on Manny's chest. "Where was the *heart*?"

Manny grunted, gritting his teeth as blood streamed down his chest. Corrado itched to plunge the knife in but kept his composure, not wanting to kill him.

Yet.

"You're a *disgrace,*" Corrado said. "If we have nothing in this world, we at least have our word, but you don't even have that. You swore your life on something and then went back on it like it meant nothing to you. *Does* it mean nothing to you?"

"No, I swear I—"

Corrado hauled his fist back to punch him, losing his temper. Manny whimpered as Corrado returned the knife to the bag and grabbed a small propane blowtorch, slowly unscrewing the back of it to release the gas. The hissing noise registered with Manny's ears as he started to cry again.

"God," he sobbed. "Oh, God! Not this! Please, God, help me!"

"God?" Corrado asked as the man delved into frantic prayers. "You're trying to appeal to *God*?"

"Please," he whimpered, hanging his head in shame, sobbing so hard he hiccupped. "I'm begging you."

"Go ahead and beg." Corrado shut off the blowtorch. "We'll give your God some time to answer."

Corrado leaned against the old table and crossed his arms over his chest as he stared at his watch, the seconds ticking away. It felt like an eternity as Manny sobbed and begged, praying again and again.

"Guess your God's busy," Corrado said, looking away from his watch once five minutes had elapsed. "Not surprising, considering he has Antonio up there to contend with."

Corrado ignited the blowtorch again. "Confess."

"What?"

"Confess."

"I did nothing wrong!"

Corrado shook his head. "So burns this saint, so will your soul."

He hit the trigger, flames shooting out the end. Manny screamed as the fire lapped at his bare feet as the piercing sound echoed through the warehouse. He writhed, fighting against his restraints as the sickening stench of burning flesh surrounded them. "Please! Please, God, I'm begging you! Oh, God, it burns! It fucking burns!"

Manny grew frantic, inconsolable, his pleading bordering on incoherent. Corrado flicked off the blowtorch, screwing the back in again to stop the flow of gas.

Crying, Manny whimpered under his breath, still whispering prayers. Corrado dropped the blowtorch. "Blood in, blood out. Rules are rules."

"What do you want us to do with him?" a soldier asked.

"Please let me go," Manny begged. "Fuck! I'm begging you!"

Corrado shook his head. "Get rid of him."

Manny's cries grew even louder upon those words as blood,

and snot, and tears coating his face. "Why?"

"We wanted penance," Corrado said. "You never even asked for forgiveness."

"I'm sorry!" Manny shrieked. "Please! I'm sorry!"

Too late.

"The canary sang," Corrado told the guys. "Take it to the roof and see if it can fly."

45

Stepping up on the creaky porch, Corrado knocked on the dingy red door, flakes of paint coming off on his knuckles. Shaking his head, he wiped them on his black pants when he heard noise inside. The front door opened, Maura appearing in front of him.

"I need to speak with—"

"Vincent!" she hollered, not letting him finish. In the blink of an eye, she disappeared down the hallway, leaving the front door hanging wide open.

Not one to invite himself in someone else's house, and not receiving an invitation from Maura, Corrado strolled over to the side of the porch and leaned against the railing, cringing when the wood groaned from his weight. He crossed his arms over his chest, staring at the open doorway. It was a warm fall afternoon and Corrado was sweating, his skin flushed. He'd woken up that morning with a ferocious headache. Although he popped painkillers throughout the afternoon, his head still throbbed, the ache settling deep down in his bones.

He hoped he wasn't getting the flu.

A minute or so passed before Vincent appeared, only half-dressed for the day. He tilted his head, regarding Corrado as he finished buttoning his shirt. "Why are you standing outside?"

"Your wife didn't invite me in."

Corrado merely stated a fact, but Vincent acted as if it were the funniest thing he had ever heard. He let out a deep laugh as he tucked his shirt in, motioning with his head. "Come on in, Corrado."

Stepping inside, Corrado followed his brother-in-law down the short hallway to the living room. He paused there, his eyes drawn to the empty spot in the far back.

"Piano," Vincent said, answering his unasked question. "It's supposed to be delivered tonight sometime."

"Didn't know you were in the market for one," Corrado said. "I could have given you mine."

The piano at the club hadn't lasted long. Corrado couldn't be there every hour of every day, and drunk people had no respect for others property. He'd had it repaired and put into storage, where it collected dust.

Vincent shrugged. "Carmine had his heart set on this limited edition Steinway grand piano he saw."

"He's eight," Corrado said. "He's a bit young for a grand piano."

"You questioning my parenting?"

"Of course not," he said. "I didn't ask any questions."

Vincent sat on the couch. "Yeah, we spoil the boy, but he's earned it. He's worked hard these past few weeks learning his first Beethoven song."

"Beethoven?"

"Moonlight Sonata," he said, grabbing his shoes to slip them on. "It's depressing as hell to listen to. He plays it pretty well, but I'm hoping I never have to hear it again after tonight."

Vincent was tying his shoes when Carmine ran into the room, breezing right past Corrado toward the vacant spot in the corner. Vincent snatched a hold of him before he made it there, yanking him onto the couch in his arms.

Carmine tried to wiggle out of his father's grasp. "Let me go!"

"Go where?"

"Over there!"

"Why?"

"Because I wanna!"

"Why?"

"Dad!" he whined, drawing out the word. "Let me go!"

"Let the poor boy go, Vincent," Maura said, stepping into the living room. "He's excited."

Vincent let go, and Carmine shot out of his arms. Standing up, Vincent motioned for Corrado to follow him as he strode toward the door. No business talk allowed around Vincent's kids.

Corrado stepped back out on the porch, taking a deep breath of the fresh air.

"What are we doing?" Vincent asked.

Corrado shrugged. He didn't know any more than Vincent did. Salvatore had called them up, saying he had some work he needed to do, and he wanted the two of them to go over it with him. It baffled Corrado, but then again, most of what Sal did made little sense to him.

"I'm missing my son's piano recital for this," Vincent said. "Whatever it is better be good."

"I'm sure it is." At least, he hoped. The way he felt, he wasn't in the mood for nonsense.

The door behind them opened. Carmine skipped outside, his mother right behind him. Vincent reached out again when Carmine tried to skirt around him, roughing up the boy's already messy hair. "Good luck, kiddo."

Carmine groaned and pulled away. "Must you do that?"

"Yes, I *must*," Vincent said. "You need a haircut."

"I like my hair," Carmine muttered.

"So do I," Maura responded. "It's adorable."

"Adorable?" Carmine looked at his mother with horror. "Babies are adorable, Mom. I'm *not* a baby."

"You're *my* baby," she said. "You always will be."

Carmine dramatically rolled his eyes.

"Adorable or not," Vincent said, "the boy needs a haircut."

"I guess I can take him tomorrow," Maura said. "After Dominic gets home."

"But I don't want a haircut," Carmine insisted.

"Don't you want to impress the girls?" Vincent asked.

Carmine grimaced. "Why would I?"

A black sedan pulled up in front of the house before Vincent had to answer that, a chauffeur getting out. Corrado vaguely recognized the man as someone he had used before for Celia.

Sal had proven to be a less passive Boss than Antonio. His two years in charge had spawned violent clashes with the Irish. Sal continually insisted their problems all linked back to them, despite increasing evidence that Volkov led some of it. Corrado had come face-to-face with the man a few times and yearned to put a bullet in the savage, but he never said a word for the sake of peace.

"Bye, Dad!" Carmine yelled, rushing off the porch. "Love you!"

"Love you, too," Vincent said, his attention shifting to Maura as she headed off the porch after her son. He grabbed her arm to stop her. "I know *you* aren't leaving without telling me goodbye."

"Of course not," she said, pausing beside him. "I'd never."

Vincent yanked her toward him, leaning down to kiss her. Corrado turned away, not wanting to invade their privacy. He had never seen such a public display of affection from the two.

"Hurry back to me," Vincent said when he broke the kiss. "We haven't gotten much alone time lately. I miss you."

"I miss you, too," she whispered. "You've been so busy."

"I know," he said. "Hopefully that'll change soon. It's been too long."

Medical school, on top of *La Cosa Nostra* business, kept Vincent away from his family more than he was around them. He hadn't given up, though, had refused to stop pursuing legitimacy.

"Way too long," she murmured. "I have to get going. I love you."

"I love you, too," Vincent responded. "Always have and always will."

Corrado looked at them again as Maura pulled away from her husband, smiling. She stepped off the porch and headed toward the waiting car, turning back to them.

"Oh, I forgot," she said, waving playfully. "Goodbye."

Vincent laughed. "I'll see you later, Maura."

Maura's smile dimmed as she turned to Corrado, but it didn't fade completely. "Corrado."

He froze, surprised by the acknowledgement. "Maura."

Maura slid into the backseat. Vincent's eyes followed the car as it cruised down the street, out of sight, before glancing at his watch. "Sal will be here soon."

What Corrado had assured Vincent would be important had turned out to be tedious work, the things they had moved passed doing years ago. They gathered at Vincent's house, since he was waiting for the piano to be delivered, and poured over books for hours on end, going through the other capo's records of games and bets, ensuring they weren't skimming from the organization. Corrado's head pounded harder and harder as the night wore on, the throb so vicious he could hardly read the numbers on the pages anymore.

Sal rambled on with thoughts and theories, ideas for other schemes he wanted to get in on, distracting Corrado to the point he had to redo his own work.

And he *never* had to do something twice.

The house phone rang after a while. Vincent got up. "Might be the delivery guys."

He headed into the kitchen where the phone hung on the wall, out of earshot. Corrado continued working, hoping to finish soon so he could go home. Vincent returned after a moment, retaking his seat.

"Was it?" Sal asked.

"Was it what?"

"The delivery men."

"Oh, no," Vincent said, picking up a notebook he had been working on. "It was Dominic... wanting to talk to his mother."

"Ah, he's staying with Nunzio tonight, isn't he?"

"Yes."

"Good boy, that Nunzio."

Corrado refrained from scoffing… barely. Nunzio was a neighborhood menace, but he was loosely kin to Sal, so they tolerated the immature brat.

"Yeah," Vincent agreed. "He is."

It didn't escape Corrado's notice that Vincent was distracted after that, his eyes frequently shifting away from his work to the clock on the wall. Time had steadily ticked away, hours passing as darkness swept through the city, casting everything in deep shadows.

After a while, the mind-numbing work got to be too much. Corrado shoved a notebook away from him and ran his hands down his face. He couldn't take anymore.

"You don't look so well, Corrado," Sal said. "You feeling okay?"

"A little under the weather," Corrado admitted.

"Go on home," Sal said, his expression serious. "We're almost done here. Vincent and I can finish up."

"Yes, sir." Corrado wasn't one to skirt on responsibilities, but he wouldn't argue. He was starting to feel lightheaded, darkness lingering after every blink.

Vincent was on his feet faster than Corrado could stand. "I'll walk you out."

Corrado followed his brother-in-law onto the porch. He could tell from Vincent's expression, the strain in his jaw, the shadowy gaze, that something worried him.

"Do you know a guy named Arthur Brannigan?" Vincent asked.

"Never heard of him."

"That's who called," Vincent admitted, his expression hard. "He's a private investigator. He was calling for Maura."

Corrado's brow furrowed. "What's he want with her?"

"He wanted to make sure she received her refund," Vincent said, his lips twisting with anger. "Apparently she hired him to find out more about Haven Antonelli."

Corrado's stomach dropped, making him even woozier. "You said she would stop."

"I thought she would," Vincent said. "*She* said she would."

"Make her," Corrado said, "before somebody gets hurt."

"I will." Vincent glanced at his watch. "They should've called for a car now. I don't know where they are. Anyway, thanks for sticking around tonight so long, even though you felt like shit."

"It's work," Corrado responded, shrugging as he stepped off the porch. "We do what we gotta do."

He strolled away, deeply breathing the fresh night air. The breeze felt good against his feverish skin. Definitely the flu.

The short walk to his house felt like miles tonight, his body sluggish. He needed sleep desperately. The sounds around the neighborhood—the revving engines, the blowing horns, thumping music, excited shouting—seemed magnified in his ears, throbbing along like a bass drum to the beat of his headache. Felton Drive used to be a quiet, respectable area, but times had changed. He didn't like it, didn't like the disrespect the younger generation had, with their reckless behavior and lack of civility.

Sure, they were criminals, but they didn't have to be *savages.*

As that thought passed through Corrado's mind, he heard a succession of bangs in the distance. An untrained ear would've called it a car backfiring, but Corrado knew a gunshot a mile away.

Chicago, the town his father had often called *Heaven*, was going to Hell right before Corrado's eyes.

46

The deranged banging echoed through the house, making Corrado's head pound to the beat of the knocking. He staggered down the steps toward the front door, groggy and half-asleep, wearing nothing but a pair of sweat pants. He went home because he didn't feel well, so for someone to interrupt his night took guts. There was never any telling what he'd find on the other side of the door, but whatever it was at this hour had better be *important.*

And by important, he meant life or death, because if it wasn't he'd make it so.

Somehow, as he made it to the foyer, the knocking managed to grow more frantic. He groaned and ran his hands down his face, trying to clear his head and wake up. He was agitated, and that wasn't a good thing for whoever was standing on his front porch.

"I'm coming," he yelled, his voice gritty. "Relax."

All he wanted was one night where his phone didn't ring. One night where he could spend time with his wife without interruption. One night where he didn't have to worry about who was doing what with who and why. One night where people left him alone.

One night where someone didn't come knocking.

He yanked the front door open, irritated at the disturbance, but before he had a chance to speak or even get a good look, someone rushed right past him into the house. Startled, he saw Vincent pacing the foyer.

Corrado blinked a few times, trying to clear his head. Something wasn't right. "Vincent?"

"I can't..." Vincent furiously shook his head, frazzled, his clothes askew and hair a mess. "I can't... he, uh... they... she... oh God! My fucking God! *Why*?"

Vincent turned in his direction. Corrado froze, horrified, at the blood splattering his shirt. Vincent grabbed onto his hair as if he were trying to pull it out, his legs giving out on him. He collapsed to the ground in a heap, his back pressed against the foyer wall as a piercing scream exploded from him.

Corrado flinched as a sharp pain shot through his skull at the sound, his ears ringing. For a second, he grew dizzy and worried he would collapse, too. He held onto the wall to stabilize himself and knelt down beside Vincent once his vision cleared.

Full on hysterical, tears streaked Vincent's face. Corrado had never seen him so out of control before. Vincent didn't show emotion around him. The only time he'd ever even seen him tear up had been the day Maura had been raped.

And just like that, Corrado knew. "Maura."

Vincent sobbed louder at the sound of her name. "My wife, my beautiful wife! Oh God, they got her! They got my Maura!"

"Got her?"

"She's gone!" His body violently shook. "They got her! Why her? Why did it have to be *her*?"

Corrado grabbed a hold of Vincent, trying to get him under control as he rambled. He needed to know what happened. He needed details, and he needed them *now*.

"Where?" Corrado asked. "Where is she?"

Vincent continued his maniacal muttering. Corrado shook him hard, trying to snap him out of it. Vincent grasped onto his arms tightly, like he was holding on for dear life. His hands looked like they'd been soaked in blood, stained red with some of it caked under his fingernails.

"Vincent!" Corrado shouted in his face. "I need you to talk to me. You need to tell me what you know. We need to fix this."

"We can't." Vincent swallowed thickly, choking back a sob. "It's too late."

Too late. Vincent didn't say the words, but Corrado knew what he meant. There was only one thing you couldn't come back from, one thing that couldn't be fixed. *Death.*

"She didn't come home," Vincent cried. "I was so mad. I went after her; I went to find her. I found the lights, heard the sirens, and then I saw. I saw her there, in the alley. I went to her. They tried to stop me. They tried to fucking stop me, but I fought them. I fought them, and I went to her, I grabbed her, but they wouldn't let me hold her. They wouldn't let me have her!"

"What in the world?" Celia's soft voice resonated from the top of the stairs as she started down them, clutching her robe around her. "What's going on down here?"

"Go back to bed, Celia," Corrado called out.

"What?" Celia ran down the steps. "What's happening?"

Vincent's sobs came on harder, his pleading eyes seeking out his sister. Celia, noticing him, let out a painful gasp as she rushed over, shoving Corrado out of the way to get to her brother.

"Vincent?" Her hands frantically assessed him. "What happened to you?"

He shook his head and tried to speak, but all that came out were cries, merging with the telephone ringing. Corrado stared at them, something stabbing at him through the fog.

Something missing.

Something unmentioned.

"Celia, get the phone," Corrado demanded, tearing her away from her brother. "Now."

She looked like she would argue, but his expression stopped her. Wordlessly, she bolted away, rushing for the telephone, as Corrado grabbed Vincent to try to get his attention. Vincent was slipping further and further from coherency, falling deep in the throes of grief. "Where's Carmine?"

"What?"

"Your son," Corrado growled. "He was with his mother. Where is he?"

"He's, uh…" Vincent wildly shook his head. "He wasn't there. He wasn't with her."

"What do you mean he wasn't with her?" Corrado asked.

"Where did he go?"

"I don't know," Vincent cried. "Oh God, I don't know!"

"Corrado!" Celia called from the doorway, her eyes wide with horror. "It's, uh, Johnny on the phone. Johnny Tarullo. He's asking for you."

"The pizza guy?" Corrado asked. "Take a message."

"He says it's important," Celia said. "He said it's about Carmine."

Carmine. Corrado let go of Vincent as he shot to his feet, his vision blurring at the abrupt movement. Hell of a night to get sick. He darted around his wife, going straight for the telephone. "Moretti speaking."

"Mr. Moretti, it's—"

"I know who you are," Corrado said, cutting him off. "You know something about Carmine?"

"I found him," John said. "He's, uh… he's here. At my shop."

"Is he alright?" The stark silence that followed was answer enough for Corrado. "Stay there. Call no one. Wait for me."

Corrado slammed the phone down and ran out of the room, sprinting upstairs. He threw on clothes, dressing faster than he had ever dressed before. Grabbing his gun, he made sure it was loaded before running back downstairs, shoving it in his coat as he hit the foyer. Celia was on the floor with her brother, holding him in her arms, rocking him and consoling him. Corrado wasn't sure if she even knew why, but the expression on her face, the tears streaming from her eyes, said she knew enough.

"I'm heading out," he said to his wife, knowing talking to Vincent was useless right now. "If he tries to leave, don't let him."

"How do I do that?" Celia asked.

"I don't care," Corrado said. "Shoot him if you have to. Just don't let him out of your sight."

He was out the door and to his car before she responded.

Corrado sped through the streets, giving little thought to police, nothing else mattering. It was only a few blocks to Tarullo's Pizzeria, only a few minutes time. He felt constantly on the verge of throwing up, the burn in the back of his throat, the heaviness in his lungs like air wasn't enough to keep him breathing, but he swallowed it back and pushed forward.

He hit his breaks, tires squealing as he swung his car crookedly into a parking spot in front of the pizzeria. In the distance, down the block, a few police cars were parked along the street, blocking a nearby alley, yellow caution tape tied up around the area.

Corrado forced himself to look away from it as he headed for the pizzeria. The lights were all on, the open sign flickering in the window, but the door wouldn't budge when he shoved against it. Locked.

"Tarullo!" he called out, banging on the door so hard he cracked a pane of glass. "Open up!"

John Tarullo appeared, racing toward the door, his face ghastly pale as he opened up for Corrado.

"Where is he?" Corrado asked, stepping inside, his eyes scanning the place. Pizza covered some of the tables, money tossed around. He had cleared the place out abruptly.

"In the back," he said. "In the kitchen."

"Is he dead?'

John flinched at the blunt question. "Not yet."

Not yet. Corrado could work with that. It meant it wasn't too late.

Bursting through the kitchen doors, his footsteps stalled for a fraction of a second at the boy lying on the floor, surrounded by towels. His white shirt was torn, the side of it soaked with blood. The color was gone from Carmine's naturally tanned skin, giving him an ashy hue, his lips tinted blue. *Not good.*

Corrado knelt beside the boy and grasped his wrist, relieved to feel a pulse. It was weak, but it was there. His heart was still beating. He checked him over, seeing the lesion on his side. Someone had shot him, a superficial wound, but he had been bleeding out for a while. Short, rapid breaths passed through his lips, his eyes closed. *Unconscious.*

"Did you talk to him at all?" Corrado asked.

"No, he was like this when I found him."

"Where?" Corrado asked. "Where did you find him?"

"Behind my Dumpster. I took the trash out and saw his foot sticking out. I yelled at him, told him to get out from back there, but he didn't move. And then I saw the blood."

The man sounded shell-shocked.

"I didn't know what to do," John said as Corrado ran a hand over Carmine's head, feeling his clammy skin. It was cool to the touch. "Maybe I should've called 911, but I know who he is… I know who you all are. I know *what* you are."

Corrado shot the guy a look that silenced him. "You did the right thing."

"I hope so."

Corrado pulled the limp boy into his arms, clutching him to his chest as he stood. "He's my nephew. I'll take care of him."

"Come with me."

Corrado followed the police officer down the long, dim hallway, the lights above him flickering and buzzing as he passed. It was stone cold silent except for the sound of their shoes against the hard floor. Each footstep, each thump, each flicker, drove Corrado closer to the edge.

The officer's proximity unnerved him. In their world, you weren't supposed to be anywhere near a man in uniform, unless involuntarily in handcuffs in the back of his car, and even then you were flirting with danger. This went against his nature.

He didn't want to be there. In fact, it was the last place in the world he wanted to be. But Vincent was in no condition to do it. He was too distraught and not in his right mind, glued to Carmine's side in the ICU. And Celia, well… Corrado would never want his wife to go through something like this.

There was nobody else.

Only him.

The officer led him into a small room with a large streaked window that gave a view of an adjoining room. It felt like a science lab, clinical and sanitized, with scales and chemicals and trays and tables, but it was much more than that. A room few experienced alive, but one most would be subjected to at death.

The morgue.

He felt it in the air, clinging to his sweaty skin, wrapping itself around his throat as it strangled the breath from his lungs. Death lurked here, the basement floor its playground where it taunted, torturing those who passed through.

Grim Reaper, the ultimate dealer of death. Blackness lurked within Corrado, but the source of it, the *real* monster, made itself at home down here, starring in the greatest horror story of all time: reality. Vampires, werewolves, zombies, and demons had nothing—*nothing*—on the callousness of some men.

Corrado paused in front of the window. The officer stood beside him, motioning to a man in the quarantined room. He pushed a metal table closer, grasping a hold of a thick sheet covering it. At the officer's nod, the man pulled the sheet back.

She appeared to be sleeping.

The wound wasn't visible from that angle, but he knew what it looked like from experience. There would be a hole on the back of her head about the size of a quarter, concealed by her hair. From the outside, it wouldn't seem so bad, but the damage to the brain had been irreparable. She would've died instantly.

Both men stared at him as he nodded. "That's her."

"Name?"

"DeMarco," Corrado replied. "Her name's Maura DeMarco."

"Middle name?"

"I don't think she has one."

"Do you know her maiden name?"

He shook his head. "I'm not sure."

"Her date of birth?"

"Sometime in the spring."

"What year? How old is she?"

Corrado glanced in the officer's direction, seeing he was eyeing him unusually. "She's in her thirties."

The officer jotted some notes down in a file as he shook his head. "You know, for being family, you sure don't know much about her."

Corrado turned back to Maura. The man had a point. He had

known her for decades, had shared a home with her for part of his life, but he didn't *know* her. He never had. He knew little about the girl she had been and next to nothing about the woman she had become.

He couldn't understand her, couldn't grasp why she had done the things she had done, what motivated her, and Corrado realized, standing there, studying her peaceful expression, that it was his own fault he didn't know those things. He hadn't *tried* to understand her.

He hadn't tried to get to know her.

Corrado wondered what she felt in her last moments, what memories flashed through her mind. He saw it so many times in the eyes of men, their lives playing out like a silent movie those seconds before their last breath. Had Maura been forced to relive every bitter moment, every painful memory of torture that Corrado had stood back and watched in silence?

What was it she thought about when she took her dying breath?

Antonio had always feared Maura would be the end of Vincent. Vito argued it would happen the other way around. Corrado never knew which man to believe, but it didn't matter. At the end, they were both right.

Killing one meant killing the other.

Maura's blood had been on Vincent's hands.

Literally.

But Vincent, too, wouldn't be coming back from this.

Corrado was reminded of a story he had heard long ago: *The Steadfast Tin Soldier.* The eccentric tin soldier loved a paper ballerina, despite everything that stood between them. The soldier put on a brave face and stayed strong, suffering silently through trials and tribulations, because it was what a soldier did. But his passive acceptance of his life steered him straight to his doom. Had he spoken up, they might have survived, but remaining silent, restrained, led to tragedy.

But while death can take away life, love is eternal. The soldier may have been consumed by fire, his exterior melting, but his heart remained, part of him left behind in the ashes.

Corrado stared through the window, peering at the ashen face of the lost paper ballerina, knowing, not far away, in a cold hospital room, a tin soldier gradually melted away, flames shredding him.

The man covered Maura with the sheet again before wheeling her away from the window. It was the last time he would ever see her, Corrado realized.

He wasn't sure how he felt about that.

EPILOGUE

So much had happened since the day Corrado gazed at Maura through the thick glass in the cold morgue. Celia had left him for almost a year to help raise her nephews while her brother drifted. Vincent's bloodthirsty quest for retribution, to get justice for what he had lost, ultimately led to him murdering the Antonellis.

Frankie and Monica Antonelli, that is. The others—Michael and Katrina—had died years later at Corrado's hand, the same afternoon that Miranda hung herself. The entire family had been wiped out except for one: the little girl at the center of it all.

Corrado himself even died once amid the violence, shot in the chest multiple times by Ivan Volkov. He spent six weeks in a coma after being revived. Celia stayed at his bedside as the doctor checked in on him. They told her not to expect much. The longer Corrado was down, the less chance he'd ever come back. He warned her there could be mental issues. They expected problems - sensory sensitivity, inability to express emotions. They said Corrado could lose his sense of humor and become socially inept. He'd lack communication skills and make people uncomfortable.

Little did they know, Corrado had been that way his whole life.

Most people didn't get another chance, not where mortality was concerned, but Corrado had managed to escape death *twice* since his birth.

He knew he wouldn't see a third.

Death surrounded them. *A lot* of death. Celia kept the articles still, stuffed into her old scrapbook. Between his countless arrests and trials, his name had graced the paper more times than he cared to count. His current trial, the RICO case that resulted in his first authentic 'not guilty' verdict, had filled her scrapbook until there were only a few pages left.

Not everything had been bad, though.

2005 proved to be a year of miracles.

Erika Moretti drank herself to death.

The White Sox won the World Series.

And Vincent succeeded where everyone else had failed.

He brought Haven home with him, where Maura had always wanted the girl to be. She found freedom, but it came at a steep price: Carmine had to sacrifice his future.

He fell in love with the girl.

Like father, like son.

Corrado had always been a fan of horror movies. *Nightmare on Elm Street; Halloween; Psycho; The Exorcist; Night of the Living Dead.* He'd watched them all.

Something about a plot driven by suspense, which played on the average person's worst fears, intrigued him. People feared the unknown, the monsters that lurked in the shadows, the ones that were rarely seen. It got their adrenaline flowing, their hearts pounding.

None of it scared Corrado, though. Not anymore. Not since he was a child and learned the truth about life. He feared no monsters. Nothing caught him off guard. No one pounced when he didn't expect it.

Having said that, however, there was one movie that horrified him, that haunted him for weeks after watching it.

Groundhog Day.

The idea of a single day that never ended, one that played out again and again, tapped into one of his only fears in life: the idea that this was it. That he would continue on, just as he was, no rest, no change in sight. More days, but no *different* days.

What you see is what you get.

It was the one thing about being a *made man* that unnerved him. There was no moving on from the Mafia. Nothing came next. This was it.

Someday, he'd be killed. There was no doubt in his mind.

But the dying didn't frighten him.

Living, with no tomorrow, did.

It was how he felt some days, how he felt at that moment, as he pulled his car into the parking lot of *Luna Rossa.* Sonny and Cher didn't play on his radio, but the song was the same, anyway.

He parked near the entrance and climbed out, buttoning his suit coat to conceal his gun as he strode through the door. It only took seconds to find who he was looking for… his staff had called to inform him the man was lurking. He sat at the end of the bar, a glass of ice water in front of him, as his eyes scanned the place.

He was watching.

Listening.

Hoping.

Pity for him, he'd find nothing.

He spotted Corrado as he approached, his expression a mixture of arrogance and annoyance. The man hated him, loathed his existence, but a part of him loved the fact that he was untouchable to Corrado.

Or so he *thought*, anyway.

"Special Agent Cerone, what a surprise," Corrado said. "Is there something I can do for you?"

Corrado didn't have to be a mind reader to know what the man was thinking: he could go to Hell, *that's* what he could do.

"Mr. Moretti," he said in greeting. "I'm just enjoying a drink."

"You can have water anywhere." Corrado motioned for the bartender. "I'd like a double Scotch and bring Agent Cerone here the same."

"That's not necessary," he interjected.

"Nonsense," Corrado replied. "It's on the house."

"I shouldn't," he said.

"You should. Unless, of course, you're on duty."

The agent gave him a knowing look. *Of course* this was business. It always was.

"What business would I have here?" he bluffed.

"You tell me," Corrado said. "While I was incarcerated on your trumped-up RICO charges, I was audited, my club surprise inspected *twice*, and they even tried to revoke my liquor license. It seems the government has it out for me, Agent Cerone."

"Well, I assure you, Mr. Moretti, we don't harass people. We only involve ourselves in situations if there's just cause."

"Good, because as flattering as it all may be, I've done nothing to warrant the attention. My employees are paid well and have better insurance than even your government supplies you with."

"You must do a lot of business to be able to afford that," he replied, glancing around at the other patrons. "Must be a slow night."

The bartender returned with their drinks and Corrado picked up his. "I do quite well for myself, but yes, it's a slow night. It's a special occasion, after all."

"Special occasion?" The agent raised his eyebrows as he picked up his water, ignoring the scotch. "What would that be?"

"There's a party tonight in honor of my exoneration."

"Celebrating an injustice. Yeah, that sounds like your kind."

The man might have been a nuisance, but at least he was sometimes entertaining.

It was a pity Corrado would probably have to kill him someday.

"You know, you're not the first officer to have a hard-on for me," Corrado said. "Years ago, a Chicago detective made it his mission to take me down."

"Yeah? What happened?"

"My father killed him."

Agent Cerone, mid-drink from his glass, choked on a gulp of water. "Is that a threat?"

"Don't be absurd," Corrado said. "My father can't kill you. He's already dead."

The agent sat there, clutching his glass, aggravated.

"You know, a wise man once told me never to trust a guy who orders water at a bar."

"Why's that?"

"Because they're there for the wrong reasons." Corrado downed the rest of his scotch before discarding the glass. It was the only alcohol he would be drinking tonight, but he needed the burn to pacify his nerves. "Have a great night, Agent Cerone. I'm sure I'll be seeing you again real soon."

It was supposed to be a night of celebration, a night of honor, a night about *liberation.* It was supposed to be the start of a new beginning.

Things don't always go as planned.

As soon as Corrado stepped through the door of the mansion in Lincoln Park, bitter voices greeted him. Twenty-year-old Carmine DeMarco stood right inside, ferociously staring down a smug Carlo Abate as the men spat insensitive words at each other.

It was starting already.

After his mother's death, after waking up in the hospital, Carmine wouldn't talk to anyone for months. But now, years later, the boy never knew when to shut up. Carmine was a loose trigger, and he was testing a man who knew how to apply just the right amount of pressure.

If Salvatore were a salamander, then Carlo was a venomous snake. He had been initiated into *La Cosa Nostra* less than a month after Antonio had passed away, the first man brought into the fold under Salvatore's reign. It was the first of a string of questionable actions that marked a downturn for the organization. A group prided on honor and respect had been marred by deception, friends killing friends, brothers taking down each other.

Corrado had once been Antonio's secret weapon, the one he turned to when jobs needed done, off the record, neat and clean. Carlo, it turned out, was Salvatore's right hand. He did the Boss's dirty work, but instead of cleaning up messes and keeping order, he was the one creating havoc.

Antonio had often chided Corrado for assuming to know his

thoughts, for assuming he knew *him*, but the fact was that Corrado knew the man's soul.

He knew his heart.

And he knew Antonio never would have stood for any of this.

The night felt antagonistic… or maybe the things Corrado knew contaminated his impression. He humored all the congratulatory words, all the while keeping his eye on Carmine. The boy drank heavily, throwing back shots as effortlessly as water, even drinking straight from the bottle.

Corrado had little patience for alcoholics.

The crowd thinned eventually, associates and soldiers clearing out while others gathered in the den. At a few minutes past nine, Carmine strolled over to Corrado, staggering. *Drunk*. "I'm leaving."

"Good." The boy needed gone. *Now*. "Go home. Sober up."

Corrado retreated to the den, relief washing through him, soothing his nerves, but it was short lived.

Carmine strolled back in.

No. "I thought you were leaving."

"Ah, he was, but I requested he stick around," Salvatore said, taking his usual seat and motioning toward the chair beside him for Carmine to sit.

The men chatted, sharing their usual conversation banter, mulling over business deals, but the words were lost to Corrado as his mind drifted elsewhere. Nothing they said would matter tomorrow. An unfamiliar panic stirred in the pit of his stomach, a sense of uncertainty. He had walked in the house on the offensive, prepared and ready for whatever was to come, but suddenly, he had been thrown on the defense.

Carmine wasn't supposed to be there.

He was supposed to be at home.

This time, he was supposed to be *safe*.

Instead, the boy sat there, right beside his godfather, continuing to suck down liquor as if his body needed it as much as air. The men talked murder, obnoxiously boasting, while Corrado remained silent. He had single-handedly killed more men than everyone else in the room combined.

The snake chimed in, bragging, his arrogance infecting the room. Corrado blocked him out, diving deeper into his thoughts, when anarchy broke out.

Carmine jumped to his feet, liquor splashing to the floor as he clutched his glass tightly. His sudden movement startled the others, conversation ceasing as men stood, trained to sense danger. Guns were drawn, and a chorus of clicks echoed through the room as safeties were released, the weapons pointed at Carmine's head.

Corrado didn't move. He stared at his nephew, coldness sweeping through him at the look in Carmine's eyes as he regarded Carlo with unadulterated hatred.

He knew.

Carmine knew.

He knew the secret Corrado had carried with him into the house, the secret that would be exposed before the night was through.

He knew Carlo had killed his mother.

He knew Carlo had tried to kill him.

But he didn't know it all.

No, Corrado was the only one in the room who did. Carmine didn't yet know that the man who sat beside him, the one who had stood at the altar the day of his christening and swore to God he would protect him, had ordered it all.

Salvatore broke up the standoff, demanding Carmine and Carlo follow him outside. Carlo sauntered from the room. He thought he was untouchable, infallible, but he wasn't.

The men in the den fell back into conversation with ease, unaffected, but Corrado remained on guard, straining his ears as he listened… as he waited.

And waited.

And waited.

Five, ten, fifteen minutes passed before the noise Corrado had been waiting for shattered the air.

Gunshots.

Men were on their feet, sprinting toward the door in a panic, as Corrado rose from his seat and took a deep breath. Reaching into his coat, he pulled out his revolver.

Vincent had come to end the charade.

Corrado paused in the doorway to the backyard as the spray of bullets ripped through the dark. Vincent stood in the middle of it all, firing at Salvatore, while shell-shocked Carmine hovered on the sidelines. Both men—the father he loved, the Boss he feared—yelled at the boy, Vincent imploring him to run, while Sal demanded he fulfill his duties.

Carmine seemed panicked, torn between two worlds—the world he wanted to be in, with his family, and the world he had to be in, the one he'd walked into to save Haven.

It didn't take a genius to figure out which world would win.

Carmine wouldn't run. That October day in 1996, when his mother had begged him to run and he listened, had sealed that decision. He ran, leaving someone he loved to face the fight alone.

He wouldn't do that again.

Corrado raised his gun and aimed for Carmine, pulling the trigger.

Don't make a sudden move.

The bullet grazed the side of Carmine's hand where he'd intended, singing the skin. Carmine dropped his gun reflexively, the weapon clattering to the concrete patio as he cursed out loud.

He looked stunned. Horrified. Frightened.

Frightened of Corrado, even though he'd saved him from making the worst mistake of his life.

Corrado sprinted for Carmine before the boy could think to grab his weapon again, knocking him hard to the ground. Corrado demanded he stay there as he stood back up, hoping Carmine would listen for once in his life. Corrado aimed for Vincent, firing over his head so not to hit him. Vincent knew what he was doing and fired back, bullets whizzing by.

Vincent had impeccable aim.

Not once did Corrado worry.

Men fell, bullets tearing through flesh as screams echoed through the air, incessant gunfire lighting up the night sky. Vincent's movements slowed eventually. He struggled, his breathing labored. He'd taken a few bullets, his hands covered with blood as he clutched his heaving chest.

The moment Vincent tore off his coat, exposing the Uzi strapped to his chest, Corrado knew it was all over. The final act had arrived.

It was the end.

Vincent bowed his head and made the sign of the cross, his mouth moving furiously as he prayed. Corrado was reminded of the boy's father then.

Antonio prayed for survival.

Vincent, Corrado knew, prayed for death.

Carmine's terrified screams cut through the night, his pleas falling upon deaf ears. It was too late to stop it, too late to take it back.

What was done was done.

"I think it's time," Vincent had said the last time they spoke face-to-face, a staunch detachment in his voice as the men stood on the steps of Saint Mary's Catholic Church under the cloak of darkness.

Corrado eyed him suspiciously. "Time for what, Vincent?"

"Time for me to be with my wife again."

Corrado closed his eyes as Vincent stepped out into the wide-open, his finger squeezing the trigger of the Uzi. Incessant gunfire lit up the night, deafening, terrifying, as bullets hailed across the yard, shattering glass and splintering wood, ripping through bodies and ending lives.

Corrado pinned Carmine down, shielding him from the deadly spray. The boy he had so fiercely resisted being responsible for trembled beneath him, needing his protection, relying on him for safety.

No matter how hard they fought it, fate snuck up on all of them.

When the bullets ran out, Corrado opened his eyes, watching Vincent fall to the ground. Crawling over to the side of the house, Vincent sat back on his knees. The gunfire had ceased, in its place the faint wail of sirens in the distance. They approached fast, growing louder as the seconds passed.

Nine blocks.

Eight blocks.

Seven blocks.

Vincent reached beside him, picking up his discarded pistol. Corrado, seeing his desolation, yelled in warning. "Vincent!"

Vincent glanced in his direction, his face ashen and eyes dull.

"It's time now," Vincent whispered, the words garbled.

Corrado shook his head, knowing what he was thinking. He'd expected to die tonight. Corrado had expected him to die.

But not this way.

It wasn't supposed to end this way.

Vincent nodded defiantly as the sirens grew closer.

Stubborn and rebellious. He hadn't changed.

Six blocks.

Five blocks.

Vincent raised his trembling gun, pressing it beneath his chin. Carmine screamed, horrified, but the sound grew muffled as Corrado's heart thumped wildly in his chest. The familiar fog took over, numbness seeping into his skin and coating his insides.

Vincent stared at Corrado, silently pleading for help. He'd never ask him to do it. He had too much pride. *Too much heart.* But his expression spoke volumes. It always had. Decades later, even after everything, Vincent still couldn't bluff.

Not with Corrado, anyway.

Four blocks.

Three blocks.

They were cutting it close.

Corrado grabbed his revolver as Antonio's hazy voice infiltrated his senses, a long ago memory Corrado had never forgotten.

"If you break Celia's heart, I'll make you suffer. I don't care if I'm rotting in a grave somewhere. Hurting my children is hurting me."

"I understand," Corrado had replied. "I swear on my life I won't hurt your family."

Corrado closed his eyes, bowing his head, as he pushed that memory away. Seeing the desperation in Vincent's eyes, knowing what he planned, Corrado realized he had to break that promise.

He had to do the one thing that would hurt Celia most.

He had to break her heart.

It was the only way to save Vincent's.

Two blocks.

One block.

Out of time.

"*Perdonatemi*," Corrado whispered. *Forgive me.*

He aimed, his finger on the trigger, and for only the second time in his life, he hesitated.

This time it was real.

This wasn't a game.

Vincent wasn't another target, another kill. Another number. He was his friend. No, he was his *brother.*

He was just like him.

Corrado stared into Vincent's eyes. Only a second or two passed, but it was enough for Corrado to seek out what he needed. He saw it, watching as Vincent's life flashed before him, as it all played out in his final moments, deep love and happiness shining from his eyes.

He needed to be with his wife.

And Corrado realized then exactly what Maura had seen at the end… it wasn't the pain or the misery. Those things didn't define her. It was her family.

Just as it was Vincent's.

The single gunshot tore through the air as Corrado pulled the trigger, killing his brother-in-law instantly.

Carmine bawled.

Sirens wailed.

Corrado prayed he'd done the right thing.

The days following were a blur as Corrado endured interrogation and nights in a cold, dark jail cell, confined for as long as they could legally keep him. When a judge ordered his release, he didn't call his wife. He didn't call any friends, any associates, or any family.

Instead, he called a priest.

Father Alberto pulled up in front of Cook County Jail, the familiar Cadillac DeVille rumbling. Antonio's car, come to pick him up from jail yet again. Corrado ran his hands along the hood before opening the passenger door and slipping inside.

He hadn't seen the thing in years.

The priest said nothing as he drove through town. Father Alberto parked the car at Saint Mary's Catholic Church and climbed out, not giving Corrado another look.

He didn't have to. Corrado followed, anyway.

He kept his head down as he strode down the long aisle, following the priest straight to the confessional. Corrado sat down inside of it, shoving the clunky screen out of the way. He had no intention of hiding his face.

Father Alberto sat beside him. "Whenever you're ready."

Corrado had never done this before, but he knew how it went. "Bless me Father, for I have sinned. I'm forty-six years old, and this is my first confession."

"Go on, my child" the priest said. "I'm listening."

"I lied." Corrado bowed his head. "I made a promise I knew I couldn't keep."

"About what?"

"I promised long ago that I would never leave my wife."

"And you're leaving her?"

"Yes."

"When?"

"I don't know," he said quietly. "Maybe today, maybe tomorrow, maybe the next day. Maybe next year. Maybe ten years from now. There's no way to tell. But it'll happen someday. I'll leave her."

"Why?"

"It's not my choice. I'm already on borrowed time. Men like me… we don't live forever. We don't live long at all."

"So by leaving her, you mean…"

"I'm going to die."

"We all die. It's unavoidable."

"I know, but it hasn't been enough," he said. "It'll never be enough. She deserves so much more."

"There's eternal life," the priest said.

"I'm not a fool, Father. My wife sometimes says I am, but I'm not. I know Celia and I aren't going the same place. There is no eternity. This life is all we've got."

The priest was quiet. "Have you considered the prospect of her leaving first?"

"No." Corrado shook his head. "It won't happen that way."

"How can you be certain?"

"Because God knows, if He ever took Celia from me, I'd burn the world down around us all."

Corrado stood to leave, but the priest reached out and grabbed his arm, stopping him. "That's it?"

"Yes."

"There's nothing else you need to get off your chest?"

"No," he said. "Everything else I've done, I've made peace with."

"Do you want penance?"

"Will it give me more time on earth with my wife?"

The priest smiled sadly. "No."

"Then keep your forgiveness." Corrado started out of the confessional but paused by the door. "You know, as I was leaving the courthouse the other day, a woman asked me a question. She said, 'what made you this way?' And ever since then, I just kept wondering..."

"You wondered what made you the man you are today."

"Yes."

"You know my answer." *God.*

"The world treats me like I wronged them, when really, the world wronged me," Corrado said. "The world made me this way. And maybe they all hate me, but still, they need me. Because without villains, there wouldn't be superheroes."

"Even in the story of your life, you still think you're the villain?"

"Of course," Corrado said. "We are who we are."

Corrado strolled out of the church, stalling on the top step to gaze out at the old Chicago neighborhood, his eyes skimming along the DeVille parked along the curb. Life, he thought, had been like a line of dominos, set up in a complex, interweaving path, toppling one another as things fell into place. Corrado often tried to pinpoint what had been the trigger, the first domino in the line, the one that had set him on this path of no return.

How far back did it all go?

He wasn't sure where it began, but he did know the end. He knew where the trail led to, what the last domino to fall would be.

It would be the last page in Celia's scrapbook.

Corrado A. Moretti

Corrado Alphonse Moretti, 51, of Felton Drive, Chicago, died Saturday, November 1, 2014. Funeral will be held on Wednesday, November 4 at Saint Mary's Catholic Church with the burial to follow at Hillside Cemetery.
*Family requests **absolutely no flowers**.*

Acknowledgements

This book almost didn't happen. It was shelved for reasons beyond my control, and that broke my heart. I couldn't imagine leaving Corrado's story untold. So I need to thank everyone who stood by me and fought with me to make this finally see the light of day. Thanks to superstar agent Frank Weimann, who unknowingly gave me the biggest boost of confidence when others seemed to be happy stepping on me while I was down. So much gratitude to Sarah Anderson, who listened to me bitch, moan, and groan about this book for years now.

To my amazing family, and my beautiful best friend Nicki, and to all of the readers out there who pick up my books and dedicate hours of their lives to them, knowing they could be reading so many other books instead. You make my life what it is. You helped make my dreams come true. You are extraordinary.

To my mother, who had a soft spot for Corrado. You don't know how much I wish you were here to read this book. I love you.

In December of 1946, The Fabulous Flamingo opened in Las Vegas, the dream of famed mobster Bugsy Siegel. While the hotel today has absolutely nothing to do with organized crime (this bears repeating: NOTHING), the colorful history of the place is undeniable. So special thanks to them, for letting me play in their sandbox fictitiously.

15412288R00318

Made in the USA
Middletown, DE
03 November 2014